STONES

Praise for *Stones*

"Not since Alice Walker's *Possessing the Secret of Joy* has a novel so boldly placed female genital mutilation at its heart. *Stones* does not turn away but looks directly at this ancient rite, encompassing and also challenging modernity's response to it. *Stones* is as rewarding as it is provocative."
—Professor Henry Louis Gates, Jr., Director, Hutchins Center for
African and African American Research, Harvard University

"As a survivor of female genital mutilation, I welcome the complex tale Jeanie Kortum has spun in *Stones*. On so many levels, her fiction tells the truth about a custom whose psychological density and convolution escape the rigid categories of sociology and statistics. In their place we find spirituality, tribal identity, myth, mysticism, and art—beliefs that anchor FGM in defiant emotions that must be uncovered and addressed in order for us activists to sooner see the end of a noxious tradition."
—Khady Koita, Founder, EuroNet-FGM and author of *Blood Stains:
A Child of Africa Reclaims Her Human Rights*

"Everything Jeanie Kortum writes (and does!) is informed by a huge heart, a gentle and tenacious intelligence, a fierce longing to tell truth stories, a passionate dedication to the betterment of humanity. She is a wonderful writer."
—Anne Lamott, author of *Bird by Bird, Operating Instructions,*
and *Imperfect Birds*

"Jeanie Kortum is a storyteller in the ancient tradition that she writes of—at once poet, dream weaver, detective, medicine woman, and visionary. Each sentence of *Stones* is a work of art, each word a surprise and at the same time deeply remembered from an indigenous past buried in our cells. . . . An epic poem, a healing spell, an ancient incantation, and a page-turner novel; the reader may emerge as changed and awakened as the characters and cultures in these pages."
—Kim Rosen, Founder, S.H.E. Fund and author of *Saved by a Poem:
The Transformative Power of Words*

"At the heart of *Stones* is a harsh tradition—female genital mutilation—that tethers its tribal actors to the Kenyan earth, the cradle of humanity. Tradition encroaches upon the modern as the young anthropologist intent on scientific investigation assumes the role of a messianic heroine.... Carried by the soundscape of Kortum's story, readers search for origins, struggle with change, chafe against inevitability. They are also granted the opportunity to loosen the chains of conflicted complicity through the authority of an extraordinary language."

—Professor Dr. Maria Jaschok, Director, International Gender Studies Centre, Lady Margaret Hall, University of Oxford

"Reading *Stones* made my mind sweat, like listening to poignant music can do. Partly this is because of its tasty, flavorful words, which exceed what we call 'poetry.' And partly it is because in the protagonist Emely/Amely, one experiences a human being turning into a divinity . . ."

—Shao John Thorpe, author of *The Cargo Cult*

STONES

A NOVEL

JEANIE KORTUM

SHE WRITES PRESS

UnCUT VOICES

Published 2017
Printed in the United States of America
Print ISBN: 978-1-63152-180-5
E-ISBN: 978-1-63152-181-2
Library of Congress Control Number: 2017936431

For information, address:
She Writes Press
1563 Solano Ave #546
Berkeley, CA 94707

Cover design © Julie Metz, Ltd./metzdesign.com
Interior design by Tabitha Lahr

She Writes Press is a division of SparkPoint Studio, LLC.

Names and identifying characteristics have been changed to protect the privacy of certain individuals.

FOREWORD

J eanie Kortum has taken years to produce a lyrical mystery in
the genre of magical realism that spans millennia well beyond
recorded chronicles. Like Alice Walker, Kortum places female
genital mutilation (FGM, affecting 130 million women) at the heart of
the story, exploring most intently the toxicity of the secret, the *omertà*
surrounding "ritual" torture to which (mainly) women subject little
girls. Silence is a weapon that fractures mother-daughter bonds and in
a sense excises worlds, obstructing the intimate union of mother and
child at the origin of human life. Intertwining the sacred and profane,
Stones journeys back to the beginning to recover the healing knowledge
that all things are one.

As Gustave Flaubert famously remarked, "Madame Bovary, c'est
moi," the exquisite claim of artists, who, if they have sufficient brilliance—and Jeanie Kortum does—can dissolve labels and shift iden-
tities by investing themselves in characters not at all like themselves.
Though Kortum lived for several months with a remote hunter-gatherer
tribe and observed an excision, thus bringing expertise and feeling to
her "facts" as a "witness through the imagination" (Lillian Kremer), the
author invests her own vulnerability and strength into breathing life

into Emely/Amely, her African protagonist. Not unlike Tashi/Evelyn in Alice Walker's *Possessing the Secret of Joy*, these names—and "names are small rafts pushed up the river of eternity by those who have left" (Kortum)—correspond to a clash of noxious dichotomies, Emely conjuring Emma, the secular revolutionary, and Amely inferring *l'âme* or soul. Context determines which of the two rides the apex of the seesaw.

Imbalance is in fact the default position for pseudo-opposites, those dichotomies immortalized by, among others, Hélène Cixous and Catherine Clément in *La Jeune Née* (1975). Cixous and Clément list the binaries—light/dark, strong/weak—from which discourse and philosophy derive and trace them back to the Ur-opposition not in mind but in anatomy: the convex (phallus) and concave (vulva) rigid in ascendance and subordination. Another poignant discrepancy and hence inequity is introduced at birth, separation from the mother who exiles her offspring into a world that insists on difference because it bulwarks patriarchy. Mind teamed with action, however, can first blur and then overcome desolate distinctions.

Thus, far from "coopting" someone else's narrative, Kortum transmits insights beyond the sectarian, trying to heal by envisioning the wholly human. If we are our sisters' keeper, love lies not in abandoning girls, now grown up, who want to see an injurious custom end, but in telling their story as our own, because it *is*. My vulva tells me that what happens to that child happens, empathically, to me.

Resembling African sources like Kenyan author Ngũgĩ wa Thiong'o's novel *The River Between* (1965) and drawing on cultures whose matriarchal power is inferred from prehistoric female sculpture, *Stones* paints a character burdened for a lifetime by her mother's fear of revealing the secret. Many initiates are told they or their loved ones will die should they "snitch," making the taboo against naming what is done to them an insurmountable barrier to change. Fearing for her child's life if she is (inevitably) excised but prevented by terror from revealing why, Emely's mother sends her daughter away, enrolling her at age seven in a boarding school. Deprived of maternal warmth, feeling abandoned, the girl proves a gifted pupil in order to earn her mother's love. Winning a scholarship to the University of Nairobi and a fellowship for her MA at UCLA, she has chosen to study "Narrative Anthropology," at the start of the novel, Emely has just arrived back to Africa to work on a "Land Reform Project" aimed—or so Emely thinks—at finding, interviewing, and preserving remote forest cultures. In reality, a greedy professor plans to exploit the young investigator's innocence. The remote tribe is thought to know where a sacred tablet, an Ur-script, is hidden. Purportedly the oldest document ever procured, the writing is coveted only for the price it will fetch, not for its meaning.

Its significance, however, accounts for its infinite value to the tribe and, more specifically, to the Great Mother, experienced as a craving or desire, who is purported to be dying of neglect and thus absenting herself from the flora and fauna that had fed the group. The resulting scarcity of sustenance affects the Mother, too. Needing nourishment herself, she demands it—in the form of a girl's spilled blood, i.e., infibulation, the most severe form of cutting—and the agent of this sacrifice is destined to be Emely/Amely.

The culture our graduate has been sent to study believes in serial Stone Women—those with special, telepathic gifts enabling them to communicate with the spirit Mother, and the novel's cohort of females, excepting only a few positive deviants, resembles in their allegiance to cutting, the majority of women where FGM persists. Now, Emely, having assumed her forest name "Amely," is elected to be the next Stone Woman, a messianic figure in the tribe, and though she accepts aspects of this new assignment, she continues to categorically reject the practise of FGM, which she is expected to perform in a matter of weeks on a young girl. Unlike members of her tribe, Emely/Amely's Western education banishes the inculcated anguish preventing victims from adjuring the blade. She denounces; she escapes; and Chipkorie, the youth whose vulva was to be proudly slashed and sewn, is cut but also, ultimately, not. The mystery behind this seeming incompatibility, never elucidated rationally but rather poetically and emotionally, lends the tale power and suspense.

Emely/Amely's gift allows her to respond to the agency of stones such as jet, cuprite, serpentine, halite and quartz, so that often, boundaries understood to be factually incapable of being unbound dissolve, most significantly those between human life and death. Through history and artefact, communication has been flowing for a mere five thousand years; the span of meaning to which Emely/Amely accedes is far longer. Mystical and telepathic, ancestral women, starting from the grandmother lost when the protagonist was five, hold vigil and serve as guides to the young woman on Earth.

Hence, in a lyrical tongue replete with startling, memorable metaphors, Kortum succeeds in creating a heroine with two epistemologies at war within her, one rational and Western, derived from education, and the other intuitive-maternal or emotional-traditional. These in turn represent the twin themes of separation and fusion, stasis and motion, machine and human, whereby the longing for wholeness, cosmic and personal, triumphs.

As Toni Morrison remarked about *Beloved*, "the consequences of slavery only artists can deal with . . . and it's our job!" Female genital mutilation is a subject for artists as well. Like slavery and the Holocaust, its hydra head defies a movement, underfunded to be sure, but tenacious and determined to eliminate the custom. And yet it continues. Blood, numerous cultures' beverage of choice to slake the thirst of gods, is still sacrificed to propitiate forces of the universe far more potent than the fragile human and is often invoked, like the great flood, to enunciate the fact that the peril to the whole exceeds the danger to one individual.

Ogotu, the matriarch in *Stones* who insists that Emely/Amely cuts the young girl, picks up the subject as well. "If Chipkorie's blood doesn't run long that morning . . . there will be no more births. No more children will move from the darkness that is their mother into the light of the sky. Water will rise and become our new sky. No one will float through time on the raft of their names because no one will be called by their names anymore. And what we know is that inside of the word for us, we carry the beating hearts of all who are nameless." Her voice, flicked with fear, flows rusty through the pipe of her throat.

Worlds are at stake.

Since time immemorial, as narrated in Shirley Jackson's faux-realistic tale "The Lottery" (1948), a town in the United States has drawn numbers from a sacred black box every June 27. All citizens are required to be present. Chitchat occupies the villagers, but one theme emerges. Radicals are questioning the rite.

Old Man Warner snorted. "Pack of crazy fools," he said. "Listening to the young folks, nothing's good enough for them. Next thing you know, they'll be wanting to go back to living in caves, nobody work anymore, live that way for a while. Used to be a saying about 'Lottery in June, corn be heavy soon.' First thing you know, we'd all be eating stewed chickweed and acorns. There's always been a lottery," he added petulantly. "Bad enough to see young Joe Summers up there joking with everybody."

Now, what is the prize? The "winner"—a mother of three named Tessie—is stoned to death. Why? "Lottery in June, corn be heavy soon."

Blood sacrifice for food, for procreation, for fear that, as Shakespeare wrote, "As flies to wanton boys are we to th' gods,/They kill us for their sport./" (*King Lear*, act 4, scene 1.)

Female genital mutilation is in large measure the Grim Reaper's doing. Given the longing to preempt his power, people temper terror by substituting sacrifice, less grievous and under control, for the caprice of malevolent forces of nature. Blood, the fearsome fluid, is seen as indispensable, and female blood, that of childbirth, the most precious gift of all.

In Kortum's work of magical realism, the practice of FGM itself, neither exaggerated nor sensational, is excruciatingly accurate and real. Furthermore, having made the protagonist a fledgling anthropologist, the author is critiquing the role academics play in the perpetuation of FGM. To compare "fiction" to ethnography, let's consider a typical peer-reviewed study, the report of an anthr/apologist, Aud Talle, who observes the Maasai. I've taken Talle's field notes and rearranged and condensed them to improve readability but kept in quotation marks the exact words she chose.

"As soon as the circumciser began cutting her flesh," Talle reports, "the [teen] started to fight back." . . . When attendants failed "to hold her down . . . the elder brother and guardian . . . told [them] . . . to use ropes."

The operation had to take place at once "because the cattle were restlessly waiting." But things were taking time. Efforts to lasso the girl's ankles failed, because, desperate, she kicked and struggled until exhaustion claimed her and she could finally be bound. Yet it's still not straight sailing. Without room in which to wrench her thighs apart, the actors called for back-up, and it came.

One of the men observing the scene . . . offer[ed to] help. Forcing his stick through the mud wall . . . , he made a hole, and pulled out one of the rope ends. The other rope was fastened to a roof beam at the entrance to the house (pp. 94–95).

At last, the circumciser could proceed. . . . With tiny movements she carved away the clitoris and the labia minora, while the women in loud voices instructed her how to cut. The blood rushed forward, and for us outside the actual scene, it was as if the excited voices of the women and the heavy breathing of the girl would never . . . end (p. 95).

Caught somewhere between horror and truth, Talle admits:

> *The smell of blood and sweat forced itself through the wall and incorporated us into what was happening inside. My own pulse beat more quickly. . . . [And] instantly, I understood what a personal challenge anthropological fieldwork could be. I was witnessing "torture," and the fact that I remained standing with the others outside somehow sanctioned what happened inside. . . .*

My point exactly, with one proviso: anthropologists don't "somehow sanction" FGM. Their "white coats" legitimize it and thereby vitiate activists' campaigns. Note that the original essay places "torture" in quotation marks, meaning to convey, *is* it *really* torture? No, not really . . .

But FGM *is* torture—*sans* quotation marks. And even when anesthesia works in clinics, amputations inflict lasting wounds and violate human rights.

Kortum shares this understanding but exceeds it. Appeals to human rights go only so far; statistical analyses, medical persuasion, and lofty sermons cannot address the *roots* of FGM. Only stories like Kortum's *Stones* do, with its intricate heights and depths, emotions, inventions, and insight. To my knowledge, no tale about the ablation of female genitalia has yet gone so deep, unstringing this tenacious custom's complex knots. Archetypal, biblical, redemptive, hallucinatory, psycho-theological, and ultimately breathtaking, Kortum's book takes ambitious leaps and dives into uncharted water.

Dr. Tobe Levin von Gleichen: Associate, the Hutchins Center for African and African American Research, Harvard University, visiting Research Fellow, International Gender Studies Centre, Lady Margaret Hall, University of Oxford.

January 2017

We know that much pagan thought, as exemplified in the famous phrase, "as above, so below," suggests that the terms "inferior" and "superior" are unreal. The idea "as above, so below," evokes an awe toward Nature, a sense that we share consciousness with plants, animals, stars, and stones, and that all living creatures, including stones, share a consciousness with the Soul of the World . . . or the spiritual genius of the Earth.

—Robert Bly, *News of the Universe*

CHAPTER 1

I was not an important woman when I was alive. I never owned land, and I didn't have a lot of cows. I lived in a hut made by my own hands from cattle dung and mud, and never left my village until I died.

I am not large, but the story I have to tell is large. Its distinction and importance selected me, and I've become bigger simply through its telling. I will try to use all of my words to tell this story, but I have to move carefully; I want to enter your ears and hearts a little askew—to grow the spaces for wonder this way so you can fill those spaces with what you know, and, more important, with what you don't know. There is an art to talking about what is not always easily understood.

I remember the long walk to the cave where I was born. I remember that even longer climb from my bed when I died. Death seems to turn up the volume on that important conversation: Where are we going? What are we supposed to do with this splendid gift of existence? Even in death I don't have an answer to those questions, but what I do know is this: what I loved most in life was my granddaughter, and what I love most in death has continued to be her. And she's in trouble. She has no idea what she's stumbled into, or what harm she's already done.

CHAPTER 2

Emely sees a nose, the camouflage pattern of uniforms, the sharp
glint of a gun. *Soldiers,* she thinks to herself, but it's as though
the thought has floated toward her from somewhere else. She
curls her hand around the handle of her suitcase, pulls her backpack in
close. More men move behind the cab, begin to talk to each other in
short, jagged sentences that sound foreign after her years away. One
of the soldiers leans over, shines a flashlight through the window. Its
yellow beam snakes across the shabby upholstery, touches her face for
a moment, then travels on to the back of the taxi driver's head. It's as
though the light activates her thoughts; stray, divided, unimportant re-
actions fill her head.

I hope Mama's present wasn't broken in the airplane, she thinks. *When
I get to the youth hostel, I'm going to take a long, hot shower.*

One of the soldiers speaks. "Step outside, ma'am," he says carefully,
almost formally. She thinks he might be enjoying his small authority.

"Yes," she manages to say, and fumbles for the latch on the door.
When it finally opens, it makes a sweet, rusty sound like the gate from
her mother's garden that leads to the cow pasture. And then, when she
stands and her lungs fill, she finds what it is she's forgotten. The air,

the air! It's alive with both animal and plant breath, and she's forgotten how old it is, how fragrant, how it travels across such a long distance. Even the night feels different. Long, black, almost thick, it settles like a drape across her shoulders.

"Didn't you know there's a curfew on?" one of the soldiers asks. Long holes have been punctured into his earlobes, stretching the skin several inches. Those ears, that stretched skin, fight the fastidiousness of his starched uniform. Emely has to remind herself not to stare.

"Well, didn't you?"

She hears deep inside his indignation something having to do with his position, maybe even the starched corners of his shirt collar.

"Well?"

She senses the press of other soldiers behind the leader. He's beginning to sound angry. She comes quickly back to attention.

"Yes," she replies. "They told us on the plane just before we landed."

"So what are you doing out here after curfew?"

She sifts through everything she could mention. She could tell him she's just been offered an important job with the Land Reform Movement, that she is a student just returning home from years abroad. But maybe that will make him angry; he might frown on a woman ambitious enough to dream of a life away from her cooking pot.

A familiar impatience stirs. *Pay attention!* she tells herself. If she concentrates and doesn't float away like she usually does, maybe she'll be able to figure a way out of this mess.

Emely does this all the time—talks to herself. She makes lists and schedules, gives speeches, exhorts rather than really converses. Even as a little girl, she always floated a little ways from the world; even back then she had had to discipline herself to step back into it. But all that hard interior pushing certainly has paid off, hasn't it? Long after most of her schoolmates dropped out, she has stayed in school. Her discipline won her a scholarship to the university, which in turn brought her to the attention of the professor who recommended her for graduate work in America. It brought her to this moment: home, triumphant, with a framed diploma wrapped in her favorite sweater.

But somehow, breathing this night, inhaling this old air, she can't think of the right thing to say. Heat—alive, desirous, the way it is in Africa—releases the smell of earth. She travels through that heat, down through the bones of animals, down into the ancient world that exists behind the one before her. Instincts long buried in her nervous system begin to bloom.

She knows, for instance, just from the content of the moisture in the air, what time it is.

"What's the matter with you, lady? Answer me!" Light from the soldier's flashlight blasts over her face.

"Please," she replies. "The driver and I, we needed to get to the youth hostel. We weren't trying to do anything wrong. We thought we had enough time, really."

There, finally, an explanation—and a tidy one at that. She looks at the soldiers expectantly.

But then the sky lowers, almost with a weight. It's like lying under a quilt breathing this air—thoughts, history, old stories, older dreams, all stitched into the dark. Half-remembered conversations, half-heard laughter floods her mind with memories.

Mama, she silently asks, *what are you doing now?*

CHAPTER 3

Only a few hours ago, the plane, ambitious in its descent, eagerly inhaled air, controlled hysteria as the pilot struggled to harness all that forward impulse, bring all those hours of movement into a state of stasis. The stewardess's metallic voice sounded overhead: "The use of electronic items is strictly forbidden; please keep your tray in an upright position."

Outside the window, row after row of shanties pulled away into the hissing night. Ragged palms, the bracelet of chain-link fences, a taxi cab too alert for this broken-down neighborhood humming its commercial animation through the night.

The plane finally hit the ground, the wheels shuddered, and finally Emely was home.

In the stunned silence of all that halted motion, she sat crumpling a Styrofoam cup between her fingers. Suddenly, all she wanted was to return to Los Angeles, where at least the lies were better hidden. There was a quality of waiting to her country—resentment, submission, a persistent unease—the same kind of waiting that lives behind the eyes of an abused woman. What terrible wave of violence was going to erupt next? What political uprising?

Some mornings, the people in her country woke to a whole new world, with violence so focused it could only be taken personally.

The stewardess's voice again: "Please arrive at your destination no later than eleven o'clock. A curfew is in effect."

A few months ago, the abused woman had blinked during yet another revolt from a combination of a faction of soldiers and a sprinkling of student anarchists. The revolt had been quickly, viciously quelled, but the country was still in lockdown mode. This was the country Emely was going to give her life to, and yet—unexpectedly—it repelled her.

CHAPTER 4

And now, a short hour later, a soldier is directing a flashlight over Emely's body. Carefully, almost lovingly, he touches every part of her with the light. Other soldiers line up behind their leader to scrutinize her. She sees their silhouettes against the sky. She could lose everything by what she says or doesn't say next.

She begins speaking into the flashlight's yellow beam.

"Please," she says, "it was a mistake. We just miscalculated, that's all." Her voice quivers with fear. "The drive just took a little longer than we thought it would."

The flashlight comes closer, the light grows brighter. "But you knew you were taking a chance, didn't you?" the soldier asks. "You knew you might be late."

She swallows, can't think of one thing to say. "I've been away too long," she finally manages to murmur, and in all that darkness comes a tiny sprig of a memory, another time when she was truly scared. She was around five and her grandmother, wishing to initiate her into some of her tribal secrets, brought her to a ceremony. Many women were there; most were naked, glazed with red mud. There was a young girl, Aziza, who was maybe twelve; she lived down the road from Emely.

The girl's head had been shaved, and Emely remembers how its shape drew her to it. She wanted to place her hands on it, know its curve. Aziza looked at her, and Emely knew in that moment that she was scared, but then a woman, so old her arteries lined her arms like an unfurled skein of lumpy yarn, appeared.

The old woman had braided and oiled her hair so that it protruded from her head like a ram's horn. The horn spiked over her head, pushed into the air toward the place where all this was going. The old woman reached down, grabbed Emely from her grandmother, held her so tight, she could barely breathe. The chanting grew loud, then louder, and the women's voices braided together. The voices joined the horn, pointed with it toward the thing that was coming.

And then that scream, Aziza's terrible scream. Emely joined it with one of her own. She struggled, and the old woman tried to hold her, but she wiggled away. *Got to get to Mama, got to get to Mama.*

She rushed through the forest of legs and ran all the way home, where she found her mother standing in her garden, talking calmly to a neighbor. Emely rushed into her arms, so breathless she couldn't talk . . . and later she didn't want to. Her mother held her, kept that terrible horn away. Night lowered, stars appeared in the sky, and what her mother talked about with the neighbor rumbled through her body. Heat released the smell of the river and the earth, and Emely wanted to stay there forever. Everything that was in that time, all of her child-hood, resided in each breath.

Later that night, there would be kale stirred round and round by her mother's spoon, the sweet tumble of rain, and then heavy, inno-cent sleep uncorrupted by screams. For this short time, all that she had just seen, all that was about to come—her grandmother's death a few months later, her parents' decision to send her away to the Lutheran Boarding School for the Education of Young Men and Women, all those lonely years in college and graduate school—was held in abeyance by her mother's sheltering arms.

Even today, that simple moment of belonging remained with her, unaltered by the dissonance of some fifteen years. These many years later she could still feel how it felt to be rocked in her mother's arms, made safe by love.

But a memory can't shield her from these soldiers, can it? The leader lowers the light over Emely's body. Possessive, hard, it presses through her shirt to her breasts, glides down over her waist, touches her rumpled jeans, her shoes. Her body feels as though it's not quite hers; she dares not move or change her expression without permission. And then the light comes back to her face and stays there, and that's when she realizes that these men don't view a curfew violation as something merely careless; to them, it is a potential act of violence against the government. To these men, she is already an enemy.

"We'll look through her luggage now," the leader says grimly. The taxi driver gets out of the car.

The soldiers open the taxi's trunk, and within seconds her whole life is scattered across the road: her favorite, much-underlined books; worn notebooks scribbled with private thoughts; her UCLA sweatshirt; her Mickey Mouse watch from Disneyland, so special she didn't wear it on the plane; hair oil; presents for her family; all this is strewn carelessly in the dirt. The soldiers move efficiently, murmuring to each other in a language now grown sharp, syllables that could nick the air. Books are turned upside down and shaken, containers opened, fingers jabbed into their contents—the soldiers even examine the backpack's tubing. What frightens Emely more than their questions is that what seemed to her a few moments ago to merely be procedure, soldiers just doing their jobs, has swelled into something more dangerous—a feeling that these men are bullies, or something much worse. Something having to do with them being bored.

"What country did you say you were coming from?" asks the leader.

"United States," she answers quickly.

"What were you doing there?"

"I was a student."

"Where?"

"UCLA," she answers, and then realizes he probably doesn't know what those letters stand for, might even think she is insulting him or showing off. "That stands for University of California, Los Angeles."

Does she sound patronizing? If she says something more will they punish her for being different from traditional women? She tries to fit her mind into these old ways, notices for the first time her earrings dangling from one of the soldiers' fingers.

Another soldier approaches the leader, carefully holding her Rubik's cube. "Look at this, sir," he says, handing it over.

The leader brings the cube slowly up to eye level, holding the beam of his flashlight on it all the while. He says something low that she can't quite catch. The other soldiers come to peer over his shoulder. "What is this?" he asks.

"It's a toy," she replies. "A puzzle. You line up the squares so that each side is one color."

The beam from the flashlight makes the cube's reds, greens, and yellows look aggressive, too cheerful.

Hoping to make things more ordinary, she says, "I was taking it home for one of my brothers."

The soldiers pass it amongst themselves, and Emely begins to breathe deeply, her spirits lifting. *Maybe I've just exaggerated the danger,* she thinks to herself. *Maybe everything is going to be all right after all. I could be just like the Rubik's cube to these men—a novelty, a game, just another way to pass the evening.*

Laughter erupts from the group of soldiers, and she relaxes even further. She sees that the soldiers were once boys.

The taxi driver has drawn near and when he speaks into her ear, Emely jumps in surprise.

"I know what to do," he whispers. His hands brush hers conspiratorially.

"What?" she asks, alarmed. "What are you going to do?"

"Watch and see," he says, and something about the way he wears his old worn hat, cocked so jauntily to one side, makes her newly afraid.

"No," she says. She tries to grab his arm. "Don't do anything!"

He turns and winks. "Don't worry, little miss," he says. "They expect it."

Emely knows this man's life from her student years here in the capital. He lives in one small room crowded with dozens of extended family members. He has a wife older than her actual years, who cooks on a coal pot in the alley out back, blaming him for all she's lost. He's like thousands of others living in the city trying to stay alive, his hopes reduced to earning a few coins by the end of the day with which to buy some liquor. Hoping to provide better for their children, most of the city's vast population has migrated from the countryside, but are now even poorer than before. At least in the country they belonged to a tribal hierarchy that, though rigid, provided answers, an articulate largesse that sometimes gave one value simply through membership. But here in this shrill city with nothing to belong to, people fall back on the basest of motivations. Whatever the driver is going to do next will probably offend Emely. What she doesn't know is if it will offend the soldiers as well.

The driver approaches the leader and, smiling, draws from his pocket a raggedy pile of bills. Peeling one from the pile, he tries to hand it to the leader. The soldier does nothing. The driver's smile becomes wider. He adds another bill to the first.

Emely is trying to feel the sky above her, to disappear in its breath—tries this way to make whatever is happening in front of her smaller. It doesn't work. The driver's absolute conviction that the leader is bribable—that it is simply a matter of determining how much he wants—holds a peculiar fascination for her.

"Come on, man, what's your problem?" the driver asks when the leader does not accept the money.

The leader says nothing, and the taxi driver laughs an ugly sound that has nothing to do with mirth.

"Okay, okay," he says, his smile now grown forced. "You want more, is that it?"

He bends over, takes off his shoe, and, reaching into the toe, draws out a crumpled bill. Despite her fear, Emely finds herself admiring his absolute insistence that he's running the show.

The leader stands rigid. "I don't want it," he says. "Put it back."

When the taxi driver speaks again, his voice has softened. "This is a lot of money," he cajoles. "You can buy yourself a girl, have yourself a good time!" He laughs; the sound rises and scratches the sky. "Find yourself a pretty girl like this one here."

Emely decides to use what she knows to travel away. She knows about the Land Settlement Policy of 1993. She knows how to successfully present a paper to a classroom of opinionated scholars. She knows how many feet of lumber can be cut from a large ponderosa pine—approximately twelve hundred. She knows about various farming procedures in her country, the population per square mile, vaccination techniques to prevent infant mortality. Usually she knows when to talk and when not to. She knows about different kinds of loving, how to take a child onto her lap and make him laugh, that she loves her mother and father, the professor, her grandmother who has died. All of this she reviews and remembers. What she doesn't know is what she's doing standing here in this dark night.

She stares at the leader. He's still at attention, his hands at his side. She wants to compliment him on his patience, then remembers that she is already in violation, a potential threat to the government.

"I've even got a sister," the driver cackles. "She's very pretty and very, very juicy, if you know what I mean." He pumps his hips suggestively.

She knows the script for this exchange, and when the driver laughs—he, too, has read the leader's embarrassment—she's not really surprised when the leader unstraps his gun.

The soldiers wait for some kind of sign as to how this night will go, and the driver waits with a trace of his former grin still lingering on his face. He now knows he's gone too far.

When the gun finally moves, it seems to travel in slow motion. The side of the gun strikes the driver's cheek, and his flesh looks like bread dough spilled over the edge of a pan. Emely hears a sharp crack. She is surprised to see the taxi driver still standing after the blow.

There is another moment of suspended quiet, and that is when Emely realizes there have been sounds in the night all this time—grass blades whispering, the faraway humming of insects, the distant, steady wind.

The Rubik's cube has long since dropped to the ground. The beating begins in earnest, all the soldiers joining in, bunching their fists into tight, hard weapons.

What has become of her self-confident American strut, the label on her jeans? Is this happening because she hasn't paid attention? Everything that Emely has learned in the United States vanishes, and she's once again a frightened tribeswoman engaged by forces she doesn't quite understand.

The sound of the beating continues. She hears the gasp of air being sucked in, the thud of flesh hitting flesh. The driver is no longer standing. Nothing from the world she recently left seems to exist here, none of the same rules apply. The driver was crude, that's true; he demeaned the leader in front of his men, but he still doesn't deserve to be so viciously, thoroughly beaten. Will they shoot him, then turn to her next? If she turns and runs, the soldiers will certainly follow her, maybe beat her to death.

So what does Emely do? Once again she floats away, concentrates on the sky, on breathing in its air, not this blood-red scene before her.

Breathing it in, pushing it out. She puts her hand into her pocket, touches first the stone she carries for luck then finds a ballpoint pen, begins to nervously push its tiny knob in and out with her fingers.

Fierce, hard hits now, some with the butt of the gun. The driver, his upper lip curled back, sports a new gap where two teeth recently were. Blood pours from his nose, splatters the ground.

The nub of the pen going in and out marks the beating like a tiny metronome. Emely takes her hands out of her pockets, folds her arms across her chest. Are the spots on the soldiers' uniforms the driver's blood, or part of their camouflage? She looks down at her shoes and realizes they are sprayed with blood as well.

When the soldiers finally stop hitting the driver, they turn and look at her. They draw near, the men, silhouettes, moving in a pack. Boots scrape the ground, and she stands there, not understanding—and then, when she does understand, does not want to know. She is next. She begins to back up. A low moan slides from between her lips. A slow "no."

"No," she says louder, surprised by her voice. She's suddenly angry. "What are you doing?" she says. "I'm a patriot serving this country!"

They begin to surround her.

She has an idea. "I'm an anthropologist," she says and digging into her fanny pack, pulls out her official ID. "I'm working on Professor Cambura's Land Reform project."

That seems to stop them. They look at each other. The leader takes her card, shines his flashlight on it. "Maybe we better take her to Chief Kenti," he says to the soldiers, and then turns back to her.

"Get in the car, miss. You're under arrest."

CHAPTER 5

The last time you saw me alive, Granddaughter, you were only five. I was sliding up one side of my breath, trying to bring it in, falling down the other side, trying to push it out. And what were you doing? You were clinging to my neck, squeezing so hard I could barely breathe. And that wasn't a good thing, because I needed all the air I could get for the matter at hand; I was dying.

"Don't go, don't go," you called, only inches from my ear. No one had ever left you before. "Granddaughter," I wanted to say, "can't you see I'm a little busy?"

A hygienic swish of white robes, and Father Joseph entered the hut. *What has my foolish, God-fearing daughter done now? Get that man out of here!* The last thing I needed in all the world was a priest.

He glanced at me. "Looks like I'm here just in time," he whispered. And my daughter? Well, she looked at Father Joseph like he was providence itself, everything I'd taught her chased out of her ears by church and that small-minded, bland husband she married. She didn't even keep the name you were supposed to have, "Amely," the name waiting for you chiseled on the walls of a cave deep in the forest. She changed your name to the more ordinary Emely. Never mind. You will always be Amely to me.

"I thought you could administer last rites," my daughter said, wiping tears from her eyes.

Father Joseph walked over to my bed, looked down, and laid his hand on my forehead. "May the Lord in His love and mercy help you with the grace of His Holy Spirit," he intoned.

Well, you, Amely, you weren't having any of this, were you now? You pushed under the priest's arm, climbed up into my bed, pressed your hot little body against mine. If I'd had more energy, I would have laughed.

The priest put his hand on your shoulder. "Emely," he said, "give your grandmother a little more room."

Room. Ha! Shows how much he knew about dying! The last thing in the world I needed was more room. What I needed to do was to try to get small, because I was headed toward that point of light out there. I had to get so small I could slip through it. And that was a difficult assignment, because what I was discovering in those last few moments of my life was that the bodily house is full of light, that there was a constant movement against all the surfaces of who I was. Big light, huge light, and it was just as solid as my bones.

Just a few hours earlier I had somehow managed to rise from that bed. I'd had one last thing to do. I knew I was fast becoming a "was," but I needed to stay an "is" a little bit longer. I'd moved slowly toward the garden, my pain filling the hut. "Amely," I had called. "I have something to give you beyond the ears of your mother."

In the garden, you climbed up into my lap, just as you always did, and I wrapped my arms around you. I knew I was giving you a burden—the burden to remember. The story I was going to tell you was the most holy story of all, but I needed to fortify you for the years away from me. You had the spaces inside for what the world was trying to forget. Even at the age of five, you possessed a steadfast purpose that chastened anything superfluous in your path. Everything alive was your family. Five or six dogs followed you everywhere. Everyone in the village thought you fed them, but that wasn't it, was it? Somehow those animals knew you were their home.

Holes, more light. I was fast turning to lace. I had to tell this story quickly. "The ways of Jesus are fast spreading across this land," I began that day in the garden. "They are erasing the old ways. Even your own mother doesn't believe. But the story I will tell you goes back to a time even before Jesus was born. It goes back to the first fire. You must not be careless with it, though; this story belongs to many. It's not just yours to give away."

I was wearing my favorite old brown sweater. You stuck your fingers into its holes, hooking yourself into me. Somehow, you knew this story needed all ten fingers.

"There will be a time when you will use this story to save your life," I continued, "and the lives of others. Do you promise to be careful with it, granddaughter?"

You looked up into my face, your eyes dark and serious. "Yes, Grandmama," you solemnly promised.

If I weren't dying already, the lie you told me that morning in the garden would surely have killed me right then and there.

I told you the story then, trying to tell it so well you would always have its melody to lean against. When I finished, you were quiet. "Where are you going, Grandmama?" you eventually asked. I remember looking down into your sweet face. The light behind me shone through me, and I saw some of that distance in your eyes as well.

"Far, far away," I replied, trying to soothe you. "But close enough so that I will always see you."

For the last time that afternoon, we sat together in the garden, and I said good-bye to everything I loved: plowing with my favorite ox, all the animal's improbable and miscellaneous parts moving together across the red loamed earth; cooking chapatis over my fire (how many had I made in my life, circling, circling always, crimping the edges of the dough with my fingers, making that small wheel that spun my days forward toward this, my final moment?). I remembered as well the many times I had walked to the river, the soles of my feet burning with all that inhaled sun; the talk of the women running into the water, coming back as song; the dimpled bottoms of my grandchildren spilling over my arms. I remembered taking an ax to a tree for firewood, the split-open, just-been-born smell of it all; going to the fields for maize, the dry shiver of all those unclothed sheaths, the plump sweetness waiting inside; pounding the maize at the grinder, powder leaking down . . . this village, its noisy storms, its green pastures spilling toward the sky; love given back, really.

But most of all, Amely, what I hated about dying was leaving you. You were and are my best thing. Always, my best thing.

And now, a few hours later, I was back in bed doing the hard work of dying.

Father Joseph reached down into his robe and drew out a small, green velvet bag. "May the Lord turn His countenance to you and grant you peace," he said in his important sermon-giving voice. He pulled the tassels of the bag and took out a silver cross and a small bottle. "Christ is the only true God," he said as he unscrewed the bottle. "May this pagan heart accept Him tonight." He splattered me with holy water.

Another voice began to hum in my ear. *I am waiting for you at the edge of light. Friday, September, April? You say your tiny words, mount the tiny hills of your days, and none of this matters. I love perfectly, because I love nothing in particular.* Words like lungsful of air, words that glowed in the dark. The Great Mother, the hard stone of prayer inside the blue, blue sweep of her sky.

No more pain now, I was traveling toward her, into her, becoming her. I could barely hear Father Joseph now.

Actual death is a little like floating. Loosened from the strange and wonderful grip of mortality, my body was changing. I was becoming pure movement, flowing into the curve of the sky. Women out there, many women, pulling me toward them—a hand, breasts, more hands, smiles . . . oh, such welcoming goodness! I was moving toward them, but before I was with them all the way, I turned one more time to look at you.

You knew I was leaving. Your eyes were large, and I could see that you'd reached down into yourself, to the place where you really live. And then what did you do? You leaned over the emptying husk that was my body and tried to give me your five-year-old breath. Your lips were warm and slightly damp against mine. I didn't take that breath, and that's how you knew I was dying—I had never refused anything from you. And that's also when you pressed your body even tighter against mine. Even the priest and my daughter knew now to stay away.

Climbing, climbing, I was moving away from my final stillness, riding my last singular breath far away from the deep green of my home, toward and into the great indestructible Mother. I was small now, small enough to get through that single radiant point of grace out there. One last look back, and that's how I know that in that final moment, you leaned over and pulled my last breath into you.

Mama, daughter, grandmama, the slide of those small syllables no longer fit; you don't name one breeze in the wind, one wave in the ocean, do you? Africa, Okino, I belong to so many now, I am no longer just one name. There is no separation when you're dead—no black, no white, no otherness. We all just run into each other, swirled together into one thick, rich consciousness. What someone knows in America flows into what someone else knows from Tibet. All experiences run into each other, too; lawyers, teachers, plumbers, doctors, and chefs—we have all sung our children to sleep.

And what we know is this: you're in trouble, Amely, and we, the dead, watch.

CHAPTER 6

The man the soldiers bring her to, Police Chief Kenti, is a dark force. He gazes at Emely with steady eyes that seem to be all pupils. The gray in his hair streaks from his forehead in tidy strands. He sits in a chair wearing a starched shirt, but there's a light mark on his lower lip that clashes with his immaculate, almost severe, surface. About the size of a little finger, the area makes Emely think that, at some time in Chief Kenti's life, a torrent of angry words indented his lower lip.

He stares at her so ominously that words begin to pour from her mouth. "Please, sir," she says, "let me explain. They told us on the plane about the curfew, but I wanted to get to the youth hostel. It's cheap, you know. The taxi driver assured me we could get there in time."

The chief continues to stare. His eyes reflect nothing from within. Vast, unruffled, he is so still he is almost more geography than man. He doesn't even blink.

Emely clears her throat, plunges on, decides to repeat what seemed to stop the soldiers out on the road: "I'm an anthropologist, employed by the Land Reform Movement."

More silence. Light chopped by the fan on the ceiling flicks across the police chief. Although the light grazes his skin, burnishes his cheeks, rounds his forehead, it somehow seems to remain separate from him. She can't imagine him being a boy or a father. Has he ever laughed in a movie theater, ever loved a woman, balanced a child on those massive shoulders?

He has not spoken a word, and she is more frightened of him than she ever was of the soldiers. His great silence makes her continue to babble. She throws words of explanation into the dark holes of his eyes—no discipline, no thought.

"I'm only a student," she continues. "And I can't really afford anything besides the youth hostel."

When his voice finally comes, it is so deep it seems to rumble through long corridors before it reaches the air. "What is your name?" he asks.

"Emely Matei," she answers breathlessly.

"Do you have any identification?"

"Certainly," she replies. She reaches into her fanny pack, opens her wallet, flips opens the plastic container that holds her international driver's license. He is already in possession of her passport, student ID, and official travel papers.

He glances impassively at her license. "This is quite a serious offense," he says. "It could mean a long time in prison." He speaks carefully. There is a precision in his voice, as though he never puts anything out there into the world that he hasn't already considered.

Her heart beats rapidly. "I'm sorry, sir," she replies. "I've been away for three years. This is my first time back. I just got a master's degree in Narrative Folklore. I used to live in this city and attended the university here before earning a scholarship to study in America. I've worked very hard. I'm just trying to get home." Her voice has become a tiny flame. "I haven't seen my family in three years," she pleads. "I'm from the mountains. I'm not a criminal. I just underestimated the time it would take to get to the youth hostel. That's all."

His eyebrows rise. More silence follows, and then into the quiet comes a voice.

Amely, I am here.

It is unbidden, moving up from a source deep within her, flowing past all her hard-earned, school-taught facts, the known and the proven. Her grandmother. She has finally broken through.

What? Emely asks silently. *Who's that?* She asks this, although she already knows the answer.

Step carefully, Granddaughter.

Grandmama?

It is only in the empty spaces where the living don't know everything that the dead can finally speak. You're so frightened, Amely, you're finally beginning to hear me.

Of course she tries to shake it off. *I must be really scared,* she tells herself. *Grandmama is dead. Pull yourself together.*

She tries again. "Sir," she says, "this is all just a big mistake."

You're in more danger than you know, Amely.

Although she doesn't believe this voice is anything more than the product of fear, she silently pleads with it. *Grandmama,* she says, *leave me alone. You can't help me here.*

You've asked me to come, child.

What? She wets her lips. *How could I have asked you to come?*

A small, unknown part of you asked for me, her grandmother says. *And because I love you and you're in trouble, I came. You need me, child. The man before you is dangerous. Look before you; what do you see?*

Despite the fact that she doesn't truly believe her grandmother's voice is real, Emely tries to argue, as usual. *He's just a man, Grandmama. An important man, that's true, but just a man, nevertheless.*

There's more, her grandmother says. *Much more. Look again. The man before you is one of the entities who has become so injured by life he has given away everything that makes him a man. You must be careful, Amely. He is only temporarily wearing flesh.*

Emely's heartbeat fills the room. She stares into the chief's eyes, fighting panic.

These entities will turn you into something that is theirs, Amely, her grandmother continues. *They will turn you silent and then demand to speak through you.*

Perhaps because she is so alone, Emely finally asks for help.

Grandmama, she says. *What should I do?*

Words, child, her grandmother replies. *Use your words. It's what you've got the most of. Do what you do best; use your words like planks to build a house, a house with walls he can't enter.*

What words, Grandmama?

Drop inside, she instructs. *What do you see?*

Facts, indignation, statistics . . . These?

Yes.

Emely is not conscious of breaking the paralysis that has been hold-ing her. One moment she is standing frozen in front of the desk, the next she is leaning in toward the police chief, is speaking once again. She tries a new tack.

"Sir," she says, her voice quaking, "I haven't done anything wrong, and there's a man outside who has been viciously beaten by your soldiers just for being out ten minutes past curfew. It's a definite human rights violation."

The man twists his lips into a shallow smile that speaks to both conversations: the words she has just spoken and the communication below her voice, which she somehow knows he hears.

"We aren't criminals," she says.

Grandmama's voice comes back, smooth, liquid, and sweet. *Keep going, Amely. You're walking down the right path.*

Her eyes travel to the picture of the president on the wall. "I'm not a traitor. As I mentioned, I'm part of the government's Land Reform Commission."

The police chief straightens his pen so that it is at a right angle to the desk.

"I have an assignment that begins in two weeks."

Finally, attention curves around the edges of his silence.

"My assignment is to record the Okinos' lifestyle, their stories, lan-guage, artifacts. It's the first stage in a large plan designed to unify all the tribes in our country."

"The Okino?" His eyes seem brighter. "The Okino, near Ambolmas?" She nods.

"Tell me more," he says. His tongue flicks across his lower lip.

She straightens her shoulders, tries to speak crisply. "I'm to docu-ment their way of life. The time will come when the Okino will realize the forest can no longer support their current lifestyle. The ecosystem can't sustain much game, and because of the timber harvest, eroded soil is silting up the river. There can't be too many fish left to eat."

Grandmama's voice again. *Good, child*, she says. *He's listening.*

"Is this Professor Cambura's experiment, by any chance?" he asks. He floats the word *experiment* upon a raft of disdain.

Although Emely has already sensed he knows everything about her, she's surprised at the mention of her mentor. "Why, yes!" she ex-claims. "Do you know him?"

"I've made his acquaintance," he responds. "I've even had some influence on the project."

She's surprised again. "I thought it was a university plan," she says. "I didn't know that the police were involved."

He picks up a pile of paper, thumps it against the desk. "This is a project to collect data on all of our countries and indigenous people, isn't it?" he asks.

"Yes," she answers. "We know their lives will be untenable in another twenty years or so. We'll teach the people farming, health care, nutrition, good things like that. We want to record their way of life now and prepare them for new ways of living in the future."

She recalls his use of the word *experiment* and adds brightly, "The idea has been tried very successfully in other countries." She finds herself nodding too much, smiling too often. "If everyone has access to the same standard of living, there won't be so much fighting among our different tribes. I'm only involved in the first stage, however—the observing and the recording."

"How will you communicate with the professor?" he asks. "I understand he is the lead coordinator on this project."

She doesn't know why he wants this information, but she's anxious to make a professional impression. "I'll have a radio," she says. "And we're going to establish a series of contact days. Professor Cambura changed my life, you know. He urged me to go to America, and he's the one who gave me this job."

The first time she heard the professor speak was during her freshmen year at the university. He was giving a lecture on the Land Reform Movement, and at the last moment she decided to attend. She had heard he was a visionary who was working closely with a committee of scholars, environmentalists, international activists, and politicians to develop a plan to address the needs of tribal people. Going into the lecture she had only a slight interest in the subject, but sitting in the darkened auditorium, she was mesmerized.

The professor articulated a vision of a unified country, and for the first time, Emely could imagine it. With a fair and equal standard of living for all citizens, he theorized, internal conflict could be quelled— but he also stressed how crucial it was not to lose what the indigenous people knew. He said it was critical to send scholars into the field to document the traditional way of life.

After that lecture, Emely changed her major from political science to anthropology, and in the year and a half that followed, she studied hard—writing papers, reading, and presenting oral treatises about the importance of preserving and recording tribal beliefs. Eventually, she found a tributary of anthropology that she loved: the gathering of narrative folklore. UCLA had a department specializing in this branch of anthropology, and at the professor's urging, Emely applied for a scholarship, never imagining that she would ever be actually accepted.

The next part of Emely's life was like a fairy tale. Every year the professor took some of his best students under his wing, and now Emely was one of them. When first invited to his Sunday salons, she sat shyly through the lively intellectual debates in his living room. Gradually, however, she began to speak, and—especially after she was accepted to UCLA, lit from the inside—she began to dazzle the room with her opinions, facts, clever arguments, and hope (all calculated, of course, to bring a smile to her mentor's face).

And smile he did. He told her that when she completed her studies in America, he wanted her to work with him on the Land Reform Movement. "You'll be one our first foot soldiers," he said. And when she received his letter in America formerly offering her a job, how proud she felt. Emely Matei, daughter of a tea grower from a mountain tribe, would figure in her country's future!

The police chief interrupts her thoughts. "You seem very young," he challenges. "Why were you chosen for this important assignment?"

"I was recommended by the professor," she says proudly. "My grandmother was an Okino, and she left the forest when she was twelve. I speak a similar dialect. It really is quite an honor. The professor has put me in charge of trying to find the tribe. They're very secretive and haven't been seen for years."

She puts her hands into her pockets, feels for her lucky stone then decides it's too casual a gesture, pulls them out again. "I like the concept of the Land Reform Movement," she continues. "Things in this country would be a lot different if we all lived in the same way. There wouldn't be as much intertribal conflict. I know how it feels to be looked down on. I went through a rather hard time at boarding school because I came from a supposedly backwards, more primitive tribe."

Too intimate, too female-confidential? Although he is listening closely, there is still no me-and-you in his stare.

Should I tell him I've heard about the forest from you, Grandmama? she silently asks.

Before her grandmother has a chance to answer, the chief abruptly opens up a drawer, takes out a map, and unfolds it across his desk. "When are you going into the forest?" he asks.

"Three weeks from today," she responds promptly. "That way I'll have a little time to relax with my family."

"Miss Matei," he says, "would you mind showing me where the forest is and where it is that you live?"

Again, she has a feeling that there is nothing careless about this conversation. It is as though she is following a script only he has access to.

She leans over the map. "This green is Kawani. This is Ndora, and this is—"

"The River Waduli," the chief says. "A child can float on that river, and sometimes, when the moon is high, it's like floating in moon juice."

"Excuse me, sir?"

One large fingernail is idly stroking the surface of the map. The police chief seems lost in a dream.

"The trees," he continues, "some are hollow and you can crawl inside them, and in those dark places you can breathe deep the layers of rot and hidden things. Secret things, midnight things."

Be careful, Amely. Grandmama's voice is taut with warning. *He's become a boy, but his power is still a man's. Ask him a question to bring him back.*

"Have you visited that region, sir?" she asks.

He doesn't bother to answer, but his hand stops moving. When he looks up, she sees something she doesn't think she's supposed to see. For just a second, before he resumes his mantle of control, she catches a glimpse of the wildest fury she has ever seen in the eyes of a human being. The rest of the police chief's face is still, but his eyes blaze with bright, direct, hot anger. It is only for a couple of seconds, but Emely will never forget it. She has never seen so much hate.

But then his face goes blank. He closes his eyes and breathes. "You wear palm oil in your hair, don't you?"

She looks away. Her smell is more information than she wants him to know.

He opens his eyes again and looks at her with a sense of recognition. "You're very ambitious, aren't you, Miss Matei? You think this job will be your stepping stone to future success."

She has a feeling he is collecting information so he can destroy her world. She crosses her arms and tries to smile.

"But you aren't just motivated by ambition," he continues. "You also have rescue dreams. You think you will go into the forest and save these people, don't you?" His voice is eerie, low and personal.

"It's true I want to help our country, sir," she replies cautiously.

His next sentence is as abrupt as two hands clapping. "I'm sorry, Miss Matei, for this brief inconvenience." He stands up. "I see no reason to detain you further. You may rest here for a while, and in a few hours, when it is light again, I'll have one of my soldiers drive you back to the city."

He crosses the room, lifts a coat from a hanger, and puts it on. Although he has turned away from her, she still has the feeling that his eyes—those strange, glassy eyes—are on her.

"What about the cab driver?" she asks.

He turns. "I'll see that he gets to a doctor. And Miss Matei . . ." His upper lip draws back in his version of a smile, revealing perfect white teeth.

"Yes?"

"I'm very pleased to finally meet you."

She feels the withdrawal of his mind before he even leaves the room. When he is gone, she stares at the groove his fingernail has made on the map of her home.

Why did he say he was pleased to "finally" meet me? she wonders. She looks up. The window behind the desk is divided into six small panes. She chooses the one in the upper right hand corner, stares at the small square of night. *Mama,* she thinks to herself, *wouldn't she be frightened if she knew where I was tonight?* Tears burn in her eyes, and she sinks slowly to the floor.

Grandmama, she calls. *Will you come, call me by my secret name?*

Her grandmother answers immediately. *Yes, Amely, I am here.*

Too much has happened tonight that I don't understand.

You're tired, granddaughter. Close your eyes. I'll keep watch while you sleep.

CHAPTER 7

A woman in Iraq picks up her stones, holds them until they are warm with her.

"*Khanoman, khaharan, Mishenavid? Ahange do ah be sooyeh shoma miferestam!*" (Sister Women, you who are the dead, can you hear me? I send you my song of prayer.)

We who are the dead answer immediately. *Yes, Sister, we are here.*

"What has happened?" she asks. "I'm frightened. This morning at my altar, the blue feather tore."

The good news is that Amely is starting to hear us. She was arrested coming back into her country, but now she sleeps. We're stronger inside her because she is less certain of what she knows. She's starting to fill the hollow places where she doesn't have answers with us.

"I feel so helpless," the woman says. "Is there anything I can do to help her learn faster?"

Think bigger thoughts with holes, we reply. *Make louder wind chimes to catch the wind, build taller sculptures to help our Mother receive air. In order to hear what it is she knows, Amely needs to rid herself of the world's noise. We only hope she will be ready in time.*

"Yes, Sisters," the woman says. "I choose my country's stone, jet, so that she will know courage. I warm it in my hands, push it into my family of stones."

CHAPTER 8

I t all started three years ago in a Los Angeles dormitory. Emely was waiting to meet her new roommate. She looked around the room. *So much emptiness for such a small space*, she thought, *a tourist kind of smallness.*

The walls of the dormitory had been painted a careful neutral green, the color made more significant by what it chose not to say. Twin beds, each covered with a pale yellow bedspread, a bulletin board peppered with holes, a desk wedged against each bed—what goes into the mind lives in the same neighborhood as the body.

Emely opened the door of the closet, peered inside, absorbed its wispy sadness. Six white plastic hangers. She flipped her hands across them—listened to the clackety-clack of all those knocked elbows. She sank back on one of the beds.

When did I become so different from everyone else? she wondered. None of the things she loved were there, not even light. Outside the window, a jumble of roofs, the fallen blocks of air-conditioner units, were all bathed in the bleak, disquieting smog of the Los Angeles afternoon.

The dead were surprised by what Emely did next. She reached into her luggage, pulled out a picture of her grandmother, and wedged it into one of the corners of the bulletin board. Now there she was, dark stretched power, ferocious, and smiling just a little. Her grandmother, watching, liked it.

I'll keep guard over you, dear one.

Her scent preceded her: precise pinpricks of cinnamon. Valerie Mayfield of Middleton, Connecticut—her full song and personal weather—now filled the doorway. Long neck, pink, pillowed lips, loose, flirtatious light. Blond hair swinging, scarf inclined the other way—two hellos, one to her and one to that hair.

How was Emely going to sleep in the room with all that light?

Valerie pranced across the room and spilled a drugstore's worth of beauty products onto one of the desks. She had two perfectly formed calligraphy lines of eyebrows, and one of those eyebrows raised itself at the sight of Emely.

And then, her voice. It moved up through the long tube of her throat, circling, rising, spinning, until finally it found the pink pout of her lips, and then, sugar-flaked, a tin of cookies, her voice filled the room with butter-yummy entitlement.

"Who's that?" she asked, one pink fingernail tapping on the picture of Emely's grandmother, and what she asked she seemed to taste, flicking the words around with her tongue. "Looks like some kind of witch."

Witch, indeed! her grandmother said to herself as she watched. *If I could, I would fry that girl up for dinner, because look, look what she's doing to my Amely—all that entitled shininess rubbing her down, making her small, tribal, primitive, reducing her to just the pit of herself.*

"My grandmother," Emely eventually replied. "That's who it is."

Her new roommate grabbed the wing of her hair between long fingers and, making a screw of it, began to twist it round and around, drilling down toward what she really wanted to know. "Can I have the bed by the window?" she asked.

Emely managed to nod.

Before she had climbed on the plane, Emely had surprised everyone who was watching by picking up a few stones and putting them into her backpack. Each one had a white line running through its middle. She took those stones out now, began to arrange them in a circle on her pale-yellow bedspread.

Valerie Mayfield of Connecticut looked at Emely, looked at the stones, picked up her hair dryer, and went into the bathroom. Citing asthma, she moved out the next day.

We, the ones who watch, think it probably started with those stones. Emely began to do herself up slick. Eyelashes spiked with mascara, her grandmother's photograph still pegged to the bulletin board, she learned quickly how to retail her roots, creating an allure both ethnic and modern in its exploitation of mystery. A staccato series of roommates, not one date, straight A's, of course; Los Angeles both elated and confounded her with its instant gratification, the furor of fame, the self-absorbed "I" shined up and praised.

No longer scripted to the mythology of the tribe, Emely had to continuously translate and reconfigure herself into a system she didn't always understand. But Emely wasn't stupid. She quickly discovered that even the most sophisticated scholar carried a private pack of subliminal postcards related to her country. Slap a card down, a silhouette of Maasai chiseled against a magenta sky. Another card? A herd of zebras. All the cards laid down? A kind of hypnotic suggestion at work, time manifested as matter, the promise of human existence revealed.

And Emely learned to play those cards well, presenting the stories she had been raised on as culturally significant folklore, stitching in just enough danger and mysticism to excite even the most erudite of listeners. She left people wondering, did she live here in Los Angeles, measuring the information of the world into tiny units, or did she live back in the small, smoky village from whence she had come?

She never fully answered that question; what they wondered became part of her slicked- up Los Angeles brand—that circle of stones, feathers for bookmarks, a few well-crafted allusions to a mysterious imported darkness. "My grandmother told me that stones could talk," she said one day in her narrative folklore class. Then, with a few deft strokes, she managed to subtly advertise a strange world as unseen and as private as another consciousness, and in the process became her own best story.

As Emely commercialized her roots, spilling more and more secrets into ears that couldn't possibly understand, the ones who watched became alarmed. Everything she did, every story she told, affected nothing less than the balance of the world. And then there was that fateful day when Emely stood in the Fallow Museum of Anthropological History and gave away the most important story of them all.

She was presenting her oral treatise to a rustling crowd of opinionated graduate students, professors, and PhD candidates. A flick of a switch and another photograph of her grandmother poured across the screen behind her, her face creased by the weather of her life, wrinkles lined with PowerPoint light.

"I would like to introduce you to Mrs. Natodu," she began. "My grandmother. She was an Okino—one of a tribe that is the oldest in all of Africa, and among the least documented. The Okino is a hunter-gatherer tribe, indigenous to the Nulu Forest. They speak an obscure dialect, part of the greater Lumi language. Nobody knows very much about them. This tribe is very elusive, and, as such, no current population count is available. Their traditional folklore and spiritual practices have never been documented. Because of dwindling resources, many Okino have left their traditional lives and are now integrated into the general agricultural practices of the tribes that surround the forest. My grandmother herself left the forest when she was twelve."

Her grandmother's eyes flashed from the photograph, but did Emely see her warning? No. Either that, or she chose to ignore it.

"My grandmother told me this story the day she died," she continued. "It may be the oldest story in the world, older even than the creation myth collected in the Amazon a few years ago by Dr. Gudidi. It is a story that has never been shared with the West. My grandmother's exact words were that this story goes back to the ember that holds the beginning stir of all life."

Foolish granddaughter! Silly granddaughter, careless and dangerous granddaughter! Don't do this!

We began to pound on the thin membrane that separates life from death.

"In the beginning," Emely said into the microphone, "we were all made from good mud by the Great Mother. Everyone who was alive was family. Human beings could move back and forth between the different species. The same way you decided what tie to put on this morning, what earrings to dangle from your ears, those who were alive in the morning of time could decide to pad forth into the world on bare feet or paws, or to slither across a tree branch on scales."

Amplified by the microphone, the story sailed into the darkened auditorium, each word limned with importance.

"Because we had just been born," Emely said, "we were all brothers and sisters, a vast interlocked belonging connecting us all. Even today, this mythic knowledge of origins touches us from some other place, comes to us in dreams. Ordinary moments can break open, spill the light that began us all."

Acute listening out there, and the women who watch couldn't have said they were surprised. Magic happens when new listeners are pulled into the ancient gravitational field of an old narration. *But how far is she going to go?*

"What the forest people believe," she said, "is that in the beginning the Great Mother surrounded all who were alive. She shared her light with us all. We sang our thoughts then, really lived them as they passed across our throats. We knew that certain words were so powerful they could walk out into the world, become serpents, fruits, the leaves of a tree. Other words we could lean up against. Certain words shone so brightly they could lead our way through the dark."

She looked down at her notes. "A thesis demonstrates a student's ability to define a research problem and regenerate or assemble a body of data, analyze it, and indicate its relevance to established anthropological thought, based on original field work, laboratory, or library research," she read.

"The Okinos' mythical tradition centers on a concept that a selected person will receive holy and arcane knowledge and thus attain mythical, godlike stature," she said. "That anointed person of the Okino tribe is called a 'Stone Woman.' This entity is thought to be a divine human being who can speak and sing in the old language. The Stone Woman is involved in shamanistic divination and prophecy, and is seen as a medium between the Great Mother and the tribe. Even today, there are certain women who are recruited to serve the Great Mother. They come few and far between, and do not always live inside each generation. My grandmother told me there hadn't been a Stone Woman for a long, long time and no one knew when the next one would appear."

Betrayal, shame, and a deep, deep grief fought for precedence in those of us who watched. Her grandmother observed in disbelief.

I trusted you, Amely! In all of life and all of death I've never felt so helpless. These are secrets, our secrets, too powerful to be spoken just to get your degree. Don't sell yourself so cheaply.

But once again, Emely either ignored the dead or didn't hear.

"The Okino believe the Stone Woman is the holy connector," she said. "She can rise and enter the magical realm between humans and animals, the cavern that holds both vast meaning and vast mystery. She pushes up through the many layers of consciousness, and when she is tall, one half stone, she presents the Great Mother with an offering."

She's become Los Angeles, we realized. We wondered how we hadn't seen this before. *Loneliness has leaked into her face like a stain.*

"What my grandmother told me," Emely said, "what the Okino believe, is that the Stone Woman can stand with arms outstretched and the world will come to her. She knows where in a body disease dwells, and she knows where in the dark the best songs wait. She speaks to weather and weather speaks to her. She can translate the language of wind, she can push a dying body into the sky; she knows as well when it is not yet time for someone to go. Her task then is to lure that person back to the loveliness that is this world."

She cleared her throat. "There is a secret sect that serves the Great Mother, protecting the sacred feminine. Even in these modern times, these women exist. They are the oldest pagan goddess cult on Earth. Throughout most of time, these women—mystics, priestesses, witches—have been hunted down, tortured, and killed, especially by the Church."

Though ancient wisdom flowed across Emely's tongue, it was the wrong kind of listening out there. She felt it too; we could see it in her eyes. Her audience's ears were turned only to the imprecise. But she had something up her sleeve, didn't she, something even better than a circle of stones or a few dropped allusions to an imported darkness. What she said next would out-Hollywood Hollywood!

She leaned into the microphone and, with her next words, opened the tinderbox of her own DNA. "My own great-grandmother was a Stone Woman," she confided in a low voice, "and one of the most powerful who ever lived. The stories about her are legendary. She could read every event, no matter how slight—a feather on the ground, the way a leaf falls from a tree, she could even answer the many voices of water. Everything she heard, saw, smelled, felt, or spoke had meaning. She could make a man impotent with just one look, could make a woman pregnant who had never been with a man."

For the first time, Emely saw the glass of water on the podium in front of her. She reached for its brightness, and when she took a sip, everything that water is—its tumble over stones, its quest for the sea, all of that sparkle and activity—was born into her mouth. But did the small song of water stop her? No. She merely wet her lips, returned to the microphone.

"This next part is graphic," she warned, "and may be shocking to those unfamiliar with the practice. The Okino believe that the Great Mother is dependent on the ritualistic spilling of blood by young tribeswomen. When girls enter puberty, their blood is offered to the Great Mother through the practice of female genital mutilation. The tribe that my grandmother came from performed the most extensive form of female circumcision. It is called 'infibulation.' In this procedure, the clitoris, the labia minora, and labia majora are removed. What skin remains is then stitched together, usually with animal gut. What remains is a very small opening for urine and menstrual blood. The instrument used to cut the young girls is often a piece of broken glass or a tin lid."

There were some gasps from even this educated audience.

"Female genital mutilation is one of the oldest practices on Earth," Emely went on. "There is even a mummy from the sixteenth century BC that shows evidence of the procedure. Among the Okino, the Stone Woman is often called upon to perform the cutting, because it is only after the spilling of a young girl's blood that she can rise—only by offering to the Great Mother the cut parts of a girl. When no Stone Woman is available, another tribal woman steps in to do the cutting. If my grandmother had not left the forest, she probably would have become the next cutter, inheriting the position from her mother. These cuttings often resulted in extensive blood loss and a lifetime of chronic health issues, including urinary and reproductive tract infections caused by the obstructed flow of menstrual blood and urine."

The audience was perfectly quiet.

"Female circumcision was outlawed, of course, by the Children's Act of 2001, but because no one has had contact with the Okino in recent years, we don't know if this practice still continues," Emely said. "And in spite of our repugnance toward this mutilation, it is still important to preserve the ancient beliefs surrounding this practice."

Because Emely was raised on the craft of storytelling, she understands the use of silence; it is as much a part of telling the story as the words themselves. One, two, three, four beats of silence. She waited, then once again spoke into the microphone. She had their attention now.

"And there is something else, as well," she said. "Although its existence has never been officially confirmed, my grandmother told me she saw it herself. This object, if it does exist, would be the oldest object in the world, older even than the Holy Grail. It is a tablet said to have been made by the very first human being at the beginning of time."

Her grandmother, watching, doesn't mind not having her hands anymore, but she sure wishes she had that little hammock of skin between her first finger and thumb she used to push back and forth when she was worried. No hammock of skin anymore, no more hands, just worry, worry, all the time.

How far are you going to go, Amely? she asks. *You don't know that if you make even one little rip in the web that holds us all, everything alive will shiver.*

"The tablet is said to be wiser than any person," Emely said. "The answer to all of human existence is embedded in its clay. The dropping of a young girl's blood is supposed to place into motion a series of events that will culminate in the Stone Woman finding this tablet, and when she does, when she runs her fingers across the secret runes engraved on its surface, she connects with an integrity larger than any other human being can know singularly."

Well, she'd done it. Bluetooth, smartphones, graduate students, and PhD candidates, they were listening out there, they were listening all the way. The mystery now labeled, time itself was strung between those scholarly fingers for an endless game of cat's cradle.

Emely had married the mystical properties of this old story with the exacting requirements of her thesis, aligned it all into one precise arrangement. And now, by adding some prurient horror about the cuttings, sprinkling in some old-fashioned greed, she'd convinced her listeners that maybe they could be the ones to hack into the forest and find the tablet. What would it be like to hold the oldest thing in the world?

We can't say we liked what Emely had just done, but we could certainly admire her skill. *Master's degree, here she comes.*

And now it was time to bring it to a close. "Thank you for listening to the Okino oral tradition," Emely said primly, and then she flicked a switch and her grandmother's face disappeared.

The audience begins to buzz out there in the auditorium. Emely stood behind the podium and watched them leave carrying bits of her story—bits of her grandmother, really—out into the harsh Los Angeles sun.

It was only here, watching people leave the auditorium, that Emely began to understand—the mask on her face, the interior corruption.

She turned. Handshakes then, a pat on her back from her thesis advisor, high fives from her study group. "Want to go to lunch?" someone asked.

"Maybe later," she managed to say through the cut of her mouth. Living behind her face, not in it, she left the auditorium, and was immediately made small by the aggressive American sun.

Emely made her way slowly down the street toward the store that would frame her diploma. The day looked switched on, lit with fluorescent light, everything too loud. Even the air felt like it was against her.

The story needed to be told, she assured herself. *It's of vast scholarly significance.* But what she said didn't fully inhabit her, the words moving down through her body like someone else's taste. And that's when Emely fully got it, what the dead had been saying all along.

You can't separate yourself from your own story, Amely, the dead told her. *You are never not Africa. You are your own history—not just the storyteller, but its immediate, embedded pain. What is spoken on your tongue, justified by your ambition, can still be refuted by your heart. More boundless, more intelligent than anything you can ever say, the story you have just sold for a few initials to follow your name is the cleverest hypnosis of them all.*

It's what the telling has done to you, Amely, not what it has done to your audience. Just one day, one story, and nothing will ever be the same.

CHAPTER 9

W hat the Great Mother says on the wind:
I am context, I am time. I am the beginning of life and everyone still waiting to be born. I am a continuous line of love.
The bones of the world's first man rest under my trees while my leaves exhale breath for everyone still waiting to arrive. Inside the beat of one heart is the clamor of all hearts. That sound, simply, is me. I won't be here much longer if a Stone Woman doesn't rise soon. Never before has a Stone Woman been able to rise and speak with me, but this is what I need. It's why I've chosen Amely.

My new Stone Woman must be made from both sides, the world of the sun, the world of the shade, inside, outside, old and modern; she must be perfectly balanced. If she doesn't rise soon and bring back my warnings then I won't be here much longer, and if I'm not here, you won't be here much longer, either.

I'm here in the reach of my mountains, here in the fall of rain. My language is the movement of trees against sky. The new Stone Woman . . . will she be ready in time?

CHAPTER 10

In the morning, just as the sun is rising, the soldier drops Emely in front of the main post office. She glances at her watch. 6:15 A.M. She doesn't have much time. A short visit with the professor, and then she has arranged to meet her brother, Kareem, at the bus station. Kareem is studying veterinarian science at the same university Emely attended, and is heading home for summer break.

Dawn has always been Emely's favorite time of day. When she was a student at the university, she used to get up early, make her way down to the Cafe Winthrop, and order the strongest coffee they had. As the sun rose in the sky and the coffee sent its bright exultation into her body, she would sit and watch the city awake.

There are different kinds of walks so early in the morning. Some people, still entangled with dreams, move slowly down the sidewalks. She could always tell the ones who had been up all night; they moved with a certain leftover jazziness, each step grabbed distance between their legs.

This morning she counts herself in the up-all-night group. Without the jazziness, though.

She makes her way slowly down the main street. The sunlight turns broad, more orange. Stalls begin to open. Sculptures of elephants, giraffes, and long, haughty women in tribal dress are polished. Men pedal by on bicycles with tinkling little bells, their trouser legs rolled up. Cars appear. Mercedes Benzes glide by, so white and smooth they could be well-rubbed bars of soap. Businessmen with long chins and rumpled suits stride the sidewalks with a preoccupied air.

Nairobi: wide open, gaudy, everything a soliciting call toward itself. The jumble of different languages, the mix of errands with commerce—as the city awakes, it becomes a place to feel fantastically alive.

Not this morning, though, at least not for Emely. The noise she walks through no longer seems brave; it too closely matches the chaos she feels inside.

How could I have been so stupid last night? she asks herself. *I should never have climbed into that taxi. Why did the soldiers so brutally attack the cab driver? Just for fun? And why was my crime of curfew violation so easily forgiven? And Grandmama talking to me? I must have been really tired.*

She reaches the professor's home and sees a knocker on the door in the shape of a coiled snake. She grabs its scaly body, knocks twice.

CHAPTER 11

"Come in," the professor calls, and Emely walks into a smile so familiar all she wants to do is lie down in its curve.

He's equally glad to see her. "Emely," he gushes, "it's so good to see you! Sit down. I've poured us some tea." Their long history is coiled in the syllables of his welcome.

On a low table before the professor a cityscape of plates and cups, forks and knives, a bowl filled with sliced lemon smiles. A blue-glazed dragon is out for a stroll on the belly of a teapot. Just as she used to, Emely drops her luggage at the door and sinks into the chair opposite her mentor.

He presses an immaculate half-moon fingernail against the teapot and pours a hot brown stream into a cup. When he hands her the cup, he turns it ever so slightly so that the handle will be available for her reach.

"Lemon?" he asks.

"No, thank you," she says.

He picks up a slice, squeezes it into his own cup. It weeps yellow tears. Then he leans back, appraises her carefully. "You look pretty tired, dear," he says. "A bit of jet lag, perhaps? May I offer you some pastry?"

Realizing how hungry she is, she nods. He slides a wedge of cake mottled with raisins onto a plate; she eats ravenously.

"It's good to see you, sir," she finally manages to say between bites. She presses her finger against a crumb and licks it back into her mouth.

The professor is just the way she remembered him. His face puddles inside a thin frame of a tidy beard; there's the ubiquitous bow tie, this one pale yellow, the pressed slacks, the loafers tossed with tassels. The skin of his neck falls from his jaw like the third leg of a stool, his skin not quite white . . . "International origins," he once confided. She knows very little about his life, only that he was married briefly in his student years to a woman doing postgraduate work in ethnographic studies. No children. "Some things are not meant to be," he said before quickly changing the subject.

No glassy eyes following her, certainly no instructions from the dead. Each sip of tea thickened with sugar is a remedy for her loneliness. Maybe by the time she reaches the bottom of the cup, she'll be the way she wants to be in this room, just a recently graduated anthropology student showing off for her mentor.

Emely looks around the room. Bright, buoyant, the professor's home floats so high in the air each window holds a piece of the sky. Inside the rooms, however, is the reflective heft and weight of a life seriously lived. Bookshelves teem with answers: *The Biography of Gandhi*, *Living Prayer*, *Encounters with Buddhism*. A carpet so thick one doesn't so much step across it as sink into it. A grandfather clock keeps time, a yellow chickadee clucks to itself in its cage, over the fireplace is a framed piece of Japanese calligraphy. "Good faith," the Professor once translated. The painting holds that active point of acceleration when both ink and paper, recognizing the other, rush forward—and then, as the black singularity of each letter sinks into the open hungry spaces of the white paper, beautiful, graceful surrender.

Almost a visual scale, below the painting, ranging from big to small, are five red bowls in descending order, each bowl an open, evocative mouth. As Emely's eyes move from large to small, it is as if she is participating in the collection's creation, and then, her gaze finally reaching the floor, sight spills her toward what the calligraphy and all those open mouths really want to emphasize. It is the familiar sculpture of a horse, muscles flowing in liquid bronze, mouth open either in tribulation or equine luster, she's never been quite sure which.

The professor juts his wrist from his sleeve, revealing the glint of an expensive watch. "Let's get our business out of the way first, Emely, and then we can have one of our cozy chats."

He extracts a thin notebook from his shirt pocket, thumbs through it. "Let's see," he says, scrolling down the pages with one of those half-moon fingernails. "Contact dates. September 22, September 25, and every four days after that at noon, precisely. Our first contact date will be in exactly three weeks. That will give you some time with your family before going into the forest. I'm still trying to arrange for a guide to take you in. I'm sure I will have heard from him by the time you're ready to leave. A fine young man, he used to be one of my students. Quite bright, actually. He had a lot of academic potential, but then his father died unexpectedly and he kind of lost his way. A good fellow, though, and he knows that part of the country well. I know he'll accept this assignment."

Emely listens to the professor's instructions, receives another cup of tea, pours some milk, adds sugar, circles her spoon round and round, and yes, manages to nod and smile, but she realizes she has barely spoken one word.

"I'll show you how to use the radio," the professor says, and leaning over a cardboard box, he extracts a shiny new machine. He takes out the microphone. "You push this button here, wait a moment, and then you say 'CD1245, Base Camp here, reporting in,' and then, on the other side, I'll pick it up. Remember to say the word 'Over' after each transmission. It's really quite easy. I've typed up the instructions, along with our contact dates." He hands her a slip of paper.

She folds it and put it in her back pocket. "Thank you."

His eyes are half circles of mirth. He puts the microphone up to his mouth. "You say you found the tribe, Emely? Very good. What are your coordinates?" He laughs, inviting her to play along, his pantomime as comforting as the sugar-laced tea. When he chuckles, Emely remembers that laughter can be another kind of home.

Sometimes she finds it hard to concentrate in the professor's home. There's usually another presence so emphatic, it could be another living, sentient being: jazz, great smoldering American jazz, at all hours of the day and night. Predatory, seemingly at odds with the fastidious order of the professor's life, the music of John Coltrane, Miles Davis, and others roam his home singing of never-ending sorrow, the treachery of midnight's silence. This morning, the professor has stacked the CD player with Billie Holiday. Looking for those who aren't quite ready to feel all the way, her charred voice moves through these tidy rooms, filling to the brim the bowls on the mantelpiece, soiling the carpets, causing the bronze horse to buck even higher.

"Thank you for sending me a copy of your thesis," the professor says. "Brilliant, just brilliant! I'm just so proud of you. Do you need another pillow for your back, maybe another pastry?"

And then the conversation peters out. The professor sips his tea, she sips hers, light glints from his glasses. She doesn't know what to say. Thoroughly in charge now, the professor stretches the silence between his fingers; she finds herself scrambling to stay upright on its taut surfaces.

She tells herself that last night didn't matter. She tells herself that she's tired, "jet-lagged," as the professor says, but Billie Holiday's smoky voice finds her anyway, the rusty facade of what she sings barely able to contain her sorrow. That sorrow slips between Emely's ribs. Something is different here. Though the professor crosses his legs, leans forward to pour her more tea, though there's that pillow for her back, she gets a sense that the professor's diplomacy is just another barrier to hang between them. Beneath the smiling bowties, the grandfather clock marching up the hallway, beyond even the sound of Billie Holiday's voice, there's a new occupant in this room. Silence—the fact that she can't think of one thing to say—has become the real tenant in this room.

Her eyes stray to the calligraphy over the fireplace. *Good faith*, she reminds herself, and decides to try again. "Do you mind if I speak candidly, sir?"

He smiles. "As I recall, you always have, Emely. You know you can tell me anything."

She remembers this particular skill. The professor appropriates any piece of dangling experience, in this case her nervousness, and makes it his by naming it.

"I do know that, Professor," she responds carefully. "And I've always appreciated our mutual candor. I guess what I want to say is that I feel a little unprepared for this assignment."

The professor crosses his legs, aligns the crease of his slacks so that it runs straight from his knees. "It's natural to feel a little nervous about a new job."

"Well, I don't think it's just feeling nervous," she persists. "I think it's a little bit more than that. But please, sir, don't mistake me. I'm so honored you've chosen me. But I guess that's my question as well. Are you sure you have the right person in me? I only got my master's degree two weeks ago. But really, sir, please don't misconstrue my apprehensions. I'm tremendously grateful for this job. I'm just concerned that I won't be able to fulfill my assignment in an appropriate manner. It all seems a bit unorthodox, I guess is the right way to say it."

There is the polite click of his cup being returned to its saucer. Obviously relieved, he leans back in the sofa.

"Emely," he says and his voice is soft with reassurance. "You had me worried there for a second. I thought you were going to quit or something. You just have to believe in yourself more, I've always told you that. There might not even be any living members of the tribe left; no one's heard from them for years. If you do find them, however, and they let you stay, simply record their ceremonies, ask them about their belief structure, document their stories and their songs, and then report back to me. The guide will help you, and it will be over before you know it. If you don't find them, try to find out how they used to live. Photograph whatever artifacts they left behind. They probably lived in caves. It will be a short and unhygienic six weeks, that's for sure, but really, my dear, you're going to do just fine."

"I'm just words looking for a tune, reaching for the moon . . ." On the CD player, another Billie Holiday song. The Professor cocks his head and steeples his fingers for a moment, listening. "Irving Berlin," he pronounces after a few seconds. "'Reaching for the Moon,' recorded on June 9, 1936 by Teddy Wilson and His Orchestra."

When he crosses his legs again, the world is reflected in the shine of his loafers. As if naming the song reminds him of something else he owns, he looks up, suddenly excited. "Would you like to see my new sculpture, Emely? I've just got her. She's in my back office."

"I would love to," she replies.

They both rise, and the professor, cupping her elbow, escorts her down the hall. "She's from the same area in the forest where you'll be living. The dark side of her is easily identified. It's clay from the Emboma area, probably mostly river silt. But the light side is completely new to me."

They pass the stutter of abstract prints hanging on the walls next to the salmon pink–tiled bathroom, its glass shower with the soap egg nestled halfway up the wall, the basket that hangs inside the toilet seat discreetly dispensing bleach. She detects a whiff of the professor's slightly flowered aftershave.

"I have to send the clay to a laboratory for analysis," he says, "but maybe in the next month you'll be able to find out a little bit more about what materials the tribe uses for its ceremonial objects."

More bookcases in the back room. A large mahogany desk. A screensaver on the professor's computer depicts a tiger getting ready to pounce. But Emely barely notices any of this because what catches her eye, causing her to gasp, is the statue. Rising from a packing crate, the statue is almost six feet tall, reaching almost to the ceiling. One half of her is dark clay; the other side is pale. She's naked except for a piece of cloth sculpted around her middle. A small smile, large eyes. A necklace around her neck concludes with a half circle. The only interruption to her perfection is her right arm. Though it reaches above her head, it's broken at the elbow.

The professor crosses his arms, rocks back and forth on his heels. The light of acquisition shines from his eyes. "Beautiful, isn't she?" he says softly in the same landlord voice he used to name the Billie Holiday song.

"I've never seen anything like her!" Emely exclaims. "Where did you get her?"

His reply is more oblique than usual. "Let's just say I have my sources and let it go at that." There's a shrill, piping sound behind him. "Fax coming in," he says, and walking over to a machine, he picks up the piece of paper that has been transmitted.

That leaves Emely alone with the sculpture. Feeling an unexpected apprehension, she takes one step toward her, then another. Reaching for the moon, indeed; the statue is what Billie Holiday sings—the dream of every women to reach, to touch, to finally be whole. And yet she is also pain personified—not because she is broken, but because, like Billie Holiday, she is striving for something she will never quite reach. Just as the suspended mechanism of the CD player holds the still-alive flame of Billie Holiday's voice, the clay of the statue still holds the living flame of entreaty.

And there's more. Some force drags the statue's mind into hers. Louder than the ticking of the grandfather clock, friendlier than the chickadee talking to itself in the cage, more pleading even than that bronze horse, the statue invites Emely to participate in some sort of secret yearning she's never really acknowledged.

Not quite understanding what she's doing, she begins to stretch her arm over her head. She opens her hands, spreads her fingers as wide as she can.

"I will help you," she says under her breath. "In the places where you are, I will soon be, and in the places where you aren't, I am."

Emely is pulled upward by some kind of linear force, reaching for the only thing that will fill the empty curve of her hand. When she says the word, she doesn't just say it with her voice, she sings it with her spirit. "Acalla," she says. The word floats up into the air, erotic, liberated, and free.

She smells the professor before she sees him, his factory-produced aftershave camouflaging some kind of dark agenda beneath. Instantly, she holds her breath. She doesn't even want to inhale that much of the man inside of her.

"Emely," he exclaims. "That's the old language!"

She gets a glimpse of the professor's face. Something she can only call "greed" fights scholarship in his eyes, the alchemy so potent it threatens to swim out from the tidy frame of his beard. She hears a scramble of falling-down sounds. He's looking for something. "I've never heard it spoken before!" and then a small, black microphone is shoved into her face, the red button of the recorder doing some listening.

"Say it again!" As though sliding up the volume on the tape recorder, his tongue moves swiftly from left to right. "I think it's the ancient word for 'moon'!"

Moon, Emely thinks. *Yes, that would be right.* She says the word again, "Acalla." The sound comes from her, but from the distant past, as well.

Like the tiger on the computer, the microphone is doing some stalking; it's only inches from her mouth now.

"That language is as extinct as the dodo!" the professor exclaims. "Do you know any other words?"

But Emely's ignoring him. "Acalla," she says one more time. Though her voice swirls with distance and mystery, the word fits perfectly into the palm of her hand.

The shove of another order. "Say it one more time, Emely. Let me get it clearly. "

Maybe it's the excitement in his voice, or maybe it's his assumption of power over her, but whatever it is, the spell is broken. Shielding her eyes from his bright consumer glare, Emely retracts her arm, swallows back the word. Suddenly, everything looks sordid, even the sculpture. Especially the sculpture.

"I have to go, Professor," she manages to say. "I have to meet my brother at nine."

"Of course, Emely," he says. "But don't you see how perfect this is?" The tassels of his loafers shake like little cheerleader pompoms. "The fact that you know a little bit of the language means you're just the right person to go into the forest!"

She slides her moonless fingers into her pockets. "If I don't get going now," she says, "I'll miss the bus."

"Of course, my dear." He looks down at the fax in his hands. "I have some business of my own to attend to."

Emely leaves the room, picks up her luggage at the front door, turns to the professor one more time. "Good-bye, sir," she says a bit unsteadily. "And again, thank you for this tremendous opportunity." She begins to move down the steps to the streets.

"Have a good time with your family," the professor calls after her. "I'm so proud of you."

Why hasn't she ever heard it before, that cash register sound in his voice? She moves quickly down the street. She doesn't want to be that broken sculpture rising from a packing crate in the professor's back office, doesn't want to be that horse, protest forever immobilized in bronze. She doesn't want to be that yellow chickadee talking to itself in its cage, no flight left in its tiny wings, its ancient mysterious pull toward migration forever dimmed. She doesn't want to be owned.

It comes to her then. Beyond that old word she just spoke, that word made of bone, rain, and maybe even stars, she recognized the statue. Her still lips, devout eyes—the statue in the professor's back office was a perfect rendering of her great-grandmother, Amely.

Trying to outwalk what she has just realized, Emely moves quickly down the street.

CHAPTER 12

The professor is playing his favorite game. "My beauties, my children, my loves," he murmurs as he runs his hands across each huge slab of granite. He inhales the color, exhales it as words. "Captured light," he says, caressing a golden slab from Lake Tututu. "Flame-fired sunsets, or maybe the origins of a painting." He hovers over a black stone from the south, his voice as soft as fermented fruit. "The faraway light of stars."

He runs his hands across one of his favorites, a turquoise-blue slab harvested near the area of the forest where Emely will soon be going. "Liquid music," he says rapturously.

The aesthete in him admires the granite's beauty, the capitalist admires its potential for profit, but by far the largest part of the man—the omnipotent, behind-the-scenes manipulator—admires his own brilliance, the simplicity of using a natural resource to fund his plans.

The professor is one of the wealthiest distributors of granite in the country. He has bombed the land, his machines have ripped into hills, and he has found the stone beneath the soil. Birds leave, flowers die, what is buried is revealed, and then all that beautiful stone comes here to this warehouse, the entire country delivered in slabs, lined up like corpses, row after row.

The area in front of the professor's warehouse is divided into tiny wedges, each featuring a different way to use his granite. Piped-in music for his customers merges with yellow pools of polite track lighting. One display is a tiny kitchen, but no water has ever flowed from that faucet; no one has ever taken a bite from those red wax apples.

Another wedge is a diminutive bathroom with pink walls, a mirror that opens three ways, and silk flowers blooming a forever purple. The only thing alive is the granite countertop. It's the color of the sky just before the sun drops into its evening home. Fans of brochures are spread everywhere, featuring photographs of people standing in front of their fireplaces. They wear vanilla leisure clothes, miles and miles of hypnotic, weedless, entitlement-fertilized lawns glimpsed through the open French doors.

Decorators fly in for one day. "That's the one," they say and, borrowing the gesture from their wealthy clients, point toward a $7,000 slab of granite. And yes, the glasses of lemonade are free, the chatter of ice cubes at the bottom of the glass even more suggestive than the piped-in music, promising customers a shiny, brochure-perfect life, divested of the higher and lower octaves of pain.

The professor moves slowly down the rows of granite at the back of the warehouse. He strokes a stone from the north. "Varnished light," he decides. "Yes, this one is varnished light."

CHAPTER 13

Far away from the professor's warehouse and his deadly game, a woman in France picks up her stones, holds them until they are warm. *"Femme soeur,"* she calls. *"Vous qui êtes les morts, pouvez vous m'entendre? Je vous envoie ma chanson de la prière."* (Sister woman," she calls. "You who are the dead, you who are alive. Can you hear me? I send you my song of prayer.")

The dead answer immediately. *Yes, Sister, we are here.*

"Has Amely walked yet into the full sky of her truth?"

Two names, two selves, the dead reply sadly. *She is still divided, still pushing away what it is she already knows.*

"Does she know how dangerous the professor is?"

She is beginning to suspect, but it is only a faint whisper. You know how he is. No room for generosity, no room for light to fit, and certainly no room for Amely. Syringes filled with smiles; the professor's drug of choice is empathy, but his wealth and scholarship can't disguise his greedy heart. What we know is that he asks questions only to use our Amely, to manipulate who she is with his dark, savant skill. She's only one more piece of granite he can own.

"Can we do anything?" the woman asks. "I'm so frightened."

The stones, the stones, the dead reply. *Know them when they are wet, whispering rain. Touch them when they are brushed with dawn. Travel across the sky, plains, and rivers and down through a stone's hard surfaces into its warm, waiting, inner life. Listen to their sweet spirit: it is the promise of life. Stones. Stones carry all of what we know and all of who we are.*

"Yes, Sisters," the woman replies. "Let's just hope our Amely will be able to hear our songs in time. I choose the stone of my country, cuprite, so that she will know perseverance. I warm it in my hands and push it into my family of stones."

CHAPTER 14

"Hey, man! Where are you going? Come here this instant or I'm going to smack you, child!"

Emely is walking toward the bus station through the poorer part of the city, the one tourists don't usually see. Laughter and snippets of conversations swirl around her. The streets are more crowded here. Children scuttle down muddy walkways on errands for their mothers; shop owners set out boxes filled with tea, hair oil, and combs. Gray pigeons peck dead light. Old people sit slumped, considering their next breath; young men stride by, managing to convey both eagerness and insolence with their steps.

Then the women arrive, and they are magnificent. Unabashedly beautiful, they walk into their days the way they would sing. Some have braided their hair into such intricate arrangements it looks as though they are balancing elaborate baskets on their heads. Right next to them are the fragrant, black-eyed Indian women. They seem to float down the sidewalks wrapped in the chiffon wings of their butterfly dresses. Flamboyant, sensual, backs straight, heads high—the women navigate the sidewalks as if they own them.

And then Emely catches sight of her: her first spirit woman coming through. She wears a brown blanket and parallels Emely's progress down the sidewalk, but on the opposite side of the street. What Emely notices most is her posture. She walks as if a string links her with the sky.

Emely walks fast, the woman walks fast. She slows down, the woman slows down. *My mind is playing tricks on me,* she thinks, and when she next glances across the street, the woman has disappeared.

Though it is early, the city is already alight with alcohol. Home-cooked whiskey, charcoal smoke, perspiration, bus fumes, tea, tangerine peels, paprika—odors pile on odors, sight piles on sight, noises collide, jostle, and overlap. Emely hears an assortment of languages, along with many different kinds of laughter: happy, drunk, boisterous, empty. She sees paisley cloth, Indian saris, a row of enamel cups, plums from the Rontand District so beautiful they look as if the sunsets of the world have died within their tiny globes, and skin—brown skin, red-brown skin, blue-purple skin, skin like coffee stirred with milk.

A skinny cat yawns, its triangular face like one of those paper origami puzzles children make to clump back and forth on their fingers. Dogs skirt legs, shadows flit across alleyways, doorways threaten to pull her into their dark, concentrated noise, and above it all, the sky holds claim.

It's hard to walk quickly. Emely's suitcase and the bag containing the radio are both heavy, slapping her legs as she walks. Her backpack cuts into her shoulders.

And then another woman appears. The same erect walk as the other. This one wears a dark-green blanket. Emely is close enough to look into her eyes, and when she does, she feels as though she's falling down wet, slippery steps. The woman's eyes take her right in. Is she protecting her or sizing her up? Emely doesn't know. What she does know is that when the woman sees that she's caught sight of her, she pulls the blanket quickly over her face, lowers her head, and hurries on.

The dead know who the women in the blankets are. They know because they've sent them. *Can Amely do it?* they wonder. *Reach the fertile place where America meets Africa?* They know she needs protection. The newest part of her, her fancy job and what she's learned in America, is being chased by the oldest part of her, the history that lives in her cells.

Something bangs Emely's shoulder. She turns. A woman, hair a flame of peroxide, lips squeezing a bottle of beer, says "Excuse me." Blank, drunk eyes.

Her companion comes up behind her, snakes his arms around her waist. He, too, is drunk. He wears an old fedora, its brim cocked into a jaunty grin. He's lost a button, and the straps of his overalls are held together with a clothespin. The origin of his slurred speech tips its bottleneck from his pocket. For some reason, he wears a pink necktie.

The woman laughs a high *tee-hee-hee* sound, empty of mirth. The man dips his head, kisses her neck. They're blocking Emely's way. "Honey," the man says, his words blurred. The syllables sound sucked on, like a melted cube of ice. "Honey."

Slowly, with exaggerated care, the woman lifts the necktie over the man's hat, slips it down over her own neck, and then raises her arms over her head and begins to rock her hips. People are gathering; she knows they're watching. Even if the life that swirls around her is filled with scorn, she still wants to be at its center.

More hip movement, back and forth, back and forth. Pounding her feet, she almost falls. The necktie is the only thing about her that doesn't seem inebriated; against the swayed verbs of her drunken dance, it always manages to return to a pink and vertical sobriety.

Emely is wondering how to get past this show when she sees the third woman. She stares at her from a doorway, her blanket copper-colored, a sliver of light illuminating her face. Hers is the same obsidian stare that the other women gave her, and like the other woman, when she sees that Emely has noticed her, she moves quickly back into the gloom of the doorway.

No doubt about it. These women are watching. But why?

A young boy appears, blocking her way. "Hey, lady," he says, grinning, looking Emely over. "Wanna buy an ashtray?" Except for dirty shorts held up by a piece of string, the child is naked. His chest is pockmarked with scars; a backpack hangs from one shoulder. Its bright-blue color broadcasts that it is stolen; the Air Kantara tag fluttering from one strap confirms it.

Emely shakes her head.

"Come on, lady," he says, "just take a look!" Emely tries to move around the boy, but he blocks her way. "It'll just take a second."

"Go away," she snaps.

He squints. "Just ten shillings, lady. I could get a bowl of soup then. Come on, I haven't eaten all day."

"Leave me alone," Emely says firmly. She looks for something of childhood in his face but finds only aggression. People are starting to notice, and the boy, realizing he has an audience, shines an even brighter salesman smile. He holds out a handful of rags. "Just take one look," he cajoles. More onlookers gather, and the boy begins to peel back the cloth. Brown, creased leather, fingers slightly curled, a cuff of black fur edging the wrist—it's a gorilla's hand. Rotting flesh bulges from the severed package of skin.

Emely drops her suitcase in shock, instinctively shoving the thing away.

"Ooh!" says the crowd, pulling back as one in revulsion, then flooding forward in fascination.

"Quite valuable, you know," the boy says. Flecks of blood freckle the gorilla's cuff of fur.

Emely looks into the boy's eyes. "Where did you get that?" she manages to ask.

"None of your business, lady."

The man in the fedora raises his bottle, the lady in the pink necktie still dances, the boy brings the hand in close. Emely smells dead flesh.

"You want it or not?" he challenges. His smile is canny, not a child's.

She finds herself blinking back tears. "Of course I don't want it," she says. "It's sickening!" Tears fill her eyes. Maybe it's everything that has happened in the last twenty-four hours, but suddenly she can't swallow the ball of pain that fills her throat. She sinks down on her suitcase. And that's when she sees her brother.

Glowering, Kareem shoves his way through the crowd. He doesn't even notice Emely. His eyes hard with anger, he grabs the gorilla's hand, shakes it in the child's face. "Don't you know it's illegal to sell animal parts?" he snarls. "Especially gorillas. They are on the endangered animal list!"

The crowd loves it. The man in the fedora raises his bottle. "Fight!" he proclaims to the world at large. The crowd picks up the chant as well—"Fight! Fight!"—and finally the black malice that runs beneath the surface of the city, the relentless scheming that feeds the vilest of deeds, has a place to spray. "Fight! Fight!"

For as long as Emely can remember, her brother has belonged more to the family of animals than that of human beings. Maybe that's why he wanted to become a veterinarian. One summer he built an entire pet hospital behind their mother's cooking hut—cages filled with birds with broken wings, emaciated kittens, a dog whose leg he had set. Each morning was either a celebration because a wounded animal had made it through the night—or a funeral. Everyone knew better than to talk to him if that happened.

Remembering those funerals, she remembers his anger as well; she has to get her brother out of here. She rises from her suitcase, places her hand on his arm. "Kareem," she says tentatively.

But he doesn't take any notice of her. "This is an endangered animal," he repeats. "Who gave you this?"

"Kareem!" Emely tries to raise a flag of warning with her voice, but his entire focus is on the boy.

"You know you can get into big trouble for something like this," her brother continues. "You should be arrested."

Arrested? Emely's heart speeds up. The last person she wants to see again is the police chief. She grabs her suitcase. "Kareem!" she yells. "Let's go!" Her brother finally sees her.

"Please!" she hollers. "I'll explain later." She turns to go, but the crowd has surged in close, bunched in on all sides. They won't let her through.

Sshhh . . . She doesn't so much walk as glide, the woman in the earth-covered blanket. And then another woman arrives, this one in a blue blanket. And then more women in blankets come. Without a word they move through the crowd, and suddenly a space opens up.

Emely seizes her brother's hand. "Come on!" she says. "Let's get a move on!" She begins to drag him down the street.

"But . . . ," he says, turning to look behind him.

She orders him around as only a big sister can. "Kareem," she says, "it's not worth it. Let's just get out of here."

A can rattles up against a curb; a cat turns his head sideways to get a better grip on a fish carcass in his mouth.

"Did you see those women?" Emely asks as they move toward the bus station. "The women in blankets?"

"What women?" Kareem replies. "I didn't see any women."

Behind her, the pink necktie begins to dance.

CHAPTER 15

The police chief knocks on the door and steps inside the room. The professor's back is to him, and for a moment he is relieved. That gives him a chance to get used to the chief's presence. Though the chief secretly has a plan to outmaneuver the professor, the chief knows he has to be at the top of his game.

But then the professor turns, and when he speaks his voice is so forceful it is almost a physical blow.

"Have you done it?" he asks.

The police chief nods. "The first step has been completed," he says.

The Professor flashes a smile, more muscle twitch than anything else. "Was it difficult?"

The police chief walks his fingers sideways across the brim of his hat.

"No," he says. "Not at all. When she was resting in the police station, I confiscated her backpack, adhered the device between two panels. She'll never find it."

"Let's see if it works," the professor says. He opens a laptop on his desk and clicks a few buttons, and a map of the city swims onto the screen.

"There she is," he says, pointing at a small, flickering red dot. The police chief can feel the man's excitement. "There's our Emely, leading us right to the treasure!" Though he speaks with his usual careful diction, running beneath his words is a current of anticipatory pleasure.

The police chief decides it might be the right time to bring up something that has been troubling him.

"Sir," he begins cautiously, "I was wondering about something."

The professor hangs a scowl from the hook of one raised eyebrow. He is not used to being questioned.

"Yes?" he says.

More traveling fingers on the hat. "I was wondering why you think you need this GPS signal. Couldn't you just rely on the girl's radio reports to find out where she's going to be? She would have given you a compass reading."

It's like watching a glass slowly fill with dirty water. Anger grabs the professor's mouth first, turns it downward, and then travels to the lines around his mouth, which deepen with scorn—and then, finally, the glass is full, and all that bitterness blasts from his eyes.

"I'm not questioning your plan, of course," the police chief says quickly. "And I've complied with each and every one of your instructions . . . but you know, for the sake of simplicity?" His voice trails off, his Adam's apple bouncing up and down inside the sock of his neck.

Maybe the professor's excitement makes him more generous than usual.

"The way you described the old woman in the forest influenced my decision the most," he explains. As though the answer is curled up inside its circuitry, he glances at the laptop. "Sounds like she's smart enough to instruct her not to transmit the tribe's location." He smiles, and the pink skin above his teeth looks more naked than any other part of him. "This way we'll be able to monitor all her movements all the way up to the Orianga Plains, into her village, and then into the forest. She won't be able to get away." The professor's eyes are unnaturally shiny. "She'll lead us to the tablet," he says. "No one believed that it actually existed, but now, thanks to you, I have the statue—irrefutable proof the tablet exists. If anyone is still alive in the forest, it proves the tribe still believes in the Great Mother. And Emely is just the right person to lead us to it. Right before she left my home, she said something that could only be linguistic data from the source, the old language word for 'moon.' Pure anthropological gold, it goes back all the way to the first word spoken by a human being."

That naked pink smile again. "Our plan is in motion," he says in a low, thrilled voice. "When we find the tablet, we will rewrite history. It is the symbol of the oldest pagan society in the world, a secret goddess cult that worshipped a powerful female deity. It's priceless. But we must proceed cautiously. Emely must never know we are following her."

He looks down once again at the computer, "Looks like she's almost reached the bus station," he says and closes the lid of the computer with a snap. "I want you to follow her but be very discreet. She must never know she's being watched."

CHAPTER 16

My death was the final signature signed to the scroll of my days, my life spent honorably serving the Great Mother. Though I'm proud of my life, I'm not so proud of what I left behind; my daughter so vague she can't hear the stones; my grandson turned metallic with anger; and you, Amely, you've become as thin and flat as that diploma you're so proud of.

I kept the promise I made to you, Amely, on the last day of my life in your mother's garden. Since the day I died, for all these fifteen years, I've stayed close. I watched you leave your mother's fire for those years with the nuns at the boarding school, saw the day you received the letter offering you a full scholarship to the University of Nairobi, watched you meet your mentor, who in turn recommended you for yet another scholarship in Los Angeles. I've seen you preen, strut, soar with ambition, fall into loneliness.

I've kept my promise to you, Amely, but you haven't kept your promise to me, have you? You gave away our most holy story, and look—look what is happening now.

CHAPTER 17

Emely pushes her suitcase up into the rack of the bus and wedges herself into the middle seat between her brother and a woman with a baby. Four hours stretch before her—four wonderful hours to get to know her favorite brother all over again.

Emely and Kareem have always been close, and she thinks she knows why. When he was around two, inexplicably, Kareem started to go deaf. Their mother took him to a visiting doctor.

"Nothing I can do," the doctor pronounced. Scar tissue was building up in his ear canals.

Undaunted, their mother took Kareem to an old woman in the village who still practiced the old ways. "Oil of cloves," she told her. "Warm it up and massage it into his ears."

Mama did this for what seemed like months, and gradually Kareem's hearing did return. But it came with a cruel price: sound became excruciating for the little boy. Any noise—the braying of the donkey, a conversation in the next room, even the scrape of Mama's spoon against the cooking pot—would send him into a storm of tears.

Emely was the only one he would let near him, and that was because she figured out the one sound he could tolerate: humming, as long as it was very soft. And this Emely offered him for hours at a time, rocking the little boy in her arms, the sound of her humming more air flutter than anything else. Eventually, Kareem was able hear again without pain, but Emely has always believed that though the oil of cloves returned him to the world of words, her humming returned him to the world of song.

She wonders if maybe she should try humming a little bit now. Her brother still hasn't said one word; he's just staring morosely out the window of the bus, head resting on a balled up sweatshirt. Even his smell is defiant; his perspiration smells like a newly sharpened lead pencil. She wonders when he last took a bath.

The bus inches down the crowded streets, past skyscrapers, lawns spread like the skirts of young girls, statues of important people, church towers solemn in their promise of comfort. Soon they reach the outskirts of the city, traveling through miles and miles of shanties. People sit motionless in front of their shacks. Women hold babies in their laps, the rigidity of their stretched-out legs at odds with the protective curve of their upper torsos. A few stringy maize plants rattle their leaves in the dry wind. Even the dirt looks worn out here, the color of old roast beef.

And still not one word from her brother. She steals a look. He looks like a Q-tip, she decides—his body as skinny as a stick, his head covered with a ball of unruly, puffed hair. His shirt and jeans are an indifferent blue. The only thing familiar about him is the rat-a-tat-tatting of his fingers, incessantly pounding out his own personal soundtrack. This, at least, she remembers. Whistling, bobbing his head, tapping those long fingers on tin pails, knees, fences, and walls, anything he can find, her brother has always made music. *He needs a shave*, she thinks. *Certainly he needs a haircut. Maybe he needs a big sister.* She decides to try to talk to him.

"That sure was weird back there, Kareem," she begins. "I mean, it's not every day you get to see your little brother in the middle of a street brawl." Her laugh comes out as a whinny.

"Things are so bad in this country," he says, his voice burred with anger. For emphasis, he stabs his leg with his finger. "You know what those poachers are after now? They're going after our endangered species. That kid back there was only the bottom of a great industry."

Ah, she remembers this. Politics! She knows the swing and jab for this kind of talk; one nods one's head a lot, agrees, builds slowly toward a mutual and eloquent fury. She turns slightly toward him.

"I tell you, Kareem, I'm shocked," Emely says. "I've always heard there was a black market in animal parts, but I've never witnessed it firsthand."

Another harder jab with that finger. "They're either butchering animals for their parts, like that poor creature back there, or they're selling them to unethical zoos that will pay any price for a rare one." Kareem shakes his head.

She picks up his gesture, shakes her head as well. "Terrible," she says. "Short-sighted, really."

"I've been meaning to talk to you about something, Emely," he continues. "I almost wrote you about it. I think you should reconsider this new job of yours."

She is genuinely surprised. "What?" she asks. "What are you talking about?"

"Well," he replies. "How much do you really know about it? Do you really think you can trust your precious professor?"

Billie Holiday, "Reaching for the Moon," tossed tassels on the Professor's shoes . . . no, she's not sure she can trust the professor, but she's not going to reveal this to her brother. "He's not my 'precious' professor," is all she can think of to say, "and anyway, it's a great opportunity. I'm lucky to have been chosen."

It's as if Kareem isn't even listening; his anger is regulated, tapped to by his long restless fingers. "The Land Reform Commission isn't what it seems to be on the surface," he says. "I have this from trustworthy sources." He rubs his hand across his chin. "It's really just an excuse to move indigenous people off their land. A lot of people have misgivings. Some people I've talked to actually believe it's a cover for cultural genocide."

"Cultural genocide?" she exclaims. Now he's gone too far. "Kareem, who's saying this? That's absolutely not true. It's all about scholarship, documentation. We're going in with complete respect for indigenous cultures. In fact, we're trying to save what the tribes know."

Bruised eyes, thrusting thoughts, and thumping fingers—*who is this young man?* she wonders. He's not even pretending he's glad to see her—no "How was your flight? Are you tired? Here, let me carry your suitcase." No, there is only this tension she can feel but can't quite name. Something larger than loneliness settles in her stomach.

She decides that Kareem is two people. From the front, Kareem's features are soft; he is still the brother she hummed to long ago. But his profile is a different matter altogether. It is there, in its sharp ridges, that his anger rests.

She decides to address his anger. "Things are a bit more complicated than your two-bit radical politics, Kareem. The professor would never be involved with anything that's corrupt. He has an international reputation. This plan has taken years of preparation, and it will be a model for efforts around the world."

Again, it's as if he hasn't even heard her. With both thoughts and fingers, Kareem continues to stab. "You're just being used, Emely. *Greed*." He pops this last word out with ferocious assurance. "Fat cats. Rich people just trying to move poor people onto reservations. They exploit them for cheap labor, and they end up working on tea plantations grown on the very same land they once owned."

Lowering her head, Emely places her fingers on either side of her forehead, tries in this way to make a shield against his words. Mama told her about this new brother. "I'm worried," she wrote in her careful schoolgirl penmanship. "Kareem's become angry, sees conspiracy everywhere. I think he might be falling in with the wrong people at school."

Emely was quick to appease her. "I wouldn't worry too much, Mama," she wrote. "A lot of young people go through this stage, and who knows, maybe his anger is a good thing. Kareem might use his passion to start a reserve, form an organization to save endangered animals."

She knew something of what she was talking about, for she went through a similar stage herself during her first year in college. Her own particular fire, however, was for women's rights. How many conversations did she sit through at the Cafe Winthrop, burning a hole in her stomach with too much strong coffee? Women's rights, economic empowerment—thrilling conversations piled high with alarm, strategy, an easy invention of sides. Gradually, however, especially when Emely began to recognize that militant sisterhood didn't necessarily constitute friendship, she outgrew her one-note diatribes and decided instead to focus on what she could actually *do* for her country.

As though sucking on secrets, Kareem bunches his lips. Emely tries to address the soft brother she used to know. "What's happened to you, Kareem?" she asks. "What kind of homecoming is this? You haven't even said you're glad to see me!"

He doesn't answer her questions. "This country is going to hell," he snarls. "But we're going to get it back. Blood is going to drop."

Her heart speeds up. "What are you talking about, Kareem?" she asks. "You're scaring me."

Kareem knows he's gone too far. Like pulling a string tight on a drawstring satchel, he closes his mouth, nooses his secrets deep inside. He turns away, stares out the window.

Down the aisle, a woman holds a dead rabbit by its ears. Every time the bus hits a bump, the rabbit's legs jump. Another woman carries a box containing a live rooster. Children doze, their heads resting against their mothers. "Did you see the color of the kale at the market?" someone calls over the straining sound of the engine.

"Beautiful," a women in a red scarf responds. "Deep green. Must have been grown in the mountains."

Outside the bus, old men sit before their shacks, too tired or uncaring to fan away flies. Children sit like the old men. Their eyes follow the bus—not out of any curiosity, it seems, but because it's the only thing moving.

Emely takes a deep breath, reminds herself to be patient. There is a mightiness in her family, a magnificent love that is unflinching—and much of that love has always been for Kareem. He was the best of them. Even as a little boy, he was chivalrous. He would be the first one to jump up to get water for their mother. When kids were turning a jump rope, he would hop in and make everybody smile at the crazy rhymes he made up on the spot. He would play for hours with Emely's little brothers and sister until their voices rang with laughter. One morning when he was around six, their mother accidentally cooked up a fish he was trying to save. The scene that followed was terrible; Kareem cried for hours. And inside his weeping was a note of intense tenderness. How could people he loved so much hurt him so much?

Maybe this new anger of his is just another way of crying. Emely decides to try one more time.

"Are you all right, Kareem?" she asks. Sympathy rocks at the end of her question. "I remember my first year at the university was kind of hard. It's difficult to go from a small village in the mountains to a big city." She knows Kareem has all but abandoned his allegiance to this conversation, so she tries to load concern, big-sister solicitation, into her voice. "Did you get along with old Mr. Ramrod in advanced calculus? God, what a terrible teacher. I hated that class!"

Down the aisle from her, the dead rabbit takes another hop.

"I hate going home," he mutters in a low voice. "You better prepare yourself, Emely. Things are bad."

"What do you mean?"

For the first time, Kareem seems uncertain. "Mama," he says slowly, "she's changed."

"In what way?"

"Remember a few years back, when she did that whole thing with the blood of chickens? Remember how weird that was?"

Emely nods. "I remember," she replies. "But that was a long time ago."

"Well, I think she's taken up that stuff again. One day I caught her in the kitchen, and she was squeezing blood all over some dirty little stones. I mean, how crazy is that?" He shakes his head. "It's like she's living a hundred years ago. Maybe Father's right and she is possessed. One moment she's talking to Auntie or someone else from the village and she's all happy and smiling, then someone will say something and she's crying and nobody can find out what's wrong."

"She's gone back to her stones?" Emely asks, worried. She remembers the last time she witnessed this. It was right before she left for boarding school. No more open doorway with the light shining through; some kind of dark thing had claimed her mother. Silence grew inside her, and then those places froze. There was no room in her private, aching world for any of them.

"I had no idea," she says. "I got a few letters from her, but they were mostly upbeat. Have you tried to talk to her?"

"Yes," Kareem replies. "One morning I even got mad and told her to stop all this nonsense. But she refuses to listen to me, or anyone else for that matter."

"Have the other kids noticed?" she asks.

He shakes his head. "No, you know how little kids are—they don't notice anything. She still does all the Mama things, like cooking and working in the fields, and that's all they see."

"What does Father say?"

"You know his answer. It's church, church, church. That's always his answer. He wants the priest to come over and sort her out. I just want to get the hell out of there."

No long fingers rattling a tune anymore. Maybe his hands can't find the music for what he has to say next. "And there's something else," he says, voice low—but then he stops speaking. His silence distresses Emely more than any argument could.

"What?" she asks, alarmed. "What is it?"

"Mama . . . says she's waiting for you. She says you're in trouble."

"Me?" Emely is astonished. "What does that mean?"

He shrugs. "How am I supposed to know?" Then he crosses his arms, leans his head against the window once again, and closes his eyes. The boy who was once shut out from the world by silence has now learned to use silence to shut out the world.

CHAPTER 18

But he's not asleep.

What would Emely do if she knew I had the makings of a bomb in my backpack? Kareem thinks to himself. *Instructions downloaded from the Internet, rather elegantly stated—to my mind, at least: "PVC pipe, enclosed at the bottom (duct tape works), about a pound of dynamite tamped down tight; include nails or something else sharp." Country going to hell, big sister being used, and I'm going to do something about it. I don't have the dynamite yet, but when I get home I'll go to the quarry. They use dynamite to extract granite from the hills.*

Kareem remembers when Mobwab first introduced the idea for this action at a secret meeting back at the university. He slid forth the strategy like a knife drawn from a sheath. "Five people, five points of the star," he said. "Let's make a statement!"

Kareem has never met anyone as smart as Mobwab. The man used his intelligence to trail blaze the world he wanted to step into, and when he spoke of it, for a few elucidated seconds, one could almost see it with him. Mobwab talked in outline form when he is excited. "Eradicate corruption, equal rights for everyone, return to tribal rule," he proclaimed.

The twins Tracy and Kuckoo are two points of the star, mischief and tomfoolery in their comingled blood. At the age of ten, one of them told Kareem, they crept into a church early on a Sunday morning and rang all the bells; thinking they were late for church, the whole village popped up from their beds. A few years later, and now the twins have exchanged church bells for PVC pipes loaded with gunpowder.

But that's not the reason he's sitting on a bus with the makings of a bomb in his backpack. It's Eshe. Just the sound of her name and his heart speeds up. Eshe is the fourth point of the star. She always brought her knitting to their meetings, the sound of her needles clicking a tiny metronome behind Mobwab's outlines. Kareem has never known what she's knitting and is too shy to ask; he just saw endless stripes of color the consistency of stewed fruit stabbed into existence by those needles.

But that's not what fills his nights or his loins—not why he sits on this bus today with a secret. It's the time he saw Eshe dance that changed everything.

Long before the music even started she began, staring toward some far-off source. And then—lightly at first, then stamping harder—she took the orderly rhythm of those knitting needles down into her feet. Eyes dark, hands liberated doves, each stamping foot proclaimed what she has never needed to say with words: "Never apologize, never explain, I am triumphant and here!"

Her dance turned the men who watched into wood; she became their flame, and in that moment, Kareem remembered becoming frightened, perceiving for the first time how strong women actually are—so strong, in fact, he would bet anything that on the night of the action, when five people crawl forward to ignite the sky, Eshe will not be the least bit afraid.

"To the Five Point Star," she said in their last meeting, all of that hot, mutinous power tucked away, just the clicks of her needles ordering the silence.

Emely and her corrupt government job, Kareem thinks. *Wait till she sees what I'm going to do!*

His bomb tonight will be a stamp on the letter he never sent, written extravagantly across the sky. "Look up, Eshe. Look up, Emely. I am brave. Do you see me now?"

CHAPTER 19

The bus hits a hole in the road, and Emely is thrown against the soft arm of the woman sleeping next to her. The baby in her lap begins to cry.

"Excuse me," she says, quickly righting herself.

"It's all right, child," the woman says. Lowering her dress, she pushes her nipple into the small valentine mouth of her child. The baby places one dimpled hand against his mother's breast, his tiny, tear-lined cheeks sucking like little bellows. "Where are you going, daughter?" the woman asks in a friendly way.

Emely smiles. "I'm going home to Elbomus," she answers.

"Oh," the woman replies. "You're an Okino?" The tribal name is full in her mouth.

"Yes," Emely says, and for the first time in three years hears how someone just saying her tribal name can make her feel at home.

"My aunt on my father's side was Okino," the woman says. "But she came out of the forest when the land was being cleared for cows and more tea fields."

"That's when my grandmother came out as well," Emely says. She takes a deep breath, begins to relax. The baby on the woman's lap sleeps, his puffy legs stretched out across Emely's lap. His mother closes her eyes and, remembering how easily people touch in her country, Emely lets her shoulder and upper arm rest against hers. Two kinds of Africa here—her brother's shrill, angry one and this soft one, spoken by this soft woman.

Unlike Emely, who feels punctured—hunted, even—by her brother's remarks, the women on this bus seem happy, their lives so defined that they are free. Their dreams are the same as their mothers'; they know what they are going to be doing next Wednesday, because it's the same as what they did last Wednesday. Very few have been farther than the capital, let alone to the United States. Not one of them knows or cares that Emely's diploma is wrapped in a sweater inside her suitcase. No one knows or cares that she can name all the states in America, cook pasta al dente just right. Not one of them knows or cares that she knows how to apply pink nail polish thin and delicate as a shell. None of that matters.

For the first time in three years, Emely is only an Okino woman going home.

CHAPTER 20

When Emely next looks out of the window, there are no more edges left in the world; the land and sky blend together, as soft as chalk. A bedraggled moon, exhausted from its encounter with the night before, shines pale in the sky.

Amely.

She looks up. Lulled by the motion of the bus, most of the travelers sleep, even her brother. The woman who sits next to her rests her head against her baby; her eyes, too, are closed.

Amely. Almost a song, a voice pulls her toward the place where a woman stands outside the bus. Another spirit voice coming through, but it's not her grandmother's voice this time.

The Sister Women are talking about you through the stones, the woman says.

Trying to remain moored to the ordinary, Emely presses her arm firmly against the woman who sleeps next to her.

I've posted myself here to pass you along.

The woman's song is alive in her ears, but Emely doesn't want to hear it. She gazes out the window, tries to focus on an impala. She studies its nervous tail, skinny legs, but then another slides into her view, and then another, and soon, like stars in the sky, there are hundreds.

No purchase here, certainly no singularity. She can't help it; despite her resistance, her eyes are pulled toward the woman.

Shoulders parallel to the horizon, she stands on a hill, feet spread wide as if to better grasp the planet's curve. She is old; her eyes rest in a web of wrinkles. A long braid cascades almost to her waist. She wears a brown blanket, holds a staff in her hand, and is speaking.

You will bring into the forest a small cup of light, Amely. If you hold it carefully between your hands and learn well, that small, cupped light will break open and spill light, and your life will become as large and dazzling as the sky. What the woman says, she seals with fiery eyes.

She fills Emely's mind with the same kind of knowing that happened when she stood before the statue.

But Emely doesn't want to know these things. It's time to talk back. She grips the seat of the bus between her fingers. "Leave me alone! I don't want to know you."

She thought she said this in her head, but perhaps she spoke aloud; her brother moves in his sleep. Regardless, what she says doesn't work—and in that moment, Emely understands. It doesn't matter that the woman is older, that her hair is much longer, that one vein runs down the side of her forehead, that she has given birth and Emely hasn't. Their differences dissolve; something drags Emely's mind into the woman standing out there wrapped in her blanket until there is only a common vortex of belonging.

And then, from out of nowhere, a young girl materializes next to the woman. She, too, wears a rough blanket, discs of sky in her ears.

She looks up at the older woman. *Pearls, shells, puddles, skulls, feathers, bones, footsteps,* the young girl sings. *Things over?*

The old woman shakes her head. *No,* she says firmly. *Things left behind.*

Figments that aren't quite there, statues talking, thoughts that run like water, voices from people she knows with certainty are dead . . . Emely is suddenly so exasperated by mystery it makes her angry.

"Leave me alone!" she says one more time. This time she knows she spoke out loud, because the woman with the baby in the seat next to her is startled awake. She sits up and rubs her eyes.

"Leave who alone?" she asks sleepily. "Who's bothering you?"

Emely doesn't answer, but her gaze is still entangled with the woman and the girl. Her seatmate follows her eyes out of the bus.

"There's no one out there," she says, mystified, and then her eyes widen. "Wait. I know that way of speaking! My mother told me about it. Halfway to song, it's the old language that speaks to the dead!"

Covering her baby's head with her blanket, the woman rises quickly, then leans over and picks up a bag of vegetables from the floor by the seat. Staring at Emely with frightened eyes, she reaches for the cross that hangs from her neck, brings it up to her mouth, and kisses it.

"Devil sight," she hisses. "May God be with you." Then, turning quickly, she hurries down the aisle of the bus to another seat.

No more belonging anymore, no sweet tribal alliance. But it isn't her diploma wrapped in a sweater that makes Emely different. It isn't those footsteps she took on another continent. It is the occupation of these strange voices, the way she keeps seeing and hearing things that aren't there. And now other people are beginning to take notice.

Emely looks out the window. The woman and the young girl are no longer there. Around her, conversations resume—or maybe she's just come back to listening.

Mama, she thinks to herself. *Another couple of hours and I'll be back at her fire. She'll make all of this go away.*

Mama. Round cheeks, sitting inside a round hut, she stirs food in a round bowl, all her round loving shaken to, made percussion bright by the *chucka-chucka* sound of her bracelets. Mama. Inside of all that round loving, she'll finally be whole.

Just another couple of hours and she'll be home. Despite everything that has happened, despite what Kareem has just told her, Mama will make everything all right.

CHAPTER 21

I *will tell you what being dead is like. You are at once who you are*
and everything else you see: white stars behind the moon, Rift Val-
ley below, Kareem with his tiny war, Amely who doesn't want to
encounter the large breath of what she already knows.

Worry for my granddaughter has grown strong now—I worry all the
time, in fact. Because I watch her so constantly I even worry that the force of
my watching will make her slight, less herself.

Being dead is not so fun when the one you adore is in trouble and can't
hear you through the stones.

The bus has long since passed when the woman with the long braid
squats and speaks to the young girl beside her. Trouble puckers the skin
of her forehead. "We must drop our stones," she says. "The dead are
speaking."

She reaches into the folds of her blanket and brings out a small
pouch. One, two, three, she places three stones on the ground before her.

The first stone is green. A thin line runs through it like an equator.

The second is an ordinary brown, like the meat side of a thumb; the third sparkles a tiny rainstorm within the edges of its diminutive globe.

And we, the dead who watch, begin to sing. *Pale moon behind us, send us your one eye. Watch the one coming. She is in trouble . . . doesn't yet know her story.*

The young girl gazes at the older woman with steady eyes. She's seen this all before.

The woman clusters the stones together so they touch. *Like a family,* she thinks, stroking them gently. She picks up the stone with the line running through it. In the cavity of her lined hands, the smooth orb looks like an egg resting inside of a bird's nest.

"The dead are speaking," she says. "Something is following Amely, something dark. I will try to talk to her mother through the stones."

The young girl next to her reaches over and picks up the other two stones, jostling them together until they clink. "Will Amely's mother be able to hear us?" she asks. "After all, she's pushed us away for some time."

The woman shakes her head. "I don't know," she replies. "For so many years that woman has been caught in the in-between, but she's frightened now, knows already that something is happening to her oldest daughter." She raises her face, catches some of the sky in her eyes. "If we join our voices with the others, what we say will become a long ribbon of song. Maybe then she will hear."

Together, they turn, and in the empty space left by the old woman's words, they begin to sing: *Dada wanawaki wi amabio ewafu unawasa kesia imi mini kukutia wimbau yongu asala.* (Sister women, you who are the dead and you who are alive, can you hear us? I send you my song of prayer.)

Of course we answer immediately. *Yes, Sister,* we say. *We are the dead and we are here.*

"One of us is moving," the woman replies. "Her name is Amely. She came from the place of the sky, is now moving into the forest shadows. Please help Amely's mother Ebele hear us through the stones. The old ways slumber deep inside of that woman. She has pushed us away for many, many years, but she has to listen! We have something important to tell her. Her daughter is the next Stone Woman. She must prepare Amely to find the tablet and rise into the Great Mother's sky. It is the only thing that will save us."

The woman and the girl turn their faces into the gauzy light. "Yes we hear you, owl that is forest thought," they sing. "Yes we know you, green that is shadow. The one with the light is moving. Help her mother pick up the stones. With our hands, our thoughts, these words, we pass her along."

The moon begins to roll, and no one can stop it. Not the spiders who knit nets across the sky, not the branches of the trees probing evening's edge. No one can catch the fast-running ball of the moon.

CHAPTER 22

The dead watch as Ebele, Amely's mother, works the field with her ox and plow. The animal is the color of bone, deepening to tan where its stomach gives way to its legs, where ears connect to skull. *Three stones laid on the red soil. She must pick them up. Nothing less than the fate of the world rests on what she does next.*

As the plow cuts the ground, red earth foams on either side of the blade. The smell of soil rises and mixes with the odor of ox. A long, green sigh of a weed wraps around the blade of the plow, stays there for a moment, then falls to the ground.

Somewhere between sky and Earth, Ebele floats. Steering with one hand, she brings her arm across her forehead, catches her head in its V. Plowing on this day is more a matter of following than any kind of initiated movement.

But then she sees the three stones laid before her, so purposeful it is impossible to imagine they aren't important in some way.

"Whoa," she says to her ox—whoa to the flies, to the ox's swishing tail, to the hands that grip the polished wooden handle of the plow. The animal stops.

And we the dead sing louder. *Lean in, Ebele, rest against our songs. You are not alone. Pick up the stones. We have something important to tell you.*

One of the stones flickers with a scattering of white lines. The next blasts an emphatic white line across its middle; the last contains a glitter of white spray. Ebele knows immediately what they mean. The scattering of white lines is fire; the stone cut clean across with the white line is earth; the one with the glitter of white spray is water. Fire, earth, water, in exactly that order.

Fire? No. Water? No. Maybe she wants to hear from the earth. Ambivalent as always, she reaches down and picks up the stone cut clean across with the equator line. At first, trying to contain its tiny eloquence, she wraps her fingers around it tightly; then slowly, heart pounding, she opens her fingers, exposing the stone to the sky.

We are pleased. *Well she's taken the first step at least,* we tell each other. *She's picked up the stones. She wants to know, needs to know. She can already sense that something is happening to her oldest daughter. But will the stones talk to a woman who still believes in Jesus?*

Nothing—only silence. And why not? Despite her husband scolding, her church scolding, despite the rebuke of her very own mind, Ebele was hoping the stone would speak. After all, isn't she as open as a cry? But why would the earth want to talk to a woman who has tried all these years to push her belief away?

She doesn't remember the next step.

Ebele, we yell. We would wring our hands if we still had them. *Don't you remember you have to begin with the prayer of the stones?*

Has she heard us? As though she's reaching back into memory, she closes her eyes. Something new has arrived on Ebele's face.

And then, slowly at first, she begins: "*Dada wanawaki wi wi amabio ewafu unawasa kesia imi mini kukutia wimbau yongu asala,*" she says haltingly. ("Sister Women, you who are the dead and you who are alive, can you hear me? I send you my song of prayer.")

The dead are elated. *It's working, it's working!* we cheer. *She's finally singing the prayer of the stones, her voice cleaned of lies!*

"Please let me step back into your circle," Ebele continues. "My daughter is in trouble, and I don't know what to do."

Far away in the forest, sitting at her stones, the old woman delivers the news. *Ebele*, she says somberly, *listen to what I have to say. Only your daughter can save us. She is our next Stone Woman. If she doesn't find the sa-*

cred tablet and rise into the Great Mother's sky, a terrible darkness will come. It is already close. No more will small ones roost in tiny places. Nothing will lap our mother's waters, no animals will curl in her shadows, nothing will leave behind the marks of hooves. If there is no one left to dance, to draw, or tell this story, will our Mother still be here?

Ebele isn't really surprised. The words match with what she has always known but has tried so hard all these years to push away. But she's terrified. She knows what being a Stone Woman means.

She clutches the equator stone. "What do you want me to do, Sister Woman?" she asks.

Try to talk to your daughter, the old woman responds. *Just as you are now awake, the parts that have been slumbering deep inside of her must awake. But you must send her to me empty, cleaned of the world's noise. Can you do that, Ebele, send her to me clean? Maybe then she'll be able to hear what it is she needs to know.*

A bird cuts the air, leaves whisper, the land vibrates with heat at the edge of the field, and the woman in the forest waits. The dead, watching above, wait as well. What will she say? The words a mother speaks to her daughter are the most potent words of all.

Finally Ebele replies. "Yes, Sister," she says softly, "I will try."

She puts the stone back into her pocket, reaches one more time for the handles of the plow.

But though she has just made a holy pledge, the dead hear what she's thinking.

Bulu, Afrua, the other women in the village will never let an unclean Stone Woman go into the forest. If they find Emely, they will cut her. They will scrape and stitch her lower private lips in the most horrific procedure of them all. It is very likely that my sweet daughter will bleed to death.

Ebele knows she can't warn Emely. Her mother drilled that into her long ago. Guarded for centuries, the cuttings are the most holy secret of them all. Grave repercussions occur if one tells the holy secret to someone who didn't believe. She will have to figure out some other way to get Emely away from the woman's knives.

She had tricked them once before; can she do it again?

Listening, we are horrified. *Ebele,* we say, *the world is finally waking up! At long last we have a Stone Woman, and we haven't had one for a long, long time! Foolish woman, silly woman! You actually think you can stop the world's yes with your tiny and incidental no? You are trying to trick destiny itself!*

CHAPTER 23

We, the dead, have gathered to know our fate, and while we wait, we brush each other's hair, oil the creased geography of our skin. We pray with shells and feathers, bones and stones.

We are one mind up here; we are not separate from each other, we are each other. There is no individual I.

And we are powerful. We need Amely's blood. Does Ebele really think she can outsmart all the women throughout all of time?

Down below, Ebele is pleading with a young man named Mentegai.

"Please take my daughter into the forest tomorrow," she says. "She'll be home tonight, and I'll have her ready to go by morning. The professor won't say no to you. You're the only person around who really knows the forest."

Ebele. Strong arms, big holes cut into the lower parts of her ears, a reddish glow to her high cheekbones. Flared nostrils and something still girlish about her legs. Her hair sticks out in points from beneath her faded headscarf.

"I told you, Ebele," Mentegai replies, "I'm not going to do it! I don't want to have anything to do with that man."

The dead, watching, approve. *Don't taste her words, young man. Don't taste her night.*

Mentegai is the young man the professor hoped would be Emely's guide into the forest. Long dreads fall almost to his knees. He's chewing on a twig of evergreen; his tattoo runs vital across his otherwise immobile face. He holds a bird in each hand, one gray, one white.

We know what she's up to, the dead say to each other. *Ebele thinks if she can persuade Mentegai to take Amely into the forest early, she will escape the other women in the village. She knows if they find her daughter, they will cut her in order to prepare her for her Stone Woman's duties.*

But what's a little blood in the grand scheme of things? Does she really think she can outthink destiny? There's never been an uncut Stone Woman.

Silly woman. Too much Jesus, too little of us.

Ebele lays out a row of bowls; then, picking up a bucket, she slops water into each.

"The professor isn't a good man," Mentegai continues. "I learned that years ago. And anyway, you can't just go and change the timetable. Knowing him, there's an exact schedule."

Mentegai received a letter a couple of weeks ago embossed with the name of the man he turned his back on two years ago. "From the office of Dr. Cambura," it read. "Dear Mentegai, I hope this letter finds you well. Please be informed that The Land Reform Movement would very much appreciate if you served as a guide for Miss Emely Matei. She is trying to find the elusive Okino tribe. Because of your family's association with this tribe, you are the appropriate candidate to escort this young woman into the forest. The country would be eternally grateful if, for six weeks, you would serve as her guide." And then, at the bottom of the letter, the professor mentioned a sum larger than anything Mentegai's father has ever made in a year.

Emely Matei, this woman's daughter. Word of the professor's offer has evidently leaked out.

Ebele squeezes a rag between her hands. Tears begin to run down her cheeks. "Please Mentegai," she says, "I can't tell you why, but please do this for me."

Mentegai watches her. *She still has the little girl in her*, he observes. The birds in his hands are restless; he tightens his grip. *It's in the way she sits, one knee drawn up to her chest.* He sees it also in the way she rubs her tears, hands balled into fists. But mostly he sees it in the way she pleads with him; the woman before him still believes in the dream of rescue.

"Please, Mentegai," Ebele says one more time. "Please."

Though his hands are filled with captured flight, Mentegai himself is still. He wedges one word from between the bars of his hair, "Why?"

"I told you," Ebele replies, "I can't tell you."

Like some kind of royal insignia, the lines of Mentegai's tattoo crest up from between his eyebrows. A line of musical bars just waiting for notes engraves his forehead; more lines circle the apples of his cheeks, then fall down to lick a wave below his lip. Somehow, as if the artist found the rhythm of his skin, his tattoo looks natural.

More tears. "Please, Mentegai," she pleads, "just get her out of here!"

He transfers the evergreen twig to the other side of his mouth. "I'm sorry, Ebele," he says, "but I don't want to have anything to do with that life anymore. I'm trying to find my own family in the forest—if they are even still alive."

Mentegai discovers in this moment that fear can send out a light all of its own. Eyes burning, Ebele sends him a fierce look. "Is that really the reason, or are you just as much intimidated by the professor as Emely is? Are you trying to get away from him?"

And we the dead, watching, scold, *Go easy, Ebele. Don't question that young man's motivation. Mentegai just wants to become a child of the trees again, go where the world is kind. There are stories inside of every tattoo, he just hasn't found his yet.*

Mentegai shakes his head, thumping the long ropes of his dreads. He's not going to answer her question. "Ebele," he repeats softly, "I won't do it." The sorrowing words he speaks are accompanied by the bitter taste of evergreen. "That's my answer. I'm sorry."

Watch out! When a woman begins to remember things she has tried a lifetime to push away, when she finally steps out from the cloud of duty and has something to protect, stand back. A new look comes over Ebele's face, unadorned and fierce.

"She can't be in this village for even one day!" she screams. She picks up a bowl, slams it to the ground. It breaks into a dozen pieces, each whirling wooden chip saying what her words can't reach.

Fear mingled with an instinct for self-preservation causes Mentegai to take a step backwards. He releases the birds; they fly up into the trees above. White and gray watching from two pairs of bland, round eyes.

The ground is jigsawed with shards of the broken bowl. Ebele sends Mentegai a look so hard it is as if her eyebrows' sole responsibility in life is to offer some mitigating kindness for the intensity of her stare.

"If they find her they'll do something so awful . . . " Ebele's voice trails away.

"Who?" Mentegai asks. "What are you talking about?"

She doesn't answer, just turns and begins to walk away. "How can I save my beautiful daughter?" she asks herself under her breath.

CHAPTER 24

We've been watching that young man for some time now: we know his story is somehow entwined with that of our new Stone Woman. He is time lived backwards. Though he lives in the modern world, he's trying to swim back into the story of us all. Like our Amely, he's dim, caught in the in-between. He thinks if he drapes his father's divining bag across his shoulders, makes fire with two sticks, he will find his family. What he doesn't know is that destiny is more complicated than that. He won't find his family unless we want him to.

Years ago we watched Mentegai and his father leave the forest. Mentegai was only four; looking for stronger drink, his mother had left the forest the year before. Mentegai's father knocked on every door of the village looking for her, holding his son's hand. "Is my wife here?" he asked, again and again.

"No" was usually the answer, though once or twice it was, "She was here, but she left."

The trail grown cold, Mentegai's father decided to put down roots in the village.

At first, their life was good. The farmers' collective taught him how to drive the only tractor in the village, and he made a decent living clearing brush. To this day, Mentegai looks out at the pastures his father cleared with pride. And the tribespeople liked him, too; he was the first person called upon when a cow needed help giving birth, he dammed the river further upstream so the women didn't have to go so far for water, and no one else knew how to get the grinding machine up and running when it was stuck.

But most of all, Mentegai's father loved his son ferociously, and poured everything he knew into him, imprinting him with his way of looking at life. They took trips into the forest together. He taught him how to hunt, catch birds with snares, make bows and arrows, sharpen spears, and train a hunting dog; he taught him how to swim, including something as primary as noticing where the current is most alive.

"Embrace it here," he told his son. "Then it will carry you toward wherever it is you want to go."

The two of them speared Mentegai's first forest hog together. They were inseparable—and Mentegai needed his father all the more because he didn't have a mother. At night they would lie under the sky and talk. His father would point to the constellations above them. "That's Eight Bright Eyes," he sometimes said. "Maybe your mother is one of them."

"What was she like?" Mentegai would ask then.

His father would snap the top of a beer can before answering. Then, with a voice as soft as flower petals, he would begin to pile up the words. "Beautiful, loving, tender, smart," he would say. "You could hear her laugh even when there was no sound."

And Mentegai would try to pile the words higher, into someone as tall as his mother.

On those star-crested nights, his father would tell him about life in the forest, including how children were named after the ones who came before. "In the forest, you learn from those who live in the sky," he would tell him. "They come and talk to you in your dreams." He would crush another beer can and throw it on the growing pile beside him. "Everything made sense in those trees, everything fit," he would continue. "You became larger somehow just because you belonged to something. Boys like you were taught to be men. There were ceremonies." He would point to the tattoo that gamboled across every inch of his face. "In the forest, when you became a man, you were engraved with this tattoo."

Mentegai always knew when his father was sad, even when he acted happy. We, the dead, knew it too. There was a game they used to play together. Mentegai would say one word—dog, yellow, elbow, anything that popped into his head. As he said the word, he would flutter his fingers. His father, popping out his eyes, would say the word as well, and flutter his fingers, too, and then Mentegai would jumble the word, say something else. Then, his father would jumble that word, and then all of that jumbling would grow so high it would make them both laugh—until, suddenly, just as they reached a height beyond play, his father would tumble off of all of their giddiness and reach for a beer. And then another.

A few years later, there was no money. Mentegai's father was losing work, staggering home drunk. No more lying under the stars, no more soft, flower-petal voice—it was beginning to appear that alcohol was the only thing that could erase his father's feeling of loss. Gray thatched his hair, his eyes became hollow, his chest caved in, and he seemed to forget that he even had a son. Face swollen, deep-etched lines in his cheeks, his mouth was reduced because now he spoke only the smallest of thoughts.

Even the dream of finding his wife had evaporated—and sometimes it seemed that even his love for his son had dried up as well.

The women in the village took care of Mentegai. They washed his clothes, fed him, listened to him when he needed to talk. He always had a place to sleep. And then, spurred on by the Women's Christian League, the village decided to send Mentegai to boarding school—the same one our Amely attended.

We, the dead, didn't like this. All that talk of hell and salvation; one more convert for Jesus. But we did see something good come from it: Mentegai did well in school. He discovered he needed a force to live against, and somewhere along the line decided education would be it. The nuns were pleased with his progress, but even they were surprised when a letter came, signed with a familiar signature that lifted dreams.

"From the Office of Professor Cambura, PhD, Department of Anthropology, Nairobi," the letter read. "Congratulations. You have been chosen to attend the University of Nairobi on a full scholarship." It was the second letter the nuns had received in two years offering one of their students a full scholarship, the first one extended to Amely.

It was here the dead took up watching as closely as we do now. We don't believe in coincidences. We knew somehow that the story of Amely and Mentegai had become entwined.

The day came when Mentegai left the boarding school for college. Just as Amely had done, he sat at the back of the bus watching the nuns get smaller and smaller on the road behind him. "I'll pray for you," Sister Mary Rose had said when he had leaned over and kissed her ancient parchment skin.

In the city, Mentegai had never seen buildings so tall, or so many people. At the university, he sat in an auditorium listening to lectures, one of hundreds. He lined up for meals at the cafeteria and slept in tiered bunk beds inside the school dorms.

When he returned on school breaks, his father was barely there; they had forgotten how to talk to each other. Mentegai pretended he didn't care—and besides, he had found a new authority to please. Back at the university, Professor Cambura had smiled at him and begun the subtle art of grooming.

"Your prayers are answered," Mentegai wrote to Sister Mary Rose. "Professor Cambura thinks there's a future for me in anthropology."

The last time Mentegai saw his father was summer, the year before last. For what seemed like the millionth time, his father was trying to get sober, and one morning he told Mentegai he wanted to make him a steam hut, purify him the old way. "It's time to become a man," he said. The dead were pleased. He wanted his son to know things, secret forest things.

Mentegai shrugged. He didn't care anymore—too many broken promises had come between them already. But then, for the next few hours, with an avidity he usually reserved for drink, his father fashioned a hut of willows and covered it with hide.

Mentegai was hardly impressed. It looked more like something made by an animal than a man. But he could tell his father was proud of it.

That evening, his father heated some stones in the fire and placed them in the middle of the hut. They both took off their clothes and crawled inside. It was damp, claustrophobic, and hot inside the hut, and when his father leaned over and poured more water on the stones, steam rose and filled the hut with heat so intense it was hard to breathe.

Half an hour, forty-five minutes, maybe an hour—the hut grew hotter, then hotter still. Sweat poured off their skin. And Mentegai waited. He waited because this man was still his father. He waited because he had made this place for him and told him he wanted to tell him secret things. He waited because despite everything, he still wanted to know what his father would say. Maybe, finally, he would say something that would make sense out of this life.

But did his father speak? No. Just that thick breathing in the dark, once or twice a groan. No words, and his father's sweat—well, it smelled of alcohol.

And then his father crawled out of the hut and plunged into the stream. One more failed promise.

What he did next, however, surprised Mentegai. His father picked up some dirt and tossed it in four directions, then leaned over and lit his ever-present cigar, the smoke as constant as the color of his skin. "See Through the Wind," he pronounced with a thick puff of smoke. "Mentegai, in the old language."

Mentegai didn't understand. "What?" he asked.

"See Through the Wind," his father repeated. "Your man's name."

Mentegai tried to follow this latest enunciation down the corridors into his father's mind. "What kind of name is 'See Through the Wind'?" he asked sarcastically.

"The name is older than those trees," his father stated, gesturing toward the forest with his cigar. "It goes back to the first fire. It means that you will always be able to see through the wind toward truth."

Despite himself, a light came on behind Mentegai's eyes; the old father-son connection clicked back into place, and suddenly he was ten years old again, when times were better.

"Mentegai," he said slowly rolling his new name on his tongue. "I like it. Mentegai."

"And you get my medicine pouch, as well," his father said.

This is the part that Mentegai later wished he could apologize for. "Some stones?" he scoffed. "Some old bones? What do I want with a medicine pouch? You might not understand it, but I'm out in the modern world now."

His father turned to him, his eyes so dark Mentegai thought that surely they would leave streaks on his skin. "Don't discount the old ways so quickly, my son," he said quietly. "These are not just bones and stones. They are magic, big magic. They are language, songs and chants, wisdom and beauty." A small pause, and then he sighed. "I feel a bit tired," he said. He stood slowly and began to walk away. "Good night, son."

Mentegai didn't bother to say "good night," and he didn't bother to say "thank you." His silence that night would be the formaldehyde that kept that last moment with his father trapped forever in his mind.

See Through the Wind? he thought. *Eyes Shut Tight is more like it.*

Was it because Mentegai had his mother's eyes that his father didn't tell him what he was going to do? And anyway, how do you tell your son you can't do it anymore, that you're tired and your body has outlived the reach of your dreams, that you are finally going to do something for yourself and that something is called dying. You don't tell your son, you just make sure he's off at that fancy school before you get on the tractor with just enough alcohol in your belly to not waver as you head off that steep hill. You don't say good-bye—no, not when your life has always been about action, not when those words would have stuck in your throat anyway.

Mentegai was back at the university when the phone call came—when Sister Mary Rose whispered, "Your father is dead." The medicine bag was in his father's open hand when the villagers discovered him under the overturned tractor.

His father's death left Mentegai wondering. Had the stars been good company those last days? Were there enough of them to hold all of him, the man his father had been, the man he had allowed himself to become? How many mornings had his father awakened so filled with despair that the only way to live through the day was to reach for another drink of absence? And then Mentegai asked what was perhaps the hardest question of them all: *Why wasn't I enough to keep my father alive?*

He changed his name to Mentegai. No carefulness; his name now flared danger. He began to stay up late, emptying a few beers of his own, wandering into class late. He didn't know he was going to drop out of school the day he walked into the professor's office, but without any preamble, surprising both of them, he just said it—"I quit."

The professor tried to talk him out of it, of course. He used words like "a brilliant future," "serve your country," "stellar career"—but Mentegai was now beyond caring, the words just made a clutter of dry leaves around his feet. A few hours later, he found a tattoo shop in the downtown part of the city, and he lay there for five hours as a needle dug into his skin. He walked out with his father's forest tattoo swirled across every inch of his face.

A few months later, trying to lessen his grief, Mentegai turned his back on his future, began instead to move back into his past. Returning to his early boyhood days, he picked up the spear he had made with his father, donned a vest he had fashioned out of bongo skin, and yes, hung the medicine pouch his father had given him around his waist. First one week, then two, then for months on end, Mentegai lived in the forest shadows. Though he knew there was a possibility that there weren't any living members of his tribe left, he spent his days looking for his mother and his father's family. He grew his hair long, hoping that if they were still alive they would know by his tattoo and long dreads that he was family.

"It's See Through the Wind," he would sometimes call. "The son of Sarutu." But his words just dropped into the full, waiting silence. No one stepped forward, and in the quiet that followed his call, he was left lonelier than before. If they were out there, even his own family didn't want him.

CHAPTER 25

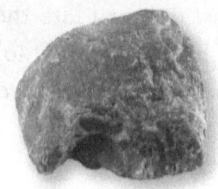

*I*t's a fight for our new Stone Woman's soul, between that man down there wearing his two crossed sticks, the dead up here wearing the sky, and Ebele, that foolish woman, who is still trying to trick destiny, scheme her way out of this dilemma. She couldn't get Mentegai to take her daughter into the forest early to escape the women's knives. Let's see what she does next.

"I've asked Father Joseph to come over and pay you a visit," Emely's father says. Though his voice is quiet, warning lies buried in its curves.

Ebele shakes her head. She doesn't like this. "What?" she asks. "Why?"

"What else was I going to do, Ebele?" he replies. "You aren't sleeping, you pace all night. I'm worried about you."

She stares at her husband for a moment, then lowers her eyes.

The man Ebele married is ruthless about order. Sometimes she thinks that life for him is just one big mathematical graph. Look at him now. He's wearing a shirt checked with stripes, his tea plants cover the land in ruler-straight rows; as if to control his own personal wilderness, he gets up every morning and shaves his head. Two lines indent each side of his mouth so deeply, it's as if his face has been folded. Sometimes Ebele suspects even his devout sense of religion is just another form of mathematical tidiness, a prescribed and orderly cause and effect.

But this evening she's going to talk back to all those stripes. "This isn't about me, Apunda," she says quietly. "Please try to understand." As if the words are too big for her throat, she speaks slowly.

"What do you mean?" he asks.

She responds enigmatically. "We can't slash the body of the Earth without killing ourselves."

Her husband makes an impatient husband sound, jingles the coins in his pocket. "Where are you getting all these ideas from, Ebele?" he asks.

Firelight flickers in her eyes. Her words are slow, reluctant, and thick. "I hear them from the stones," she says slowly. "I've returned to what I tried all these years to push away."

"Oh, Ebele," her husband responds. He spreads his hands. In the dust of the hut, they glow like two cave paintings. "Please give Father Joseph a chance. Remember old Mrs. Grenu who used to live down the road from us? Remember how she went out of her mind for a while? She also said she heard voices from stones. What craziness! But then Father Joseph came and prayed over her, and she went back to church. Doesn't she head up the choir now?"

Her husband stares at her for a moment; then, lighting the tip of an arrowhead with love, he stretches back the bow, tries to shoot true. A note of pleading enters his voice. "What I'm trying to say, Ebele, is that I miss you. You barely sleep, you're mumbling over some dirty stones all night. You're falling apart."

Apunda. Three parts, three sides. He's got his business part so organized, it makes him the best farmer for miles around. Then, there's his religious part, the part that he's using now. Hovering off to one side of his face is the secret third part of him, the one he doesn't reveal to very many people, and that's how much this man loves his wife. Is he self-righteous? Yes. Rigid? Yes. But anyone who knows him well knows that hiding beneath all that inventoried information is a very frightened but very loving man.

That's the part Ebele addresses this evening. She draws herself up, pushes her head scarf back on her forehead. "Listen to me, Apunda," she says. New softness threads her voice. "Our daughter is going into the place that holds the beginning of us all, and I think she may be in danger. Please, please listen." Their long marriage is coiled in the curve of her voice—all the children born, the people who have died, the hollow place worn in the maize cob mattress from all their years together, all this love and history she tries to wedge into her husband's unyielding brain.

She raises her head defiantly. "I have returned to the old ways, Apunda," she says. "I no longer believe in the words spoken by a white man in sandals. I believe in the Great Mother. Everything is connected. Those who made the world are still inside the trees, everything and all knowledge is woven together." Staring into her husband's eyes, Ebele begins to sing the old words she has tried for so long to extinguish. "Women are circles carved from the moon," she sings, slightly swaying. "We are eclipses, one part of the sky. We know the truth that lies between the stars." She matches these old words with the beat of her fingers on the bowl she uses to boil milk.

The faces of her children glow in the hut like little moons. Their eyes move back and forth from their father to their mother. There's no animation in their listening, however; fear has turned them silent, pressed them frozen against the walls.

Trying to stand at right angles to this chaos, her husband draws himself up. "I know where you are getting all this nonsense," he snarls. "All this craziness comes from that batty old witch, your mother." His voice holds the phlegm of disdain. "What's going to happen to your soul if you continue this way, Ebele? You don't listen to the priest anymore. You don't read your Bible."

She shakes her head. "You aren't listening to me, husband. Finally, after so many years of not believing, I can hear the Great Mother. She's in the wind, in the trees. If I could hear more clearly, I'd be able to protect our Emely. The voices will tell me what to do."

But her husband has something up his sleeve, something that will weigh down his wife's crazy, jazz-rising thoughts. He has names. Names are Apunda's personal possession. Planted right, names can be fluttered over everything that is his.

"The field that looks like a blanket," is one of his names. "The stream like a crooked finger," is another. And his children are the most possessed of all, their names long fabric of sound. Emely's name alone could own a country: Emely Baako Kesia Matei.

Trying to work his proprietary magic, he unhinges one finger from its set, points it at her. "Ebele Matei," he solemnly pronounces. But it doesn't work; she doesn't come back to him. Instead she raises a finger, speaks a name all of her own.

"Tsholofelo Zoa," she says.

Her husband doesn't understand. What's his wife's best friend got to do with any of this?

Though her husband doesn't understand, the dead who have gathered to watch do. *No, Ebele,* we whisper. *Don't do this. Just one name spoken this way can rip a seam in all mystery.*

But Ebele's not listening. "Tsholofelo Zoa," she repeats, then kicks over the water bucket. It makes a complaining, falling-down sound. "Tsholofelo Zoa!"

What she says sets fire to everything her husband believes, everything he has built and owned; all those names are now engulfed in smoke. Two warring fingers, two names.

Because Ebele's remembering the worst day of her life. Her best friend, Tsholofelo, was in the birth hut trying to push out her baby. The midwife was working frantically, trying to cut the scar tissue surrounding Tsholofelo's infibulation to make an opening large enough for the baby to come out. She started first with a tiny knife, then moved to a larger one, and then finally scissors. Tsholofelo's baby finally slid out, and then there was a familiar silence as everyone waited. No wail of life this time; the baby had been trapped too long in the birth canal. Another stillborn to be buried in the red clay of the hills.

"A girl," the midwife whispered, and the women who watched knew what her life would have been. She would have seen every nightmare on Earth, the seasons of her life measured in the dropping of the blood. After her first cutting and sewing, she would have had to spend up to two hours just to pee. When her period came, she would have had to hide, blood building up inside of her, the smell terrible. On her wedding night, she would scream with pain as her husband penetrated what would become an open wound. And if she, in turn, gave birth to a girl, it would start all over again.

"Tsholofelo, Tsholofelo, Tsholofelo!" Ebele screams. It's a sound with its own teeth, its own life pulse and knowledge, a sound as eloquent as any throat can produce. And it's dangerous, too. Ebele traces her friend's name across an entire geography of women's secrets, all that has lain at the bottom of her too long—unfettered, unsaid, unleashed, untamed—all those *un*'s spray against the correct diagram that is her husband.

For Tsholofelo died that day. "Complications at birth" was the official reason. Loss of blood from her second re-stitching was the secret reason that all of the women in the village knew.

Laid next to the body of her little girl, one more woman to be buried in those hills.

"I've tried to follow the ways of Jesus, Apunda," Ebele says. "All of our children have been baptized, haven't they? I wore a head scarf to show the world I was a good Christian woman and went to church every Sunday. But our daughter is coming home, and I don't know what will happen if they find her." Remembering the terrible pain from her own excision, the secret cuttings every women in the village has experienced, her voice trails away.

"Who?" her husband asks. "What are you talking about?"

Ebele doesn't answer. She can't speak the secret aloud. She was taught from an early age that if anyone talked about the secret ceremonies, there would be grave repercussions. But what can she do to protect Emely? It's only a matter of time before the other women in the village find out that her oldest daughter is the next Stone Woman, and as soon as they know they will begin to prepare for the most severe cutting of them all. She tried to get Mentegai to take her daughter into the forest early, but he refused. She has to do something. If she doesn't figure something out, Emely could become the next Tsholofelo!

Blood, she thinks, suddenly. *The song of blood.*

When her daughter lived inside her body, she sent her a steady stream of nutrients and oxygen in her blood. Maybe she can do it one more time, keep her daughter alive this way. It will be runner's-up blood, that's for sure, but it will be blood nevertheless.

Turning away from her husband, Ebele picks up her kitchen scissors, separates them into two ballet legs. The air is suddenly charged with intensity.

"What are you doing?" her husband asks, alarmed.

Too many secrets, too many unsaids; she takes a deep breath, spreads the legs of the scissors apart, then slides the blade across the skein of veins on her wrist.

"Take what it is that makes me, Great Mother," she says under her breath. "Let me show you how beautiful I am."

Blood then, ruby-red abruptly spurts. Her children scream, her husband rushes forward, and Ebele smiles just a little. Prayers pulse on her heartbeat. Pure light, pure love. She has reached that calm center where everything is all right.

The dead, watching, are disgusted. *What has gotten into you, Ebele? Trying to bargain with the Mother by offering your own blood instead of your daughter's? No matter how deep you cut, she doesn't want your blood. She needs Amely's blood—rich and fierce, holy and good.*

CHAPTER 26

"Looks like I'm here just in time," Father Joseph says. He's silhouetted against the door, the sky, the sun, and clouds balanced on his shoulders. He enters the room with a swish of his white robes and nods to Apunda.

Ebele's husband watches him like providence, the children watch him like he's a magician. Ebele doesn't watch him at all. The priest calmly turns to Ebele's husband. "Apunda," he asks, "do you have something clean to wrap around Ebele's wrist?"

Moving in a trance, Apunda hands his wife a rag, and she wraps it around her wound. Blood creeps slowly onto the white cloth, the pink sky of a reluctant dawn.

"Give us this day our daily bread," Father Joseph intones, his deep bass voice surprisingly strong in a body so frail. Apunda bows his head as well. "And forgive us our trespasses," he says. From some secretive fold of his robe, the priest draws forth a communion wafer, snaps it in half. "Put this under your tongue, daughter," he instructs, but Ebele shakes her head.

There is a resolute quality to the priest that often occurs in people who have chosen a life of celibacy. It's as if he stands still and commands the world to move around him. It is only through vigorous discipline that he has won the war against carnal appetite. That victory, combined with the conviction of his faith, lends him an unbending certainty. He fills this little hut with absolute authority.

But Ebele's not finished. Before anyone can take them away from her, she picks up the scissors again, moves to the other wrist. "Blood is the only language for my thoughts," she says dreamily. "Take it, Mother, my most personal, traveling me."

A quick slice, but not too deep this time.

But the priest has got some magic of his own. He extracts a small green velvet bag from his robe, pulls on its tassels, takes out a silver cross and a small tear bottle of holy water.

"Christ is the only true God," he says solemnly, unscrewing the lid of the bottle.

Ebele's husband nods gratefully. "Amen," he says.

The priest tosses holy water against Ebele. It splashes on her skin, rains down on the dirt floor. Then he throws some against her husband. Wet spots splash against Apunda's faded gray shirt. "It's a sin to kill yourself, Ebele," he says. "Your soul will always hover between the worlds."

Ebele shakes her head. "I'm not trying to kill myself, Father," she tells him. "My blood is a plea. I am writing my fear in blood, trying to make more of a space between who I am and what I need to know."

The priest splashes more holy water against her. "Let the everlasting Father of Our Lord, Jesus Christ, help this woman throw aside her devil ways."

There is a tremendous skill at work here as the priest drops these old words into the deep well of Ebele's flickering faith, inviting Jesus into this small hut.

But Ebele's not having any of it. She holds the scissors tight. "This is my history, Father," she says, "not Jesus's truth. All the killings, all the fallen, live in my blood."

The children stand in a scale from big to little, crying orphan tears. The dead also watch. There is more at stake than any of the living can know.

"Let me have those scissors," her husband says firmly, but one more time his wife shakes her head.

"Let us confine that fallen tyrant to the flames of hell. Let them cry unto thee," the priest says. "Me, your unworthy servant." Hands so pale and crusty they look as though they are the first part of him that has died, the priest kisses the cross, holds it so that its shadow flickers across Ebele's face. "Help this woman see the purity of your ways," he continues. "We are your humble servants."

But Ebele has now moved deep into the Great Mother. "I've tried to listen to you, Father Joseph," she says. "I've tried to listen to my husband as well. But these teachings I follow now are older than Jesus. They go all the way back to the first fire. I'm sorry, Father, but we have no more need for Christ."

Her husband inhales a shocked breath, but the priest doesn't appear fazed. Another splash of holy water. This time he appeals to nothing less than God.

"Do not let this woman fall into the pit of fire, oh Lord," he prays. "Don't let her soul roast in the hands of the tyrant."

"In the old days, we were part of the same family," Ebele says. "We were relatives of everything we saw. We ran with the animals, not from them. The gorilla was our grandfather."

"Tsk," the priest says, one hot syllable of disdain. For the first time he seems personally affronted. Color rises to his face. "That's devil talk. We come from Adam and Eve, not the animals. You know that, daughter." He bows his head. "Help this woman renounce these tribal beliefs, oh Lord. Snatch from ruination this pagan soul."

One foot on God's glory train, his deep voice swirls the insides of the hut.

But Ebele has more to say. "We used to be able to sit down and share the same tree with the tiger," she says. "We spoke with those who had gills, scales, fur, wings, and beaks, and when we looked inside another, we always found ourselves."

One foot on God's glory train, last call for Jesus—the priest is determined. "Save this human being made in your image, oh Lord," he says in his best conductor's voice. The red leather of his Bible rebukes the dirt walls of the little hut, the book more fingered than his own body.

God's glory train begins to shudder on its rails, all those souls bound for heaven. Ebele makes one more cut. Searing pain, heart rate slowing, she's almost there. Each beat of her heart pumps more blood from her arteries out onto her skin.

"The Lord sent his only begotten son into the world to train the lion," the priest says—white man's words that hunt the vines wrapped around Ebele's heart.

She is careful down here; panic can burn up her chances of survival.

Her husband's voice is soft and pleading. "Don't, Ebele. Don't do this. You've lost too much blood already. Give me the scissors."

Ebele holds her bleeding wrist. "You love me in secret, Apunda," she says weakly. "But you must love all of me, even what I believe."

Her husband can't control himself any longer. Hollowed out by fear, he slips into patriarchal scorn. "How do you expect me to be respected in this community if you're crouched over some rocks muttering to yourself?" he yells. "Let me see what you're holding in your hand."

Ebele slowly opens her fingers to reveal a small stone, sliced through its middle with one thin white line. Her husband plucks the stone from her open palm, holds it to his ear.

"I don't hear anything," he says mockingly. He holds it up to his children. "Do you?"

They are silent.

He goes to the door and, with all of his might, throws the stone as far as he can.

A thrown stone, the swollen words of a priest too large for her family's little hut, the buried life in her mother's eyes—this is what Emely encounters the evening she arrives back home from America.

Hardly the homecoming she imagined.

CHAPTER 27

B efore her, her mother's riotous garden. Flowers sail scent into the air, blooms glitter hoorays against the sky, pods hang like various musical notes. And before her, glowing warm and familiar, her mother's kitchen hut. Home—Emely's finally home.

"See you later, Emely," Kareem says behind her. "I've got some stuff to take care of."

She turns. "Aren't you coming inside?" she asks. "Don't you want to see Mama?"

He shakes his head. "No. I told you. It's always weird coming home. You never know what you're going to find." He slips out the gate of their mother's garden, heads toward the hills.

Emely leans her rolling suitcase against the wall of the hut, flounces her nylon parka, and in opposition to all those years away—all those degrees, lined-up facts, papers, and treatises—ducks her head and enters her past.

It's dim in here. Silent, too, and for some reason she doesn't understand Father Joseph is standing right in front of her. Here too, pressed against the walls of the hut, stand all of her brothers and one sister. *Is that really Nunu?* she wonders. *She's so tall!* The last time she saw her she was cradled in her mother's arms. And that man in front of her has to be her father. Though his back is to her, she recognizes his faded gray checked shirt.

"Hello!" she says. No one answers, but the fire cackles, and somewhere, the slide of someone's foot across the dirt floor briefly cuts the silence. But then her father moves and Emely sees the source of everyone's silence. Her mother. Washed out skin, a cloth tied around one wrist stained with blood, lips moving but emitting no sound.

"What's going on?" Emely demands.

Nunu pops her thumb into her mouth. Again, there is no answer. Her mother picks up a bowl, slants it toward the firelight, and, finding a small scab of food adhered to one edge, begins to scrub it clean with her fingernail. When she is finished, she puts the bowl down, picks up another. More scrubbing.

One more time Emely tries her bright call. "It's me, Emely!" she says. "I'm home!" The children glance at her, but no one else does. All eyes fall back to Mama.

Firewood is the next to order. Moving slowly, Mama stacks, restacks the wood, as though in all the world only those few obedient straight lines will keep her sane.

Clothes are next. Though obviously weak, she folds them first by color—then, dismantling the pile, she piles them up by category: pants, T-shirts, small Nunu dresses. She does this with a ceaseless, driving energy that burns.

She is doing Mama things, trying to make the world clean for her family, but it doesn't feel like love. There is none of the joyful exuberance of her garden, either. Her flowers out there are an ardent, sloppy celebration of what she can't control; this, on the other hand, is only stern, wedge-cut air.

As her father has just attempted to do, Emely tries to bring her mother back by saying her name. "Mama," she says. "It's me, Emely." And this time it works. Mama stops folding and refolding the clothes. When she looks up and finally catches the eye of her oldest daughter, she sends her a look so achingly pure Emely's heart moves. Then, fist clenched, heart shocked, Mama falls to her knees, all the things left inside of her for too long, all those fermented secrets, expelled into one long, gasping sob.

"Owl Feather," she says, calling Emely by a name she used to call her when she was a little girl. "Owl Feather, you're home." Then she does something Emely doesn't understand. She reaches over and picks up her scissors.

"No!" Father Joseph immediately says.

"No!" her father says.

"No!" says every eye watching.

When her mother pulls the blades of the scissors apart, holds one of them against the veins of her wrist, Emely matches their "nos" with her own. "No!" she yells, springing forward. "Mama, what are you doing?"

Her mother's eyes are frightened, feverish. "I must drop my blood in order to save you," she says. "If anyone comes one step closer, I'll go deep."

Behind her, Emely hears the rumble of Father Joseph and her father beginning to pray. "Almighty Lord, help this woman tonight," they say together. Emely remembers what Kareem told her earlier—that Mama has changed, that she spends her days mumbling over a pile of dirty stones.

"What's going on?" Emely whispers to her father. "Is Mama trying to kill herself?"

Her father shakes his head. "I don't know," he replies. "Something's obviously gone haywire." He speaks as if his wife isn't in front of him. "She was acting so crazy tonight I had to ask Father Joseph to come over. She's been . . ." he searches for the right word, "sick."

He dips his head, blows his nose in a handkerchief. "I just don't know what to do anymore. We have to get the scissors away from her."

The blades of the scissors hover over her mother's wrist. "I send what is inside me back to the Sister Women," Ebele says, her eyes glassy. "I use no words, no stuck-together sounds. Only my blood will take me back to what we all need to remember. It will carry the deepest part of me back in time from one grandmother's head to another."

Her skin is dewed with sweat. Emely's eyes lock on those blood-caked blades.

"It's only my blood that can help you, Owl Feather," Ebele continues, and in the suspended moment that follows, mother and daughter gaze into each other's eyes, and everything they are to each other and everything they aren't fills the space between them.

This is my mother? Emely asks herself. She can barely believe it. *This place is my home? It's so small and curved, it could be the inside of an ear!*

All the geography she's traversed rises up between them. All those mountains, savannas, and oceans merge with the hard-won habits of thought she has used for so many years to shape herself into the scholar she's become. She remembers her suitcase leaning against the wall of the hut outside, the two parallel lines grooved by its wheels down the dirt road to this place.

We're made by completely different forces. We're not the same. I'm not this blood-soaked woman mumbling to herself on a muddy floor.

None of what she says to herself works entirely, however. Emely can't separate herself from what her mother is trying to tell her. Something floats slightly beyond her understanding, a thing that frightens her even more than those blood-caked scissors. It's like picking out one note from a piece of music, one brushstroke in a painting—she hears the one singular bit of intelligence inside her mother's jumbled thoughts, something of sense that refutes the priest and her father's inventoried, entitled world of faith and sin.

Her mother, recognizing that she has understood, nods her head. "There's something I need to tell you, Emely," she whispers, "but not in front of all these people. Can you tell everyone to leave?"

Emely immediately seizes the opportunity. "Yes, Mama," she replies, "but only if you let me take the scissors."

"All right," her mother says, and relinquishes the scissors to her daughter. They are warm and slippery with her blood. Emely tucks them quickly into the pocket of her backpack, then turns and addresses the room.

"Mama says she has something to tell me," she says to everyone. "She has asked everyone to leave."

The priest smiles. "You're probably the best medicine of all for your mother," he says, picking up his cross and Bible. "I'll check in with you tomorrow, Ebele. And Emely, welcome home. I'm sorry this isn't exactly the reunion we all had in mind. May God be with you." He leaves the hut with a ceremonial sweep of his robes.

Her father is the next to speak. He addresses his wife. "Maybe now that Emely's home you'll see that everything is all right," he says. He turns to the rest of his children. "Let's let your mother and big sister catch up a bit."

But just before he leaves, he turns, and the careful mask he usually wears for the world falls away. Not even the gray-and-white checks of his shirt can hold his sorrow. "Please try to get better, Ebele," he says in a low voice. "I ache, just ache for you." And then, with newly hunched shoulders, he ducks out the door. The children follow in a somber procession.

In the silence that follows, Ebele looks at her daughter with exhausted, haggard eyes. "Even with all the warnings, I thought everything would still be good between us, Emely," she says softly. "I thought that you and I would walk arm in arm down the road together, work in the fields, and everyone would know from our smiles that it was good between us."

As if to maintain the verbs of her life, her constant, ever-loving care, her hands flutter nervously before her. "I thought that you would help with Nunu, and my firstborn and my last would make a circle around my life. But the warnings are coming too strong. I'm beginning to hear things. I know you're in trouble." Tears begin to spill down her cheeks. "Something has happened to you, and the only thing I can think of to do is offer my blood."

"I'm okay, Mama," Emely says, a bit unsteadily. "Something did happen to me in the capitol that was kind of scary, but it's over."

Her mother shakes her head. "I don't think it's over."

It seems to come with her mother's gaze: a cool, lonely landscape. Galaxies tossing, time burning through the planet's crust, land and mountains running molten while rock, mud, and rain mix together in a pottery of weather. All this is transmitted from her mother's two watching eyes. But then she blinks, and it is gone.

"I think it's only just beginning, Owl Feather," she says quietly.

Suddenly tired, Emely sinks to the ground. She remembers she barely slept in the police station last night. "Mama," is all she can think of to say. First one tear, then another, and soon her cheeks are streaked with tears. "Mama," she repeats, her mother's name the only thing in all the world she wants to hold.

Is it her tears or the fact that she said her name? Emely doesn't know, but suddenly Mama—the soft, loving, reassuring Mama—is back in front of her. She reaches out her arms, pulls Emely into her lap, and, rocking, begins to croon the song she used to sing to help her sleep when she was a little girl.

"Let the cows be happy," she sings. "Let them all go out to the field in a row. Let them be happy so that they will give us milk." She has a smooth, rich voice that sometimes seems to be several voices at once;

what she sings rumbles through Emely's body. "Open the gate," she sings, "so that the cows will follow. Oh yes, they are fat and happy."

The old song sings away all that is intemperate, worried, and weak, promising that if people can just love well enough, trust well enough, sing loud enough, everything will work out after all. "Let the cows go out in a row," she croons, and Emely, held inside her mother's arms, inhaling her particular dry-grass smell, follows the song back to childhood.

"Go out into the fields, cows, all go out in a row." Her mother's voice sails out the door of the hut, twines across the village, snarls for a moment in the upper branches of a large tree, then gradually fades away.

And for a moment, that is enough.

CHAPTER 28

We the dead say good-byes in this night, good-bye to the used-to-be. In the old days, because we knew each other so well, we were each other. We talked about everything across endless cups of tea. There were secrets, of course, but everyone knew the rules. When we gathered in the cave where the gold woman danced, it wasn't because we were hiding from the world, it was because the Great Mother belonged only to us. We didn't want to share her.

Not anymore. Women like Ebele no longer honor the secrets of the blood. There are even those who want to stop the holy cuttings—more and more of them are coming after us every day. They are breaking away from the old ways; they believe in that white man born halfway through time. These days we have to hide our secrets deep underground.

No matter how many have dropped away, we still have to cut. It is what the Great Mother wants: rich, rich blood. Will our new Stone Woman's mother outsmart the women in the village, get her daughter away from their knives?

The dead can only watch, can only wait.

CHAPTER 29

Scarves tied around their heads, skirts that bellow printed gardens—the morning after Emely comes home, the women of the village are working in the fields, turning over the soil before spreading seed. And they're gossiping, of course, speculating about which new wife will become pregnant, whose husband has a roving eye, who has a fondness for drink, and so on and so on and so on. Oh the glad speculation, oh the great sweetness when they finally hit the marrow of true scandal!

And then, maybe because it's the same thing after all, all that gossip turns gradually to song. "We hoe these fields for plants to live," the women sing, pacing the rhythm of song with the swing of their hoes. "We hoe these fields for life"—and when Bulu adds her voice and all that carbonated happiness comes forward, the sound becomes so rich and full, it's enough to make everyone want to bow down.

Formidable, upright, Bulu is a woman so large, it's as if her very excitement about being alive has caused her to swell out of her own body. Her cleavage is so deep her body looks folded. Great flags of flesh hang from her arms; every time she raises the hoe each of those flags waves a patriotic zeal. Taut seconds then as the hoe hangs suspended above her head; next a long giddy slide down; and finally, when the hoe cuts the soil and the dark smell of the underneath explodes into the air, Bulu's great sigh of satisfaction, the sound splendid with her choice of working this field, raising fat children, eating food grown from the seeds, singing this song of gossip.

Venerated daily by her very own flags, Bulu is a woman so complete she could be her own country.

"Ebele's daughter got home from America last night," Afrua says. Unlike Bulu, Afrua is skinny. Burn marks the size of small coins blaze on the inside of her arms—remnants of childhood, when she and the other children dared each other to take a stick fresh from the fire and press it against their skin. One was considered brave if one didn't cry out.

Clump. The hoes cut the soil. "Doesn't she have some kind of fancy government job?" one of the women asks.

"Yes," Afrua says. "Ebele told me about it. She's going into the forest to do some kind of government survey."

The women pause and, bracing their weight on their hoes, stare for a moment toward the forest. Wind slaps their skirts against their legs.

"There can't be anyone left in those trees," one of the women says. "No one has talked to us through stones from the forest for some time."

A collective long sigh that has more to say than the wind, and then, one by one, the women pick up their hoes, resume the music of talk paced with work.

Until they catch sight of Ebele, that is—coming up the road, her head down, walking slowly, rags wrapped around her wrists.

As Bulu catches sight of the rags wrapped around Ebele's wrists, shock slackens her face "After all these years you're dropping the song of blood?" she asks. She takes a few stuttering, matriarchal footsteps foreword. "What's happened, Ebele?"

The mutation of fear jumps quickly from one woman to the next. Even the coins on Afrua's arms, can't remind her that she's brave.

The women circle around Ebele, all those hoes meant for excavating weeds now sharpened for something else, "What's happened?" Bulu asks again. "You're dropping the song of blood when for years you've told us you don't believe?" She squints her eyes, trying to put it all together. "Does this have anything to do with your daughter being back?"

Ebele, crowded now, begins to cry. She can barely get out the words. "The Mother," she sobs. "The Great Mother. For months now I have felt the storm of her, and then finally yesterday an old woman in the forest told me through the stones that she needs my Emely in the forest. She says she needs not only what Emely knows, the tiny green shoots of it, but the empty spaces of what she doesn't know."

Suddenly defiant, she raises her head, looks Bulu straight in the face. Her eyes flash with pride. "The old woman told me that Emely is the next Stone Woman." She raises her arm and thumps her chest. "*My* daughter, *my* Emely!" She streaks her eyes across the faces of all the women. "Not your amputated, slicked up, cut down, obedient nursemaid daughters! No! *My* Emely, the one who has walked farther with her mind and feet than any of you could ever imagine!"

The silence that follows Ebele's announcement is profound, all the women struggling to understand what she has just said. They can barely believe it. A Stone Woman has grown up right beneath their watchful eyes? How could she have come from a woman so indistinct that she had walked away from their holy teachings years ago, even tricked them by sending her daughter to the nuns at the boarding school?

"Our Mother help us!" Bulu finally exclaims. "What unholy chain of events is in motion? How can someone who hasn't been cut be a Stone Woman?"

One more time Ebele begins to cry. "I know what you're going to do, but it's already been taken care of. I've given the Mother my blood instead of hers."

Bulu narrows her eyes. "Silly woman," she says contemptuously. "Don't you know you can't make a bargain with the Great Mother? One more time you're trying to alter what should be. She doesn't want your blood. If you hadn't rejected the old ways so long ago you would know this."

The devastating implications are settling in. "We can't let this happen," Bulu says. She turns to the other women. "We are guardians of the ancient secret. If Emely is the next Stone Woman, she must find the tablet, rise, and enter the Great Mother's sky. This is the way it has always been since the beginning of time!"

Those coins on Afrua's arms, the deadly look in Bulu's eyes—Ebele knows what they are thinking. "Please don't hurt her," she whispers. "If you cut her she will die."

But Bulu has already made up her mind. "We need to meet tonight in the holy place," she announces. "We must figure out what to do." She narrows her eyes and turns to Ebele. "And you must not speak of any of this, particularly to Emely. You know what happens when someone spills our Mother's most holy secrets. People can get hurt."

She turns then, leaving Ebele standing in the middle of the road. The threat she is just spoken lingers in the air.

Excavating secrets, banishing anything careless or unwanted from their lives, the women return to work, using their hoes to cut the soil. One more time the wind begins to blow, but this time it's no pasture-laden breeze.

"We knew something like this was going to happen," Afrua comments. "I remember the day Emely was born. She had the light even then, but Ebele managed to outsmart us by sending her to boarding school."

"Foolish woman," another woman comments. "What makes her think that the Mother would want her blood anyway?"

"Could she be wrong about her daughter being the next Stone Woman?" someone else asks. "After all, for so many years she didn't believe."

"The stones don't lie," Bulu responds.

"But what are we going to do?" someone else asks. "We are the guardians of the most holy secret of them all."

The women swing their hoes, their questions metered with distress. A long moment passes, then Bulu stops working. She raises her head, weighs her next words carefully. "We can't send an unclean Stone Woman into the belly of the Great Mother," she say. "We will meet in the holy place tonight and prepare for the largest cutting of them all."

Behind her, the sound of all those hoes agreeing with her. A rooster's raggedy cry rends both sky and field.

CHAPTER 30

Tonight, under an almost-full moon, Mentegai sits deep in the forest by a small fire. His eyes are closed, and, as he often does these nights, he visits the dream tribe that lives behind his eyelids. He can see them clearly. Old men sit naked, dreadlocks piled so high on their heads they resemble the burls of a gigantic tree. Young girls shimmer with giggles; a beautiful woman who resembles his mother is making a sculpture, pulling features from the clay.

Where are you? his heart asks. *Are you even still alive? Why won't you let me find you?*

Even his dream tribe doesn't recognize the separation implied by this question. "We're always here with you," they respond. "We live always behind your eyelids. You are a part of us" . . . and so, when Mentegai opens his eyes and sees an old woman standing right in front of him, he thinks at first he has imagined her.

But then she speaks, the moisture in her voice holding great sorrow. "Mentegai," she says softly. "Son of Sarutu." She smiles a sad smile and takes a step forward. "I have something to ask you, son of Sarutu." No singularity is left in her arthritic fingers, but she still manages to convey the authority of a pointed digit as she raises her hand. "We need Amely, the one you call Emely. I want you to bring her into the forest when the moon is round. She is the only one who can save us."

She stares for a moment out into the forest, her skin as creviced as a stone. "Our way of life might be over," she says softly. "Where we are going, not even my magic can reach. There is only one last womb left in the forest. We need Amely to perform the sacred ritual and then rise tall." Light from the fire runs molten into all of her wrinkles.

Mentegai floats on the melody of the old woman's voice, remembering things he never even knew. "My mother? My father?" he asks dreamily. "Do you remember them?"

As though borrowed from another, younger season, the old woman's eyes flash. "Yes, of course I remember them," she says. "My hands rounded, always hold family. I will make you a promise. If you bring in the girl, I will tell you everything you want to know about them. But I need her soon. I want her under my hands by the time the moon is round. Do you understand?"

Mentegai glances up at the sky. "That's the day after tomorrow!" he exclaims.

The old woman nods her head. "I know," she says. "We don't have much time. I need to teach her quickly. The womb of my granddaughter is almost ready to drop woman's blood. The Great Mother so long silent, Amely the new Stone Woman . . . it is the perfect delta where all signs connect. I am old and close to climbing to the sky, but this is what I know. We have only this one last chance. Do we have a bargain, son of Sarutu?"

He nods, and she smiles. Placing her hands against the trees for balance, she begins to move slowly away. "Bring Amely to the tallest mountain in the forest," she says over her shoulders. "The way has a little wander to it." Her hands twist in the air. "We will leave a few signs along the way."

Right before she disappears, she throws back her head and sings a strange melody. Mentegai isn't sure, but he thinks it might be the old language his father sometimes spoke on those star-crested nights when they lay together looking for his mother in the sky.

Mentegai can't believe it. After months and months of seeking, he has finally found his parents' tribe. Finally, the promise behind his eyelids matches up with the promise of what he has seen.

Though the old woman no longer stands in front of him, the song of her still gleams bright inside. *But Emely is the ticket*, he says to himself. *I have to get to her mother and tell her I've changed my mind.*

CHAPTER 31

A few miles away, Ebele is standing over her sleeping daughter. She has found the equator stone her husband tossed into her garden last night. She holds it in the palm of her hand. In the other she holds a few fox teeth, a long rope she has twined from dry grass, and a rib bone from a cow, curved like the bottom part of a vowel. And oh, yes, her scissors retrieved from her daughter's backpack, their blades still crusted with blood.

She wants to go out into her garden—push her fingers into its moist, receptive dirt, something so old it was made before anything had a name—but she can't leave her daughter. She is standing guard. There are people out there who want her.

Oh, Emely, she thinks as she watches her sleep, *what have you gotten yourself into now?* Though her daughter was exhausted tonight, she did not want to sleep with the others in the sleeping hut. She has learned a different kind of sleep in her years away. At night, alone, under blankets as warm as a second skin, she has learned how to drop deep into the bowl of who she is, and when her dreams rise, they grasp her alone.

But this is what Ebele knows: on this night Emely's dreams will spill her back into a world full of pain. Because they are coming, those women out there, and when they find her they will hurt her in ways that are unimaginable.

Ebele rakes her mind. What can she do to protect her oldest daughter? The old woman in the forest told her she wanted her daughter cleansed of the world's noise. What can she possibly say to Emely to get her to listen? They don't use the same words or believe in the same god, don't even sleep the same sleep. *She even smells different, like the nuns.*

Only one thing left to do. Denying even her need for dirt, Ebele holds her stones, waits until they are warm with her, then whispers the words spoken by the faithful around the world. "*Dada wanawaki wi wi amabio ewafu unawasa kesia imi mini kukutia wimbau yongu asala,*" she chants. (Sister Women, you who are the dead and you who are alive, can you hear me? I send you my song of prayer.")

Her stones now warm, she sends her deepest fear through their hard surface. *Am I hearing you right? Is it true this beautiful young woman sleeping before me is our new Stone Woman? If it's true, please, please, don't punish her for all my years of not believing.*

For this is what Ebele knows: if her oldest daughter is the next Stone Woman, it is her destiny to find the oldest object in the world, a stone tablet made thousands of years before Christ was born. And when she finds it, she must be clean enough, pure enough, to follow the instructions engraved on its surface.

And Ebele knows what being clean means to the women in the village.

She casts her eyes toward her daughter's face, then her gaze travels down to her tennis shoes—shoes so animated they could be invited to dinner as two jovial guests. *My mother used to say that mountains never meet,* Ebele thinks hopelessly. *Is this the way it's always going to be with my Emely? Two lonely mountains? I can't even talk to her!*

There is only one thing left to do. If she just goes deeper, maybe the Mother will accept her blood. Maybe Bulu was wrong this afternoon.

Emely's face is a cameo against the night as Ebele picks up the scissors. Everything else falls away. It is only by focusing on her daughter that she can hang on for even one more second. *Please, Mother,* she says. *Though the women out there said you don't want it, please take my blood instead of hers. It's the only thing I have to give.*

Thunder rips the sky, rain hits the earth. One more cut.

Isn't blood beautiful?

CHAPTER 32

A woman in Japan picks up her stones, holds them until they are warm with her. "姉 [妹] のような人, 女の親友," she says. "あなたの生きている死んでいるあなた、私は私の歌祈りの送信." ("Sister Women, you who are alive, you who are dead, I send you my song of prayer.")

We, the dead, answer immediately. *Yes, Sister,* we reply. *We are here.*

"Yes, our world is in trouble," the woman in Japan says. "Rich men bomb our land with dynamite. All that buried light revealed, and then stone is harvested, cut into tidy slabs for rich people's kitchen sinks and bathrooms."

Amely's mother's cutting herself again, the dead respond, *Kareem's down there with his tiny bomb . . . that boy is right, but he is saying it wrong. Writing on the sky with fire is not the way to get people to listen. The only thing that will stop the wrong is for our new Stone Woman to rise with the sacred tablet into the Great Mother's sky.*

Dynamite, mother's blood, or ancient songs. Which is more powerful?

The woman in Japan moves the stone of her country closer to the others. "Sisters, mothers," she says, "we need the stone of serpentine for protection. Just one night used wrong can smudge dirty fingerprints across all of time."

Sunlight leaning on daisies, lulled by soft wind; Kareem, languid and dangerous all at the same time.

He sits on a hill overlooking the village. A rib-chiseled dog wanders up and down the dirt road. Chickens peck the hard crust of the earth; the roofs of a few huts twirl their grass skirts; old men sit in the wispy shade of the few sparse trees, gray hair revealing the calendar of their days.

Everyone who goes by the old men receives a snappy joke, riddles that go so far back they are almost homes in themselves. "You can't kill a flea with one finger," is today's free handout.

Tonight at eleven o'clock, when the watchmen slips away to visit his girlfriend, Kareem will crawl down the hill toward the quarry, slide under the barbed-wire fence, break the padlock on the shack, and fill his PVC pipe with dynamite. Read the sky then, folks! Five simultaneous explosions at five government-owned businesses around the country.

I will be strong, purposeful, move into this night with sound and fire, Kareem silently proclaims. *No more exploitation of the land. A match to the night—do you see me now?*

The sun up here on the hill is blazingly hot—no singularity left in the trees, grass blades, leaves, everything just different stanzas in summer's song of light. Kareem leans over and picks a yellow daisy, begins to drop its petals one by one into the bottom of the PVC pipe. *This one's for the Five Point Star. This one's for my big sister, Emely, who hasn't got a clue. And this one's for me.*

Doomed petals washed in dynamite; Kareem knows if he's found with the makings of a bomb he will be thrown into jail and executed.

"I love you. . . ." Three aching notes cut the air with longing. It is the call of the red-necked grebe. As usual, Kareem's heart gusts toward Eshe. *Maybe an explosion in the sky will help drain the pain from my heart.*

He leans over and picks another petal, drops it into the pipe. "For Eshe," he says quietly.

Day is now only a seed of light. It is almost time.

The dead are incredulous. *Oh Kareem*, we moan. *All this for a girl? Because of the longing of your body you are going to hurt the body of the Earth? What dark thing have you made of yourself? Just the sound of her name and your penis rises.*

Shame on you. Where is the boy who used to cry when one of his animals died? You've become part of what you are trying to fight against!

Not even our love can keep you safe.

CHAPTER 33

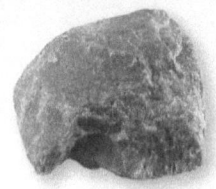

Not too far away from where Kareem sits on the hill, another conversation takes place—strategy, effortless and cruel, spoken into a cell phone. The police chief is talking to the professor.

"Emely is with her family," he reports, "and her brother is close by. I have both of them in my sights."

The police chief has just received information from the police unit monitoring student cells that along with four others, Kareem is planning to blow up a government-backed business. "A Five Point Star" is the name of the student action.

"An unexpected piece of good news," he says, and tells the professor what he has just learned. "It wouldn't hurt to have a bargaining chip if Emely doesn't turn over the tablet."

A momentary pause before the professor responds. "This is indeed good news," he finally replies, "but we have to proceed cautiously. This tablet is the symbol of the oldest pagan society in the world, a secret goddess cult that worships a powerful female deity. It's sure to attract some powerful women who will do anything to protect its existence."

A slight pause, and then, in the commanding tone of a supervisor giving orders to an underling, the professor outlines what needs to happen next.

CHAPTER 34

Day has turned to night—not just with the announcement of stars but with the deepening color of the sky. In a few moments, the watchman will leave his post at the quarry to go and visit his girlfriend, and Kareem will crawl down this hill, enter that shack, find some dynamite, and make a bomb.

Learning firsthand the grace of a listening sky, Kareem speaks the inconsequential stars of his own story into the dark as he waits.

This world is so beautiful, he thinks as he stares across the land. *Trees, stars, the breathing of everything alive, even my own death is stitched into the filigree.*

Huts glow in the deepening dusk, cooking fires trace smoke across the sky. "Yoohoo," someone calls.

"Yoohoo," someone else responds.

The sound spreads into the evening sky, becoming as round as the hills themselves. Tonight faces will glow in the firelight, food will be passed back and forth, solitude will be chased away with talk of the day, and then, in the dark, there will be that thicker, sweet sleep of joined bodies.

Only I'm on the outside, Kareem reflects bitterly. *But if I do what I have to do tonight, maybe soon I'll have Eshe. Fifth point of the star reporting in for duty! Tonight, a struck match, I will write on the sky with flame.*

"Eshe," Kareem says aloud. His voice does a little dance. "Eshe." But then he becomes terrified by how large his voice has become, and he doesn't speak again.

The watchman stands in front of the shed that holds the dynamite. Like lines drawn with a compass, the red glow from his cigarette circles from his mouth down to his knees and then back up to his mouth again. Sure enough, at eleven fifteen, romance calls. The watchman abandons his post.

It is time.

Kareem makes his way down the hill toward the shack. When he slips under the barbed-wire fence, he is careful not to leave any bit of identifying cloth in its teeth.

Darkness so thick it pulls in everything. One step, two steps more down the hill.

A brass padlock secures the door of the shack. Kareem bends down, picks up a stone, smashes it against the lock. The sharp sound that follows startles him, enters his body as a question. *What the hell am I doing?*

But then her name comes to him again. *Eshe*, he reminds himself, and he picks apart the dismembered padlock and steps inside the shack.

To his left, about a dozen shovels sleep one against the other. Beside them, plastic containers ribboned with cautionary words— "Flammable," "Dangerous," "Use with caution." The serious and consequential smell of dynamite.

Kneeling, Kareem opens one of the buckets, begins to scoop the dynamite into his PVC pipe. The pipe is almost full when he happens to glance out the door and sees a quick rip of light against the dark hills.

What is that? He thought he was the only one planning to write with light on the sky over his village tonight.

Another run of light. *I'd better investigate.* He grabs the PVC pipe and heads out the door.

CHAPTER 35

That cave down there so bright with women—I was the first to touch many of them as they slid from their mothers. But they're frightened. They sing their ancient songs, calling to the Great Mother, asking to be used. "We are the daughters of the trees," the women sing, "we are love, water, sky, fire, and earth." Even the one grooved into the cave's crevices jumps with light.

I watch my grandson crawl through the night toward the cave. Nothing less than the fate of the world rests on what happens next.

There it is again: a quick rip of light against the bush right in front of him, the light making jewelry of its leaves. Still holding the PVC pipe, Kareem approaches cautiously and reaches what appears to be a large crack running through a wall of stone.

He waits, clutching the PVC pipe. One, two, three, four . . . on the fifth beat, light shines once again and he peers at the source. It's a cave—a deep one at that. Far below, he can see a fire and the shadows of many people moving against its flames. And then, so regular that it sounds for all the world like the Earth's heartbeat, he hears the sound of a drum.

What's going on? He thought he knew every cave in the region, but none he's seen are as deep as this. And those voices. He crouches, listening hard. Yes. Coming from deep below the earth is the sound of strange singing.

Not sure if he wants to confront another secret tonight, Kareem has already turned, ready to get back to his task—Five Point Star shining bright—when he hears a cry. It's a sound without the compression of an alphabet, and he recognizes the voice immediately.

Mama! Mama's down there, and she's in trouble!

He drops the PVC pipe, squeezes through the crack, and begins to creep down through the dark.

CHAPTER 36

N̲o light from ancient stars, no reassuring conversation from the wind. Except for the occasional finger of light when light from the fire below reaches the cave's upper regions, the darkness is so complete in the cave it is almost solid. The cave narrows, the air grows cooler, and Kareem inches forward.

Darkness, gunpowder thick. He hears another wrenching cry from his mother and wonders if he should turn around and try to go get help, but decides he might not have much time. He is now crawling on his knees, moving toward a great space illuminated only when the fire below leaps up.

Pressing his hands against the walls of the cave now for balance, Kareem creeps forward. He is so frightened he finds himself shaking. What is he going to find? Like the bomb he just left behind, the secrets down here in this cave are ignited only with fire.

And then once again the fire leaps up and light spills back into the upper arteries of the cave, and for a moment sight opens out. Kareem jumps in shock. Embedded into the dirt of the walls of the cave are hundreds and hundreds of skulls. Porcupines, bongos, hippopotami— the walls are lined with them. Were they sacrifices? Is that what is going to happen to Mama? What is this unholy place?

Got to hurry. Got to get to Mama.

As he inches forward the voices below become clearer. "Women push back waves, we changed the seasons. . . ." Women's voices, a full chorus of them. "We are the before, we are the after, we are the amazing overlap."

Inching forward, Kareem finally arrives at the edge of what appears to be a giant chamber. Trembling, he peers over the edge. In the glow of the fire he sees twenty or so women standing in a circle in the middle of the cave holding hands. The strange singing grows louder.

"We are the alive, we are the dead," they sing. "We have guarded the secret since the beginning of time."

Their singing is both beautiful and strange; he's never heard any like it before. Wondering if it has some kind of hypnotic power, he crawls even closer to the edge. He's straining to see more of what is below when suddenly a gigantic women carved into the walls of the cave comes to life, hovers dreamily in the air. Kareem stares in astonishment. In the few seconds when the fire burns high, light bleeds into lines carved long ago in the dark walls, so luminous and gold, it is as if the gigantic woman is singing as well.

Still holding hands, the women below begin to bunch in close, and in that moment Kareem sees who they are approaching. His mother! She sits on a large stone in the middle of the cave, head down, shoulders shaking with sobs. Her wrists are wrapped with cloth stained with red. Is that blood? Horrified, a cold sweat breaks out across his forehead.

The singing grows louder. "We will follow the Great Mother back into time," they sing. In the next leap of fire, with an insouciant toss of her gilded head, the golden woman carved into the dirt walls once again springs into life.

The women take another step toward his mother. Their voices rise and fill the cave. "We are the guardians of the ancient secret," they sing—and then, from somewhere at the back of the cave, someone soars a note so pure, so present, it seems to tremble with light. And now Kareem's not wondering anymore if the singing has some kind of hypnotic power; he knows it: the niagara of song meets the niagara of fire, that one note opens out, becoming two, then three, the song now geography. It is a place that pulls him right in.

And he's not surprised when the woman who stands in the middle of the crowd turns, and it is Auntie Bulu. More a monument than a woman, this aunt of his inhabits every encounter the way a mountain inhabits a savanna. She bends over his mother.

"We can't send an unclean Stone Woman into the belly of the Mother, Ebele," she snarls. "If you had listened to your mother long ago, you would know this."

"Please don't hurt her," Kareem's mother whimpers, face in hands.

Aunties, friends, women of the village materialize out of the gloom—women so familiar they gave him the sky of his childhood— and Kareem wants to cry out, ask them what they are doing, but something in what the drums are saying warns him not to.

"We are the sentries for the oldest secret in the world," Bulu continues in her gritty voice. "The rightful order must be restored."

"No," his mother responds. "Please, don't. I told you. I've given the Mother my blood instead of my daughter's."

Bulu leans in close to her. "I told you before your blood is too thin, Ebele," she hisses. She shakes her head contemptuously. "You should have given her to us years ago!"

Blood? Cutting? *What are they talking about?* Kareem wonders, and a feeling of terrible foreboding comes over him. He never knew that his mother belonged to anything other than the world of Mamas—cooking, working in the fields, tending her garden. He remembers what he told Emely on the bus ride home—that Mama had changed, that she was worried, worried all the time. Is this why? A secret so terrible it needed to be buried underground?

Drums patter as soft as rain. Once again the golden woman on the wall jumps forward to declare her part in this conversation.

"It's hard to believe that after all this time, the next Stone Woman has been living right beneath our noses," Bulu continues, "especially since she is a young woman who hasn't been cut. But the stones don't lie. The ancient wheel has turned. This situation has to be repaired immediately."

She swallows hard, then raises her head. "We have no choice. We can't send an unclean Stone Woman into the forest. All the parts that are parallel to the mother's belly must be scraped and cleaned. Her private lower lips must be stitched and her blood must run thick. She will spill the red that is the hope of the uterus—and this time, Ebele, you must not stop us!"

Blood? Cutting women's parts? Kareem is beginning to understand.

Horror and disgust mix in his mind, along with something else—Eshe. The memory of all those long, hot nights punctured by knitting needles, thrashing with longing, Eshe's flamingo stampede taped forever on his heart. Eroticism, secrets, stones, and pubic bones—both entrance and destination, caves are tunnels pointing inward, holding both the plunge and the spill of arrival.

Drawn forward, repelled back, Kareem is now barely able to breathe. Suddenly the diminutive violence of his tiny bomb seems so childish.

"It will be a beautiful red, clotted with private passages," Bulu continues. "She will bleed because she is turned upside down, and it will run from the inside of the jar she is."

"Please don't hurt her," his mother whimpers softly again. Is it his imagination, or has more blood soaked into the rags tied around her wrist? Behind him, the skeletons grin their toothless grins. "*We are the dead,*" they seem to taunt, "*while you, on the other hand, are still rhymed with breath. Tell us, scared little boy, what are you going to do?*"

"If we don't do this a great darkness will come," Bulu says. As if to underline what she has just said, her shadow grows larger against the cave walls. "It is already close. The darkness will gather in everything, all of our children, all hope for the world."

She raises her head one more time. "We will cut her the day after tomorrow. We need to prepare the herbs, find the perfect piece of glass to use as a knife. Our new Stone Woman will stay in this cave until she heals, and then she can enter the forest clean."

His mother is now sobbing so hard Kareem can barely make out her words. "Emely's too old for this cutting," she wails. "She will lose too much blood and die."

Emely! They are talking about his big sister? These women are going to keep her prisoner in this cave and do unspeakable things to her? Kareem now knows what he has to do. He has to find Emely, tell her to get out of this village before these women find her. It's what his mother would want him to do if she knew he was listening.

He turns and, trying to touch just the dirt and not the skulls, begins to climb out of the cave. He has almost squeezed out of the entrance when his arm is grabbed, cufflinks snapped onto each wrist. A man's voice speaks in his ear.

"Kareem Matei," he says. "You are under arrest for plotting to overthrow the government."

CHAPTER 37

The Great Mother wonders if she has chosen wrong.

I am the strength that lies inside of surrender. I am the silence that lives beneath quiet. I am the world before the tick-tick-tick *of clocks.*

But mostly what I am is love.

Is my new Stone Woman going to be able to hear me in time? I am not the lie; she is still the lie.

Sometimes my trees talk of the men who passed through them. They burn and cut the great trees, hunt people and animals, pollute the streams with the thrown carcasses of the dead—sometimes animals, sometimes human beings.

She will die, we will die, if she does not understand what it is I have to say in time.

She's being carried into something larger than herself, but if she is going to understand what I have to tell her, she will have to extinguish what it is she thinks she knows and fill herself instead with me.

There is no room in the world for a false Stone Woman.

CHAPTER 38

I t is morning. Glimpsing dawn through the slits of the kitchen hut, Emely lifts the doll a little higher. "Nunu," she says, "she's yours, really." She fluffs out her little pink skirt. "Brand-spanking-new, fresh from America."

What Emely says does not uncork her little sister from the doorway. Thumb in her mouth, eyes enormous, she simply stares.

Emely unhinges one of the doll's arms, wedges it stiffly back and forth through the air. "Want to be my new Mama?" she croons. An almost involuntary tone of Christmas morning greed has crept into her voice.

Nunu doesn't move.

More enticement now. "Look, Nunu," Emely says, "she's even wearing a slip. Want to see?" Revealing a confection of ruffles and eyelet lace, she lifts up the doll's pink dress. But Nunu still does not take one step closer.

Nunu. A thin, ragged shift blooms with a pale pattern of what was once a field of yellow flowers. Bare feet. A galaxy of red and yellow barrettes orbits her head.

Emely's leg is beginning to thump up and down, up and down, in a nervous tic. With everything inside her, she wants Nunu to reach over and take the doll into her arms. That's family—when everyone wants the same thing.

"She can even close her eyes," Emely says, laying the doll down on her lap.

Her little sister's gaze now pierces the dusk of the hut with want, but she still hasn't moved.

Emely next stands the doll on her leg. Its two marbled globes immediately clack open—shockingly blue, and a little bit deadly.

One step, two steps . . . Nunu is finally coming toward her, toward the doll in her fancy going-to-church dress. Some part of Emely watches in suspension. Dimples encircle the spoiled rose of the doll's mouth; plastic arms reach up, but not with any kind of tenderness—no, more like seduction, take me, want me, change for me. And always the stare of those two blank eyes.

"Hydrochloric, metrobolic, heart palpitation." All those hours spent transcribing all that turgid medical jargon just for this moment. As Emely watches the hands of her country reach toward the commercial enticement of Los Angeles, the scene she had imagined during all those hours of typing at that dreary part-time job doesn't make her as happy as she thought it would.

Nunu's here now, and with more caution than she would use to pick up a baby, she takes the doll into her lap. As she reaches for her present, what she was clutching in her hand drops, then rolls away. Emely bends over and picks it up. It's a dried corncob still bubbling with a few kernels of corn, tied around its middle with a purple rag. Emely recognizes it immediately. These are the same dolls she made when she was Nunu's age. But is it a grandfather cob, uncle cob, or mama cob? She can't tell.

A few moments later, her brothers storm into the hut. Unlike Nunu, they have no trouble at all accepting what she has brought back for them. Oba rips the cellophane from a package containing a jigsaw puzzle of a castle. Kuku whoops when he is handed a miniature tow truck parked inside a small cardboard box. Mobiel immediately begins to bounce his orange basketball, the word *Warriors* scrolled across its surface.

Remembering Kareem's present, Emely extracts the Rubik's cube from her backpack and places it on the ledge above the fire.

Drumming a modern *thump, thump, thump* sound, the Warriors ball butts heads with the wall, the sound very different from the slight suck of Mobiel's usual ball, fashioned from a blown-up pig bladder. The tow truck is a small, alert presence standing at attention on the stones circling the fire, its tiny pulleys and chains ready to go, with nothing in the world to rescue. With no intrinsic knowledge of either puzzles or castles, Oba is trying to connect several jigsaw pieces of cardboard into a wobbly whole.

Far away from the world of cobs, Nunu rocks her new pink doll in her arms, her former doll family returned to what they've been all along, just a few rotting vegetables. "Baby, baby, baby," she croons.

Blond blood, flesh the color of unbleached sugar, lips squeezed around some kind of imported American secret . . . *There's no Africa in that doll's face,* Emely realizes. *What words can Nunu possibly place inside that factory-molded smile?*

Trying to blow the African part of herself alive once again, Emely leans over the fire and releases her breath gently. Smoke curls across her face.

Mama enters the hut in a small whirlwind of efficiency. Though her wrists are wrapped in rags and her eyes are still shadowed, she is happier than she was last night. Mentegai has just told her he will take her daughter into the forest tomorrow morning at dawn. She might, after all, be able to keep Emely safe from the women who are after her.

She still has to keep her promise to the old woman who spoke to her through the stones, however. She still has to convince her daughter to empty herself out, to clear the way for the Stone Woman's teachings. And she can't tell her daughter about what the women will do to her if they find her. Her mother has warned her about what happens to anyone who speaks the holy secrets into ears that don't believe.

"Oh, you got the fire going, Emely," she says, pleased. She manages a smile, and her children, caught up in a lather of manufactured happiness, smile back at her.

Even riddled with worry, Mama has the voice of love. One summer, knowing she had to return to boarding school, Emely took one of her mother's sweaters. Back at the school, when everyone was asleep, she pressed her face into its weave, tried this way to breathe her way into her mother's days. Every so often, she would get a clear picture. Sometimes she saw her mother drawing water. Prodding the piece of tin off the hole with her foot, Mama would bend over and pass the bucket slowly down into the dusk below, breathing all the while the water's secret chill. Then finally, far away, a splash, and the bucket would fill—and then, hand over hand, Mama would bring the pail up, pour the water into a pot, place that pot on her head, and then slowly, elegantly, glide her way back to the kitchen hut. All of this from a sweater.

Hoping the strangeness with her mother is over, Emely smiles. *Will she ever know much I love her?* she wonders.

Her mother sits down by the fire, unfurls a piece of cowhide, and pours some wheat from a bucket onto the skin. She tosses the hide, blowing continuously. As the grain falls, the lighter wheat flies into the air and the heavier grain falls to the skin.

"I have a present for you too, Mama," Emely says.

Her mother's face shimmers behind the small sky of tossed grain. "Hold on a second," she says between breaths. Pausing a moment, she slants her face, grips the end of the rag wrapped around her wrist with her teeth, and pulls the knot taut. "I need to get this to the grinder."

"Have you seen Kareem?" Emely asks.

Grain floats on the bellows of her mother's breath. "I saw him for a moment the night you got home," she says, "but I haven't seen him since." She flashes a familiar smile. "You know how that boy is. He's probably gone off to get reacquainted with all those animals he loves. He'll be back when he's hungry."

The in-and-out rhythm of her breath, quiet tossed with grain— this is the lullaby of her childhood, but it doesn't make Emely quite as happy as she thought it would. Maybe what happened the other night isn't over. Is it her imagination, or did the children dim their flurry of words when Mama walked into the hut? Not one of them has offered to show her their new toy, and there has been no comment from Mama about the exploded Christmas-morning commercial filling the floor of her hut.

Thin white lines rim the pupil of each of the children's eyes. All those rims float in the dusk of the hut like a constellation of half moons. *They know something*, Emely thinks. *They don't trust this warm, food-making Mama body.*

She used to know what love looked like. Big, beautiful love looked like Mama. Every day of her life, her mother poured herself into whatever, whomever stood in front of her. And her laugh? Well, it climbed the hills before her.

When it got really bad at school and Emely got so lonely she thought she belonged nowhere and to no one, not even Mama's sweater, she would take her roommate's cat into her lap and try to give to the animal what no one was giving to her.

This morning the cat she takes into her lap is Nunu. She ducks her head toward her. "What are you going to call your new baby?"

The tang of tea oil Mama has used to keep Nunu's hair from breaking rises to mix with the doll's slightly sinister plastic perfume. Pieces of chaff have landed on the doll's pink skirt. Nunu's small, dimpled hand quickly brushes the grain away. "Emely," she replies softly. "After you."

Emely hugs her tight.

Her mother rolls the cowhide into a tube and pours the heavy wheat she has just culled into a bucket. Then she reaches behind her for a large bowl and settles it on the stones by the fire, the stones as familiar to Emely as a living room couch would have been to one of her roommates back in Los Angeles. She pours some water into the bowl and adds a couple of handfuls of maize; in short order the porridge begins to bubble. Mama stirs it with a spoon.

Kulu runs his tow truck up and down Mobiel's legs. "Here's part of the door," Oba says to the world at large. "But where's the rest of the puzzle?"

A good house is like a good face, Emely thinks to herself as she hugs Nunu tight. *It takes many years to grow.* She looks around her childhood home. *This is a good face, but do I really belong here?*

She remembers how it used to be. Mama's favorite shawl was veined with silver, and its tassels fluttered behind her when she walked. Her earrings sparkled, she threw her head back when she laughed—everything Mama did altered light. Until it didn't anymore. One day, when Emely was around seven, all of Mama's swirled, stirred joy abruptly came to an end, and now there was only watching—cold, cold watching all the time. Untouched, unloved, all those *I love you*'s swallowed forever, an assertive emptiness began to fill Emely's days. The autobiography of a good home? At the age of seven Emely, entered her mother's house of pain. Her mother even took away her name, replacing the soft name given her by her grandmother, Amely, with one with a new, angular beginning.

"Your new name is Emely," Mama had just announced one day. "Emely."

When this happened, Emely decided to sweep her way back into her mother's lap. Every morning she rose before dawn to sweep out the hut. Next she brought water from the well; then she chopped so much firewood the imprint from the carrying strap was grooved into her forehead for hours afterward.

But none of this industry worked. The sharp prongs of that new E at the beginning of her name punctured any last, lingering bit of childhood; Mama kept her love hidden deep inside of a pocket Emely could never find.

"What's wrong?" she asked her mother over and over again, but she never received an answer.

And then the new nothingness spread to the other women in the village. They, too, watched her all the time. She was only a little girl. What had she done to disappoint everyone?

Then one day Emely was given the map back into her mother's arms. It turned out it wasn't sweeping, chopping, carrying water, or plowing. Her *mind* was the ticket. Her mother and father sat her down. "We've decided to send you to live with the nuns at the Lutheran Boarding School for Exemplary Young Men and Women," they announced. "Father Joseph has arranged for a full scholarship. We want you to study hard and make us proud."

And so, in the years that followed, that's exactly what Emely did. Surprising the nuns, her parents, Father Joseph, even herself, she had earned straight A's and then, as though in a dream, there was the offer of a scholarship to the University of Nairobi, and then another scholarship to graduate school in America, and now this fancy job representing the government's Land Reform Movement. "Do me proud," indeed! Full visibility, full Mama love, only seconds away. *And wait until Mama sees the present I brought back for her!*

Softened by hope, holding Nunu in her lap, watching her mother stir the maize, Emely finally relaxes, dropping back into information that has nothing to do with school-taught facts or highlighted paragraphs in textbooks. She knows, for instance, that Kinti over there doesn't like burnt maize. Tutu, the skinny one smiling at her now, talks in his sleep; Oba suckled longer than anyone else on Mama's breast; Nunu sleeps wild and loose at night. Five summers ago, Mobiel had measles so bad he almost died.

She's rested now, having slept the entire day yesterday, and she thinks about how she's going to spend her day. *I'll work side by side with Mama in the fields,* she thinks happily, *and remember once again what it is to really work. Dresses bright against the green hills, our laughter incandescent; one more time I will hold a hoe, the handle smooth from all the other hands that have used it. And then, later in the afternoon, I will reacquaint myself with rain—not just the sweet afternoon kind, but the kind that bruises clouds and rips thunder into the sky—and then maybe, just maybe, by the time I see the first star in the sky, I will have returned fully to who I really am: just the oldest daughter of Apunda, a man who once harvested more tea than anyone else in the radius of thirty kilometers.*

The fire leaps up, dies down again, sometimes pushing back the gloom just enough to reveal Oba's forehead, Kulu's knees, the slant of someone's thighs. And now that arrogant little tow truck.

Some of the maize flour has sprinkled Mama's face. Against her dark skin the speckled flour looks like tossed stars. She takes a bit of maize into the palm of her hand, cools it with her breath, pushes it between Mobiel's lips, then one more time takes up her spoon to stir the pot. "Once, twice, three times around the moon," she begins to sing. Her spoon scrapes the sides of the bowl, smoke from the fire swirls against the mud walls of the hut, and soon there are no more edges in the world, no more hollow spaces left between factory-painted dolls and a few maize cobs, no distance left to disturb the years away and what is now, everything Emely loves is inside the circle of her mother's spoon.

It is time.

Emely stands, walks over to her backpack. "There's a saying in America," she says over her shoulder. "When a daughter graduates from college, a little bit of her mother graduates as well."

The spoon stops moving.

Emely reaches into her backpack, slides out the diploma she had framed in gold. "This is for you, Mama," she says proudly, and lays it carefully on her mother's lap.

It's like one of those paintings Emely used to make as a little girl. Dabbing a bit of paint on a piece of paper, she would fold it and press the sides together and then when she opened it, behold, the same image would be there twice. This morning there is her mother's actual face, and then, as if folded and rubbed, her reflected face swims across the glass of the framed diploma.

Wet circles begin to fall on the glass, distorting and magnifying the letters. It takes Emely a moment to realize that her mother is crying.

"I hope those are happy tears," she says, stroking her mother's back. "Look!" She points to the letters on the diploma. "It says Emely Matei: Master's Degree in Narrative Anthropology."

No baby, baby, baby anymore; no *putt, putt, putt* from the tow truck either. Some of the unease from the night before has entered the hut, and the rims of all those eyes are once again watching.

It was an easy formula, actually. She has jumped higher than Mama told her to, climbed farther, some of those footsteps even on a different continent, so by that calculation she deserves even more of Mama's love . . . isn't that right?

And so she waits, a stone to be chosen, a shell on the beach. Long seconds pass and then abruptly, the two Mama faces separate. Her mother looks up, and it's as if she is seeing her daughter for the first time. She slowly passes her eyes over the cross Sister Rose gave Emely a long time ago, next sees her UCLA sweatshirt and her jeans, and finally her gaze falls to her running shoes, the tiny thunder of those Nike stripes. Then, seemingly in a daze, Mama moves her eyes beyond her daughter, and seems to see for the first time the lather of manufactured happiness filling her kitchen hut.

No more circles around the moon anymore. Emely's mother picks up the diploma and, turning it over, places it carefully against the wall. Emely sees the tiny plastic bag scotch taped to the wire on the back of the frame. It's filled with little brass nails.

"You have to leave, Emely," her mother says in a low voice. "Tomorrow at dawn. It's all been arranged. I've asked Mentegai to take you in early."

"What?" Emely asks. "What are you talking about?"

"An old woman who lives in the forest spoke to me through the stones," her mother responds. "There are a hundred stepping stones between being alive and being dead, and when you reach that final stone you are both dead and alive at the same time. The old woman will teach you how to place your feet on those stones, walk back into the dead. She says there is not much time. The Great Mother is in trouble."

Darkness, death, and stones . . . what is she talking about? Emely is suddenly so angry she can barely breathe. She has just handed her mother her diploma, and this is how she responds? She has followed her instructions perfectly—"Study hard, do me proud"—has spent all those hours, days, months, and years sharpening her mind.

"The forest holds the beginning of us, when we were close to the animals," her mother continues. "The old woman will show you how to lose the form you now inhabit, the form I gave birth to, and become another. You must grow beyond all the facts you've learned in school, Emely." She casts her eyes toward the diploma leaning against the wall. "You must even grow beyond this. Grow wings of sight, touch the far-away light of stars. I want you to do this for me."

Her mother stands and moves to the flat rock that is her chapati-making stone. Pouring some maize flour and a little water onto its flat surface, she begins to knead the flour with her fists, pacing her words with the thrust of her hands. "This will be larger than anything you've ever done before, Emely." Her hands are now white with flour. "The Great Mother is very sick. You must make room for what it is you don't know, move into the intelligence that lives in your cells. Your body remembers our beginnings when we were all linked as one. I am just coming back into this knowledge myself."

The thump of her hands kneading the dough fills Emely with a fresh loneliness. Even after she's gone that sound will fill these walls.

"You'll be frightened, daughter," her mother says, "more than you've ever been frightened before. You might even feel that your life is ending. But the old woman will teach you. Let what she says, the beauty of the old teachings, run liquid into your heart. Women who see through fear are always safe."

When her mother's words come all the way inside they seem to swell, leaving Emely with so little room inside she can barely breathe.

"I'm sorry, daughter," her mother says. A jagged white line of flour slices lightning across her face, points to what she says next. "All these years I've kept you from what you need to know. I should have listened to my mother, but it has taken me all this time to understand." Saying more to the dough then she has ever said to her daughter, she rocks the flour beneath her hands. *You are mine*, her fingers say.

Emely's mother's strange words pour off of her. Not one "I'm proud of you, daughter." Not one "Congratulations" . . . All that work and she's sending her away one more time? *No*.

Emely explodes.

"I thought that maybe when I came home this year I could spend some time with you," she says. "I thought that finally we could be close like other mothers and daughters. We could work in the fields together, tell stories, laugh. But we'll never be close if you keep talking like this. You know I don't believe in any of that stuff, and I didn't think you did either! Father's right. You *are* crazy!"

The air between them is as pounded, kneaded, and altered as the dough. Emely swallows, continues. "We live in the twenty-first century, Mama. That stuff is from Grandmama's time—even from before that, from Great Grandmama's time! In America we just thought of it all as a good story—important academically, of course, worthy of documentation, but that's all. Hey! I have an idea! Maybe I can interview you!" She looks at her watch. "Let's see, July 20, ten fifteen. Tribal woman on the subject of goddess fertility, the sacred feminine."

Something has gotten loose inside of her, and she doesn't think she can ever put it back. She is surprised to find that she's weeping. "But I don't want an interview subject," she wails. "I want my mother!"

But her mother just shakes her head. "Please listen to me, Emely. I tried to believe in Christ like your father wanted me to, but the voices are coming too loud. They're telling me that you're in danger."

Suddenly furious, Emely stands. She is going to hurt her mother before her mother hurts her again. She ducks down, curves her fingers into zeros. "See this?" she asks. "This is what I get from you. A big fat nothing." She chokes back a sob. "All I've ever wanted was you, Mama, but no matter what I did, I wasn't good enough. Do you know how hard it was to get a scholarship, not once but twice? You know how hard I had to work? And now I've landed this incredible job, but one more time you're pushing me away. I thought that surely now"—and here she glances at the diploma—"when I've proven to you how hard I worked, you would tell me that you're proud of me and finally, finally we would be close. But nothing seems to be good enough." She swabs away tears with the back of her hand.

"Well, you're not going to be able to control me anymore! This time it's me who's going to walk away, and let me tell you, I'll be just fine. Did I tell you that the professor wants me to help him curate the West Wing of the Anthropological Museum of Nairobi? And I'm going to use the field research in the forest for my doctoral thesis. And don't worry, Mama, you'll get your wish. I won't be back here anymore." Though she tries to speak fiercely, sobs threaten to break her open. "But I do have one last question for you, something I've wondered about all these years: Why did you send me away in the first place?"

Her mother's eyes fill with unshed tears. She replies quickly. Too quickly. "You know the answer to that, Emely. It was to get a good education."

Emely squints her eyes. "I don't think that's entirely true," she replies. "You wanted Kareem to get a good education, but you waited until he was twelve to send him away."

Mama drops her head into her hands. "This is all my fault," she says, her voice muffled. "My mother warned me, but I just didn't listen." She, too, chokes back a sob. "I kept you from the things you should have learned and now it is only those things that will keep you from danger." She looks up at Emely, her eyes streaming tears. "I love you so much. That's why I sent you away, and that's why I'm sending you away again."

Emptied out but swollen with sadness, finally Emely hears what she's always wanted to hear, but somehow it doesn't make her feel better. "I don't believe you!" she shouts. "What mother sends a little girl away? I was only seven. Do you know how scared I was?" Her words are rough, but now she's beyond caring. She's discovered that anger is an easier emotion than sorrow. "You don't know me—and what's worse, you're lying to me even now!"

Umbrellas, computers, elevators, mascara—she is suddenly overwhelmed by the gulf between them, all the things her mother doesn't know. She recognizes now how far she's moved away from this life, so far away, in fact, that she might never be able to come back. Just blowing on a few embers in a fire isn't going to bring her home.

But her mother has one more thing to say. She reaches down into the front of her dress and brings something out in her hand, then slowly, one by one, unlocks her fingers, revealing the necklace Emely's grandmother gave Emely on the day she died. The great stone glistens in the gloom of the hut. "I know you think that all of this is just superstitious nonsense, but I want you to wear this necklace in the forest. Wrap your fingers around it when you are most afraid." Leaning forward, she drapes the necklace around Emely's neck, tucking the stone down inside her T-shirt. It is cool against her skin.

"Hold it in your hand and when it is warm with you, you can send us your thoughts. We will hear them, and then all who are alive and all who are dead will come to you."

Grandmama's necklace is now right over her heart, and somehow that feels just right.

"I know you are angry with me," her mother say, "but you need to listen. The stone will protect you." She's now so close Emely feels puffs of air on her cheeks when her mother speaks. "In the forest you will be frightened beyond anything you have ever felt before, but you will also be loved beyond anything you've known—not just by my one small flame, but by all the women who have lived before and the women alive now." She kneels and peers into Emely's face, grips her shoulders tight. "Are you listening to me, daughter?"

Emely's hands are clammy. She rubs them against her jeans. She remembers the last time she saw this necklace. Grandmama gave it to her the day she died. One morning, a couple months after her grandmother died, just after awakening, Emely held it in her hands and her grandmother appeared. The old woman smiled and then disappeared. Emely remembered how excited she was. "Grandmama's still alive!" she yelled, rushing to find her mother. "I just saw her! All I have to do is hold her necklace and she comes to me."

She still remembers the frightened look that came across her mother's face. She grabbed Emely so hard it hurt. "That was only a dream, Emely," she said, shaking her shoulders. "Don't talk of those things again."

And then she reached down and took off the necklace. Emely never saw it again until today.

She is now even angrier than before. Mama took Grandmama away that morning, and now she's trying to give her back again? And what kind of mother loads a daughter up with all of her dark superstitions right before a big trip? A cold stone to protect her? This isn't love.

Well, she will give her mother a cold stone all her own—the cold stone of her heart, where she no longer lives.

She stands up, looks down at her mother. "Walking on stones back to the dead?" she says. "That crazy blood stuff last night, and now this necklace? It's pretty clear. You're making all this stuff up because you don't want me. It's all just an excuse to send me away one more time." She draws herself up. "Well you've got your wish, Mama," she announces stiffly. "I'm leaving." She blasts her mother with her eyes. "Excuse me," she continues. "If I'm leaving tomorrow, there's a bunch of things I have to do. I need to contact the professor and I have to organize my things." Another dart shoots from her hot, hurt eyes. "Goodbye, Mama. You won't see me again."

Her shoes leave a row of corrugated ridges in the dirt as she crosses the room and ducks out the door.

CHAPTER 39

Hoping Emely hears her, Grandmama speaks to her on the wind: *When I lived in the forest, the flawless dream of you lived inside of me. Only one generation away, you slumbered deep inside my body. But now I am on the other side of my life, only a skeleton smiling at you from beneath the dirt, only this pure, pure watching from the sky.*

You're going home, Amely, home to a cave halfway up the sky. Everyone who has come before you has walked through those old trees. You are one part in a long line of women flowing endlessly behind you, endlessly after, moving forever across time.

This world has made you who you are. I hope you can hear what it is telling you.

The women who talk through the stones, the women who are alive and the women who are dead, are worried. Even my daughter, who for so long pushed our knowledge away, is listening, but I wonder, is it too late? You've inherited the vast, cold spaces of your mother's fears; everything I tried to teach her has been extinguished by her husband and the Church. Raised on her many demanding and complicated silences, you see life through her foreboding.

Turn your receiving heart toward the place that made you, Amely. Let the ancient animal part of you come alive. Find and light that lamp deep inside of you, that beautiful lamp that holds the first ember of life. It is only this that will keep you safe.

CHAPTER 40

"Are you going to stand there all day?"

Emely turns, sees her guide for the first time standing at the edge of the forest. Five or six hunting dogs sniff at his feet. Her first thought? *Wow, I get to spend six weeks in the forest with him?* Body buffed and strong, naked except for a small fringe of buckskin covering his vitals. A carved walking stick in his hand, long dreads hanging almost to his waist and covering his face.

She spreads what she hopes is a dazzling smile across her face. "I'm Emely Matei," she says, extending her hand. He doesn't accept it and that's when she gets her first clue about how it's going to be with him. And then his dreads part, and she gets a glimpse of his face and gasps; what has been done to his face is as familiar to her as her own hands. Her grandmother's tattoo gambles and cavorts across every inch of his skin. "A tattoo is to be found," her grandmother once told her as she traced her little fingers across its lines. "It's as natural as the veins on the leaf." But now, an old memory superimposed on the new sight, that tattoo she'd love to trace with her little fingers frolics across someone else's face—someone who, by the looks of him, doesn't like her much.

But that body! The vigor and appetite of the man. A powerful blast of physicality. It's as if his body is a stopped axle of thought, will, movement, and purpose.

She talks to him as only a sex-addled young woman can. "I really don't appreciate you moving up the timetable for this expedition," she says. "I should have been consulted." She stabs her aluminum walking stick into the ground. "Fortunately the professor is a flexible man. I checked with him, and he says it's all right to go in a few weeks early."

The sky behind the lines of her grandmother's tattoo scowls. He tosses one dread across his shoulders—the long rope of it immediately gives Emely's eyes a vertical hoist—then glances at the high throne of her backpack, her sleeping bag encased in nylon, her aluminum walking sticks. He turns his head, spits. She turns her back to him.

One last time she runs her eyes across the poem of her village—then, slipping on the straps of the backpack, cinching the belt around her waist, she turns around. "Let's get this show on the road," she says, using an expression she learned in America.

CHAPTER 41

Within seconds, Emely understands why people from her village don't enter this place: it's another world. Sunlight as green as the forest itself filters in at illogical angles; ferns form a soft green mist. Tangles of rubber leaves coil aggressively across the path. Even the air is different. It leans against her so heavy with moisture it makes movement forward almost a push. She remembers how she used to love wet, steamy days in Los Angeles, the odor of woolen coats rising to sour the air with their honest animal smells. This air is not that sleepy, sweet kind of damp, however—it's heavy, carries the smell of the underneath.

Right in front of her a large bird breaks free of its perch, cuts the air with a cry. Flung wings, a sharp sound—something has died.

For a while she tries to focus on what is separate and white. There is one flower so delicate it seems that just her stare alone will cause its petals to fall. She searches for them, tangles her glance with them when she finds them, searches for more as she walks farther. But then the flowers disappear. No more white engagement anymore—just many variations of green.

A skinny-legged bird with a round belly lands right in front of her and looks just like a paragraph sign. She almost laughs out loud.

But then, one more time, she's reminded that the game here is survival. The bird sees a lizard, tweezers it between his beak. She hears the chewing of bones.

The smell of rot rises to curse the sky; nothing is familiar here, everything is an almost, bathed in an Alzheimer's haze. Leaves, their wet rattle. The bud of one flower, a barely visible line of pink, enclosed between thick rubber fingers. Orbs of strange fruit, their skin barely containing their swollen flesh.

They climb quickly up the hills only to descend rapidly down again, often in a mad, careless rush. "Slow down," she manages to pant, but either Mentegai doesn't hear her or he's not listening.

Aching for breath, keeping upright soon becomes Emely's primary occupation. Mentegai easily skims through this entangled world, at peace, even exultant, in these trees. There's a flow to the man; she envies his ease. The soles of his feet go up, go down in rapid succession, his forward movement not an aggressive push but instead a sinewy dance. Things that appear in front of him—that branch to duck under, that puddle to jump across—stream together into one long, lush verb, while she on the other hand sees a fractured world, impediments that are separate and inconvenient. She tries to imitate his confident grace but almost immediately loses the rhythm, falls quickly back into the middle of the path and its omnipresent mud.

Use this place, don't let it use you, she tells herself. She tries to see the forest as a spreadsheet, as boxes to be filled with information. *Mud is merely bacteria, enzyme, and decay.* She remembers reading about the ancient conifer trees in Lebanon. There are only five hundred of the great trees left, twelve of them over a thousand years old. They have been used by every civilization. The Venetians used the tree's wood for shipbuilding; its resin was used by ancient Egyptians for mummification. *Are these trees that old?* she wonders. But though her eyes search for computer printouts, her heart breaks open with fear at the world she sees before her. The forest, the living, breathing, sentient being of it, makes her feel guileless, unprotected, and soft.

Mentegai flickers before her like a dark moth, and then suddenly he doesn't anymore.

"Mentegai?" she calls. No answer. She is alone.

Emely returns to the angry hum of her thoughts of Mama; mud in her mind to match the mud in the path. When she heaved herself out of the door of the cooking hut after their argument, she took with her their complicated history. *Mama never cared about me*, she thinks to herself as she stumbles forward. *She doesn't even know me. All those lonely years away, the sharp roofs of all those A's. "Study hard," she told me, "make me proud." Well I did just that, didn't I? Used my books, my mind to pry open the door of her mud hut. I left the village, blew into the larger world—and all at the tender age of seven. But does any of that even matter? Has Mama ever acknowledged how hard it was for me, how scared and lonely I've been all those years away? No, not even when I handed her my degree!*

She stabs the path with her walking stick. *Bragging rights, that's all I am to her, just a paper cutout supplied with my very own cardboard triangle. The only person I can trust in all this world is the professor, even with that little bit of weirdness between us during our last visit. Tomorrow I will unhinge the microphone from the radio and hold it to my mouth. "CD 1245, base camp here," I will say. The professor will immediately answer, and then high above this small tangle of trees, in the clear, far-reaching sky, our voices will join hands.*

CHAPTER 42

Time has begun to blur. Have hours passed? She doesn't know. All she knows is that she's stumbling down the path when she almost runs into her new employee. Mentegai is more tree than the tree he stands next to. Snarling, verdant foliage, his dreads pop out in all directions, his face only a thin sliver between them.

"There you are!" Emely snaps. "Where have you been? What kind of guide leaves a person alone in the forest—and on their very first day, no less?" She doesn't know which entity to address, his hair or his face.

Mentegai is silent, and in that moment, Emely realizes something: he isn't afraid of her. And he certainly doesn't seem to care that she's in charge. Maybe it's because he lives mostly here in death's territory, but he's a man who always carries his own counsel, fierce and confidential. In the few seconds she can see his face, she has the impression of peering into a secret repose.

"Don't leave me alone again," she finally says.

As if seeing itself is a tentative act, he picks up his dreads and parts them with an almost girlish grace. "Look up," he instructs.

Shading her eyes, at first she doesn't see anything—just trees, trees, and more trees—but when she lowers her hands she discovers, to her horror, that they are covered with blood. She looks from her hands to Mentegai, then back to her hands again.

"It doesn't appear that the sky is bleeding," she says, trying to appear unafraid. "Where is this blood coming from?"

As usual, Mentegai is sparse with words. He points upward. "It's a forest hog," he says. "In pieces. See? It's hanging from those trees."

It's like one of those puzzles when you look at a drawing of the house and you're supposed to find a fish, and you look and you look and you only see the house until finally vision clicks, your eyes clear, and that's when you see it: fish, fish, fish. That's what happens. Emely finally sees it: pig, pig, pig. Pieces of a giant hog are strewn across several branches above her. Four limp hooves hang from a branch to her left, a belly bristling with black hair hangs from a branch to her right, and directly above her is the hog's face, indignant even in death. Huge, fatty bulbs protrude from under squinty eyes, short tusks curve from the side of its mouth, its snout is scarred, its eyes are open and filmed with death.

"I killed it," Mentegai says proudly. "It will help us find the Okino. I'm sure they need meat. But you're going to have to help me get it down."

Emely is standing so close to him she can smell his particular smell, something like wet stones. "How am I going to do that?" she asks.

He answers with his body. Leaning over, he quickly cuts a few leaves from a banana tree and places them on the ground next to her feet. Then, grasping the trunk of the tree between his two bare feet, he begins to inch his way upward, his strong body moving with the easy, think-and-do grace of an athlete. When he reaches the belly he draws a knife from the pouch tied around his waist.

His eyes rise over a chunk of bloody meat. "The dogs are going to want to eat this," he says. "Kick them if they get too close." He begins to lower the piece of meat toward her. Class ring sparkling in the gloom, she wills her hands to rise and meet it. When the chunk finally reaches her, she touches the blood-crusted fur, curves her fingers around its cool flesh, feels the weight transfer to her, then lowers the chunk onto a banana leaf, air-kicking at a dog that comes too close.

"This one's heavy," Mentegai says, untying the head. He plays out the twine and the head moves toward her, circling around and around. Twelve, seven, six feet . . . She watches her hands as though they belong to someone else, someone confident and unafraid. The hog's face revolves above her, looking for all the world like a decapitated despot, its last expression one of indignant fury.

The head is about four feet away when the despot decides to stick out its tongue. A thick gray rubbery slab slumps from the side of his mouth. She jumps back, can't help but shriek. The face hits the ground with a thud. The dogs dive in, too many, too greedy to kick away; they fall on it in an orgy of slurps and grunts and growls. Above her, Mentegai begins to laugh—an ugly sound, derision on its draft. He climbs quickly down the tree, kicks the dogs away, and, still laughing, kneels over and begins to cut up the meat.

It's the most inside flesh she has ever seen, indecipherable babbles and pearls she can't translate as part of a body. Within minutes Mentegai has divided the meat into tiny hills. This done, he stands and expertly fashions a small raft from the limber branches of a nearby tree. Still enjoying the festivity of his laugh, he ties the chunks of meat to the raft and, hoisting the entire arrangement over his shoulders like a backpack, begins to walk once more down the trail. Emely barely has time to slip her arms into the straps of her backpack before he disappears around a bend.

Her number one thought? *I should be filming this.* Her number two thought: *I'm tired, I don't want to see raw, bloody flesh, and I certainly don't want to deal with this young man's impertinence.* She decides it's time to speak up again. She runs to catch up with him.

"Let's get something straight," she snaps. "You're working for me. Do you understand? If we're going to get along at all together, you're going to have to pay me some respect."

What she says doesn't stop Mentegai from snickering, and now it's even worse than before. As he moves down the path before her, the hog's face, tied to his back, glares at her, its tongue bobbing rhythmically up and down.

A memory washes back to Emely: the perfect, popular girls at the boarding school. They too stuck out their tongues. "Mountain girl, mountain girl," they taunted, and then, over the months, that nickname morphed into "monkey girl." *Monkey girl, monkey girl.* She's almost relieved when both the tongue and Mentegai disappear once more.

She hates this place, feels swallowed alive. She even finds herself craving the linear sense of rain. No edges or boundaries, no place to rest, everything bursting with its own declaration, the forest is intensely physical; everything she sees before her blurs, swarms, plumes, or sprays, becoming something else. Her senses are all mixed up. Birds interrupt the air with the dissonance of their wings, but as soon as they've passed through, the tawny air resumes its arrogant occupation. A thick smell like someone giving birth enters Emely's nostrils; then, floating across it, as thin and as delicate as a gauze scarf, the fragrance of cumin, the smell at once careless and precise.

Four hours, five hours, ten hours . . . she's really not quite sure. She's making her own way down an incline so steep she has to hold on to the branches on either side of the path to keep from sliding down when she loses her balance and falls. Sharp stones, thorny branches, she tumbles faster and faster, cutting her hands when she tries to grab something, anything, to stop her fall.

Finally, at the bottom of the hill, she comes to a stop.

She folds her body in as tight as she can and begins to cry.

CHAPTER 43

T he Great Mother speaks on the wind:
The latest thought, the newest philosophy, a high, gleaming concept
that will save us all . . . I am what stones say to each other at the
bottom of the river. Fur, scales, feathers, and now Amely's own soft
flesh—everything that slithers, walks, coils, or sprays is me. Will my new
Stone Woman lose what she thinks she knows, fill herself instead with me? I
don't know. Just as with people, the greatest fear of all is intimacy.

It is time for her to know me. I will call her name with the voice of water.

Memory exhausted, body cut and bruised, hands bleeding, Emely rolls
over onto her stomach, closes her eyes. She can barely remember the
color red.

It's a dog's frightened yelp that jars her awake. She opens her eyes,
sees Mentegai standing at the edge of a large river, rib-kicking a dog.
The dog's legs are shaking; he backs timidly into the river, staring at
Mentegai with frightened eyes.

Another vicious kick.

"Stop that!" Emely yells. She jumps up. "What are you doing to that poor animal?"

The current catches the dog; he loses his balance and is quickly pulled into the middle of the river, his face a tiny chip of fear embedded in the great flow of brown water. The dog tries to swim, but the current is too strong, and soon, rounding the bend, he disappears.

"What are you doing?" she shouts again. "How could you do that to a poor, innocent creature?" She springs across the distance between them and grabs Mentegai's arm, but he shrugs her off and approaches another dog, kicks him in the ribs as well.

The dog too backs into the river, is instantly lapped into the river's flow.

Fury mixes with exhaustion. "You're nothing but a bully!" Emely screams.

The same insolent, increasingly familiar shrug. "He's just an animal," Mentegai responds. "And anyway, have you thought about how you're going to get across? Am I going to have to kick you too?"

That stops her. "We have to get to the other side of the river?" she asks disbelievingly. "It's huge!"

Mentegai laughs. "Don't worry," he says, "there's a bridge."

"Where? I don't see anything."

"See that white tree over there?" He points up the river. "By that big boulder?"

She nods.

"Follow it up a bit with your eyes and you can see some bamboo staves woven into its upper branches. Right?"

She nods again.

"We'll follow those branches out across the river, and then there's a green birch on the other side. See how it rises to join the bamboo?" Eyes sparkling, he turns to her. "That's our bridge!"

"Will the Okino be on the other side?" she asks hopefully.

That shrug again, but this time she thinks she hears a trace of kindness threaded through his voice when he says, "We'll find them tomorrow."

She takes this opportunity to ask about the dogs. "Will the dogs be okay?"

"Yes," he responds. "The current slows just around the bend. They'll be waiting for us on the other side." He begins walking toward the bridge. "Looks like you took a tumble back there. Want me to take your backpack?"

Maybe it's the memory of him kicking that dog, but she answers more shortly than she intends to. "It's all right, I can manage."

"Your call," he says, and begins to climb up the tree. "Just a word of warning, though. When you're at the top of the bridge, don't look down."

She negotiates the first tree, reaches its upper branches and crawls out onto the scaffolding of bamboo staves. So far, fairly easy. Slow, though. The bridge is a complicated multiple-choice test in which she has to think about everything she does—which branch to grab a hold of, how far to swing her leg—before she actually does it. She soon wishes she had let Mentegai take her backpack. It's awkward, makes her top-heavy. Her hands are scraped with cuts from her fall. *But I can do this,* she tells herself. *I just have to think about everything I do before doing it.*

You can't really trust the world when your so-called floor is only six inches across. She has reached the platform of bamboo branches; she cautiously places her knee on its scaffolding, then reaches for a branch to steady herself.

The branch is covered with moss. Her fingers sink into it. She pauses, considers her next move. That branch over there would make a good handle. Slow, ever so slow, she stretches out her hand. Her fingers disrupt a red leaf. In long, lazy circles, it spirals down until, with a muted roar, the water reaches up and licks the leaf down into its muddy flow. In that moment she realizes she's made the mistake that Mentegai had warned her about. She's looked down.

All her velocity, the many miles she's traveled—all that activity bunches against her skin, trying to push her forward.

Mentegai's voice floats back from somewhere in front of her. "Let's go! It's going to be dark soon, and we still have to find a place to sleep."

But she's not listening anymore. The air is hazy with all that speaks. Traces of the sun and moon float on the surface of the water below her. A branch protrudes from the river; where water passes through it makes a great, crinkly V. Far away, thunder claps.

The warm, empty air begins to fill with something she can't see but can sense. The surface of the river goes black. A new feeling comes on, something behind the sound of the river and its roar, behind the insects and birds, behind the ordinary sound that is. The thing coming floats at the edges of her listening, old, hard, and insistent.

Voices then—or have they been here all along? She hears her other name. *Amely.* It's there on the pour of the river, there on the rush of air where the shadows are most old, there, too, coiled inside the trunk of that tree.

Amely. The sound grave, vibrational.

Her heart speeds up; she can barely breathe. "What?" she asks, for a feeling of incredible malevolence is beginning to sift down over her. "What?"

No more inside and outside anymore. Leaves, flies, that piece of moss over there, they're all just disconnected chips of seeing, vision stripped of meaning. What she sees below her has breath and thought and will, and wants to know her.

"Please," she calls. "Sister Mary Rose? Someone, something, send me some kind of protection. . ." For now she's sharing the hard, coarse breath with the thing that is out there.

The river now begins to seem like her very own body with its movement of blood—the beating of her heart, cells, lungs, and tissues all united into one organism. Not understanding how air, something that is not there, can be so poignant with loss, Emely looks at the empty spaces between the trees; whatever it is that is out there, whatever the thing whispering her name is, it wants the sky to be just that—sky, not a place that used to hold a tree.

She even reaches for her grandmother's necklace. "Grandmama?" she calls. "Can you come?"

No one answers, and that's when she gets what she thinks of as her big idea. It's really quite simple, after all: she can just drop into the great, featureless world below, let those voices out there come inside and coexist with everything she already is.

Hallelujah! It's a great idea. No more story of herself.

Forget this stupid job, forget the bruise in her heart that her mother left, forget the color red—she will never be lonely again. How could she not have thought of this before and, more than that, how could she ever have resisted it?

The thing that waits out there is excited. *Amely*, it repeats seductively, the syllables stretched, radiant, and long. Emely wants to answer, but she can't seem to talk back anymore, and anyway, how do you talk back to something that is already a part of you? Your leg doesn't have a separate conversation with your arm, does it?

I'll have a new family! she thinks to herself. No more longitude or latitude anymore. Her body wide open to the thing that wants her, she stands. The only thing that surprises her is how easy it is to say goodbye. A little gust of wind tries to pry her from the branch. *Yes, Amely, that's it.*

She unties her sweatshirt, drops it into the river. A big, beautiful bloom, it floats for a moment on the surface of the water then disappears around the bend like the dogs did earlier.

"Just do exactly what I tell you to do, and I'll get you down." Another voice out there. Mentegai has climbed back into the trees, is now only inches away from her.

The voices out there seem to swell from a million throats. *Amely, Amely,* they call.

"Grab that branch to your left. I'm going to take your backpack, all right?" She feels a weight lift from her shoulders.

Maybe it's the way Mentegai's eyelashes spike above his eyes or maybe it's a new gentleness she hears in his voice—whatever it is, she decides to follow his instructions. He guides her carefully from one branch to the other, and finally they reach the ground on the other side of the river.

Filled with a sense of loss as difficult and cratered as her longing for her mother, Emely sinks to the ground, puts her head in her hands, and closes her eyes.

Is someone out there? she asks silently. *Please, please, can someone help me? I don't understand what is happening, and all I have is this paper-thin boat of prayer to keep me afloat.*

CHAPTER 44

The old woman who lives deep in the forest begins a new sculpture. As she's waiting for her new Stone Woman, her gnarled fingers pulls forth her story from the clay. A few miles away, Amely is trying just as hard to extinguish her own story. Making herself as small as possible, she sits so still her mind barely flickers. No hard edges, no speculation, thoughts only lightly sketched in. If I'm not myself anymore, she reasons, whoever, whatever is out there won't want me anymore.

What the dead know is that this isn't going to work. The spell of the forest is already at work. A conscious world waits beyond everything Amely sees before her, and it has already laid claim to her.

The Mother called her other name on the bridge. She wants her emptied out and emptied out soon.

CHAPTER 45

A few feet away from where Emely sits, two rows of trees have lined up as if preparing for an Irish rail dance. Leaves swishing, skirts raised, the shadows of the trees touch. Chaperones nod their long beards of moss; the dance begins.

"Shut up!" she wants to yell. Sometimes the world is too loud.

"Are you all right?" Mentegai kneels down before her. Beneath his boisterous hair, his face remains a place of stillness. "It looked like you were going to jump up there, and then when you took off your sweatshirt . . ." His voice trails away. "What's going on?"

Somewhere between her well-groomed, scholarly self and this sloppy, unwashed self, she balances. The only place to look is toward the ground. She doesn't know what to say.

When she doesn't respond he shrugs, then stands. "Suit yourself," he says, walking away. "This will be a good place to make camp. We're close, but night is coming."

Bloated with a kind of comic-book vulgarity, once again the forest begins to show off. "It's my birthday," says a tree, shaking a million golden hands. An antelope appears in front of Emely. Against the sky its silhouette looks for all the world like a handle ready to pick up the suitcase of the hill.

Emely doesn't understand what's happening. It's as if she's dragged the most ludicrous of Western associations into this ancient place, everything she has seen on two continents crockpot-simmered, softened, blurred, and mixed.

An existential invitation? Her other name whispered by the dead? In the end it's none of these things that finally get her to her feet; it's the smell of the beef jerky that Mentegai is eating. Upon catching the scent, she realizes how hungry she is.

"Trade you a package of dehydrated beans and rice for some of that," she says, trying to muster an engaging smile.

His twin expressions then—a hard stare, and then that smirk, and then of course another sideways spit. "You call that food?" he scoffs, but he does hand her a piece of his jerky.

She takes a bite. Farmland, sun, grass, all those days spent under an immense sky, the animal's wonderful energy roars through her. She stuffs the entire piece into her mouth and extends her hand for more. "This is so good," she mumbles.

Mentegai hands her another piece, then kneels, ties his dreads in a knot behind his head, and, reaching into the pouch around his waist, extracts two sticks, one dimpled in its middle by a small bowl. He lays the dimpled one on the ground pressing it down between his bare feet, places the other one down perpendicular into its bowl. He spits on both hands, then splays out his fingers and begins to rub the upright stick up and down between his hands. A gentle wisp of smoke emerges.

He's making fire in the old way! Emely realizes.

He places a bit of dried moss into the small bowl for tinder, leans over, and begins to blow.

She can hear the professor—"Record, record! Pure history!"—but she's too tired to reach into her backpack for her camera.

Mentegai adds more moss, then a few dried leaves, and soon a brisk fire is burning. Standing, he breaks a branch over one knee, adds it to the fire.

The dogs look from him and up to the trees above in some kind of mute solicitation. Emely looks up as well. The grotesque orchid of the forest hog's head blooms in the trees above, draped with the long, limp vines of its legs. The red buds of some other nondescript meat flower on another branch.

Mentegai climbs the tree. Not for a second wondering how a simple human being can reach into the sky and pull down meat, the dogs watch adoringly. He throws some chunks of meat on the ground which they devour, before creeping toward the fire and resting their faces on their paws. Whiskers soon twitch with dreams.

Mentegai returns, sits down by the fire, and stares into the flames. Emely moves closer to the fire as well. It's quiet now except for the occasional snap of the fire. No moon yet. Red flowers extend the essence of flame up into the trees, but only for a few feet. Night's indifferent expanse rejects the tiny civilization of the fire. She wishes Mentegai would say something, wonders where his deep stillness comes from. Is it the innate discipline of a hunter, or the quiet of someone who just wants to slip unnoticed through the world?

Beady eyes, a little smile, a porter, a doorman, a guide—the door opens in the form of Mentegai's walking stick. He notices Emely looking at it.

"His name is Kifimbo," he says.

She smiles, dips her head. "Pleased to meet you, Kifimbo," she says playfully.

Mentegai pours a little water from a piece of bamboo on the ground before him. "He opens the way for me," he says solemnly. "When I have it, I offer him honey."

Emely smiles. There's something so innocent about Mentegai's homemade devotions. It's as if he's discussing a member of his family—and indeed, under his spell, the shabby walking stick takes on that polished, insolent look of a well-protected, much-loved child.

Mentegai reaches for a dog, pulls him into his lap, scratches his ears. "What are you going to do with the Okino, anyway?"

"Didn't the professor explain it to you? My assignment, our assignment, is to record the forest people's way of life—their ceremonies, what they eat, stories, things like that. As you know, the professor's big push is to document the lives of our country's indigenous tribes before they become extinct."

He doesn't say anything.

"Have you camped here before?" she asks, just to keep the conversation going.

"Yes," he replies. "Many times." He points toward the area where the moon is just beginning to rise. "I once found a turtle at the top of that mountain." He stretches out his hands. "It was nearly two feet long, can you believe that? At one time this forest was all underwater!"

Hugging her knees, Emely secretly thanks the turtle for swimming into this night. "That's amazing," she exclaims. "I wonder how old it was! What did you do with it?"

"What?"

"The turtle. Any museum in the country would have paid a fortune for it."

Wrong thing to say. Mentegai scowls. "I left him there, of course," he replies curtly. "It's where he wanted to be. It was a creature that lived and breathed long before there ever was an us." As if to shield himself from her commercial glare, he disappears behind the bars of his hair. One more time, he's lost to her. Even Kifimbo can't help her now.

Is this the way it's always going to be with him? Six weeks of this silence? She doesn't want to feel this alone. But just as she's thinking he will never speak again, Mentegai asks a question about the one thing she doesn't want to talk about.

"What happened up there on the bridge?" he asks. "Are you afraid of heights? Is that it?"

"I think I was just really tired," she manages to answer.

Another bout of silence. Silhouetted against the fire, he looks imported from another time. "All of your modern gadgets—" he says, casting a hostile look at her luggage, "video camera, still camera, recorders—aren't you worried you'll be contaminating them with all your outside ways?"

"It's important to record history," Emely responds primly. "And anyway, who are you to criticize? You took this job didn't you?"

Moonlight outlines the plains of his face. "Let's get something straight," he snaps. "I'm not taking you in because I believe in what you're doing. It's not for the money, and certainly not for the professor."

"Then why did you accept this assignment?" she asks.

His answer is as smooth as sucked-down candy; he's obviously thought about it quite a bit. "The day before yesterday, when I was here in the forest, an old woman appeared before me. She told me to bring you in. Her exact words were, 'She's the only one who can save us.' I think she was talking about you!"

"How can that be? She doesn't even know me!"

"I don't know, but she seemed to know everything about you. She called you by a different name, though—Amely, I think it was. I wasn't going to accept this job until she showed up."

Smoke drifts across the trees, the only thing to move. Emely remembers what her mother said in their terrible quarrel yesterday. "An old woman spoke to me through the stones," she told her. "She's waiting for you in the forest."

She decides to try to talk some sense into all this mystery. "Maybe someone else from the Land Reform Movement has contacted them."

Mentegai shakes his head. "No one has seen this tribe for years. And certainly not your so-called Land Reform Committee. I looked for them for over a year and never found them. I was even beginning to wonder if any of them were still alive."

"You've never even seen them?" she asks incredulously.

"No," he replies. "Not until the old woman appeared. I'd never even gotten close. Once I found a hollowed-out honey hive, and one time I came across a stick with three moons."

She watches his mouth as he speaks. "What do you mean by three moons?"

"It was a branch that had been broken, and leaves from another tree were pushed down on some of its twigs. My father told me how to translate signs from the forest people. The leaves from the different tree meant they were hungry. Three round moons of leaves meant they had been traveling for three moons, or what you would call three months."

Standard ethnographic communication, Emely thinks. *I'll have to remember to jot it down in the morning.*

As if enticing forth his next thought, moonlight plays across Mentegai's face. When he continues, he's almost talking to himself. "I used to think I wasn't pure enough to see them," he says. "And that's why they wouldn't let me near. The forest people can see into your heart, you know."

She nods. "The people of Siberia believe their hearts can be seen as well. They consider certain groves of trees so sacred they always walk through them in silence."

"Maybe I'm like the people in Siberia," Mentegai says with a small smile. "Sometimes I almost felt them watching me, and one time a few months ago I thought I could hear them. There's a sound out there in the trees. It's not just one voice, and it doesn't seem to just come from one place."

Maybe that's what she heard up there on the bridge. "Is it scary?"

"No." He rubs his hands across his face. "It's more . . . exploratory."

He brings in his lower lip, raises his eyebrows, and, as he must have done when he first saw the old woman, surrenders to a spill of wonder. "And then after so long looking for them, suddenly, the day before yesterday, an old woman is standing right in front of me, and she's talking about you! She told me where to find them. I never even thought to look in that part of the forest. It's really high in the mountains, and so overgrown I thought that only something as slender as a snake could slip through its undergrowth. But it's close by. We'll probably find them by tomorrow morning."

She catches it then—a quick insight into Mentegai's life. His self-sufficiency an armor he's used to seal himself off from the rest of the world, he spends most of his time alone in this forest, looking for a glint of hope, a clue. "Are you there?" he calls continuously, his voice a thin sound falling. "It's me, Mentegai." And then even that thin hope disintegrates into all the silence.

He's like a crescent moon, she thinks. *One slip of light curved against a private, unknowable shadow.*

"Did you understand the old woman?" she asks. "What language did she speak?"

"It's probably a dialect close to ours. If you soften your ears just a little you can understand it. And then at the end she sang the pure language my father used to sing when he was"—Mentegai gropes for the right word—"relaxed. Part talk, part song, my father told me it goes back to the time when animals and people could sit under the same tree and talk. My name, Mentegai, comes from that language."

Emely is suddenly so excited she can hardly breathe. "They have their own language?" She rifles through the file cards in her mind. It will be a language that has never been documented before! But even as she's looking through those file cards, there's also a memory of her grandmother leaning over her and singing a beautiful song, like water running over stones. She remembers her grandmother's ghostly voice when she warned her about the police chief in the police station, the word she herself had spoken as she gazed at the statue in the professor's back room, what she had spoken and heard in the bus traveling through the Rift Valley. Is it possible that what seemed like song was actually a different language, one she could even speak?

"You mentioned that your father left this forest," she says. "How long ago was that?"

"About ten years ago. He lost his spirit when he came out of these trees."

"I'm sorry," Emely says. "The professor told me. The transition from a nomadic life in the forest to an agricultural life is a difficult one."

"Guess you could say that, Dr. Matei," Mentegai says sarcastically.

She's quick to defend herself. "I'm a long way off from becoming a doctor. Quite a few years, actually. But you're right, that is my long-term goal. And what we find in the next few weeks may even be the basis for my doctoral thesis."

For a long time, Mentegai is silent. Moonlight sifts through the branches of the trees above them, sprinkling a filigree of powdered sugar on the ground. Emely wants to dip her fingers into the light, taste the sweetness of the moon.

When Mentegai finally speaks again, Emely is surprised to find he has returned to the subject of his father. "My father loved this forest so much," he says. "He used to say that all the light on the outside burned holes into what he knew."

"What about your mother?" she asks. "Did she leave the forest too?"

Wrong thing to say. Mentegai's face closes like a fist. Without another word he unrolls a bundle of fur, turns his back to her, and lies down.

She looks out across the mountain range of his body toward the moon. *Guess he and I have something in common after all*, she thinks. *We both don't want to talk about our mothers.*

CHAPTER 46

The dead watch as Emely returns to the place that began them all. To help her remember, they push the stone of halite closer to the quartz. *Sister Women*, her grandmother says, *you who are alive, you who are dead, we sing you our song of prayer.*

Women around the world immediately respond. They pick up their stones, warm them in their hands, then speak. "Yes, Sister," they reply, "we hear you."

When Amely was over the river our Mother tried to talk to her with the voice of water, but the girl was too frightened to hear.

The women take up a chant, speaking all together: "Flinders Range in Australia, Stonehenge, Machu Picchu, the Greek island of Crete . . . these are our sacred holy places."

But none are so holy as this place, Emely's grandmother responds. *It is Amely's first night here in these trees. It's time for her to hear the voice of air.*

CHAPTER 47

The wind that begins that night seems personal, as if it's looking just for her. Embarrassed by the urban rustle of her sleeping bag, Emely burrows deep into her small piece of night. The wind finds her anyway. *Chaka, chaka, chaka*—there's the wind, but there's also the sound of bells, a slight perturbation of the night air.

No to the wind out there, no to the brassy challenge of those bells. Deep inside her sleeping bag Emely lies very still, listening to the pounding of her heart. Whatever it is that is out there can stay out there. She just wants to be left alone and go to sleep.

But then she hears her name—her other name, that is. *Aaamely*, the syllables stretched long. *Aaamely*. And this time she recognizes the voice—recognizes as well that she doesn't have any choice in the matter. Grandmama is out there and she's calling for her.

She raises her head, stares into the dark, and now sees her. She's coming forward, a small wedge of light out there. What Emely sees is more an idea than anything she could define as actually real. It doesn't matter in the least bit that she saw her die, or that she's hovering a bit off the ground. Grandmama is coming toward her and she's shining—but not with any kind of light from the stars and the moon, not from any exterior light; she is shining with an emphatic interior glow.

And now Grandmama's here, standing right in front of her.

Knowing her granddaughter is watching (and somewhat theatrically, to Emely's mind), Grandmama slowly lifts the veil from her head. Death does not become her. Her eyes are sunken, her cheeks more hollow than the last time Emely saw her, her bones exposed, her hair more climate than anything else. But what is really different is her headdress. Festooned with giant pearls, it rises from her ashy forehead; there is more heft, more volume in those pearls than in anything left in her face.

Emely inhales a shocked breath. "Grandmama," she exclaims, "what's happened to you?"

Her grandmother smiles, revealing skeleton teeth. *Death*, she says matter-of-factly. *Death is what's happened to me.* Her soft light spreads into the darkness, and there's a smell, too, of flowers. And then she begins to extend her hand, her fingers barely upholstered with flesh.

Emely knows she's supposed to be frightened, but what really matters is that Grandmama is back. Remembering burns away any lingering bit of fear. She doesn't care if Grandmama is a ghost; the only thing she cares about is that she's here, and that those are the hands that rimmed her childhood.

Lovingly, her grandmother runs one finger down the side of her face. Her touch is cold and it makes Emely's skin smart, but she closes her eyes anyway, even turns her head a bit and lays her cheek in the icy cradle of her grandmother's hands. Never mind that Grandmama's face is lace, the light of the moon shining through it; finally, here is a heart into which she can fit.

Maybe the way to bring someone back from the dead is to truly remember. Just as she did when she was small, she begins to talk, pouring everything she doesn't understand into Grandmama's listening ear.

"I was so frightened coming into the forest, Grandmama," she says. "You should have seen me. Everything seemed to know me and call me by my name, the one you used to call me before Mama changed it. I got so scared I just froze, and then Mentegai had to come and get me down."

Just as she had when Emely was five, Grandmama shushes her with one finger. *Amely*, she says. Her voice is hollow and slightly dislocated. *We have places to visit this night. It's time to teach you how to fly.* She reaches down, wraps her bony fingers around her granddaughter's wrist, and with a mighty heave, pulls her up into the spilt conversation of the stars.

Activated by dreams, the sky bursts forward in a livid rush of wind and magic. Emely is quickly carried into an expanded sense of night, the division between sky and Earth, death and life, flight and normal mammal sobriety by the moment evaporating. Flying seems to be a succession of brief, exuberant moments, one right after the other. Awestruck, she can barely speak.

"Where are you taking me, Grandmama?" she finally manages to ask. She can already sense that this night's flight is some kind of spiritual initiation.

I'm taking you to the place of origins, her grandmother replies from somewhere in front of her. *It's the place that begins our songs. You'll start your journey into the forest from there.*

"I don't understand," Emely says. "Is this a dream?"

Her grandmother shakes her head. *Stop trying to understand everything with your tiny school-girl mind!* she snaps. *Tonight you will learn the voice of wind and air.*

Almost too loud to hear, her grandmother's voice echoes in the night. Everything she says she emphasizes with the rattle of her bells. *Wind*, she continues, *Sister Wind. It pushes us through our stories until we aren't any more. Alive, that is. Have you ever wondered what happens to the you that is me, and the me that is you? Death is what happens. Death swirls us all together until we become the great, rich consciousness that is all of us. But where does wind go? What happens to air? Have you ever asked yourself that question?*

Just as she did when she was alive, she answers her own question. *It goes to the place I'm taking you tonight.*

"But I don't want to know these things!" Emely cries. "It's all way too strange!" Even in a dream, nothing her grandmother says makes sense.

It was just as it was when she was five. The look her grandmother flashes over her shoulder rips a seam in all the moonlit peace. *Stop whining*, she scolds, and there's a sound in her voice that extinguishes any further argument from Emely. There's also the sound of those bells—bossy, like the woman who wears them.

And then, with a thump, they land.

CHAPTER 48

How can Emely describe this place her grandmother has brought her to? She has left one world flying, and entered another where everything flies. More music, art, and homage than anything that is actual geography, even for a dreamscape, this place has outdone itself. Right in front of her, shining in the moonlight, a giant web is stretched between two trees.

Stepping closer, Emely sees that the web is entirely woven by leaves stitched together with tiny thorns. The veins of the leaves shine in the moonlight like tiny fish bones.

And circles. Circles are everywhere. Some are made with yellow leaves, some red, some made with stones that eventually spiral into an intricate labyrinth. Some of the lines are made of feathers, but not the way a bird would grow them—no, these wildly lyrical lines twist across the ground, each feather bordering about an inch of space so that space is rippled by feathers, and not the other way around.

On the crest of a hill is a series of middens. Each clump of stone interferes with the sky, has something to say that is gnarly and impolite. There are arches, too—everywhere, in fact. Some are made with gray stone, some are laced with a deep, lamenting blue. Each stone that forms an arch flirts with light, illuminating the stone next to it, dimming for a moment when a cloud passes over the moon.

The same kind of whimsy that has invented birds' nests and shells operates here, but like birds' nests and shells, it is a serious kind of play.

"Grandmama," Emely says, reaching for her hand, "this place is amazing! Who made it?"

There is no answer, and in that moment she discovers she is alone. Alone, that is, until she sees what is floating toward her. A chorus of women. Like Grandmama, they hover a little bit off the ground, and like Grandmama, they wear their own party. Shaking their bells, they create an entire orchestra of sound.

But no amount of party sound can disguise the fact that these women are dead. Light shines through their bones.

One more time, very quietly. "Grandmama?"

One more time, no response.

As the women come closer, Emely sees that though they are ghosts, they are beautiful; even the most vague have faces that let her in.

Amely, they say, clustering around her. *Amely*, they repeat.

One woman extracts herself from the others. Light slants from her cheekbones, and her smile reduces any lingering bit of fear Emely might still feel. She peels a piece of string from some bark, knots the string on each end of a small bone, then hangs the contraption from a tree. Leaning over, she blows gently. The diminutive swing moves back and forth with her breath.

And then another woman, hair so thick it could be a meadow to lie down in, comes forward. It's as if one part of her body is trying to walk away from the rest of her, Emely thinks, and then realizes that she has a bad hip. She stops at another tree and, rising on her toes, hangs what appears to be a small mobile on a lower branch. The mobile is fashioned from two blue feathers, one bone, and one gray pebble. Like the first woman, she blows gently. Spinning with miniature importance, it becomes its own galaxy.

The woman's silence spreads across all the moving things, and slowly all that breathes, even Emely, begins to be pulled into the rhythm of her breath. She is a woman who has borne her infirmary, even her own death, with patience.

This isn't just about air, she says, turning to Emely. *This is about feeling. Do you understand?*

Emely shakes her head. "No," she murmurs. "None of this makes sense."

Another woman wades into the middle of a small lake, throws

out what appears to be a string. It floats on top of the water. Stepping closer, Emely sees that the string is actually a row of leaves—hundreds of them, maybe an entire tree's worth—stitched together with tiny thorns. The string moves and flows across the surface of the water; the lake has becomes its author, what it has to say can only be read by water.

The woman leans over and, curling her hands, tries to lift the reflection of the moon. It spills through her fingers, splinters into millions of pieces of silver, mirrored light.

Object, motion, the assignment of emptiness, the gorgeous need of the singular to belong finally to the plural—Emely is beginning to understand. This is three-dimensional play. Vacancy her sketchbook, every woman has an invention that is her own. In this place of air, even emptiness is understood.

As though they have known Emely her whole life, the ghost women begin to speak in unison. *Beautiful sister Amely, you, too, turn on air. Like one of these mobiles, you balance thoughts and action, hang the rational against the sensual.*

Once again the question: *Do you understand?*

One more time, Emely shakes her head. "No."

Our Mother is inside of each breath, the ghost women continue. *It is she who breathes us. But if she is no longer, you won't be, either. If the Mother dies, this beautiful, vast world will not exist anymore.*

A silky sound, the women coming closer. *There are many worlds beyond the one you think you know, Amely. When you were over the river, the Mother tried to talk to you with the voice of water. Tonight she is speaking with the voice of wind. We are here to help her.*

The more the women talk, the less she understands. Stones cracked with silence, silence rimmed with stones, holes that breathe, a tree that stands dark and serious against the sky's inquiry, and somewhere at the edge of it all, Emely senses her grandmother.

The woman who stands in the lake begins to bend a limber piece of wood into an arch. The lake answers with a half circle of its own, and now, holding water and air, moon and wave, a new cameo rests against the night.

The women begin to twirl their hands in a circular motion, first to the right, then the left. Emely can't seem to look away. The hypnotizing activity of each individual pulls her eyes into the common vortex of the whole. *You must learn the story of air, Amely*, the women say. *We alone can't breathe our Mother. We are only the dead.*

The woman with the hair like a meadow separates herself from the others. *There's an old woman who waits for you in the trees, Amely*, she says. *When you become quiet enough she will teach you, but if you don't listen, you will become one of us. Your sister, your brothers, your mother and father will become one of us. No wind, no stars, no motion—all that is human will be no more. No plants, no trees, no animals, no hellos, no yellow flowers, no more somersaults of hope.*

Something too large to understand with just her mind is falling across Emely; a space is slowly opening between what she knows and what she wants to know. She rubs her eyes but can't rub comprehension into her mind.

And now the women's faces are changing. No longer beautiful, a new darkness flickers in their eyes. There is a smell, too, of rot.

Everything that connects us is breaking, Amely, they say. *Only you can restore the filaments of life.*

"No," she moans. She doesn't want to be here anymore. Why is everyone saying she's the only one to save them? The push of the women's eyes match the memory of her mother, those strained words of prophecy she spoke yesterday.

The women's faces, black now, are charred in the kiln of death.

"Get me out of here!" Emely shouts. "Please, let me wake up!"— and suddenly Grandmama is standing right in front of her, a familiar net of wrinkles surrounding the black pools of her eyes.

Without a word she takes Emely's hand, leads her to the surface of the dream, and finally, she wakes.

But though the women have left this night, the dream is inside of her now. Even one breath connects her to the reality she has just visited; one breath and she can match the world outside of her with the dream's different tonalities of air. Objects, motion, movement, and weight perfectly balanced, nationless wind harnessed by nationless minds . . . the women in her dream played seriously with what the world has given them.

Amely. Touched and caressed by the hands of the dead, Emely finally hears the air that blows through her Grandmama-given name. She burrows deep into her sleeping bag, but her breath, her own small piece of owned air, catches in her throat.

She doesn't think she can sleep, but finally she does.

CHAPTER 49

She's here, finally, in the old trees, say the dead. *Let's introduce her to those who made her.*

When Emely wakes her dream is still vivid in her mind. Her memory of her grandmother is still so clear she wonders if she actually was with her. Did she really go flying last night? And that place so ebullient with air, does it actually exist?

Above her, the sky. No demarcations, just a blank, inexhaustible blue. Until she comes across her name, that is, the one the ghost women whispered to her last night: A M E L Y . . . the letters are scrawled carelessly across the sky with magic's nonchalance.

Fingered by the wind, the letters bloom, widen, spread; it takes a moment for Emely's dream-addled mind to translate what she has seen. Smoke. Smoke has written her name in the sky, and if there's smoke, someone human has lit a fire.

"Come back, come back." Far away, she hears Mentegai's voice. "It's me, the son of Sarutu. You told me to bring in the girl, and here we are!" His voice is a thin thing against the activity, wealth, and mystery that is this forest.

When Emely was a little girl, when she belonged to that other name, she could travel into anything she saw before her using only her mind for locomotion. With her head resting on the crook of her arm, for instance, she could enter a tree many yards away, follow the heartbeat of sap down into its core. Using only her eyes, she could pull rain down into the tree's thirsty roots, become the hungry response of leaves.

She would lose herself this way—lose her separate self, that is—until finally, heart and mind united, she would join the pulse of the world. She called it "flying" back then, but really it was "becoming."

And so it is, already softened by the dream of the air from the night before, with this other way of knowing, she knows that a powerful presence waits for her in the mountains above. She has no choice in the matter. She has been summoned.

She climbs out of the sleeping bag, collects all her things, slips her backpack straps over her shoulders, and begins to climb.

High, then higher still; the foliage is so tight in some places she has to crawl on her knees. Hours spent climbing. Her face is cut by underlying twigs and still she climbs toward whatever, whoever is waiting for her at the top of the mountain. And then finally, late afternoon, breath ragged, face bloodied, T-shirt ripped, she arrives at a small clearing.

Thick green grass, the stewed smell of summer. To one side, a waterfall cascades an endless supply of shiny silver pins. And there's also a cave, the dusk inside its rock walls beckoning. Again, she has no choice. The thing that waits for her is inside.

How do you knock on the door of a cave? Once, twice, she slaps her hands on the rock. "Hello?" she calls, squinting into the gloom inside. "Anyone home?"

No answer. She steps inside, and when her eyes adjust to the dark, she gasps in astonishment. Paintings—glorious vibrant paintings—cover every inch of the cave walls. People dance, hunt, make love; there are stick figures holding spears, a series of handprints one right after the other, injured animals, dead animals, little boats, births, deaths, and hunts.

It's a serenade of life. Everything that could be hoped for, grieved over, celebrated, and lived, spills its story across these rock walls. Her academic mind immediately kicks in. *What a discovery! This might be the oldest place on Earth! What will the professor say? It rivals even the Lascaux Caves in southwestern France or the Altimira Caves in Spain! I wonder if my flash will work. PhD, here I come.*

But then something else happens. Standing in the cylinder of these long-ago-narrated lives, whirled by the echo of time, the woman who had been stroked by ghost hands last night, the one who knew that something waited for her at the top of this mountain, recognizes these stories. These drawings, painted thousands of years ago, were not just made with hands, they were dreamt alive with love. Their inexhaustible quarrels, gossip, stories, and celebrations live deep in the marrow of her bones. Though the sunlight that pours through the opening of the cave is turbulent with heat, adventure, and modern-day motion, deep inside this cave, Emely stands still. This is a place for rest. This is a place for breath. She has returned to the place that began her.

But then the E that begins her other name returns; she begins to notice evidence of modern-day occupation and reaches for her camera.

A small fire burns in the center of the cave.

Click.

Three skin bags loaded with what appears to be liquid are mounted on sticks halfway up the walls.

Click.

Sleeping furs are coiled neatly to one side, and near them sits a row of clay pots, plump with domestic importance. There are baskets filled with feathers, plants, and roots. The dirt floor has been swept recently; corduroy stripes from a twig broom groove the dirt floor.

Click.

And always those paintings, those spinning, glorious paintings.

She's clicking away with all her might when she hears a sound in the back of the cave. She turns. "Hello?" she calls. "Anyone there?"

She begins to follow one of the swerves drawn by the twig broom back into the cave's dark recesses. "Hello?" she calls once again.

And that's when she first sees the creature curled inside a small hollow halfway up the cave wall. White domed head, two waxy smears for eyes, body festooned with an assortment of bark, scales, feathers, and furs. No movement. Just the steady gaze from two dark, implacable eyes.

Emely states the obvious. "I've come from the outside," she says, her voice draped across the craggy ridge of an unsteady heartbeat. "My name is Emely. I've come in with Mentegai. Maybe you know him?"

Knowing already there's no map for the space that lies between them, she tries coaxing mildness into her voice. "His father and mother used to live in this forest."

Maybe what she says works. Extracting what appears to be a very ordinary human hand from its assortment of furs, feathers, bark, and scales, meticulously, with delicate, feline grace, the creature begins to lick each digit, one right after the other, with a pink playground slide of a tongue. When it has finished its grooming, it opens its mouth and spills sound down that playground slide. The sound moves quickly into something that could almost be called a "song"—a discernible melody with a discernible beat. Next, as though trying to dock the melody, the creature begins to clap its hands—once, twice—and even snaps its fingers.

But still there is nothing in those strange eyes that says, "Stay with me!"

Emely can't move. She can hear the professor's voice in her ear— "Chronicle, chronicle, chronicle"—but she doesn't reach for her camera. Because now the melody is deepening, the song has become pure feeling, and the part of Emely that rested in the community of long-ago-lived-through paintings begins to listen with an ancient, tribal ear. She begins to see hands, millions of hands, reaching for light, and suddenly the emotion born from the creature's song reminds her of her own loneliness, her life spent only inches from her mother's lap. Just one sound from one throat and yet the world turns.

When the singing stops Emely doesn't understand the strange new longing stirring deep inside of her. She remembered what her mother told her. "Be careful," she warned, "the ones who live in the forest can get a hold of your mind by singing just one song."

Is that what has just happened? All she knew is that she wants more.

"Please," she says reaching out with both of her hands. "Please don't stop. I love your singing." But she already knows no words can cross the distance between the creature's loneliness and her own. Nothing can fill the evolutionary space that lies between them.

It turns out those two black smears are not eyes, they are eyelids painted black. When the creature opens its eyes, fresh, girl beauty fills her face, never mind the savagery of her ash-white skin.

Emely's heart skips a beat. One more time she smiles. "Hello," she says again.

With a giant scream the girl leaps from the small hollow, sprints quickly across the floor, kicks Emely hard in her stomach. She immediately doubles over in pain. Another scream and the painted warriors frozen for so many years on the walls of the cave, awakened by the bloodlust in the girl's cry, raise their tiny spears, sends them flying into the hearts of all those painted antelopes. Animals fall, babies are born.

Gasping for breath Emely crawls on her knees out the door of the cave, falls to the grass outside. The girl doesn't follow.

She clutches her stomach. *Another stupid mistake*, she thinks as she rocks back and forth in pain. *I should never have approached the cave without Mentegai. Now we might not even be able to stay.*

Except for the sound of the waterfall's falling pins, there is silence. Silence brimmed to the top with the echo of that scream.

CHAPTER 50

All things that have been alive still speak. I am only a button made of bone, my round disc carved from the antlers of a bongo but I have something to say. I travel back through time to the animal I was when vast herds of us thundered across the savanna. Thousands of hooves shook the world.

All of this said with my one small eye.

I'm only a button made of bone, but I am the whole that fills the hole. When I slip into place I hold pieces of the old woman's furs together: my job is to keep people warm. This is the old woman's work as well. The new Stone Woman has just arrived and tomorrow the old woman will begin a new sculpture, her fingers barely able to contain her ferocious, romantic anger. "Why, why, why?" she will ask with each stroke of her hand, the words she speaks tender flames. "Why are people hurting the Mother I love so much?"

But let me tell you when both woman and bone become something else. It's when her granddaughter, Chipkorie, enters the cave. "Grandmama?" she calls, peering into the gloom. "Grandmama, you there?" The glad flush of the old woman warms both her and me. "I'm back here, Chipkorie," she answers and everything the girl is to her, the baby she had been when her mother left these trees thirteen years ago, the old woman's daily love for her each day after, shining, shining, polishing her up into the beautiful young woman she has become, lies between them.

She knows that soon her granddaughter will be in so much pain her little body will tremble and shudder uncontrollably, and draws her in for a hug so tight for many minutes afterwards Chipkorie wears the imprint of my tiny moon on her cheek. "You're my brave girl," she whispers in her ear.

Chipkorie. The old woman's most radiant work of art.

Minutes later? Maybe it's an hour? Emely's not quite sure, but at some point another song begins inside the cave, this one banjo bright, so solicitous that it impels Emely immediately to her feet. One more time she approaches the cave, one more time she slaps her hand against the rock. Once more she cautiously takes a step inside. . .

And almost trips over an old woman lying on the ground.

The girl creature is crouched at the woman's side. She doesn't even look up at Emely's arrival; her entire focus is on the old woman.

Is she dead? An enormous quiet at her core. Naked except for a leather skirt buttoned with a small sphere made of bone. Breasts slumped with time, hands a collection of bones crossed over her stomach.

"Chaka, chaka, chaka," the girl sings—then, reaching into a clay pot behind her, picks up what appears to be a sponge and begins to pass it across the old woman's body. Every inch of the woman is soon dewed with water, between the delicate flying buttress bones of her neck, a tiny lake. The water trembles, rises, and falls with breath; though unconscious, the old woman is alive after all.

The girl sees it, too. Her sound bites speed up and become chatter, happy and bright. She reaches into another basket to bring out some yellow flowers and begins to weave them in and out of the old woman's thin gray hair. Another bowl and the girl's fingers emerge blue. She slides that color across the old woman's cheeks. One stripe, two stripes, and now the blue lines hold the woman's quiet the way a cup holds liquid.

Blue fingers slide one long line across the old woman's forehead, a place to hold the sentences of her thoughts. As though whirled by the wings of a million bees, the girl's song thickens. *Don't die, don't die*, each wing says.

Spellbound, Emely just stands still, not even thinking about her camera now. This day began with her other name written across the sky with smoke, spilled from her dead grandmother's hands the night before, a cave where species mingle, where a scratching, violent attack becomes an hour later loving ministration, a place at the top of a mountain where the seemingly dead can awaken with only the humming of a song and some animating principle of blue. . .

There is magic here, yes, deep magic.

So lulled by those flower-weaving hands, senses clotted by the girl's friendly bee hum, Emely doesn't notice what all the spears raised on the walls of the cave are trying to convey—another attack.

Like some distant ancestor born from the stories on the walls, a creature springs across the floor, yanks Emely's head back, and places the point of a spear against her neck. Strange golden eyes, a row of sawblade teeth, its breath is an elixir of decay.

Emely can't move, she is so terrified; it takes a moment for her thoughts to separate and become her own again.

Animals don't carry spears, she finally reasons. *This has to be a man—a man who, by the looks of him, doesn't like me.*

Seeing that she has recognized this fact, a look of brutal gratification crosses the man's face.

Maybe it's because her body is held captive by the point of the spear, but the word, a pejorative used in childhood to mean half-animal, half-man, slips through the filter of her school-taught semantic fairness. *Animan*, she recalls, feeling oddly liberated. *Animan*—her own point of the spear.

It's as if he can hear her. A low growl begins deep in his belly and floats upward on the fermented wind of his breath; the point of his spear cuts into the flesh of her neck. Blood, sticky and warm, begins to flow down her neck.

It's at this moment that Mentegai arrives at the entrance of the cave.

His quick, smart eyes immediately take inventory: old woman on the ground, girl crouched at her side, man holding a spear to Emely's neck. His hands, pale, rise to join the hallelujah chorus of all the other handprints painted on the walls.

"Please, Mashulu," he says, using an Okino term of respect for elders.

"Please don't hurt her." Supplication threads his voice. He takes one step forward. "The old woman," he continues—and here his eyes flick toward the woman lying on the ground—"said we could come. She told me to bring in the woman you are holding at the point of your spear." He is staring into the old man's face. "We mean no wrong," he pleads. "You can trust me. I'm the son of Sarutu. Did you know my parents?"

Anger creases the old man's face, deep ravines on each side of his mouth. "I do remember your parents, son of Sarutu," he replies in a low, strange voice. "And I even remember you when you were a little boy. But look at my wife." He glances at the old woman lying on the ground. "She has become so exhausted waiting for this woman to arrive, she's barely alive. All we can do is wait for her to come back to us."

Emely wants to swallow, but can't. If she moves even just a little, the spear will cut deeper into her flesh.

"This morning when I held the soil of our Mother in my hands," the man says, "I poured it in four directions. First I offered it to the sky, then to the earth, then to the river, then once more back to the sky. Sometimes just putting my feet in the river brings me to the Mother; some mornings all I have to do is raise my face to the sun. These are my daily prayers. But this morning our Mother wasn't there. I knew it immediately."

From the corner of her eye, Emely sees for the first time that the man, too, is exhausted. His eyebrows, bushy, too animated for his tired face, look like they want to jump off and join someone else's expression.

"Our Mother," he says, shaking his head, "our Mother so vast she trembles sunsets with just her breath. Our Mother so slight she disappears at the edges of the day, only to reappear in her stars at night. Our Mother. I only want her to be all right."

Mentegai has a hunter's respect for silence. As if listening to music, his face softens; he crouches and places his chin on his hands.

"Aren't you going to do anything?" Emely wants to yell. Maybe she can borrow the old man's eyebrows for what she wants to say.

But then the old man begins to speak again. "Our Mother," he says softly, "she spreads out her arms, and we who are her flesh children live in the hollow between."

Though his grip on the spear doesn't weaken, the intensity of his anger gradually begins to diminish. He's finding a rhythm in his words, as steadying as if two hands have been placed on his shoulders.

"Son of Sarutu," he says, "because I know the people who have made you, I know I can speak to you with my heart's truth." His ruined face, cratered with worry, begins to emanate a new, tender light. Even his eyebrows, those fierce animals, lie down.

"I've never seen our Mother so unhappy. My wife there on the ground and my granddaughter"—he nods at the girl crouching at the old woman's side—"almost ready to give her blood, but there's no one left to perform the sacred rite."

Once again the leap of a live flame in those gold eyes. His anger has returned. "This morning when I spoke to our Mother, she didn't answer. She was flat and dull and quiet, and now I know why." Another push of the spear against Emely's neck. "It's all because of her! My wife says she is the next Stone Woman, but I don't believe her. We've had many arguments. How can a Stone Woman come from the outside, I ask? The world is out of balance, and my wife is not thinking straight. Unnatural sounds fall across our Mother from the sky. Eggshells no longer rim life. Lights come from the outside and take away our dark. Animals are born too soon or not at all, and wrong fills our rivers with tastes that make our fish sick."

The sour smell of worry explodes on the old man's breath. Emely tries not to breathe it in. Even more than the smell, she doesn't want this forlorn story to come inside, become her.

"Wrong words enter our silence and claim all the time between them as their own," the old man continues. "Animals stalk the night, hunting beyond need. Though we who live in this cave dance and sing and pray and make our art, we are not strong enough to push back this wrong. It is more dangerous than anything we have ever fought before."

"Last times," he says, laying his own story across all the other stories chronicled on the cave walls. "Last time for the wind to slough through these trees. Last time for water to sing across stones . . . last times."

Another jab of the spear. "And all because of this woman! She is the tip of the arrowhead bringing into the forest all that is wrong."

As she listens, Emely finds herself almost grateful for the spear. Though it cuts her neck, it keeps her pinned to the upper edge of the hole where her darkest, most concentrated questions live. Because she knows something. The man is right; the words he speaks match up with what all those painted spears are saying, what all those deaths chronicled on the walls say as well. She *is* wrong. She had stumbled into this cave and upset the bird girl. She had thought that ugly word, sucking all the while on its sour judgment. She is the tip of the arrowhead bringing in all that is to come. Maybe not this year, maybe not next, maybe not for fifty years more, but the outside world—its golf courses, granite countertops, university-taught progress—is coming.

The words, already alive, move deep inside her. She says them softly at first: "I'm sorry." Then one more time, a little louder. "I'm sorry."

And then no more piled-up words anymore, no counterfeit smiles; everyone just stands, separate and still.

It is a long, strange quiet. Outside the cave, stars begin to appear. In the trees close by a monkey howls, a flock of vultures chafe the sky with paparazzi resolve, but inside the cave, air dim and kind with creaturely comfort, it is quiet.

Evening arrives, slowly fills the cave with its sad, blue light. The air smells of fire and a little bit of dirt, and the waterfall, silver and constant, continues to drop its pins outside.

The old woman opens her eyes. "Oh, good," she exclaims, staring at Emely, "you're finally here. Now we can get to work!"

"Wife . . ." the old man warns.

The old woman's eyes flash. "Husband, I told you," she snaps. "She's the one who is going to save us."

The button made of bone on the old woman's skirt catches some of the light from the fire. Potent with animal knowing, the small sphere seems to wink.

CHAPTER 51

D ay has long since lowered into the deep barrel of night; evening is beginning its slow slide toward tomorrow. An almost full moon, the clouds so hefty they could be another country. In the river a fish swims up to the surface of its world, pushes rings against the sky of water. A monkey swings from tree to tree, investigating everything with its tiny hands. An anteater scratches an anthill then pushes the long point of its nose into the hill. Darting its long, sticky tongue, it begins to slurp its night's dinner. A leopard, so dark it is the color of midnight, moves through the trees, lightly touching its nose against leaves. Only the gold of its eyes is reflected in the moonlight.

As the moon rises, the forest passageways fill with traffic, the branches, trails, and streams throb with movement. Though it's a rich and interlocked ecology, it is not a sentimental wholeness—the night is spent hunting, killing, and devouring.

The people in the cave draw near to the fire, the heat almost a second skin. The old woman tosses a small stone back and forth between her hands. The old man, frowning, stares into the fire, and the young girl, when she thinks Emely is not looking, casts curious glances her way. Though her face is still white with ash, the scales, fur, and feathers that covered her body earlier were apparently only a cape, which she has removed to reveal a demure body.

Mentegai is hard at work using the commerce of meat to buy his way back into his family. He arches limber branches over the flames, each one adorned with a chunk of the forest hog's meat. One, looped with the pearls of the hog's intestines, looks like the bejeweled neck of a fancy lady.

The smell of roast pig soon fills the cave. Like one of his adoring dogs, the people watch everything Mentegai does.

When the pig is done cooking, Mentegai hands a lollipop of meat to each person. The forest people eat ravenously, barely chewing the meat before swallowing, cheeks bulging, grease running down their chins.

Emely is handed a chunk of meat, still sprouting here and there some of the hog's black, wiry hair. She has leaned over to take a bite when the young girl slides over.

"Don't," she says, and points to a pebble buried deep in the fur.

"What?" Emely asks.

"It's a tick," the young girl replies.

Revulsion fills Emely's throat. As discreetly as she can she places the meat behind her, hears the rattle of a dog's nails as he approaches, the quick snap of his jaw.

Mentegai's voice then, a dark bruise. "Don't feed my hunting dogs."

She's tired, she's hungry, she's been hypnotized by song, kicked hard in the stomach, held captive by the point of a spear. "You wouldn't even be here if it wasn't for me," she shoots back. "Who do you think paid for that forest hog?"

A long, tangled stare then across the flames.

"Can I have another piece of meat?" she eventually asks.

Not saying a word, he hands her another piece. She leans it toward the fire, inspects it carefully before taking a bite.

It's so good. Soon she is eating as voraciously as the forest people, tearing the meat with her teeth, cracking the bones to suck the marrow, hands shiny with grease. She finishes the first piece of meat, has mutely extended her hand for more when suddenly she's caught by a gust of homesickness so acute it brings tears to her eyes.

Her mother's meals were always affirmations. Vegetables cooked by the very same woman who had planted their seeds, the gossip and stories spoken over the chopping of the stalks as much a part of the cooking as the food itself, when the meal was finally served, it was simmered in community, family, belonging.

No affirmation here. Appetite is as vulgar and unadorned as the tick's. Just the holy trinity narrated in the paintings on the walls: kill, dominate, eat.

The girl turns to the old woman. "Don't eat too quickly, Grandma," she says. "Your stomach might not be ready for new tastes so soon after being gone."

"I'm all right," the old woman scoffs, but Emely notices that after her granddaughter's warning she does try to eat more slowly.

"What is your name?" Emely asks, turning to the old woman.

"Ogotu," she replies.

"And your name?" Emely asks, turning toward the old man.

Head down, he strips meat off a bone with a hard, taunting appetite no food could begin to address. He doesn't answer but his granddaughter does. "His name is Tempi," she replies. "Old Tempi. He's my father's father."

Emely is about to ask the girl what her name is and where her parents are when suddenly she jumps up, begins to pace back and forth before the fire. "This is so good I can't eat it just sitting still!" she exclaims. Firelight stammers copper radiance against her graceful body.

The old man chuckles. "Well, mine is so good I wish I had another mouth!" He reaches behind him for another piece of wood, throws it on the fire. The log slumps heavily into a small city of gold.

The girl walks over to one of the leather bags hanging from a stick on the cave walls, carefully pours some of the contents of the bag into a bamboo tube. Returning to the fire she sits down, raises the bamboo to her mouth, and drinks. She then hands the tube to the old woman, who drinks as well; then it is in the old man's hands, next Mentegai's, and now Emely holds it between her two hands.

After the tick she is leery. She cautiously raises the tube to her mouth, waiting for whatever it is that is at the bottom to reach her lips. An inside smell comes from the tube, slightly dirty, like water left too long in a barrel. She tilts the bamboo at a steeper angle and, when she finally swallows, discovers to her surprise that she likes it. Cool, quiet, it's like drinking the space between trees. Again and again she drinks—until finally, realizing she is being greedy, she reluctantly hands the tube to the young girl.

The night becomes the wait for whatever it is that is inside the tube of bamboo to finally return to her hands.

Three times, four times, she drinks deep the bamboo's taste of calm—and then she happens to glance up and sees for the first time, high on a ledge cut into the cave walls, a small, intricately woven basket articulating a pattern of upward-pointed arrows. The basket carries its own concentrated sense of gravity; Emely can't seem to look away.

And that's when she gets her first great idea. These paintings, this endlessly repeated tune of animals circling forever inside the perimeters of this cave—well, she could be the one to release them.

It's a great idea! Another drink from the bamboo. She can see it now. The grand opening of the anthropological wing of the Museum of Natural History in Nairobi. Photographs of these very same paintings mounted against the walls. That little basket, its concentrated, fertile silence, resting inside a Plexiglas cube, a discreet tag at its base: "Okino artifact, 174, collected by Doctor Emely Matei. See catalog for further exposition." Her elegant, slightly understated speech. "I would like to thank the Professor, my parents, Sister Mary Rose," she would say. Lights from the museum's newly designed glass wing would blaze their victory in pushing back the primitive night, even if only for a few hours; history, even the basket's silence, would be owned, displayed, arranged, and catalogued.

It's a brave thought, a glorious thought. But then, floating towards her from whatever is inside the tube of bamboo, comes another different kind of thought: *I won't be lonely here. I have returned to the beginning of myself. These are my ancestors. Look, their bows and spears rest against the rock walls. They eat their day's work.*

Suddenly the Doctor before her name doesn't seem so important anymore. Some photographs mounted on a wall, that basket resting inside a Plexiglas cube—they could never articulate the fullness of life here. Savoring the warmth of her new insight, she wants to go to the old man and kneel beside him. "Let me tell you about all the people you have helped be born," she'll say.

And so it is that when Ogotu looks at her and asks, "What is your name, new one?" the word pops out before she can catch it: "Amely," she responds. The syllables of her Grandmama-given name send her skipping like a stone across water.

"Amely," Ogotu repeats, jostling the weight of her name on her tongue—and in that moment, Emely learns how one word, spoken by just the right person at just the right time, can absorb all of darkness.

She retreats quickly from having that much right. "I'm-I'm sorry," she stammers. "I don't know where that name came from. My name is Emely, Emely Matei."

Ogotu looks at her for a long time. Emely shuffles uneasily in her position on the floor. She doesn't think the old woman has ever experienced doubt in her whole life. *Maybe that's how she has managed to grow so old*, she thinks; *she always knows where she was going.*

Ogotu appears to make up her mind about something. Placing her hands on her knees, she stands slowly. "Follow me," she says over her shoulder, and she walks to the back of the cave. "It is time for you to know your story."

When Emely stands she finds she is dizzy. She has to brace her hand against the cave walls in order to walk. For the first time she realizes the drink in the bamboo might be alcoholic. She might even be a little bit drunk.

She has no time to think any of this through, however. Ogotu stops at the back of the cave and stares at her, her eyes strange and pale as though blanched from too much seeing.

"Is this your name?" she asks, and there it is again—A M E L Y, the letters chiseled deep into the stone. A M E L Y, the name the ghost women called her last night, the name that was written on the sky this very morning.

Her usual divide. First thought: *Oh Lordy, Lordy. It's an anthropological gold mine! These people have a written language!* Second thought: *What is the name my sweet grandmother gave me so long ago doing chiseled into the walls of this cave?*

Ogotu taps her fingers against the letters. "Your great-grandmother carved this name," she says. "She too was named Amely. She predicted this day would come. When the world is dark and our Mother is in trouble, she foretold, another Amely will rise into the sky. She will save not only the trees but the Mother herself." The old woman stares deep into Emely's eyes. "Names are small rafts pushed up the dark river of eternity by those who have left," she pronounces. "They carry the heavy freight of divination. Do you understand?"

No to that raft floating toward her, no to this other kind of knowing. Emely, staring back into Ogotu's eyes, tries to keep her voice calm and steady. "I'm sorry," she says. "I told you, that isn't my name. It was a mistake. I got it wrong."

A bit unsteadily she returns to her place by the fire and reaches for her backpack. Its steel frame and right angles comfort her. *I will belong only to the name Emely Matei*, she tells herself, clutching it tight. *Especially if one day that name will begin with the small engine of the word "Doctor." In fact, I'm going to start up that engine right now, practice what I'll report to the Professor tomorrow morning.* She finds a piece of Velcro and, comforted by its tiny engagement, presses, releases, presses, releases.

Base camp here, I will say. CD1245, come in. First contact made, sir. I'm proud to report that though I've been met with some initial hostility, the interview subjects have decided to let me stay. The offer of meat seems to have facilitated their decision. She scans her eyes across the girl, the old woman and the old man. *Field subjects appear to be a small band of hunter-gatherers. I have yet to appraise if there are others. Perhaps this is a small breakaway group, formed to better share what appear to be meager resources.*

Press, release, press, release, oh yeah, oh yeah. Doctor Emely Matei, arranging the information of the world in alphabetic order.

A long, drawn-out howl brings her back from her thoughts. The sound fills the sky then falls back once more on the land. The people in the cave raise their heads.

"Leopard," Old Tempi says, and then there is silence so dense it could be another person.

Outside the cave, the moon, smudged but smiling, sails farther up into the sky. Inside, the forest people began to sing. "It is good to eat," they sing. It's a strange song but it brings more expression to their faces. "And tonight we will make the pig dance. Once again it will rut and push its nose into the soil and find tubers." Catching all the stray radial lines of the song in the low net of his voice, what Old Tempi sings runs beneath everything else.

Emely leans forward to tie her shoelaces, finds herself humming along.

When the song ends Ogotu reaches into some secretive fold of her furs and pulls out a pipe. Taking a stick from the fire, she lights it and then, raising her head, exhales a large gust of smoke.

Emely breathes deep. Her grandmother smoked a pipe, too.

Ogotu addresses Emely again. "You have something on you that talks to people the way smoke talks to the sky," she says, staring at her across the fire. "It lets people know where you are."

"What are you talking about?" Emely replies. "I don't know what you mean."

"It's there," the old woman says and points to her backpack.

Emely moves her hands across the flap of the backpack, feels something hard beneath the cloth. Leaning it over, she sees for the first time that the seam of the flap has been ripped. She tweezers her fingers between the ripped cloth, feels between the folds, and extracts an object about the size of a watch battery. She knows what it is immediately. A GPS unit. But who put it there? Who would care about where she is?

"We will throw it into the river tomorrow," Ogotu says. "Then the ones who follow you will only know the home of fish."

So much mystery in this place. How did the old woman know it was there?

She has no chance to think any of this through, however; the young girl is tapping her on her arm. "You haven't asked me what my name is," she says.

Emely turns to her. "Well then," she says with a smile. "I will ask now. What is your name?"

The young girl doesn't return her smile. "Chipkorie," she replies seriously. "But it's soon going to change." Her voice brings with it light flickering across trees, the soft smudge of shadows.

"Why is that?" Emely asks.

"Because soon I'll be a woman, and then I can marry."

Emely is not really that surprised. People in her country are so poor it is common for girls to marry at a young age for the price of a dowry.

"Our Mother is so unhappy," Chipkorie says. She leans over and rubs some of the forest hog fat from her fingers onto her legs. In the firelight, her skin glows red-brown. "On the morning I am cut, if my blood doesn't run long, the world will grow dark again and we won't be anymore. The time is coming close."

Emely remembers the cultural information she presented in her master's thesis about the Okino traditionally practicing female genital mutilation. They couldn't possibly still practice that barbaric ritual, could they? One more time she reaches for the oblivion that waits for her inside the bamboo. Maybe they are talking about cutting themselves on their arms the way her mother did.

Ogotu, listening, picks up the subject as well. "If Chipkorie's blood doesn't run long that morning," she says, "there will be no more births.

No more will children move from the darkness that is their mother into the light of the sky. Water will rise and become our new sky. No one will float through time on the raft of their names because no one will be called by their names anymore. And what we know is that inside of the word for us, we carry the sound of all the beating hearts who are nameless." Her voice, flicked with fear, flows rusty through the pipe of her throat. "The stories spoken long ago in this cave have come true." She stares across the fire at Emely. "Tomorrow I will sculpt your face from time's pale clay. Then you will rise and talk to the Great Mother."

She dips her head, sucks on the pipe, exhales a great cloud of smoke. "I'm not frightened for myself," she continues. "I'm too old to rise tall again. I already have one foot in the country of death. But I am frightened for what I leave behind." Another puff on her pipe. "Did your grandmother tell you anything about the ways of the Stone Woman? I know you didn't learn much from your mother."

Emely doesn't know how to respond. How does this old woman know anything about what she learned from her mother and grandmother? "Grandmama did tell me some things but I don't remember too much," she eventually says. "I was pretty young when she died."

"The first time I grew tall was during a time of no water," Ogotu says. "It was just after my cutting and my marriage. There was no rain. Sun beat down on us day after day, moon followed moon, day followed day, but the sky was silent. The soil of the forest became dust and though we sang our most sacred songs trying to pull down rain, nothing came. It grew so hot that just drawing in breath was like breathing fire."

She glances at Emely. "Rain means that you are being touched by the sky, you know. Each of us missed that feeling. My father walked with a new stoop and my mother grew listless. She was one of the most holy, had been a tall one even at a young age, and yet when I looked into her eyes there was no color." She sighs. "Animals began to die. When we walked the paths of our Mother I would think I saw a sleeping animal but when I leaned over and picked it up, whatever it was—rabbit or mouse or baby antelope—it had dead, glazed eyes."

The old woman sucks on her pipe for a moment then seems to reach her voice back toward the time when she lived this story. Chipkorie moves over, sits down by her feet.

"The time our great river shrank and became just a thin trickle with no music under its skin was a sad time for us all," Ogotu continues.

"The river became shallow, rose only to my ankles. All that should have been underneath was seen. Stones that had never known the heat of the sun were suddenly exposed and grew hotter than some bellies. The birds grew fewer in number. At first I heard thin music from beaks, and then nothing at all. Our people began to leave. They strayed away one by one, and if they returned at all, they talked your talk, Amely. They smelled different and chattered of the blank world. We blamed them, the ones who had left, for the sky's continuing punishment.

"As though the sun was trying to boil them out of us, our beliefs grew small and our songs grew faint, and when the river became just a slim line running between our stones, we even began to forget to thank our Mother.

"One day I went to a place that had once been a lake but was now only a pond. I saw below me, half in, half out, a great, stranded fish. Its mouth was still under water, but its body was in the air. Sky's color glinted on its scales. I knew it would not live much longer; when I picked it up it didn't even resist, but its sides heaved with the need to be alive.

I held the fish as though I was holding a special secret. I placed it in a cradle of green leaves, carried it carefully to water that was deeper, and lowered it in. The great fish slipped out of my hands, circled twice, then sank back into the mystery of its world.

The next morning I looked at my mother and I knew she was dying. I ate nothing, loved nothing, dreamt nothing, and then, one sorrowful morning, I gave birth to nothing. It was a small pain that gradually became a greater pain that caused me to kneel, and then the pain pushed something out into my hands. It came out half formed, an almost-daughter without eyes. I stared at this almost-daughter, looked at the sky, and howled."

There is the glint of tears in Ogotu's eyes, and when she continues her voice is moist with feeling. Chipkorie leans her head against her grandmother's knees.

"The day after I gave birth, my mother chose to die, and I became the holy cutter. There was an initiate ready to be cut. I was empty. No longer did I carry my daughter, no longer could I hold my mother. But I knew we needed our world to be in balance again.

"It was a good cut. The sharp piece of glass slid easily through the initiate's skin, and though her little legs shook violently, she didn't cry out. Then, as required, I danced, but nothing came up from inside me to join the sky."

Though Emely knows she shouldn't interrupt, she does. The alcohol in the bamboo has made her brave. "Excuse me," she says cautiously. "I just need some clarification on a little matter. What kind of cutting are you talking about?"

"Don't stop the story with your silly questions, new one!" Ogotu barks. "You should know these things!" The look she sends Emely is almost physical, pushes her back into silence.

Ogotu swallows, begins again. "The initiate's offering had been placed on a banana leaf," she continues. "I danced in a circle around the leaf. The blood she had dropped still stained the earth. Our guests began to leave the holy clearing, but I continued to dance.

"The moon rose and sent its light down on her offering. My feet began to find a rhythm. As the moon rose higher I began to sense that I was connecting with something above me. My husband came back, wanted me to drink water, but I shook my head; I did not yet deserve to drink.

"I did not realize at first that I was being lengthened. It was only when I put back my head and opened my mouth to try to swallow moon's light that I felt it. One side of my body was hard, the other soft. I knew then what I was becoming and joy rushed through me. My mother had convinced the ancestors to choose me to honor the forest; I was becoming the new Stone Woman.

"As I danced that night I came into a great power—a power that could cause the sun to set, the moon to rise, a fish to surface in the river. All the graves of all my ancestors were inside of me. I looked down from a great height. The tender offerings of the initiate were resting like a bird's nest on the green leaf, and suddenly from between them came blood—bright red, jewel-like blood.

"I grew longer, wider, tried to dance higher. The flesh placed on the leaf before me became clasped hands holding what was fast becoming a red geyser. It was a beautiful red—not the red from our wombs, not even the red from our cutting, this richness came from the earth itself, life-affirming and thick."

Emely shifts uncomfortably. She doesn't understand much of what the old woman is saying, and finds herself hoping this is a story about any other sort of cutting than female genital mutilation. Not wanting to alienate her host, however, she suppresses the urge to ask again for clarification.

"The blood rose until it lapped against my ankles," Ogotu says. "I bent over and put my hand into it. My hand brushed against scales, and then, breaking the surface, came a great fish, the same fish I had saved. I saw moonlight on its scales. I looked into its eyes, and it looked into mine, and when it began to speak I knew that nothing ever died, for it spoke to me in my mother's voice.

"'Rain will soon come,' my mother told me. She told me that night not to grieve for her, for she was still here. She said that if I lived the right way, I would have a son, and this baby would live. 'Don't keep your loving careful,' she told me. 'Don't stand inside the lines of what is alive and what isn't. With your husband you have moved from one to two, but soon you will be three, and all the space between you will be filled with family. Remember to speak to your son daily, for then he will choose you and be born.'

"She told me that there is a fierce beauty in a mother's wait to know her child's face. 'Dream your secrets and wish your wishes until they bloom,' she told me that night. 'For just as surely as you choose the furs you wear, you choose the person you allow yourself to become.'

Ogotu smiles. "The next morning it began to rain, and I began to live differently. I began to live my life as a river, knowing always I would be carried toward answers, and I've never again allowed myself to become so small that I couldn't bring down rain from the sky." She reaches out and strokes her hand across Chipkorie's head. "These are powerful female teachings, granddaughter," she says softly, "and I have tried to use all my voice in these words. As I speak so does my mother, my grandmother, and all the ones who came before us, all the way back to the great river. They are gathered here too, sitting beside us, listening as well."

She looks up at Emely. "I'm giving you these words, and they are warm with me. I am too old to climb the sky anymore but I still remember what I learned that day long ago. The day my mother appeared to me as a fish, I learned that the womb and the ancestors are all one and my thoughts alone can bring down rain. That day I began to listen. You must do the same. Only the river remembers from where we came. If we ever forget as we did in the time of no rain, the river and its creatures will remind us, if we just become listeners again."

Old Tempi stands, takes a stick out of the fire, and walks to the door of the cave. He draws the stick across the sky, and Emely almost expects whole chunks of the night to fall. Looking almost like written language, the red lines linger for a moment. Just as she thinks she can read their message, however, they disappear.

I really hope she isn't talking about female genital mutilation, she thinks to herself one more time. *Chipkorie would be just about the right age.* She stares at the young girl. *So perfect, so lovely. How could anyone think of cutting any single part of her?*

The thought is as violent as assaulting moonlight. She brings her knees in close, clasps her arms around them tight.

CHAPTER 52

The Great Mother sends her voice lamenting through the trees:

My new Stone Woman will soon ride the song of remembering, and when she rides this song she will begin to cry. This is my prayer this night. Let her one solitary tear be an opening through which she can pass and then, quiet, humble, and listening, may she enter my sky and be so loved she will finally become all kind sky.

No cuts of red against the night sky can explain what happens next. As though it has stepped out of the old woman's story, an enormous creature arrives at the mouth of the cave, and it doesn't matter in the least that Emely had seen separate parts of it hung in the trees, had carried its liver on her back yesterday, an hour ago had even ate its meat. The forest hog is alive, the expression on his face as fierce as it was yesterday when she saw it hanging in the trees.

Emely staggers to her feet. "Run!" she says, but no one listens.

Its great domed head magnified against the wall, the forest hog moves to the center of the cave. Old Tempi reaches behind him and pulls out an instrument fashioned from a dried gourd, strung with what appears to be animal gut. He places the instrument on his lap, begins to strum. "River current we love," he sings, "leaves we love, stones singing to the sky." He smiles at his wife and granddaughter. "Yes, yes, we are wild."

Though the old man's back is straight and his fingers are sedate, the music he strums on the gourd is anything but. Almost giggling to itself, the song travels forward. Chipkorie rises and approaching the hog, raises her arms, begins to swing her hips back and forth.

Emely sees for the first time the woman the girl is going to become. She is already beginning to swell from some parts of her body. But Chipkorie is innocent of this new power beginning to occupy her; never having been used, she doesn't yet know how to use.

Taking gigantic steps, she begins to run around and around the cave, stirring the stories of the paintings on the wall with her body. "We are wild, we are hope," she sings in time with Old Tempi's strumming. "Soon the animal of the world will live again." Then she stops in front of the forest hog and takes a mighty jump. Branding the night, she hangs in the air—and then, landing on her feet, she begins to circle the cave once again, pausing only to turn and smile briefly at the woman she had momentarily become.

Home rasps against homelessness, knowing rasps against unknowing, everything Emely knows suddenly contracts—the girl has just jumped on the back of one of the painted horses. Traveling forward in time's endless loop, the horses painted on the walls of the cave toss their manes. Emely tries to look at boundaries, but animals and humans have merged with the story of evolution painted on the walls and Old Tempi, sweating, pulls the song from the center of the earth. There's a sound in his voice that searches for the part of Emely his wife had just tried to call alive with her story.

As Emely listens to the old man's song, she begins to see pictures. Water slides across the bow of a ship, light shines through beveled stained glass windows, a heavy gray sky, and the slide of snow. How can a simple vegetable that has known only forest dirt, string that has known only the insides of an animal, sing the song of snow?

She glances over at Mentegai. "We are wild," he sings, eyes half closed. "We are hope." Then he, too, stands and begins to dance with the forest hog. As though to make his acreage greater, he pulls his dreads up over his head, a small smile on his face, as if he is remembering something he doesn't quite know.

The bamboo is once again in Emely's hands. She dips her head, swallows deep the taste of longing. It doesn't take a GPS unit to tell her she is as far away from what she knows as she could be.

One more time the leopard pulls the long howl of his voice across the trees. A wild frenzy fills the cave. Past and future spin into the night. Old Tempi puts down his instrument and, approaching the forest hog, begins to pump his body against the animal in a way that long ago he made the parent who had in turn made his granddaughter. The smell of roasted meat mixes with human sweat.

Emely has reached the hard stone buried deep inside the song's mirth. The forest people's dreads swing; the hog, glad to be standing on two legs, turns its great head. Emely would swear she sees its eyelids going up, going down.

Floating somewhere between what she thinks she knows and what she is soon to know, Emely stands unsteadily as well, joins the strange singing. Without even realizing it, somehow she knows the words. "Stones we love," she sings. "We send our song into the sky."

Cheeks rouged with fire, she has dropped deep into memory's well. She is what the paintings, kind and human, are telling her; she is their story alive. She is here with her great-great-ever-so-great grandmother, spinning her shadow against the walls. Like the old woman's story, she will make rain with her body, turn a storm with song.

All propriety, all boundaries disappear. Part of this amorous dark, Mentegai's face glows before her. Emely wants to stay in this strange, limbic dream forever; this new, thoroughly occupied version of her surges with lust. She wants to mingle her breath with his, swallow all the parts of him, taste his skin, see his eyes shine just with her. She could live by firelight alone as long as it was alongside this man who could make her daughter, who could make her daughter's daughter, who could make her daughter's daughter's daughter. . .

Pushing against the great possibility of this night with the promise of her body, she approaches him and, standing before him, begins to match the swing of his hips with her own.

She reaches up to touch his face. Bemused, he stares at her, but doesn't rebuff her hand.

Chipkorie wraps the chain of forest hog intestines around her neck.

"When I finally drop my blood on the morning of the cutting," she announces, "it will run full and rich and glad. I won't cry out, and then our Mother's love will drift over us once again."

A knife appears in the girl's hand. Old Tempi begins a new chant. "Cut, cut, cut!"

The forest hog comes close. "Cut, cut, cut," it says, voice muffled. "I need blood in order to live again."

The chant moves into the time between the words. The young girl's pretty face becomes tight with concentration.

"Cut, cut, cut!"

The knife hovers over her arm and Emely notices for the first time that both her arms are laced with cuts. Maybe this is her answer; they don't practice female genital mutilation after all. But just as she tried to stop her mother from cutting herself a few days ago, she has to stop the girl from hurting herself. She turns away from Mentegai. "Don't!" she yells and, springing forward, tries to grab the knife from the young girl.

Chipkorie's face turns hard; she turns her back to Emely, slides the knife across her arm. Bright red blood immediately flowers against her skin.

Old Tempi throws his fist up into the air. "Yes!" he cheers.

The girl begins to spread the blood across her beautiful body. "This is only beginning blood," she murmurs, "but soon there will be more."

The song begins to slide downward, the fire burns lower, and the people in the cave gradually become silent. When Ogotu takes off the head of the forest hog and throws it into the fire, for the first time Emely understands the mechanics behind the illusion. The old woman's face is scabbed with blood. Without saying a word, she goes to the back of the cave and lies down.

Music no longer racing through their bloodstream; the people in the cave seems lost to Emely, unjoined. Even the moon seems less round. Mentegai doesn't even look at her. Crawling toward different places in the cave, they all go to sleep, curling around themselves, not each other.

Floating down the river on the tiny raft of her name, Emely stares into the fire. She is the only one to see flames enter the forest hog's head and dance in the now empty eyes, and the dead, watching above, are the only ones to see their new Stone Woman dip her head and begin to cry.

CHAPTER 53

What the dead do all the way through time is sing, dreaming that you, the alive ones burdened with flesh, will hear. Our new Stone Woman heard us last night, but will she hear us in the bright light of day? It is her destiny to find the oldest object in the world, a stone tablet made thousands of years before Christ—and when she finds it, she must be clean enough, pure enough, to follow the instructions engraved on its surface.

The next morning when Emely wakes she thinks she is in her grave—walls closing in, mouth dry, headache coming on, her Great-Grandmama-given name chiseled into the stone above her head.

Wait a second; if you're dead you don't have a headache, do you?

And then she remembers. Wild, lyrical singing mixed with blood, head thrown back, hips grinding against Mentegai's, the place where her body was inhabiting the place where her mind wasn't. Sexuality, lust, hope . . . last night she wrote desire on the cave walls.

There must have been strong alcohol in that tube of bamboo.

How could she have been so stupid? Drinking with the very same subjects she is supposed to be studying, hung over on her first real day . . . she closes her eyes. *I'm going to have to be a lot more careful.*

But she also admits something else to herself. *I don't like this place. I don't like any of this.* Because she knows something. It wasn't just alcohol that loosened her last night. Some kind of otherness caused her to climb out of what she knows. There is another world here, a world of shadows she wants nothing to do with. And the story about cutting and blood? She doesn't want to think about what she has stumbled into.

Six weeks, she tells herself. *Get in, get out. Just do your job.*

She sits up, brushes a few leaves from her hair, looks around her. The cave is empty. She goes through her bag; her equipment all seems to be okay, thank goodness. She pulls out her recorder. "First-Day Interview," she writes in big, bold letters on a Post-it. She takes off her bloody T-shirt, puts on a fresh one.

In and out, she thinks again. *Just do your job. Time to talk to the professor.*

When she turns the radio on, the thick hum that immediately rises from the machine makes her feel brave. "CD1245," she says, extending the antenna. She turns up the volume, speaks into the microphone. "CD1245. Are you there, sir? Over."

The machine is silent. "CD1245, base camp here," she repeats, more loudly. "Are you there? Come in. Over."

The radio gives off a crackling sound. The professor's smooth voice rises from the box. "I hear you, Emely. How are you? Over."

Delighted, she smiles. "I'm very well. I'm here in the forest. Over."

"Fine, fine." The professor's voice is hearty. "Have you met the Okino yet?"

"Yes," she replies. "I'm here with them now. We brought them a forest hog as a gift, and they're going to let me stay."

"Have you been able to do any documentation yet?"

"No, not yet, sir; it's only the first day. But I don't think it's going to be a problem. There's plenty of rich folklore, and they seem fairly comfortable with me. As I said, we brought in a butchered forest hog, and last night the Okino honored the pig with dancing and song." She knows she should tell him about the story of blood, decides to summarize it as best as she can: "They seem to practice bloodletting in some kind of coming-of-age ceremony. Last night a young girl cut her arms. I don't know too much about it, but I'll get back to you with more information."

"Fascinating, Emely. Why weren't you recording?"

"I'm sorry, sir." She doesn't want to tell him about the alcohol. "I was very tired from the journey in. I'll get the next ritual. It won't be a problem. Another thing that was a little strange is that the old woman somehow knew there was a GPS unit hidden in my backpack. She had me take it off, and she's going to throw it in the river, but do you know who would have put it on me?"

Silence then. She turns up the volume button. "Can you hear me, sir? Are you there?"

His voice charges in, robust and clear. "Yes, I'm here, Emely," he replies. "I have no idea who would have put that GPS unit on your backpack. Do you have your coordinates?"

"No, sir. Again, I'm sorry. I'll get them to you the next time I report in to you. I just wanted to tell you I've arrived safely."

"I'm glad to hear that, Emely. Just be sure to get me those coordinates. We need to keep track of you."

"Yes, sir, I understand. I think I'm going to be able to bring you back some amazing documentation. I've already been able to ascertain that their god seems to be a relatively benign Earth mother archetype. She is called the Mother, and is both entreated to and appeased, and what can't be explained seems to be attributed to her. According to a rather grim story the old woman told last night, they believe in a deity called the Stone Woman, and they seem to believe that she is chosen from the tribe to serve this Mother. The belief structure I'm learning about here seems to match up with the little we already know about the tribe. As I learn more, I'll be getting specific reports back to you."

"Very interesting," the professor responds. "Sounds rather like the Jivas in Polynesia. Their religion is based on a concept of an interpersonal supernatural power called the Gakarna. Just remember your main objective is to study their beliefs, record their stories. Let me know of any rituals you observe. We are in a rare position to study a tribe that has lived so close to dominant culture and yet seems to have remained relatively intact."

"I'll do my best sir. I do have a question for you," Emely says. "The old woman, the tribe's matriarch, seems to feel that I'm here for a special reason."

"What do you mean? Explain."

"She says she called me into the forest and that I have some kind of role to play in the tribe's belief structure."

"That's wonderful!" the professor exclaims. "They might reveal more to you now. Get in there, record their stories. Record their ceremonies, find their artifacts. Have you had a chance to ask them about the sacred tablet?"

"They haven't mentioned it yet, sir, but as I said, I've only been here one night. I know it's a high priority for you. I'll ask, I promise."

"All right. As soon as you hear anything, contact me. I need results. Again, your role, Emely, is to record, record, record. Get me your coordinates in your next report. I'm signing off now. Good luck. Over and out."

His voice cuts off, and the radio is silent.

CHAPTER 54

Looking none the worse for wear, the forest people and Mentegai are sitting by a small fire out in the middle of the clearing. No hog's head in sight.

"Good morning," Emely says brightly. No one answers. Trying not to look at Mentegai, she sits down on a rock.

"Thank you for letting me stay with you," she says tentatively.

No answer, but she does notice that the old man scrapes the stick in his hand a little faster.

She pushes on. "I'm sorry things got a little bit out of hand last night. I think I must have been really tired." A pause, then a smile. "And maybe I had a little bit too much to drink."

No one responds. She will have to think of another way to start this conversation. She remembers the professor's instructions: "Record, record, record."

She turns to Chipkorie, holds out her recorder. "You said last night that your name is going to change because you're going to become a woman. Does that mean you are soon going to marry? Are there others living in this forest?"

The mountains are steeped in morning's blue air, the moon dim in the sky. The girl doesn't answer.

Mentegai looks up and coos a soft sound. Two pigeons fly out of the sky and land on his hands; no flicker of gladness in their round bland eyes, telegraphing nothing about where they came from or what their journey was like—they are simply home, home in Mentegai's hands.

He bends down, tenderly brushes his lips across each feathered head.

"Your father could do that," Old Tempi says. "Pull birds from the sky."

And then, quiet indented only with the sound of the old man's knife against a stick. No one speaks for a long time.

Why hasn't Mentegai said one thing or at least looked at her? She finds herself wanting to rest in his two hands. This man who clutches feathers in his hands, holds flight and stay, here and gone, come, stop, and go—suddenly she wants her gone captured by him. She finds herself staring at his bare feet. There's a large space between his big toe and the next; just as his toes bracket space, his few words bracket silence.

Immediately she is mortified by her thoughts. *Stop it*, she tells herself. *Stop this nonsense right now! Last night was one thing, but now it's time to get control. Don't let some barefooted hippie with an overly romantic idea about his ancestry distract you. Six weeks, that's all. Get in and out. Just do your job.* Again the professor's voice echoes in her ears: "Record, record, record."

Holding out the recorder, Emely turns to Ogotu. "Last night you said the forest hog came alive," she says. "Do you believe that animals come alive when you dance?"

Hair like coiled winter, the old woman has the face of endurance. She looks at her as though she knows something about her, just hasn't decided whether to fill her in or not.

"And this entity, the Great Mother," Emely persists, "do you sacrifice animals to her?"

"Nothing empty in her," Ogotu mutters under her breath. "Nothing inside that hasn't already been claimed."

Mentegai shakes his head as well, and like the old man begins to scrape his knife against the piece of wood. Each cut says what his words don't have to: "I am not this woman. I am not like her in any way."

No! She will not be deterred either by the old woman's mutterings, the space between Mentegai's toes, or the sound of that knife. First-Day Interview, bold letters.

She turns to Chipkorie. "Did you make that bracelet on your ankle?" she asks.

The girl doesn't seem to mind answering this question. "My mother made it for me," she responds softly. "She has one just like it." When she leans over to pat some of Old Tempi's shavings into a small hill, the rough lion mane bars of her hair slide forward, all the more severe because each dread leans against the soft plumpness of her cheeks.

Emely wants to ask where her mother is, but something in Ogotu's face warns her not to. There's also the fact that the old woman has once again picked up a small stone, is beginning to pass it back and forth between her fingers. And she's muttering again. "I don't know if I can do this," she says under her breath, staring at Emely all the while. "Everything she knows is only a shout. She can't hear what is being whispered."

Words tossed, stones tossed.

Don't look, Emely tells herself. *Don't get caught in that small melody of stone.*

But she can't turn away from what Ogotu says next. "A part of you remembers when you were a frog and lived in these trees," she says.

Emely's eyes widen. "What?" she asks. She even forgets to turn on the recorder.

"Yes," the old woman says, nodding her head. "A long time ago, a large chunk of soil carrying some frogs broke away from this place and floated down the river to the big water. The frogs landed in faraway dirt. After a long time they grew longer legs, climbed into trees, and became something other than frogs. Then, after even more time passed, those frogs became you. That part, deep inside, is what I am trying to call alive."

She puts down the stone and, reaching into her leather skirt, once again brings out her pipe. Lighting it with a small stick from the fire, she lifts it to her mouth, sucks deep, releasing a cloud of smoke through her nose.

"Do you know how important you are to the world's story?" she asks, squinting through the smoke. "The world's first breath is still inside of you. Do you understand?" Her eyes are deep, penetrating.

What Emely understands is that she's going to do some bragging to the professor when she next gets on the radio. "Subjects communicating, sharing their world," she will report. She wishes she weren't so central to their stories, but she remembers what he urged her to do: use any mistaken belief they have about her to garner trust.

"When we were born," Ogotu says, "we needed air. Our Mother sent us trees to clean our air so that we could breathe."

"Yes," Emely says eagerly. "Is this a story your mother told you? Did her mother tell it to her? How far back do you think this belief goes?"

The old woman gives her a disgusted look. Everyone grows quiet.

The sun rises high in the sky. Heat crushes the silence like a giant French press. *What would Margaret Mead do in this situation?*

The rumble in her stomach reminds Emely she is hungry. She remembers the meat Mentegai offered last night. "I brought some millet in with me," she offers. "I'd be happy to share with you."

Not even a glance in her direction. No one responds.

Wait a sec. She has another trick up her sleeve. Trying to catch everyone's eye, she holds the recorder out toward Chipkorie. "Say something," she says with an encouraging smile, and presses the red recording button.

Turns out people all over the world say the same thing. "What should I say?" Chipkorie asks.

Emely rewinds the recorder, plays it back. "What should I say?" floats into the clearing, not even as loud as the waterfall.

The girl's eyes widen. "Who's that?" she asks.

"That's you!" Emely says. "That's why I'm asking so many questions. It's so I can take what you say out into the world and people can hear it."

"But why would they want to hear what I have to say?" Chipkorie asks.

"That's not my granddaughter," Old Tempi snarls, a cold rasp in his voice. "She would never be caught inside that thing. It's like a honey hive. It only holds what is left behind."

After staring at the young girl for a second, Emely agrees. Her full innocence spills in on her. This girl who hums to bees and is hummed to in return, this girl so lovely that even at this very moment the plants behind her are scrambling to grow vines strong enough to hold the perfect berry of her face—yes, the old man is right. This little box she is holding could only contain the honey of what is left behind.

But then her eyes wander down to the cuts on the girl's arms, and another memory spills in on her. The slice of the knife the night before, the flowering of her blood. And what did she say? "This is only beginning blood."

She puts down the recorder.

A lather of white feathers, and a large bird lands on a rock a few feet away. Two steely eyes, a sharp beak, the bird looks Emely over for a moment. Along with everyone else in the clearing, it apparently doesn't like what it sees. Seeking freedom and expanse, it takes off into the sky, flying so close to her as it goes she can feel the wind from its wings, and for a moment she lives its expanded version of the world.

But only for a moment. Once again, the descent of that French press. No motivation, energy, or verbs; even the waterfall's splash doesn't sound like music anymore. She watches Chipkorie twirl the bracelet on her ankle, tries not to look at the old woman who is once again tossing that stone back and forth between her hands. Flies move across the dirt.

It's boredom that's going to get to me.

But when Chipkorie begins to talk again, Emely's response is so careless she almost wishes they could return to silence.

"Why do people on the outside always want to know where we are and what we are doing?" she asks.

The answer pops out before Emely can catch it: "It's the government who wants to know."

"What's government?" Chipkorie asks.

It doesn't take Mentegai's hiss to know she has made a terrible mistake. "What an amateur," he scoffs. "Everything you do and say brings the outside world into this place. Getting Chipkorie to talk into that recorder, introducing the idea of outside ownership . . . you're showing off, that's all. Ever heard of contaminating pure field research with the mention of an oppressive outside source?"

Emely remembers now that he studied anthropology with the professor, too.

"Oh, shut up," she snaps. "You wouldn't even be here if Ogotu hadn't told you to bring me in," she reminded him once more.

But though she has defended herself, she knows he's right. She is an amateur, and she has made a mistake. The only question remaining is, what is she going to do about it?

She begins cautiously. "The people on the outside have decided that the people who have occupied the land the longest will own the land. If you tell me your stories, people on the outside will know that you've lived here for a long time and they will let you keep the land." A solicitous smile; she's building steam. "Think of it!" She passes her hand across the clearing. "All of this could be yours. Then no one will be able to come in and cut down the trees. They might even name it after you!"

But she is only making things worse. Mentegai turns his back to Emely and scrapes harder on his stick. Ogotu joins his contempt with scrutiny so intense it's like a spiritual MRI. The look she sends Emely should by all rights knock her over. "Don't you know if you name every-thing, you break the world into pieces?" she asks scornfully. She thumps her walking stick. "The only land we will ever own is the land inside our stories." Rising slowly, she walks over to a bag slumped against the side of the cave. Unfurling a piece of skin, she pours the contents of the bag on the ground. It looks like pale clay. She sits down and begins to knead the clay between her strong hands.

"Maybe if I get her face, I can add more quiet to it," she mutters.

Chipkorie, as usual, doesn't mind responding. "But we could never own the forest," she says, the two small lines on either side of her mouth like dainty quotation marks. "That's like saying somebody owns the raindrops!"

For the first time that morning, everyone laughs. Even Emely joins in.

"Why does everybody from the outside want to tell us what to do?" Chipkorie continues. "Remember Unduly? He left the forest for a while, and when he came back from the blank world he wanted us to cut down all the trees, grow food in straight rows. He said that anyone who believed in the Mother would burn in a hot place filled with fire. He even said that all our ancestors were in that place."

"No wonder the Mother pushed him out," Old Tempi says. "I think the blank world swallowed part of his brain."

"He smelled like the blank world, too," Chipkorie says. "Sweet, but something fake underneath." She turns to Emely. "You don't smell that way, though."

Not quite sure how to respond, Emely smiles politely. "Thank you."

"I'm not like Unduly," Chipkorie says. "I would never leave this for-est. This dirt holds all of those who came before. If I were ever to leave this place, my ancestors would miss me when they walked at night." She turns to Emely. "A person never really belongs to the land unless a part of him is buried under the ground, you know."

"Interesting," Emely says, encouraged. As discreetly as she can, she turns the recorder back on.

Ogotu, in the meantime, is working the clay furiously. She flattens the clay into a sheet and then, pinching her fingers, pulls it upward into a point. With a slice of her hand, she cuts a line of tension, and miraculously, a human being's rough shape emerges. More tugs and two cheekbones are stroked into being. Could that even be a smile? The old woman stares at it a moment, decides it's not quite right, and with the smash of her hand returns the clay to its elemental existence of sand and moisture; then, leaning over, she begins all over again.

More faces emerge, then disappear. Rolling, punching, kneading, discarding, she's completely immersed in the rhythm of her work, building then dismantling all over again.

Chipkorie still seems to be musing about the outside world. "The ones from the outside think that every story begins with them. But what Grandma says is that every story holds all of its yesterdays."

Emely nods her head. "Go on," she says with a smile.

"The blank world doesn't know that the world is like a person," Chipkorie continues. "It remembers everything. Those from the outside come into our trees and don't even walk across our Mother with bare feet. They stand in our streams and shoot our animals and don't say thank you for what they take."

She glances up at Emely. "They're like you. They say they are coming into the forest for our animals, their meat and tusks, but what they're really searching for is themselves."

Old Tempi jumps in. "And what about that animal?" he asks. "The animal that talks to itself? It makes smoke and cuts down our trees and sounds so lonely."

Probably a chainsaw, Emely thinks, but she's learned her lesson from dropping the word "government"; she decides to keep this insight to herself.

"Our green is only as small as the pupil of an eye," Chipkorie continues. "But Grandma says when I drop blood the Mother will grow strong again."

Emely doesn't want to hear about blood, but remembering the professor's edict, she keeps the red button of the recorder turned on.

Fortunately, the young girl doesn't stay on that subject. "We haven't had meat for a long time," she says. "For a while, we found the bones of animals, and that gave us animal energy, but now even those are gone. Grandpa makes carvings of the animals he wants to come to his spear. Show her, Grandpa."

Apparently the old man would do anything for his granddaughter—even engage with Emely. Reaching into a small bag tied around his waist, he extracts a small wooden bird so perfectly carved she is immediately drawn into its diminutive world. Light shimmers across its miniature feathers.

"It's wonderful!" Emely gushes. "Perfect!" She reaches for her camera, begins snapping pictures. "What an artist you are!"

Though Chipkorie casts an uneasy eye at the camera, she still smiles proudly.

Old Tempi's eyebrows are salted with white, and his large ears are like a little boy's, alert and looking for secrets. Safe behind the lens of the camera, Emely studies him closely. A mole beneath his right eye is so emphatic it becomes the destination for all glances. His hands are beginning to knob with arthritis. And his hair! Dreadlocked into one long hose, his hair leaves his body and curls across the ground like a primordial tail.

"Are there any more carvings?" she asks.

Clearly reluctant, Old Tempi nevertheless reaches into his bag and pulls out a carving of a forest hog. He places it on the dirt next to the bird. Light shines from its beady eyes and small, vicious tusks.

"These carvings are amazing!" Emely exclaims. Can it get any better than this? Emely Matei, almost PhD, doing her job. No more yielding now—she's clicking away with all her might, moving back through the arteries of the camera into a darkened auditorium, a PowerPoint presentation glazing the screen with this very photograph, "First-Day Interview" written in bold letters across the screen.

The old man produces another small carving, this one of a dog, nose pointed upward as though he's sniffing the air. He places it on the dirt beside the other two. He slides one finger across the dog's back, and his smile breaks the template of his usually severe expression.

"Each carving I make is like finding a new love," he says, "but this one I like the best." His voice reaches back to the time when the dog was alive. "I loved this animal so much. He died before you were born, Chipkorie. I loved him so much that now I have many dogs, so I don't have to feel that one single feeling again. It was too hard when he left."

Suddenly, he looks up. A monkey has appeared in the trees above, is staring down at them with small, lively, intelligent eyes. "Don't move," Old Tempi whispers. He reaches behind him, grabs a long tube of bamboo, and then, raising the tube to his mouth, he fills his cheeks with air. A quick spitting sound, and his body lurches forward. The monkey springs away.

It's a continuous line of motion. Old Tempi throws down the tube, and in two steps is at Ogotu's side. "Wife," he yells, "can't you see what is happening?"

The old woman, head down, fingers working furiously, doesn't answer.

"I warned you," he says. "The new one is taking away our animals. She used her magic to swallow our granddaughter's voice!" He points toward Emely. "She made me miss the monkey! Raise your eyes, wife!"

Chipkorie catches some of the old man's agitation. She too stands, begins to pace back and forth in front of her grandmother. "Grandpa's right," she says. "It's all my fault!" Her thin cry pierces the air. "I'm not clean anymore. I've made myself wrong, and now it won't be a good cut." Her shoulders shake with sobs. "I was in that talking thing, and it made me dead!"

Once again she's being blamed. But this morning Emely is going to talk back. She might have used that careless word, "government"—and yes, last night she crossed professional boundaries—but this morning she's going to defend herself.

She places her hand on Chipkorie's arm. "Please," she says. "Please calm down. Let's sit down and talk this over."

The girl's arm is trembling. Her eyes burn with rage. "Don't touch me!" she snarls. "I don't want to be wrong again."

Ogotu is not paying attention to anything her family is saying. "She's almost ready to dance," she says to herself.

Old Tempi's gaze hardens. "Wife," he warns, "can't you see? The new one's making us wrong."

Still trying to defend herself, Emely takes a step forward, but when she sees what Ogotu has created, she stops dead in her tracks.

What in the name of God? She's staring down at a perfect clay sculpture of herself. "I-I can't believe it," she stammers. "It's incredible!"

Me-myself-and-I fully captured, the face staring back at her looks just like her. Relaxed now, Ogotu sits back, places her hands on her hips, and smiles.

"Now that I see you, I can move what I see down into my hands," she says. She smiles even wider. "I think I've finally got it."

One arm and one leg are just roughed in, but it doesn't matter.

The clay is infused with here; Amely/Emely roars through the clay. So much beauty and promise. The sculpture has more to say than anything Emely has ever allowed herself to feel in life. And what is that around the edges? Hope?

Staring down at the sculpture, she is filled with a simple love for herself. It's as if for the first time, she really sees herself alive, and just seeing herself alive makes the strange fact of being alive known to her all over again.

"I've awakened the clay," Ogotu says proudly, "I found what it wanted to say as it lay for thousands of years along the riverbank." Her next words come out in a sudden rush of excitement. "Now that I've made you, you can rise tall and talk to the Mother."

Old Tempi doesn't like what he is hearing. "I told you, wife," he snarls, "someone from the blank world can never be a Stone Woman." Eyes flashing, he lunges at the sculpture and, turning his hand into a claw, reaches down, gouges the clay, then heaves it against the cave walls.

In dreamy slow motion, Emely sees one of her eyes slide down the wall, linger for a moment on a little ledge, then slip all the way down to the dirt floor.

CHAPTER 55

A river filled with storms, wind-swayed trees, this is what she knows, the dead say. *It is time for her to meet the people who stand still.*

❦

Ogotu doesn't seem to be too upset that her husband has destroyed her sculpture. "I'll make a new one tonight," she says, turning to Emely. "There will be more in your face after you see the others." She suddenly grabs Emely's wrist between her strong fingers. "The ones who have come before want to meet you."

Emely is not sure she wants to see what the old woman wants to show her, but it appears she doesn't have a choice. She barely has time to reach down for her fanny pack before Ogotu begins dragging her across the clearing to a high wall made of stone.

Hunching over, Ogotu spider-walks her fingers across the rocks until she finds one that is loose. She pulls on it, drops it to the ground, and pulls on the next. Soon the hole in the rock wall is people-sized. She climbs inside and turns toward Emely.

"Amely," she says, her face as creviced as the stones, "step inside. The ones who made you are waiting."

Amely doesn't want to climb into that hole, but remembering the professor's instructions—"Observe, record: this is the opportunity of a lifetime!"—she tightens the belt on her fanny pack and steps inside.

A dusty inside smell permeates the place, and it's so dark she can't even see what is right in front of her.

"Ogotu?" she asks tentatively. The sound of her voice echoes in the gloom. No answer; her words have been absorbed by the great silence of the place.

She tries again, this time fighting panic. "Ogotu?"

In the resounding gloom of the cave, the syllables of the old woman's name sound dropped.

Nothing. Where has the old woman gone?

And then a man appears before her. Staring straight at her, a spear raised over his head, he is completely white, the look on his face as pointed as that spear. Is he a ghost? Where is the old woman?

Another visage materializes behind him, this one an old woman holding a baby, one eyebrow raised in an arch of challenge.

"Ogotu?" she ventures one more time, heart hammering in her chest. No answer.

Who are these pale people? Are they another race made of stone? She wants to turn back and crawl out the hole back into the sun toward people who are the right color. She wants to see movement, any kind of movement.

This time she says her name softly. "Ogotu," she whispers. "Where are you?"

No answer. Another woman appears out of the gloom. Head back, her dreads fly in all directions. And then, behind her, a young girl with plump cheeks. As her eyes adjust to the dark, Emely realizes there must be hundreds of these still, white entities. As more men, women, and children appear before her she begins to feel as crowded as she used to feel riding the bus in Los Angeles. And she's beginning to understand. Desire, yearning, sexuality, grief immortalized, these are sculptures just like the one the old woman had just made of her.

"You see any part of yourself in any of them?" Ogotu reappears suddenly, stepping toward her. She sweeps her hand across the many faces.

Relieved, Emely turns to her. "They're astonishing!" she says. "Who made them?"

"Many, many women have made them," the old woman responds. "We pull their faces toward us from the clay."

"But why?" Emely asks. "Why do you make them?"

"To remember, of course," the old woman responds. "Some go back to the morning of time." The leaves that veil the opening of the cave shudder in a gust of wind. "Would you like to meet them?" she asks with a smile.

"I would love to," Emely says. She wishes she had brought her camera, wonders if Ogotu would let her go back for it. It's pretty dark in here, however, and she has never liked that shocked light of a flash. Would the old woman let her enlarge the hole to let in more light? *Don't push it*, she tells herself. *Establish trust. This is all pretty good for my first morning.*

Serving as a kind of hostess at a party, the old woman begins to lead Emely up and down the narrow aisles of the cave, introducing her to each sculpture. She nods toward a sculpture of an old woman smoking a pipe. "She was my great-great-grandmother," Ogotu confides. Even the delicate plume of smoke emanating from the sculpted pipe has been meticulously conveyed. "When I smoke my pipe I sometimes hold the shape of her old words in my mouth," Ogotu says.

She points next to a sculpture of a young woman holding a honey hive. "That one there is my great-grandmother."

"She has your eyes," Emely says.

Under Ogotu's direction, the cave begins to buzz with life and vitality; even the furs the sculptures wear transmit the dynamic force of long-dead animals.

"Who is that?" she asks, pointing to a sculpture of an old man. His back is to her, but the delicate, interlocked petals of each bone of his spine have been meticulously rendered.

"He was my grandfather," Ogotu responds and pulls Emely around to his front. He has uneven teeth, a wild and rakish smile. She snorts. "He was a bit of a rascal."

"I can tell," Emely says. She is so excited she can barely breathe. These statues are an inventory of people long gone. She wonders if the old woman would consent to be interviewed about each one. The sculptures are like a giant scrapbook chronicling the lives of everyone who has ever lived in this forest, a genealogical flowchart—a perfect vehicle to record the tribe's history. If the statues are as old as she thinks they are, this discovery is as important as King Tut's tomb. Her first piece of fieldwork will light the world on fire!

A familiar dream fills her head. In the National Gallery of Anthropology, these hundreds of lives, chronicled in alabaster clay, peer out from behind glass at the millions of people flowing by. A discreet brass plaque mounted on the wall declares, "Discovered and curated by Dr. Emely Matei." Maybe these very same faces can even grace the cover of *National Geographic*!

She turns back to Ogotu. "The artistry, the poetry!" she exclaims. "What incredible artists you are!" She has to work hard to dim down the commercial sound in her voice.

The old woman smiles proudly. "We try hard to find out what the clay has to say." She points to a sculpture of a young man. "You recognize that handsome fellow over there?"

Unlike the person who sits outside, Emely can look directly into his face without flinching. "That's Old Tempi," she exclaims.

"Yes," Ogotu responds. "His mother made that sculpture right before we got married."

She pulls her down the aisle toward a beautiful sculpture of a young woman smiling down at the baby she holds in her arms. Though made of bland, colorless clay, the sculpture radiates captured light. "You know who this is?" she asks with an almost girlish smile.

The artist has perfectly rendered the look of wonder a new mother feels when she finally meets the child grown under her heart for nine months.

"It's you!" Emely immediately exclaims. "You're so pretty."

"Thank you," Ogotu replies. "It was just after I gave birth to my son."

"The son your mother told you you would have," Emely says, remembering last night's story. "Is he living in another part of the forest?"

The old woman doesn't answer, but the next statue they pass by answers for her. This one also portrays Ogotu, but a new melancholy has entered her eyes.

Emely stops in front of it. "What happened?" she asks. "Why are you so sad?"

Wearing some of the sculpture's sadness on her face, Ogotu stares into its eyes. "Sometimes we have to tell people to leave these trees," she responds slowly. She seems to be wrestling with some question deep inside; then some new resolve passes across her features. "Come," she says. One more time Emely's wrist is grabbed. "I need to show you something. I think it is partly why you are here."

She pulls Emely to the back of the cave, where a cluster of sculptures stand. One depicts a toddler—plump, dimpled bottom, legs tiered with fat. The statue next to it is a little boy holding a bow and arrow; the last is a sculpture of a teenager, his lean, strong, muscles beginning to appear.

They are beautiful, of course, but what causes Emely to gasp is that each sculpture has no face. The place where their features should be have been obliterated.

"Who is this?" she asks. "What's happened to him?" The clay still resonates with the violence of slashed fingers.

The old woman crosses her arms. "This is my sister's son," she replies sadly.

"But why does he have no face?" Though the sculptures have no features, the terrible "I" of him still fills the cave.

"I did this to him," the old woman answers.

"But why?" Emely asks, and she's not asking anymore as an anthropologist; she's a person who wants to hear this story. She glances around. "He's the only one with no face."

The old woman is silent again, thinking. "I'll tell you," she says finally. "If you try to listen the right way."

She lowers herself slowly to the ground, pats the dirt beside her. "Sit down here," she says. If she notices that Emely has reached for her recorder and turned it on, she doesn't say anything.

"When that first sculpture was made," Ogotu says, nodding at the sculpture of the toddler, "six of us—me, Tempi, my sister, her son, my son, and the girl who would eventually become my daughter-in-law lived in the forest. We moved from place to place, and we always had fur to wear and meat to roast at night. The berries were so fat and sweet in those days, eating them was like eating songs. We took long journeys then, carrying our hunting knives, spears, fishnets, and fire sticks. Because there was no wrong, our Mother always sent us much to eat. It was a time when our children could eat from bones larger than any they had grown within them; there was always food in their tiny flower-bud hands. There was so much food we didn't have to live with our feet standing on two times, now and tomorrow. We didn't have to store our food or smoke it; we ate what was in front of us. We knew the next day would be the same as the last."

Something insinuating and dark moves beneath her words, and she is silent for a moment. When she begins again, her voice is lower.

"I knew from the beginning that my sister's son was different. Even as a little boy, his eyes held such emptiness, his gaze would make you feel lonely. He played with bones, not stones, liked to sit inside of places rather than out beneath our Mother's sky. He found the tightest caves to crawl into, the smallest caverns inside the trees. He talked to himself, but not to others.

"Once he brought me a lizard he had tortured. He had ruffled its scales, twisted its tail, tried to pull out one of its toes. The lizard was still alive, but barely, and the boy wanted to share with me his amusement at the creature's agony. I was so angry with him. I spoke to him about respect and kindness for our Mother's creatures, but I knew he wasn't really listening. After that, he just learned to hide his appetites from me and the others.

"Time grew taller," she continues, "and I watched wrong grow in my nephew. I could tell that my sister had begun to notice, as well. Her son would disappear, and when he returned to our fire he would smell like death. When he was almost a man, almost ready for his ceremony, I wanted to tell him to leave, but he was my sister's son and my hands, rounded, always hold family."

When Ogotu looks up, Emely sees a softer side of the old woman. Her eyes glisten with unshed tears. She has the authority of someone who has faced many hardships and, though she has always managed to slap them back, still grieves. "You see, Amely," she says in a moist voice, "my sister had known such sadness. She poured light into everything before her, but her husband had still left her. She had only this one child left to love." She shakes her head, speaks low. "But I will always carry a great burden for my silence."

Ogotu swallows, begins again. "Animals began to disappear. Our Mother wasn't happy. When I rose tall at night and asked her what was wrong, she told me I had to tell my nephew to leave. She told me wrong was growing in her belly and moving into her night.

"I was in agony, but still I didn't do anything. We began not to have enough to eat; the Mother was so unhappy with us, she began to keep her animals. But still I didn't do what our Mother needed."

Ogotu pauses for a moment, and when she speaks again her voice is filled with shame. "Then I found a gorilla with its hands cut off. I thought perhaps someone from the outside had entered our forest and had done this to one of our animals, but then the next moon I came across another, and then a short time later, another. They were sprawled on their backs, each with no hands. I knew then why we had no meat to eat. Our Mother was terribly angry; she was punishing us for what was being done to her creatures."

Emely remembers the gorilla's hand the boy had tried to sell her in the city. Had that animal lived once in this forest?

"I knew what our Mother needed," the old woman continues, "but I was trapped between my love for my family and my love for the Mother. I told my family to sing the song for gathering courage, but when we sang our songs they only scratched our throats. They didn't reach out far enough. And then Tempi came to me one morning.

"He's killing the gorillas," he told me. "Wife, it's our nephew"— and I knew then I had to step forward.

I finally spoke aloud the words I knew I had to say. "You must leave," I said to my nephew. "You must leave our trees and never come back. You have violated our Mother's animals, her people, and the teachings spoken under the great trees. You touch the bones of our creatures rather than their breath. You are wrong, and you are no longer family."

Her eyes shine with memory. "In my nephew's eyes I saw the beginning crawl of a new power—the same thing I see in you, Amely. But your power is good. My nephew's power was wrong, bent, distorted. He turned that morning, and without even kissing his mother good-bye left our world. It was then that I came into this cave and scratched out his face. I took his sleeping furs and burnt them over fire, making sure that the smoke sent every part of him straight up into the sky. I even swept the dirt where he had slept.

"My sister was generous in her grief. She didn't blame me. She understood why I had asked her son to leave. But she did blame herself, and I had no answers for her. I stayed with her as she grieved, and though I loved her, it wasn't enough. In the end, she chose to die.

"We never saw the Wrong One again, but sometimes when I walk through our shadows an old cold will enter me and I know then that I've just walked through one of his midnight schemes. I quickly leave those places, never go near them again."

Ogotu laughs a curious sound, but buried deep is a sound that holds tears. "We are the ones who remember," she says, slowly standing up. "We go back to the morning of time. While the rest of the world out there stumbles and falls, we are the ones who stand still. That's why I have told you this story."

Her right hand begins to circle the slack skin of her left hand. "One last womb, one last Stone Woman. Everyone else has either climbed the sky, dissolved in the light of the blank world, or been told to leave."

All those blank, staring eyes. It is the silence, even more than the clay, that keeps the statues frozen—a deep, reverberant silence as solid as a mold. *Don't look at those circling fingers,* Emely tells herself. *They will make you gone.*

But then she experiences another kind of gone. Ogotu suddenly throws back her head, closes her eyes, and releases a note from her throat so pure, so present, it seems to have its own physical form. That one note gradually swells, becomes two, then three. Heart hammering, rimmed with circles of gone, Emely stands as transfixed and still as one of those statues. Almost too loud to hear, the sound seems to come from the center of the Earth, visiting the old woman for only a moment. It's the kind of singing that needs a big sky behind it, and though it certainly is strange to be standing in a cave surrounded by hundreds and hundreds of immortalized lives, Emely finds that she's not frightened anymore. The singing has a predictable, remembered pulse as familiar to her as her own heartbeat.

Still aerobic with the movement of their lives, the faces of the sculptures begin to stream by—some young, just beginning their lives, others more emphatic, their faces graven with wrinkles like a dry creek bed. And now, just like the shape of the people in the cave emerged from the unformed clay, words begin to arrange themselves before Emely.

"Cold clay, warm flesh, living, dreaming, birth, and death, we flow into each other's lives," Ogotu sings.

Is it her imagination or are all those alabaster ears listening as well?

She is beginning to understand. The statues narrate what they learned in life, culminating in this, their final, eloquent statement carved with clay. Voiceless yet singing, sightless yet seeing, frozen yet expansive, grandmothers, great-grandmothers, toddlers, first loves, these lives are the living stories of those left behind.

These sculptures aren't bullet points for her resume—they are biology, personal. Each has something to tell about the long, arduous journey that has brought her to herself. Staring into their eyes, she realizes with a start that she is actually looking for the thread of herself.

The singing drops down, becomes a barely obedient hum, and just as she did when Chipkorie stopped singing in their first encounter in the cave yesterday, Emely reaches out to touch the hand of the person who has made the music. "Please," she pleads, "don't stop. It's like . . ." She searches for the right word. "Hope."

Ogotu nods, pale-gray eyes watching. "You're beginning to understand," she says quietly. "Parts of you are beginning to awaken. But it's too soon for you to know more."

"But what is this?" Emely asks, mystified. "It's not just singing, it's something more."

"It's the mother language," the old woman replies. "Here in these old trees we sing the contours of our world—its mountains and valleys, our ravines filled with water. But those old words can't live on the outside. Sound just straightens out, becomes as tired and useless and empty as the blank world."

Emely shakes her head. "I don't understand."

"The old language has great power," the old woman says. "All history, all graves, the beginning of life and its endings—all lie inside its rhythms. In time, you, too, will learn to speak this language. Its full rhapsody will cross your throat. But it's too soon for you to know more. You don't know yet that you are separate from the sound. You would fall right into its rhythms and disappear."

The old woman's eyes blaze as though they are the only reason to grow a face. "What I have to say next I will speak in my flat voice—no mountains, no valleys, no lush, running water. Those who are dead and those who are alive have passed you to me through my stones. They are gathered here with us this morning."

Her voice thunders against the walls. "You are made from the history in this cave, Amely, from bodies forced to leave this green, sweet home. Our stories run through your blood. Beneath all your noisy shininess I can see it—see the old ways. They are crouching low, but I see them nevertheless. When you become quiet enough I will make another sculpture, and then you will rise tall with offerings for the Great Mother—and then, thick and rich and proud, her love will flow back into our world once again."

Emely reaches for the comforting efficiency of her fanny pack. "I told you, Ogotu, I'm just here to observe," she replies. "I'm just going to record your stories, watch you prepare food, and make your art. Six weeks, that's all, and then I'll be gone."

Even she hears the lies in her voice. She remembers the fantasy of just a few minutes ago, of all these statues being transported to the National Anthropological Museum. She knows when she goes out and reports what she has found in this forest, the world will not be able to leave this discovery alone.

But the old woman isn't listening. "My husband is wrong," she says. "When the male parts of our world are no longer held in balance by female voluptuousness—when there are no more songs, no love, no breath—a terrible silence will come. You are the next Stone Woman. This is why you are here: to rise into the Great Mother and stop that silence from coming."

One more time Emely's wrist is braceleted between strong fingers. "Come," Ogotu says, "I have something to show you."

She pulls Emely down the aisle toward a sculpture of a young girl.

It doesn't matter in the least that she is only a statue made of clay. Emely recognizes her instantly. Her grandmother stands before her as a young girl. Some kind of vital flame still flickers deep inside the clay; instantly, Emely wants to walk into her embrace.

Ogotu watches her closely. "This is your grandmother," she says, "And those are her parents, your great-grandparents."

A handsome man stands behind the sculpture of her grandmother, a big smile on his face. Dreads are wound round and round on top of his head like a turban. A woman stands next to him, slim and beautiful with high, firm breasts. Though made of clay, both of them glow with the fact that they have made this perfect little girl.

"If your grandmother hadn't gone into the blank world and dissolved her powers," Ogotu says, "she would have been one the most powerful Stone Women that ever existed. Stories are still told about her courage."

Searching for her own story locked inside the statue's anatomy, Emely stares into the face of the young girl who eventually left this forest and bore her mother, who eventually, in turn, bore her.

"Hers was a magnificent cut," Ogotu says. "When her private lips were cut, blood flowed from her for a very long time. Everything she had she gave."

Lightheaded, Emely feels as if she's going to faint. What she had been dreading since the events of the night before was true. She drags the words slowly across her throat. "Cutting?" she says, barely able to phrase the word. "You mean female genital mutilation? Where you cut and stich a girl's vagina?" She remembers the ceremony her grand-mother brought her to when she was a little girl. She still remembers that terrible scream.

Ogotu smiles brightly and nods her head. "We don't use the blank world's words for it but yes." She sweeps her hands across the statues in the cave. "All the women in this cave have been cut. It's why you are here. Finally, the perfect constellation. A Stone Woman, and an initiate ready to drop blood. You will soon find the stone tablet, carved at the beginning of time. It is the way the Great Mother calls to her Stone Women. On a morning not too far away, when we have prepared Chipkorie with songs and dance, I will hand you the piece of glass—the same glass that cut your grandmother and all the women in this cave. You will bend between Chipkorie's legs, and with one slice cut first the guardian of her village and then the sheltering lips on either side. They will fall, and I will hand you the needle made of bone and strung with animal gut. You will scrape her inside skin, and then stitch back and forth, back and forth, until the opening is only about the size of my little finger. Chipkorie will be in terrible pain, of course, but I will have placed a stick in her mouth, and she won't cry out and curse the cer-emony—no, she will be as silent as the statues here. You will then place your hands on the tablet and rise and offer the Mother her cut parts. Chipkorie will bleed everything she is for the Mother. Blood will run into the soil, and our Mother will drink long and deep, and when she is gorged full she will be happy and send us animals again."

Emely's throat constricts. The cave fills with the silent screams from all those cut women. She stares into the old woman's face. "It's time to get something straight," she says as firmly as she can. "I'm not your Stone Woman, and I'm certainly not going to participate in any kind of mutilation of a young girl. You say you love your granddaughter, but do you know she could die from loss of blood? And even if she doesn't die, she could get really sick from infections? Scar tissue will build up around the wound, and it will take hours for her just to pee, and when the time comes for her monthly blood it will build up inside of her and won't come out. She will smell rotten—and there's even more risk of infection. What you are talking about has been outlawed in the so-called 'blank world.'"

She knows she is criticizing a cultural practice, stepping far across the line of deliberate social science objectivity, but she will do anything to save Chipkorie's life. "If she gets married," she continues, "her husband will penetrate what will become an open wound, and even if she does get pregnant, her baby could die in the birth canal trying to push through all that scar tissue. I've heard stories of midwives trying desperately to cut through all the scar tissue that has grown up around the edge of the opening just so that the baby can get out, but it's so dense and impacted the baby dies anyway."

She draws herself up, stares into the old woman's eyes. "It is a hideous, barbaric practice, Ogotu," she pronounces, "and I won't have any part of it. I'm going to find Chipkorie right now and use all my so-called 'flat words' to try to convince her not to go through with it."

She is just beginning to crawl out of the opening of the cave when the old woman addresses her one more time. "You carry a stone in your pocket, don't you?" she says. "It's green with a white line running through its middle. It's from the day you saved your mother."

Surprised, Emely puts her hands in her pocket, feels its familiar form. "How did you know that?" she asks.

She remembers the day as though it was yesterday. While home from boarding school for a few weeks, she was walking to the grinding stone with a bucket of maize when she first noticed the stone. She leaned over, picked it up, and held it in her hand. When it was warm from her skin, the stone spoke—not so much with words as with pictures. She saw clearly that a few fields away the blade of the plow had just run over her mother's foot. It was a severe cut, and blood was everywhere.

Emely put that stone in her pocket and ran as fast as she could to find her father. "Mama!" she exclaimed when she found him. "Mama's hurt!" And she pointed toward the field where her mother lay wounded.

When they had arrived, her mother had lost so much blood she was barely conscious. Emely's father took off his shirt, tied off the wound, and rushed her to a missionary clinic a few villages away. The wound took many months to heal, and Father Joseph told Emely that if she hadn't found her mother that morning, she would have died from loss of blood. Her mother asked her once how she could possibly have known she was hurt when she was so far away.

Emely avoided answering.

She kept the stone, however, and it became her secret ritual to use it when she was most frightened—like when she took her first plane ride, and when she had to give a presentation at school. In fact, the night she was arrested she had used it to talk back to the police chief.

Today, she uses it to talk back to this crazy old lady with sorcerer eyes. "I'm not your Stone Woman," she repeats. "And the last thing in the world I would ever do is cut Chipkorie."

She turns and crawls out of the cave into the sunlight's warm, waiting arms.

CHAPTER 56

I am only small, the stone says, *but let me tell you what I know. I know that we move from existence to existence, taking many forms along the way. I know that somehow we continue—in our songs, our stories, the militant sculptures the old woman creates, sounding why, why, why . . . in the hearts and minds of everyone the Great Mother loves. Live better, dream higher, become the magnificent person you are capable of becoming, she tells us.*

Stones, feathers, shells, and bones, all things speak with the alive intelligence of the Great Mother. Listen to these old words spoken by a diminutive stone. There is no hope for us if we don't remember. When you kill even one fish, one tree, one bird or animal, you kill also its children and its children's children. But what happens if all the fish are killed, all the birds and animals are gone?

In order for the world to become what it needs to become, we have to reach back in time, touch the Great Mother. We must remember the past in order to go forward.

I am only a small stone speaking these few cool, gray words. Will our new Stone Woman hear me in time?

CHAPTER 57

I t is late afternoon now, and Emely is sitting on a rock in the middle of the clearing, jotting down a list of items to report to the professor. Though she knew he would be excited to hear that the old woman had mentioned the existence of a stone tablet while talking to her in the sculpture cave, the object was too tied into Ogotu's false assumptions about her; the old woman's belief that as the tribe's reigning Stone Woman, she would cut Chipkorie, place her hands on the tablet, rise and present the girl's cut parts to the Great Mother. She didn't want the professor to think her work was contaminated; pure anthropological documentation should be a devoid of any kind of influence from the outside.

She would find a way to refute the old woman's beliefs and clear the path for pure objective observation. Maybe she could even think of a way to talk Chipkorie out of being cut as well.

She has just scrawled a sentence about the kind of baskets they make when she hears a low growl behind her.

She turns. A skinny, rib-chiseled dog has found its way up into the clearing and now stands only inches away from her. Its eyes are too shiny and drool falls from its jaws.

Fear immediately fills Emely's throat. She can barely breathe; it's like looking into the heart of a storm.

"Don't move," Ogotu says behind her. "That animal is sick. One bite and you'll catch its fever."

"We have to kill him," Old Tempi says, reaching for his spear.

"Give me a second," Mentegai says. Fluid, slow, with a hunter's grace, he's now at Emely's side. "Get up," he whispers. "I'll take your place."

She's only too happy to comply, quickly stands and moves into the cave. Mentegai takes her place on the stone. The dog still hasn't moved. The pages of the notebook Emely has been using ruffle on the ground.

Fur matted with blood, wounds flecked with flies, the dog stares at Mentegai, and Mentegai stares at the dog. The entire clearing fills with this silent conversation between species. Mentegai passes his eyes across the dog's wounds, reads what has happened to him, and the dog, knowing he is being observed, stands still.

No words are said, but a primal conversation has sprung up between the man and dog, everything spoken through the eyes. Knowing that there are some kinds of pain you can't talk away, through the beautiful art of silence Mentegai is slowly bringing calm back into the animal.

But not for long. That growl again, and suddenly the wild thing that lives inside the dog awakes. He lowers his head, paws the ground.

Old Tempi raises his spear.

"Wait," Mentegai hisses.

The animal begins to move, pacing in long, loping circles around Mentegai. The sun glitters on his wounds like they're medallions. Though the pacing has a quality of the hunt, Mentegai still doesn't move. He knows he has become a man in the dog's world, not the other way around. Emely remembered how upset she had been when they were coming into the forest and Mentegai had kicked his dogs at the edge of the river. She remembered his explanation that it was the only way to get them into the water so that they would swim across. She hadn't believed him then, thought he was merely being brutal, but watching his gentleness with this animal this morning, wondered if perhaps she should have trusted his explanation after all. This man had a magical way with animals.

How much time passes is hard to tell. The long grass in the clearing moves in the wind; leaves shiver on the trees; clouds occasionally burst forward in bright declarations of self-centered glory.

But still, round and round go those paws.

It's only when the shadows have lengthened to almost people size that the revolutions start to slow, the orbits begin to be sponsored by the man and not the other way around. And then, just as abruptly as the pacing had begun, it stops. The dog puts down his head and sniffs the grass.

But still Mentegai sits quietly, no wound too ugly to observe. Behind them the mountains are blue with twilight, the long, silky grass whispers, and still nothing happens. Though the animal seems to be completely immersed in his own world, a contract is being negotiated. Who will belong to the other? Who will finally be owned?

It's when the clouds darken and evening finally arrives that the animal begins to move again. As though he has taken some of the evening's heaviness into his paws, slowly, deliberately, he approaches Mentegai, not in submission but clearly in partnership. Paw over paw he steps forward until he stands only a few feet away from Mentegai.

It is only then that Mentegai stands, his face open not in triumph but in respect for the miracle that is happening. Slowly he approaches the animal, reaches out his hand, and cautiously begins to stroke the animal's wounds. No words are spoken; all of his voice is in his hands, mothering, fathering, trying to smooth away a lifetime of suffering to bring the animal home.

Who knows whether it is the possibility of food or simply the fact that now, finally, this animal can lean into someone and for a moment at least allow some of his hurt to be carried by another, but whatever it is, when Mentegai finally walks toward the cave, the dog follows, their mutual silences forever entwined.

"That boy's got some of the old ways in him," Ogotu says, watching him approach. Pressing her hands against her knees, she slowly stands. "I'm going to go put these tired feet in the river," she announces. "I want to give thanks for what I've just seen. I might not be able to rise tall anymore, but I can still have conversations with other parts of the Mother."

Emely stares at this man who is now feeding the dog a few of the forest hog's bones. Despite her persistent warnings to herself not to fall for a coworker, despite his dismissal of her just about every time they've spoken, she finds herself irrevocably drawn to him. She thinks of her own wounds—her mother casting her out, not knowing where she belongs. She's homeless, really.

If he can so easily take that animal's pain and make it his own, what would he be able to do with some of hers? She doesn't have an answer, but it's a totally new and wonderful thought.

CHAPTER 58

That night, Emely travels far in her dreams. Stone, flesh, silence, noise, history leans against the future, the city presses right up against the forest, her body is a union of opposites. And she runs, runs through the intricate night.

Those berries over there hold wine, that slim line beyond the trees will soon crack open with dawn; by the complexity of the sky to her right, the way it feels against her skin, she knows that underneath it, people sleep. The air on her other side comes from America and carries the lean of intersections, traffic, corners.

As she runs, Emely is filled with a huge, proprietary love for all that she sees. She hears a metallic rattle of nails: a crocodile has pulled itself up onto the riverbank. A bushbuck has just been born in that clearing, slick and steamy with birth juices. Over there, flowing liquid and sinister against a branch of the tree, is a snake, but she's not frightened the way she would be if she were the daytime Emely.

And now here come about a dozen monkeys, gossiping, chuckling, pushing things over with their tiny hands. She smiles, spreads out her arms. *Mine,* she thinks. *All mine.*

Cutting the young girl? An old woman with eyes that push? This Emely of the night will outrun all of those orders. Though she knows it is not a sentimental darkness out there, that it is hazardous, filled with conquests and killing, nevertheless everything still fits—even this gigantic woman jumping rivers with one leap.

CHAPTER 59

Emely has been in the forest about a week now. Every night the same dream reaches for her, and she rises and moves into the night—leaving behind all of the questions that plague her days. Sand, water, spiders, monkeys, rain, the moon . . . filled with love for all that she sees, in her dream she becomes big and brown and fierce, heavy on both sides with all that she sees before her.

These are her nights—beautiful and rich and inclusive. Not so her days. There is no running in them, and certainly no lush belonging.

Every morning she wakes to Ogotu's withering stare. The old woman never seems to sleep. She works all night long on her sculptures, feverishly making face after face, none of them quite right. The entire floor of the clearing is littered with bits of Emely's face—her nose over there, a few of her eyes slapped up against that rock. Their talk, too, is broken like shards from an archaeological dig—only the surface of thoughts revealed, not the meaningful underneath.

"You're not living behind your eyes," Ogotu says one morning, ripping apart what must be her four thousandth face. "Your mind and your body aren't talking to each other." She dips her hands into the clay and one more time begins to knead and pound, saying to it what she can't fully articulate to Emely.

Emely always transcribes these personal observations, and though there isn't any truth to them, they somehow always manage to bother her. As much as possible she wants to maintain her role as a passive observer. This is groundbreaking work, and she doesn't want it sullied with any kind of assumptions from the forest people about her role in their lives.

Every morning Emely pours water into a pot, then millet, and stirs. Everyone eats except for Ogotu. The old woman is losing weight at an alarming rate. They are all mostly relying on the millet Emely has brought in and the few roots and berries Ogotu and Chipkorie find in their wanderings. Emely follows Chipkorie and Ogotu each day when they go to collect firewood and whatever food they can find. They always bring their digging sticks and a leather thong to help carry the firewood. She brings her recorder and asks her questions in what she hopes is a professional and courteous manner.

"How large was your tribe in your youth, Ogotu?"

"We were as many as the blades of grass."

"Have you ever been outside of the forest?"

"Why would I want to?"

"Can we go back to the cave with the sculptures, and would you let me interview you about all of those lives?"

No answer. Just a forceful jab on the path with her walking stick.

"Questions, always questions," the old woman mutters. "Too much talking. You haven't learned to let wonder ripen in the sun like berries."

But sometimes (and these are the best times), the old woman feels like talking. She always seems to begin in the middle of a thought.

"We are all part of the Great Mother," she states one morning. "The story of life peers out from everyone we see."

Emely remembers the professor's dictate and hurries down the path to catch up with her, the red light of the recorder on. "Can you describe the Great Mother?" she asks eagerly. "What exactly does she do for you?"

The look Ogotu sends the recorder could sear the machine, but today she's in a good mood—they found some honey made by ground bees this morning. She doesn't directly answer Emely's question, of course, just begins to talk in her deep voice.

"A long time ago, life was only a tiny speck of light. Then, after time passed, that light grew into a fin, and then after much more time passed, that thin fin became a body and then became a fish. The breath from that first creature is still inside us. As though it had shoulders and could smell, this fish moved through the water and eventually climbed from the sky of water into the air of the land."

Emely is so excited she can barely breathe. *Wait until the professor hears about this! An evolution myth! Could it get any better than this?* She checks her recorder to see if it's still on.

"Then one skeleton thickened up," Ogotu continues. "It grew stubby legs, began to stumble across the ground. Eventually it raised its head, sent sound across everything it could see. Then it began to drop eggs. Those eggs cracked. Tusks, horns, a new thing was born; constant stare, heavy, swaddled walk. And then it, too, lengthened and stood upright so that it could see farther across the land."

"More creatures were born. Color began. Soon, life was teeming. Scales and lungs grew, teeth sharpened, tails elongated, our world even became a little crowded. And then—wouldn't you know it?—war began. Life split into different tributaries—the tall against the short, claws against scales, those who stood erect against the hunched. What to kill became the largest question."

She pauses, hands coiled like roots around her walking stick, a faraway look in her eyes. Her words have spilled her back to the time when the story first began.

"Then what happened, Grandma?" Chipkorie nudges, eyes lit with a tell-me-a-story shine.

"Life always moves toward the now," the old woman says when she begins to talk again. "Eventually the life that would become us stuttered forward, until one day—glorious arrival! The we that was almost us stood up."

Anthropological gold, Emely thinks. *This is as precious as the sculptures.* Ethnographic folklore with a narrative storyline. One more time she checks the light on her recorder. The red light is shining, the volume button's high.

But then the old woman suddenly turns to her, eyes glowing fierce. "You think this is only a story, Amely," she says ferociously, "but it's actually the breath of life itself. What we call a human being is only this temporary now. We are not only this arrival but the many thousands of bodies forming in the dark, the fanned happenings of all of those in-betweens. We come from every spurt of that becoming."

Her eyes narrow. "But if you don't listen well, the long story of us will end." She casts a scornful look down at Emely's recorder. "You ask all the wrong questions with your talking thing and that watching red eye. That constant monkey chatter you make keeps you from dropping into the full quiet and essence of Stone Woman knowledge." Her eyes harden, her good mood now gone. "Maybe one day these words will lift you. Until then you are living only in the sad, thin light of the in-between." She turns, begins to walk rapidly once more down the path.

"Too much worry in my hands," Emely hears the old woman mutter as she walks away. "Maybe that's why the clay won't speak to me."

CHAPTER 60

And so it goes: days of sullen activity, plagued by lectures from the old woman, and little physical sustenance. She felt dissipated—proof of which lay in dozens of disposed pieces of mangled clay. But still Emely tries to do her job. Every morning she puts Post-its on all of her recordings, which correspond to the page numbers in her field books. Then she transcribes all the recordings she made the day before, marking everything with the date glowing on her wristwatch. That usually takes a couple of hours. Next, she polishes the lens of the camera with the special cloth she brought. The camera was quite expensive; she keeps it in a plastic bag to protect it from the forest's humidity.

And, of course, she makes sure to report in regularly to the professor on the dates they had arranged before she came to the forest. She rehearses for hours before their call what she's going to say. There was one subject however she has avoided. She was uncomfortable mentioning to the professor her so-called Stone Woman status, and the fact that the old woman thinks she was going to cut Chipkorie. Was it that she didn't want the professor to think her work was contaminated with the tribe's assumptions about her, or was she uncomfortable talking about FGM with him? She didn't know.

Between her dreams and the old woman's lectures however, as the days went by she began to feel more and more pressure. Though she had thought she could refute the old woman's beliefs and get back to pure anthropological observation, nothing she had said so far seemed to budge Ogotu's belief that she was the next Stone Woman.

It was time to confide in the professor. No matter how uncomfortable the conversation made her, she needed help. "CD1245," she says briskly one morning, holding the microphone of the radio. "Base camp here. Come in, sir." She tries not to look at the scraps of her face littering the ground.

The professor responds immediately. He must live by his radio.

"Emely!" he says. "It's good to hear your voice."

She remembers to give him her coordinates. She checked the compass this morning.

"Are you getting a lot of stories?" he asks eagerly. "Any word yet on the tablet?"

"Actually the old woman briefly brought it up when I talked to her in the cave filled with statues, but that's also partly what I need to talk to you about this morning. I'm afraid I'm in a bit of a quandary."

"Go on," the professor says.

"About a week ago I learned that this tribe still practices female genital mutilation. It's all woven into the beliefs around the tablet, and that's why I haven't brought it up before. I'm sorry I didn't tell you earlier, but I thought I could handle it. I didn't wanted to disappoint you by sullying perfect research. But it's getting a little messy, and I guess I need some advice about how to handle everything."

"Go on, Emely," he responded smoothly. "You know you can tell me anything."

"Well . . ." she began hesitantly, "as I've told you before, there's a young girl here who is about twelve or thirteen. In a matter of weeks, she's going to be subjected to the most brutal kind of cutting there is. To make matters worse, the old woman insists that I'm the one who is going to cut her! She says I'm something called a 'Stone Woman' and that once I find the tablet I will cut Chipkorie in the most savage form of FGM there is and then after I cut, I will place my hands on the tablet, rise and offer the Great Mother the girl's cut parts. Complicating everything else, I'm not getting much sleep. I'm having these crazy dreams. I know that doesn't sound very important, but every night it's the same dream." She hears the tremor of fear that has entered her voice. "I don't know what to do, sir. Can you give me some advice? How should I handle this?"

"What do you mean you don't know what to do, Emely?" he asks. "This is a marvelous opportunity. As I've said before get out your recorder. That's your mandra! Record, record, record."

"But, sir," she protests. "Of course I won't cut the girl, but what if the old woman decides to go ahead with it? It's hard for me just to stand by and shove a camera in front of people's faces when this young girl is in peril. She's probably going to be cut with a piece of glass. She could die!"

The professor's voice is sharp. "Just do your job, Emely. This isn't some kind of women's cause; this is scholarship. Our main objective in the Land Reform Movement is to chronicle the lives of our indigenous people, not alter them. Very few have been able to record the teachings surrounding this ancient practice."

A short pause and then he asks: "Do you know where the tablet is?"

"No," she answers. "The old woman just says that when I know enough I will find it."

"Well find out," he responds shortly. "If they think you're the Stone Woman and are going to cut, they'll reveal more of their beliefs to you. They might even tell you where the tablet is. There will be greater good extracted from quietly and intelligently observing their practices than from imposing your own personal value structure on them."

Horror washes over her. "You mean you want me to pretend to be the Stone Woman?"

"It's all worth it if you find the tablet. If you had more years under your belt, you would understand this." She can almost hear the professor's fingers impatiently drumming the table. "Place your work in a larger context," he continues. "This custom has been practiced for thousands of years. It goes back to the Egyptians. Are you really going to hold up all that scholarship for the sake of one little girl? It is arrogant to think that your job is to change a culture. You might end up jeopardizing greater knowledge with your shortsighted sympathy. Do you understand?"

Emely chokes back tears. "Yes, sir."

His voice softens. "I know that this is hard for you, but think of what's at stake. If the old woman leads you to the tablet, even the pain of a little girl is worth it. It would be the most important discovery of all time! We would have to have it carbon dated, of course, but it could possibly be the oldest artifact in the entire world."

His voice holds the expectation of obedience. "Report back to me in a week, and I hope I hear something more than the metaphysical ramblings of a first-year university student. Do you hear me, Emely?"

"Yes, sir," she replies quietly.

"Good luck. Over and out."

Emely turns off the radio, turns off as well the sound of ownership in the professor's voice. Two leaves, one brown, one gold, meet in the wind. For a moment she watches them frolic—then, gently at first, then hard, tears begin to flow down her cheeks.

CHAPTER 61

*H*orizons, says a woman already dead. *Horizons provide an edge we can rest against. Move in a little closer to your life, they tell us. Poets speak poems to them, sailors use them to steer their ships. Horizons* separate our home from infinity, who we are, from the ever-expanding cosmos out there.

"We have a horizon," says a woman in Greenland, warming her stones with her hands. "I see it now, shining against the ice."

"So do we," replies an Egyptian woman. "It is there where sand meets sky. Every morning I steady myself by gazing out long."

There's no horizon here in these old trees, Emely's grandmother responds. *Nothing for our new Stone Woman to lean against. No line separates her from the vast night out there, the Mother just spills right in. She needs to rise with the cuttings of a young girl in her hand. Will enough of the Mother fill her in time?*

Despite her statement to the professor about professional objectivity, two days later, the conflict that has been smoldering beneath the surface of her days explodes.

Chipkorie is oiling her legs when it begins; Emely is close by, transcribing her notes from yesterday; Ogotu is as usual thumping the clay behind them. The men are off hunting.

There is no preamble. "On the holy day," Chipkorie says, looking up at Emely, "when the sun is rising, and I have prepared myself with songs and oil, you will bend between my legs and cut first my berry and then the two long sides of me. Then you will stitch me together, and when I am no longer an open jar pouring, pouring out, I will be so tight I will be only one small hole."

She calmly pours more oil into the palms of her hands. "I don't want to be dirty," she says. She begins to smooth the oil across her upper thighs, just beginning to hint of a woman's curves. "If you don't cut me, my long sides will grow and drag on the ground." Balling one of her hands into a fist, she circles it round and round on her nose, the gesture sweet and childish.

Emely decides to put one big toe over the line of anthropological objectivity. "You know you could die from loss of blood, Chipkorie," she says. "And even if you don't die, you'll be affected by this cutting for the rest of your life."

Just one toe, that's all. Behind her, soft yet vigorous, comes the pounding of Ogotu's hands on the clay. Emely knows the old woman is listening, but she can no longer hold back her concern for Chipkorie's well-being.

"It's the only thing that's going to save us." Chipkorie rubs more oil on her upper legs. "When I am cut, our Mother will be happy. This is the way it always has been." Her oiled skin adds more luster to the day, glows red-brown in the sun.

Words bubble up faster than Emely can speak. "You don't have to sacrifice your body," she blurts out. "This practice has been outlawed on the outside. It's barbaric!"

But Chipkorie isn't listening. She stares into the far-off trees and smiles. "It will be a good cut," she says, mostly to herself. "It will bring the animals back to the forest."

More listening than thumping behind her now; Ogotu's hands have slowed.

Bile rises in Emely's throat. *She's so beautiful! Even if she doesn't die, her life will be forever diminished, everything sexual cut from her as though ardor itself is a crime.*

Emely knows she is moving far away from the professor's counsel about trying not to stop the ancient ritual, but she can't help it. How could anyone think about cutting away any part of this girl's loveliness?

"Scraping and sewing your private lips is not going to bring animals back into the forest," she says. "That's propaganda, Chipkorie, and it's deadly."

The girl shifts her delicate frame on the rock she is sitting on. "You're not going to make me change my mind, Amely." She pours more oil into her hand and begins to smooth it across her arms. "You can't possibly understand any of this. You're from the blank world."

Emely feels engulfed by a terrible helplessness. What can she say to this girl? "It's just a made-up story, Chipkorie! A story that could kill you."

She knows she has now stepped way over the line, but she can't help it, she's careless with her anger now. "The planet doesn't need your blood!"

It's as though Chipkorie hasn't even heard her. "On the morning of my cutting I won't cry out. My blood will run so long and rich our Mother will receive it and drink it in, and everything will be as it should be."

Emely wants to shake the girl. "Please, Chipkorie," she pleads, struggling for calm. "Please listen to me. This is brainwashing, pure and simple."

"Grandma's disappearing into worry," Chipkorie says. "She's getting smaller and smaller, and she never smiles anymore. Grandpa's always watching her. He's like a hunter looking for the woman he married. My blood is the only thing that will bring her back." With something close to aristocracy, she raises her head. "On the morning of my cutting, Grandma will place a stick in my mouth so I won't cry out. Then she will hand you the cutting glass, and you will bend between my legs and do what a Stone Woman is supposed to do. And all will be right in our world again."

She smiles then and stretches, the languorous gesture at odds with the severity of the words she has just spoken.

It is that nonchalant stretch more than anything else that convinces Emely to step all the way across the line of passive anthropological objectivity. "Your grandmother doesn't know what she's talking about!" she explodes. "She's just a scared old lady. Yes, she loves you, but she's also using you to feed some kind of sick fantasy."

All goes quiet behind her. Not even the sound of thumping. No smiles or languorous stretches anymore, either; Chipkorie is angry, too. She rises on her two well-oiled legs, places her hands on her hips. "Grandma says the only reason you're here is to cut me," she says, anger blooming red on her cheeks. "This is the way it's always been, since the morning of time. Do not speak this wrong to me again. I must be clean inside for the dropping of the blood."

Emely stands as well. She extends her hand towards the girl. "Please listen to me, Chipkorie," she says softly. "I don't want you to be hurt. I care for you."

As though trying to disengage from the conversation, the girl steps backwards. "Wrong, wrong, wrong!" she spits. "My mother said the wrong word, 'no,' and Grandma had to send her away."

"What are you talking about?" Emely asks.

"When it was time for her re-sewing, my mother said 'no,' and that little word brought down the sky." Chipkorie casts her eyes toward Ogotu. "Tell her, Grandma. Tell her what happened. Maybe if Amely hears the story, when you hand her the piece of cutting glass on the holy morning, she will do what she's supposed to do."

The old woman smiles at her granddaughter. "Come here," she says and pats the ground at her side. Chipkorie hurries over and sits down so close to her it's as if she's trying to climb inside the old woman. "You, too, Amely," Ogotu orders. "Come sit here, and I will tell you how one small bone of word brought down the sky."

Great, Emely thinks. *Another story.* She knows she has just gone way too far, and all she's achieved is making Chipkorie angry with her. Maybe it will help to sit down and just record. Reaching into her fanny pack, she extracts her recorder.

As though to ride the story she is about to tell, the old woman begins by placing her feet far apart. "We live in the roots of the world with the bones of our grandmothers, our great-grandfathers, our mothers and fathers," she begins. "Our remembering keeps the world in balance. These teachings go back to the beginning of the world." She strokes her hand across Chipkorie's head. "'No' was the word your mother spoke that brought down the sky. It was also why she was sent away from the forest." She pauses for a moment, and when she speaks next her voice is rich with feeling. "Your mother, my daughter-in-law, had just given birth to you, Chipkorie, and it was time for the re-sewing of her private parts. It was a good time. Our laughter rose to touch the stars. When we walked, we found many arrowheads made from black stones. They were like footprints left from those who walked before. There were many different kinds of food, not just the nuts that hid deep inside their husks or berries sweet from the sun. Unlike now, we had a lot of meat. We would take the liver of antelope and wrap it inside of leaves, put it in the ashes of the fire, and cover the ashes with a layer of hot rocks. The meat would cook all day, and when we ate at night we thought we had never tasted anything so good.

"When it was time for the re-sewing ceremony, we gathered our sweetest berries, cooked our meat, invited our guests, and made liquor from honey. My sister was the holy cutter, but I was the one to guide the ceremony forward, announce its many phases. When the sun rose on the morning of the ceremony, my daughter-in-law placed herself on the ceremonial furs. Her breasts were heavy with milk, and she held you in her arms.

"I had sharpened the needle well," Ogotu continues, "and strung it with animal gut. I began to sing the re-sewing song, and I saw how the sky received it. The clouds came lower. I sang the song well that morning, and my sister did as well. We sang as our mother and her mother had. 'You will be sewed,' we sang. 'You will make yourself tight, offer more of your blood for our Mother.' My voice gusted out, the notes rose, and I was pleased. The morning was becoming good magic. But when my sister went in to do her work, your mother, Chipkorie, wouldn't allow it. She kept one foot tightly over the other.

"We sang the song a little louder, tried to give more curves to our words, but though we sang, and our ancestors had come to watch, though the Mother was waiting, she did not unwrap her clenched legs.

"'My daughter,' I whispered, coming close. 'What are you doing? Our guests watch. Let my sister cut.' But still she didn't answer. She just clung tighter to you, Chipkorie. I turned to my son, worry in my heart. 'Can you guide your wife?' I asked, for I was beginning to feel a great fear. But my son did not meet my eyes with his, and I knew then that if my daughter-in-law's answer was 'no' and my son did not support me, there would be very grave consequences.

"I turned back to your mother. 'You have to do this,' I demanded. 'You have to be restitched and drop blood. This is the way it always has been.' But my words did not affect her. She sat straight up, raised her head, and looked me in the eyes. I saw fear there, but I also saw a new determination. She looked at me with this new rebellion, and I grew frightened of what she was going to say. I was right. When she spoke, the words she said were a great wrong. I can barely speak them this morning in the retelling.

"'No,' she said defiantly. 'I never want to feel that pain again. It is worse than anything, even childbirth.'

"My heart was beginning to beat fast. You must have sensed the tension in the air, Chipkorie, for you began to cry. 'Please,' I said. 'You must do this. It is what you have been taught.' But she shook her head again, and once more said the word 'no.' 'I will not endure that pain again,' she said, clutching you tight to her chest. She put her head down, and I no longer saw her eyes, but I heard the word again: 'No.' She spoke the word softly. And when the first drops of rain fell on my cheek, I knew it was different from the rain that had fallen the day before."

Caught by her story, Ogotu falls silent, her silence a wedge keeping open the door to the great beyond.

Chipkorie rests her head against the old woman's shoulder. "Go on, Grandma," she says. "Then what happened?"

The old woman begins to speak again. "The clouds that had gathered to witness the ceremony darkened and began to leave. I had to speak loud to be heard above the sound. 'This is happening because you have not allowed yourself to be cut!' I warned your mother, but still she did not listen. She stood up, gathered you to her chest, and ran through the rain back into the cave. I followed slowly, my heart heavy.

"When I entered the cave, I saw her deep in the shadows. She held her head in her hands, and your father Chipkorie, stood next to her. Nothing was said. I already knew that words were too thin to alter the wrong that was coming.

"In the days to come my sorrow grew feet and began to trot. Wrong brought down more water than the river could hold. Rain was the first thing we heard in the morning, the last thing we heard at night. The water grew higher. The raindrops tasted like tears. Streams and rivers cut through our world like wrinkles on an elder's face. Animals dashed into hiding, trying to find a dry spot in which to curl up. Some of them fell into the great water. We saw their carcasses floating by.

"The moon grew from thin to fat and then thin again. Though we sang our strongest songs, our thoughts grew smaller. Rain battered the forest, sound assaulted our world. Everywhere I looked there was water, all brought down from that one word, 'no.'

"Once again I tried to speak to my daughter-in-law. 'Your giving your blood is such a small thing to ask to make this water go away,' I said. 'You must do this for your family, your daughter, the Mother. Though it's not the best blood because it's not a young girl's blood, it is still holy.' But still she shook her head. In fury, I turned to my son. 'Talk to your wife!' I ordered. 'Convince her that she must be sewed again.' But he, too, shook his head. 'I can't stand the look on her face when we make love, Mama,' he said. 'She is always in agony. I don't want to do that to her again.'

"Tears stood in my eyes as I looked at my only born. He had the face of my husband when he was a young man. But I knew I had to speak the painful words. 'You must go,' I said quietly, trying to stand tall. 'I will take care of your baby until you are settled. But you can no longer live in our world.'"

The old woman gently strokes her hand across Chipkorie's head. "Your parents left, the rain stopped, and light came back into our world again. I always expected your mother and father to come back for you, but they never did. I never heard from them again, all because of that one small bone of a word that brought down the sky." She looks up at Emely. "I hope you understand now how words, even little ones, have heft and burden. They enter the world and never leave. You use words far too carelessly. You spread them across the ground the way people in the blank world spread seeds. At first I thought I could go and sit next to you the way a listening person quiets a too-much talker. Then, when that didn't work, I thought maybe one day you would use up all your words. That hasn't happened either."

All the lines around her mouth seem to be pointing toward what she says next. "When you are fully living in your face, you will cut Chipkorie, find the tablet, rise, and offer Chipkorie's cut lips to the Mother. But until that day, all of your words will continue to push away knowing. That's why I can't make a sculpture of you. An old soul lives deep inside you, but you're preventing her from rising and living in your face."

Knowing the professor would grill her on the subject, she wanted to ask the old woman more questions about the tablet but before she can, Chipkorie speaks. "Don't worry, Grandma," she says, "I'm not like my mother. No matter how big the pain is, on the holy morning my blood will pour out." She leans her head against her grandmother, the entire language of a shared life spoken with that one gesture. "Everything I am, I will give to the Mother." She casts an ugly look in Emely's direction. "No wrong words. I won't cry out."

Ogotu smiles down at her granddaughter. "I know you won't," she says. "You're my brave girl."

Teachings packed with blood, no grandeur here. These people have created a hideous, glorified belief system around the cutting and sewing of vaginas. Suddenly overwhelmed, Emely tucks the recorder back into her fanny pack, then stands. "I have some things to do," she says, and makes her way to the back of the cave where her equipment is stored. Ignoring the urban smirk of her red backpack, she finds her field notebook and draws a series of straight lines.

"Interview questions," she writes in the first column. "Things to do," she labels the next. Discarded pieces of her face are everywhere; stories calculated to make a young girl lie down and be cut crowd her thoughts. In this green, tangled world it makes her feel a little bit better to try to live her days pushed up against these long, precise lines.

CHAPTER 62

There is one part of the day, however, that makes it all worth waiting for: when shadows lengthen and night tiptoes in, turning the world a deeper blue. Then, swept clean of the particulars of her life, full and vacant at the same time, Emely joins the others near the fire. When day finally closes its eye, her mind invites in images—long fingers, the traveled skin of faces, leaves flinched with rain. Then, as though they have been used and borrowed by somebody else, her thoughts return, filled more with sensation, feeling, and color than anything else.

Another reason she likes these evenings is that sometimes when she looks up she finds Mentegai staring at her. She remembers his gentleness with the dog. There is an attractive quiet to the man, an innate watchfulness that makes him complete and thus unpossessable. These nights by the fire they have short conversations of the eye, and some kind of question blooms in the air between them. She smiles and he smiles, then both drop back into their separate reveries.

And still she waits. Somewhere out in the night, comets collide, stars hang faithful in the sky . . . something is coming. It is close, getting closer. By now she knows what to look for. Ogotu has already begun to tap her foot, but that's not it. Almost, but not quite.

She knows it is finally here when Ogotu raises one of her shoulders—all that is about to happen announced with that slight gesture. And now here it comes; full, glorious, radiant with power, the forest language breaks against her.

When the others join in the singing, she does as well, sometimes loving the song so much that sound becomes almost physical; she stretches out her neck so the melody can spend more time inside of her.

Has it been ushered in with song? These blue evenings, she's never quite sure, but she begins to know things, night things that she doesn't know during the day, like where birds sleep after the hard work of carrying the sky on their wings all day, where hooves sink into the forest soil, where in the night a leopard watches. Not only does she know these things, but unlike her disciplined days listening to Chipkorie's clitoridectomy soundtrack and Ogotu's blood-filled stories, these are things she wants to know.

Ogotu watches her across the fire and sometimes even manages to look pleased.

"Two Amelys," the old woman says one evening.

Another difference between Emely's days and nights; she doesn't mind being talked to this way.

"One is living the fire of your physical life," Ogotu says, "while the other is who you become at night."

As though to illustrate the old woman's pronouncement, twin reflections of Emely's face swim in the pupils of the old woman's eyes.

"Dreams carry the dream for us all inside of them," Ogotu says. "They rise and place light in the night." The two watching twins in her eyes urge Emely to rise as well.

Emely burns with a new kind of intricate thought. What the old woman has just said brightens something inside. She knows she has to find a place in the dark to put this new light. She rises, begins to run. She crosses the river with a single leap; the tree right in front of her, another leap. Bushbucks arch their backs doing their high-step march, hoping to attract a mate. Plants spread spores on the wind. A fish rises to the surface of the river and touches the moon.

It is an active and wealthy world she has entered, everything alive beseeching, touching, dancing, calling to others to procreate.

Emely doesn't want clothing anymore. The future Doctor Matei strips off her T-shirt, drops it to the ground. She presses her hand against her stomach, brings it up to her breasts. One cool, one warm; her body has become a marriage of opposites—flesh, stone, silence, noise, the city pressed up tight against the forest.

Her thoughts run as silky as poems, and she runs, runs through the steamy forest air, splashes through the river. What was history and what will become the future inhabits her very own body. She wants her trees to go on forever, but they don't. Just as she becomes big and fierce and brave, heavy on both sides with love for all of her creatures, she runs out of air. At the forest's edge, where the flat world begins, she stops, gasping. She sees an enormous clot of smoke down below; she bends down and smells decay, death. Many men down there, wearing hard hats. A big truck pulls a large log up the road amidst clouds of red dust. A short distance away, a giant tree falls, exposing a skirt of roots and taking with it all the younger trees beneath it as it crashes down. A machine promptly rolls over and picks the tree up with a mechanical claw. It drops it into the river with a giant splash. A small monkey watches, its tiny hands grasping a branch. Another tree falls, and the animal scampers back into shadows.

Emely turns as well, and like the little monkey retreats back into the forest's deepest shadows. Once more her own size, she crawls into her sleeping bag and tries to sleep.

It is only here, far away from her running, that she remembers what the old woman had said. "On the morning of my granddaughter's cutting," she said, "you will crouch between her legs and cut first the guardian of the village, then the two sides. Then you will scrape the inside skin so that it will grow back together, and I will hand you a string made from bushbuck gut and you will stitch her tight so that there will be only a small hole left, about the size of my little finger."

Bloated, engorged like a blood-filled tick, these were her words.

CHAPTER 63

The Great Mother grows more concerned by the day.

My hills and valleys I use like a lap to gather in all whom I love, but despite my care, evil was born in my folds.

I worry that my new Stone Woman won't be ready to fight him in time. She must enter my night as a bird, send out sound the way my leopard does. I want her to be that brave.

I worry that my new Stone Woman isn't the kind of woman who can pray out loud, bring a cloud down from the sky with song. There are two kind of wildness. One she sees before her when she runs, the other lives deep inside of her. Will she know the quiet inside kind?

I watch, I worry, I wait.

CHAPTER 64

Something has gotten loose inside Emely. There is no place to rest, no place at all. The old woman's turbulent stories about cuttings, the dreams when she runs tall at night, the forest's wild sense of time and space are all pushed right up next to the organized world narrated in her notebook, pages titled with academic phrases like "Age Set" and "Matriarchal Deity."

Emely is drifting in the space between her two names.

One morning, she is trying to work, but what she is really doing is stealing glances at Mentegai. Gentle but emphatic, with each day that passes Mentegai seems to be coming more into himself, and when he flashes his beautiful smile it brings forth a kind of longing inside her.

This morning he sits across the clearing making spears, wrapping arrowheads with twine, attaching them to the ends of sticks. As he works, he whistles a slow melody that tells Emely more about what he is feeling than anything his few words ever reveal.

She has always looked toward conversation as a way to locate herself. Maybe he can work a little bit of healing magic on her. They haven't spoken since he called her an "amateur"; that was over a week ago.

She stands, walks slowly across the clearing, offers a smile, and asks, "Do you mind if I sit down for a sec?"

His whistling stops. He looks up and shrugs.

She finds a rock to sit on.

He reaches for another arrowhead.

"I'm not sure where to begin," she says tentatively.

He raises a stick, jostles it gently up and down with one finger to test its balance.

She decides to plunge right in. "I don't know what is happening to me," she confides, "and because you know the world I come from, you even know the professor, I thought maybe you could help me. Please don't be angry with me. I really need to talk to someone."

When he nods, the long chains of his dreads thump their encouragement as well.

"Both Ogotu and the professor are saying the same thing. They want me to find a tablet. I've heard about it before—my grandmother told me about it when I was a child, actually—but it could just be a story. And on top of everything else, I'm not getting much sleep. I'm having these crazy dreams at night. Every single night I run through the forest, and I'm huge; one half of me is still me, but the other half is stone. And when I reach the edge of the trees, I can't seem to breathe anymore. Sometimes I wake up gasping for air."

She watches a buzzard wheeling through the sky. Still not one word from Mentegai, but the gravitational force of the man pulls on her, drawing forth the next tumble of words.

"It's like something is chasing and leading me at the same time," she says. "I feel like I'm going crazy. My world used to make so much sense!" She is beginning to panic; she forces herself to calm down and breathe slowly. "As you can probably tell, I like knowing where I'm going. I like order. When I was selected by the nuns to go to boarding school it saved my life."

Why is she confiding in someone who is going backwards in time—someone who wishes to live only on what he kills with his bow and arrow, disappear into the forest? Is he even listening?

But then she looks into his green eyes, and her face grows hot. He *is* listening—listening acutely, in fact. His continuing silence is a gift—a blank page on which to pour out every part of her story.

She stumbles forward. "And Ogotu," she continues. "What a piece of work! I don't understand anything she's talking about. She is convinced I'm something called a Stone Woman. She goes on and on about that. She says she has to teach me the old ways so that I can rise tall, but it's like her words are made of liquid: I don't understand them, can't hold them in my mind for very long."

She twirls the end of one of her shoelaces around her finger, one more time tells herself that it's inappropriate to have a crush on a co-worker. When these six weeks are up, she's never going to see him again.

But she can't help it. When she looks into his green-flecked eyes, all her doubts, all her questions fermented so long in solitude spill out, an uncorked, stirred-up, splashed-out version of herself. His quiet loops her back to herself, his listening a yardstick rising inch by inch, and somehow she knows understanding fills the fractions in between. She plunges on. "I've never really belonged anywhere, you know. It's as if my whole life has been spent watching from the sidelines, and now I'm here and everyone's barking orders at me, assuming I'm theirs."

She is surprised to find her eyes welling up with tears. "And the worst thing of all is that in a matter of weeks Ogotu expects me to cut Chipkorie. And when I try to tell them that cutting a young girl can't possibly be a solution for anything, no one listens to me." She struggles to get control of the fear that has entered her voice. "If I don't do it, Ogotu probably will. How can mutilating a young girl save the world? When I ask the professor what to do, he tells me not to hold up all this valuable anthropological scholarship for the sake of one girl. He even wants me pretend I'm the Stone Woman. He says it will lead us to finding the tablet and that will make everything worth it. I don't know what to do!"

Mentegai places a finger on a green feather, ties it with a piece of forest twine. When he finally speaks he doesn't actively address her questions. "I love it here," he confides. One of his dreads swings down to remind his fingers they are not alone. "For the first time in my life, I feel like I'm home. There's something in these trees that pulls you right in, some kind of magic that's hard to explain. My father used to talk about it." The buzz of insects, the curve of roots, the movement of sunspots and faraway a white butterfly sails through the air. "People on the outside know a lot, but it's mostly just information," he says. "The people who live here know the things I want to know. It's like a whole other species of thought."

Is it a trick of the sun? Suddenly, light rims Mentegai's beautiful body the way gold honors the jewel it is charged to protect. He is so attractive Emely can barely breathe.

"I feel my father near me in these trees," he says. "When I cut the branch for this spear, for instance, it was like he was standing right next to me. When I walk these trails I feel him near me." Rattling the long chain of the dreads, he shakes his head. "I really miss him."

Emely feels a little lightheaded. What do you say when a really attractive man reveals his heart? She thinks of the hole where her mother should be, that perpetual keen of desertion. "I understand," she says softly. "I really do."

"I know it sounds crazy," he says, "but I feel like my father wants me to be here. I want to raise my children here. I want to be buried here."

"You're lucky," Emely replies. Again she thinks of her mother, the way she pushed her away from her fire for all those years. "I don't think I've ever really had a home. I've only just had places where I've stayed a while." Then she asks a question Emely the outsider would ask. "Have you thought about what you would eat if you stayed here? The ecosystem is obviously becoming too small to support much game."

A long moment of quiet then, so long that a cloud drifts from one side of the sky to the other.

"Something will work out," Mentegai finally replies calmly. He raises his eyes, stares her straight in the face. "I think it comes down to you and how large you allow yourself to become."

"What?" she asks, startled. "What does any of this have to do with me?"

He replies in the same soft voice he used to calm the wounded dog. "I know you're confused, but I think you're going to find that tablet. I think you're here to save these people."

She shakes her head. "No," she whispers. "Not you too. Even if it does exist, I don't have a clue as to where it is."

"Long before I met you, I had a dream," Mentegai says, "and you were in it. I had fallen into some very deep water, and I don't know how to swim. I was really frightened—close to drowning, in fact—and then a hand came out and saved me. It was you."

She moves, startled, on the rock. "How did you know it was me?"

He glances at her hand. "You were wearing that ring. Even underwater I could see it, see the red stone."

She stares at him, astonished. "It was only a dream."

"I don't think so," he says softly. "I think you're here to save the tribe, and you are also here to save me. When you aren't showing off, using other people's words, you're someone I really like."

And here it is, spoken quietly in the middle of this bright morning. This man who has tattooed his face in a swirl like the grain of the trees, who offers honey to his walking stick and belongs to shadows and deep quiet—this is someone she may be able to follow.

But now here come those tears she's been fighting so hard to control. Ignoring all the warnings in her mind, trying to fill her void with him, for the first time she acknowledges what she has not yet been able to say, even to herself. "Sometimes I wonder if maybe I'm the Stone Woman too."

He smiles his beautiful smile. "I know one way to find out." He reaches out and tenderly brushes away the tears now rolling down her cheeks. "It's a story my father told me one day." He stands and, tucking the spears he has just made into a bamboo container slung across his back, extends his hand. "Let's see if it's true."

Reaching more for his touch than for the possibility of an answer, Emely gives him her hand. They begin to walk down the path.

His skin speaks of his days. There are calluses on his fingers made from carving honey hives and strength from threading arrows through a bow and pulling the string back taut in his grip. There is the gentleness he used to stroke belonging back into that dog as well. All this is in his touch.

Maybe he's right, Emely reflects, *but right backwards. Maybe he'll be the one to save me*!

CHAPTER 65

Mentegai leads Emely to a clearing close to the cave, then drops her hand and begins to walk back and forth, examining the ground.

"What are you looking for?" she asks.

"A rock," he says. "According to my father's story, we need a rock, but it has to be just the right size." He leans over and picks up one about the size of his hand. "This is good." He cuts a piece of forest twine from a bush and wraps it round the rock, netting it with twine.

"What you going to do with that?" Emely asks.

"You'll see," he says. "According to my father, if you're the Stone Woman, you should be able to make this rock move just with your breath." He walks to a small tree and hangs the rock from the lower branch.

"That's impossible," she snaps. She would much prefer going back to just holding hands.

The toss of those green eyes across his shoulder. "You're the one who said you wanted to get some answers." He points to a place about six feet away from where the rock is hanging. "Stand over there."

More to get it over with than anything else she walks to the place he has designated. "Now what I do?" she asks grumpily.

"Just blow."

"This is ridiculous," she retorts—but she takes a deep breath and blows it out.

Of course the rock doesn't move.

Mentegai scratches his head. "Maybe you're supposed to think of something. Or maybe someone. My father didn't tell me that part." His face brightens. "I know," he says. "Think of Chipkorie. I know you really care about her. And close your eyes this time."

Emely knows it's not going to work, but she also understands what is behind his request: his yearning to belong to the old story his father told him so long ago. And so, closing her eyes, she thinks of Chipkorie.

The first thing she thinks of is her beautiful, expressive face; next, her liquid grace. Sun warm on her shoulders, slowly, ever so slowly, she slides her mind's eye down over the girl's body, landing on her toes. Another, deeper breath, and she pulls in the tossed ingredients of her young friend—her goodness, joy, and innocence. When she has her fully alive, eyes still closed, she releases her breath in a barely audible hiss.

A small moment of silence, and then Mentegai speaks. "It's working," he says quietly. "The story's true!"

Emely opens her eyes. Sure enough, very gently, in the middle of this still morning, spinning only on the draft of her breath, the stone is slowly revolving round and round.

Nearby, a bird calls in a voice so pure it could almost be articulating an idea. Emely puts her hand in her pocket and feels for her stone. "There must be some kind of rational explanation," she says. "Are you sure the wind wasn't blowing?"

Mentegai shrugs. "Only one way to find out," he responds. "Let's try another one, and this stone should be heavier."

Walking back and forth, he again inspects the ground and finds a larger rock. Wrapping it with forest twine, he hangs it from a different branch of the same tree. "This time stand farther back," he instructs.

She takes a couple of steps backward. "Who should I think of this time?" she calls.

His smile alone makes her want to run her fingers through his verdant hair. "Maybe the old man," he says. "Think of that spear he held to your neck the first night!"

"Very funny," she says, returning his smile.

If this weren't so strange, it would almost be fun. She finds a place to stand—about twelve feet away this time—and closes her eyes, and just as she did with Chipkorie, tries to become the curator of her own breath and fill her insides with the image of Old Tempi. She doesn't think of the spear, of course. What she thinks of first are his soft brown eyes and the long curl of his dreadlocked hair, then his eyebrows, so thick they're like awnings. But most of all what she pulls in is the feeling of him, the ferocious and tender way he loves his wife and his granddaughter. When she has him fully in her mind, slowly, through the slit of her lips, she blows him out.

One more time, silence. When she opens her eyes, the world jumps forward in brilliant white light—and sure enough, in the still, quiet air, the rock that is Old Tempi is spinning crazily, round and round.

Mentegai and Emely stare at each other. "It's true," he says, awestruck. His smile is like that of a little boy. "Let's try an even heavier one this time," he says excitedly. "Try standing about halfway across the clearing."

She knows what he's thinking. She is not just blowing on stones; she is blowing alive the ember that burned deep inside his father's stories. If it is true that a Stone Woman can make a rock move just with her breath, then the many times his father told him that he loved him were true as well.

But for her it's not so simple. The world seems bathed in a hallucinatory haze; that stone spinning round and round in front of her represents yet another rip in her consciousness. Is breath so powerful, air so sustaining, that they can influence the world so much? And beyond that question, an even greater one: Is she the next Stone Woman? Is she actually here to save the tribe, as Mentegai and Ogotu say?

When she looks up, she sees Mentegai has chosen a stone so heavy it could almost be a seat. Straining to lift it, he ties it to another tree. The branch droops under its dead weight. He pulls the vines away from the trunk of the tree and says, "This time think of Ogotu."

Her hands now clenched in a fist, Emely stares at the rock hanging from the tree. Mentegai stands nearby, his face shining with anticipation. She remembers something Ogotu told her the other day. "Live your questions well," she said. "Don't answer them too soon. Let them ripen like a berry in the sun."

Does she want to pluck this berry? She knows if she turns her back on Mentegai now, she will never return to the touch of his hands. So it is time to choose. Does she really want to know if she is the Stone

Woman? She remembers something else the old woman told her: "If you can imagine your future, you can walk right into it."

Emely takes a deep breath and closes her eyes. She sees the old woman clearly—hunched over her walking stick, hands gnarled like dark roots. Dropping deep, she feels Ogotu's full force, her adherence to that perfect piece of consciousness she believes is buried deep inside everyone from the time when everyone belonged to everyone else. But this time, pushing against the unknown, Emely gets creative. Reaching for the infinite with her breath, she sprinkles in something from her own life. She remembers the flounce of the ocean's lacy skirts when it finally arrived at the shore in Los Angeles. She adds to the force of Ogotu the propulsion of all those waves. Deep now, in a place that's both full and empty at the same time, she gathers it all in until finally, filled with something that is both Ogotu and herself, she blows out.

She opens her eyes. The stone is moving! No whisper of the wind, either.

Mentegai is so excited he's nearly jumping out of his skin. "Let's do it one more time!" he says eagerly. "But let's really put it to the test this time. This time we'll find an even heavier one, and you'll stand all the way across the clearing." He finds a rock so heavy he can barely move it. "Can you help me?" he calls.

Emely joins him, and they begin to roll the rock across the clearing. She watches their hands move companionably together across the surface of the rock. Another berry to pluck. If she can make a stone turn just with breath, what magic can a man and a woman together make?

After Mentegai has wrapped the boulder with forest twine, they strain to lift it together. He ties the knot quickly and commands, "Go all the way over to where the trees begin." Apparently he is quite bossy in the face of miracles.

She walks slowly across the clearing. Reach farther, breathe deeper, soothe the world with breath. Can she do it, inhabit the world on the other side? She isn't so sure. It's like traveling to the other side of the air. She and Mentegai are crossing the final frontier together, taking what is ordinary and combining it with some absolutely splendid idea for the world, beyond anything either of them have ever known.

She's standing in the shade now, so far away that Mentegai looks only a couple of inches high. She doesn't want to be so far from him—

but then she thinks of a way to bring him closer. This time she will think of him. She closes her eyes.

First she thinks of his calm fortitude, then his green-flecked eyes, and the thing that is beginning to dance between them. She thinks of how he seems to find himself in gentle moments—the bend of the stream, the configuration of trees sweeping the sky, the simple poem of walking. She settles her body, quiets her teeming thoughts, and drops deep inside. It's like making love without touching.

She finds a beautiful emptiness down here; quiet, too. Daring the unexplained to step forward, she blows out a gigantic gust, but this time when she opens her eyes the stone hasn't moved. Is it because she's standing so far away?

"Who were you thinking about this time?" Mentegai calls. He has to cup his hands around his mouth for her to hear.

She is reluctant to reveal her heart, but finally answers. "You," she says. "I was thinking of you!"

It seems to take him forever to walk across the clearing, but now he's standing right in front of her, so close in fact that his tattoo looks like one of those mazes children try to follow with one finger. Start at the top, try to keep within the lines, get to the bottom, don't get caught in the cul-de-sac circling the apple of his cheeks. But then she's not seeing the lines of the tattoo anymore, she sees only the tender sky behind the lines, because his face is coming near, so close it is only inches away. She feels his warm breath on her skin.

He stops, suddenly shy. "You're so beautiful," he says. He sweeps his eyes across her body, smiles at all the conversations they have been conducting; then, with exquisite slowness, he once more reaches for her lips.

Their hair twines, does their kissing before they do.

"Emely, Amely," Mentegai murmurs, drawing away. "I've wanted to do this from the first day we walked together into the forest."

"Me too," she says softly.

"I've been so alone. Living in the shadows, hunting, always alone. And then I met you." He gazes into her eyes. "Are you sure this is all right?"

"I've never been so sure of anything," she says, her eyes never leaving his face. He has the beginnings of a sandpaper beard. She runs her finger across the line of his jaw. "It's what I want."

He reaches down to kiss her again, and she closes her eyes, surrendering at last to that ancient conversation between a man and a woman.

Kissing him more ardently, she falls into a new hunger. Completely forgetting her worries, the feel of him is all she allows into her heart. A soft moan escapes her throat, husky, as though it has been strained through some rough material. "There is a wildness in women that shouldn't be apologized for," Ogotu said once, and now Emely understands. How is she going to live with this enormous hunger his mouth has ignited?

How long they kiss she doesn't know, but when they finally draw away from each other a thin moon has appeared in the sky. It touches them with a light that makes them both shine.

"Think of that," Mentegai says, smiling, and when he turns and walks away, Emely feels as though he's taken away some private, aching part of her, a precious part she can only experience when she's with him. It feels like a kind of magic that may not know the words for things but can speak with kisses.

Fortified by the touch of his lips, she decides to try to move the stone again. But this time she keeps her eyes open. Shadows are beginning to deepen into purple, the trees are bearded with moss, a bird hovers above, so slight against the sky it could be an eyelash. It's quiet, too, as if the world itself is leaning in to see what is going to happen.

She looks at the rock hanging on the branch at the other side of the clearing, makes a line of tension between it and the trunk of the tree. Then, mixing what she sees before her with the physical package of oxygen, and adding to it the new feeling of Mentegai's lips, the way the part of her body that will soon be cut from Chipkorie has budded hard, she sprinkles in a little of the flexibility and magic of her nighttime dreams. She catches, loses, then catches all over again an elusive truth, traveling always toward the possibility of finally belonging to something larger than herself. Manipulating it all with the perfect engine of her body, she takes in a deep breath and blows everything she has seen and felt out.

Across the clearing, the boulder begins to revolve.

"Emely Amely," Mentegai calls. "You've done it! You really are the Stone Woman!"

Suddenly bright and dangerous, the late-afternoon light blazes hard. Wrapping her arms around herself, Emely begins to shiver.

CHAPTER 66

A woman speaks through her stones:
We are always our best resting against air.

Tonight, when the dream reaches for her, Emely uses all her parts as she runs—her arms, her legs, and the new, wondrous spaces she discovered this afternoon while blowing on stones.

Her dream brings her to the very same place her grandmother introduced her to on her first night in the forest, the clearing where she met the ghost women. No grandmother this time—no ghost women either, thank goodness—but the same cacophony of sights and sounds, all those inventions saying hello.

Tonight Emely decides she's going to make something that greets the world as well. She leans over and picks up a red leaf, and the same way Mentegai hung rocks from the limbs of trees, she twines it with a blade of grass and dangles it from a branch. *Chipkorie*, she thinks to herself and blows lightly. Just as the rock did this afternoon, the leaf spins on her breath.

Next, she finds a stone that resembles a brown thumb. Looping it with twine, she hangs it close to the red leaf. *Old Tempi*, she decides. Mentegai, of course, is a green feather. Ogotu is a quiet gray stone that twirls close to her husband.

It is everyday play. As she hangs each object, she tries to hear everyone's voice, tries as well not only to hang the objects but to sketch the spaces between them. Because everyone loves her so much, Chipkorie revolves right in the center.

What object can she find to represent herself? She walks back and forth, and the moment she sees it in the long grass, she knows it's right. A tiny bird's skull—its fragile bones leaning up against each other, moonlight pouring through its eye sockets.

Threading a blade of grass through one of its holes, Emely hangs the skull next to the stones, feather, and leaf. It hangs in the tree like a dainty lace doily.

Can she bring the miracle of what happened this afternoon into this dream? She blew everyone else alive with breath. Can she do it for herself?

She stands a couple of feet away from her mobile and decides to try twin breaths: Emely and Amely, paired. It is a conversation between all of her separate parts. She brings in the scared little girl she used to be, made lonely and solitary by a mother's shallow love; then, remembering Mentegai's kiss that afternoon, filled with voluptuous air, she takes a deep breath and blows out.

It works. Right before her eyes, the Old Tempi stone moves toward his wife; they make a private, confidential click. Then the green feather that is Mentegai reaches out and brushes the bird's skull. And all the while, the red leaf that is Chipkorie flickers in the middle of the constellation like a tiny piece of laughter.

She stands in the middle of the clearing, smiling. With only one breath, a red leaf, a green feather, a couple of rocks, and a bird's skull have turned on air and become a family. And more than that—stone, flesh, forest, city, Emely, Amely has breathed in pain and blown herself out whole.

CHAPTER 67

But then, the next morning, a scene. Mentegai and Old Tempi are off hunting. Chipkorie is still sleeping. Emely's cleaning her camera. Ogotu watches everything she does through slit eyes.

Something's growing in the silence—a cold, dynamic dimension expanding by the moment.

And now the old woman's by her side. "You aren't listening to me, and we don't have much more time," she snarls. Hoarse voice, eyes that burn. "You are still living too much in your mind, not your heart. It is time for you to join others who breathe."

Damn it. She asked Mentegai not to tell Ogotu about blowing on the stones yesterday because she didn't want any more pressure from the old woman, but here it is, happening anyway.

"Leave me alone, Ogotu," she says. "I'm tired of all your lectures." She knows she is being rude, but she doesn't want any mystical excursions this morning. She just wants to be an ordinary girl replaying the memory of her first kiss.

It appears she doesn't have a choice in the matter. Just as she did when she dragged Emely around the sculpture cave, Ogotu reaches down with her strong hands, wraps her fingers around her wrist, pulls her to her feet, and begins to lead her down the path. Chipkorie, rubbing sleepy eyes, joins them as well.

"Where are you taking me?" Emely asks.

No answer, of course. Just the dry touch of her skin.

A few minutes later, so abruptly Emely almost bumps into her, the old woman stops. When she sees where they are, Emely gasps in surprise. Ogotu has brought her to the same place she visited last night in her dream, the same place her grandmother had brought her to her first night in the forest.

It's a little more ordinary in daylight, thank goodness—imagination-stirring, ebullient, even, but nothing that conveys the supernatural. No ghosts, either.

Right in front of her is the windmill tree, each blade slowly revolving in the wind. Cupping both land and water, the giant arch rises from the water in the lake. There are towers too—towers everywhere, in fact, glass sparkling. And there, billowing outward, the enormous sail made of leaves and thorns. It is engineered art, really, all these many inventions swirled by air. When a gust of wind strikes the clearing, the blades of the windmill tree begin to revolve; those blades in turn pluck the strings of the guitar trees, wind chimes tinkle like the civilized laughter of guests at a dinner party, and wind flows through the long throat of the flute tube.

Trying not to think about how a place she had visited in her dreams can be manifested bright and solid in front of her, Emely adds her gust of wonder to the many inventions. "This place is incredible," she says. "Can you tell me something about it?" She reaches into her fanny pack and extracts her recorder from a plastic bag. It's been so humid in the forest she's decided to keep all of her digital equipment in plastic, not just the camera.

Chipkorie taps her on the shoulder. "Can I have that?" she asks pointing to the plastic bag.

"Of course," she says. "But what are you going to do with it?"

"I'm going to use it to make more light," the girl responds, and a short time later Emely sees she has done just that. The little bag spins where Chipkorie has tied it to a branch of a tree; in this place of receptive, jubilant light, it's become just another piece of receptive, jubilant light.

Trying to talk the ordinary back into this day, Emely approaches the old woman, the recorder's red light on. "Who made this place?" she asks.

No answer. Ogotu, head down, is busy attaching a brown feather to the end of a stick. Behind her, the giant sail is boozy with breath.

"Did the same women who made all those sculptures in the cave make all of these as well?" Emely persists.

Another gust of wind tears through the clearing, instantly turning it into a moving festival of play. *Ordinary girl, ordinary questions*, Emely tells herself. "How do objects hanging from a tree honor a spiritual concept?" she asks.

The old woman obviously doesn't want to answer, but by now Emely knows she can't resist any chance to indoctrinate her with propaganda.

"All the mothers all the way back to the great river have made this place," Ogotu finally responds. "But you already know that, don't you?"

Emely's not going to answer that one.

"These trees are like members of our family," the old woman continues. "Each tree has something different to say." Despite her scorn at Emely's questions, her face fills with delight. "We share air with everything that is alive. Wait a second and you will hear." She squints, stares at the sky, then points. "In a moment that tree over there will clap, and then the one standing right next to it will spin, and soon everywhere there will be laughter, and we will laugh as well."

Sure enough, it is just as the old woman predicted. Raw, sensual, mixing the smell of leaf mold with the smell of the lake, an enormous blast of wind roars through the trees, breathing life into each invention, and now everything has something to say. The sail made of leaves and thorns swells with breath; streamers of snakeskin tumble forward; light bounces against all the blades of the windmill tree.

She can barely hear what the old woman says above the cacophony of sound.

"You were here last night, weren't you?" she says.

"What?" Emely asks disbelievingly.

An alive click behind her. She turns.

Revolving in a slow orbit right in front of her are the flickering red Chipkorie leaf, the quiet, watchful Mentegai feather, the brown thumb of the Old Tempi stone, the great stillness of the Ogotu stone, and finally, the bird skull filigreed with light. It's the mobile she made last night in her dream.

Emely's body quakes from head to toe with the same feeling she experienced yesterday when she made rocks turn just with her breath. "No," she says. "No. I don't want this." The world is leading her somewhere she doesn't want to go.

Ogotu reaches up, pushes the gray stone against the bird skull, turns to her, and smiles. "You turn on wind and space," she says, watching her closely. "Just the act of breathing mixes with the laughter of this place."

Like a human corkscrew of light, Chipkorie begins to spin round and round, arms outstretched.

"In the time before," Ogotu says, "the cutting would have been one vast, rising song. Instead of my one voice, there would have been many to welcome our initiate to our side, and she would have known from our feasting and songs what she was becoming. When a woman bleeds, it is a love letter sent to all mothers. It connects us with the cycle of the moon. The blood is holy, and we are holy because of it. This is what this place is for. When we don't have blood to offer, we try to at least give our Mother air."

No to all of this aerobic happiness! No to this counterfeit gaiety! Despite everything the old woman preaches, there will be no singing dream of the future. This exuberance is only a lie built on cut girls, the many different inventions trying too hard, the trees palsy against the sky, shadows the color of bruises. Surprised by the violence of her anger, Emely snatches the bird skull and throws it on the ground. It breaks into a dozen pieces.

"No!" she yells. "This is all wrong!" She grabs the Old Tempi stone, throws it as hard as she can. Next goes the Ogotu stone, and then the green feather that is Mentegai is sent on its final flight. Finally, the Chipkorie leaf is thrown to the ground.

"No, no, no!" Emely yells. "Shut up! I don't want to hear one more thing about cuttings or blood!" Crashing, breaking, it feels good. The destruction complete, Emely turns to leave. But just as she is beginning to walk away, she senses something. Behind the giddy shine of the place, something wrong—something sharp and serious and wrong.

She moves across the clearing, driving past Chipkorie, who is still spinning. It's over there by that tall tree with leaves the color of flames, this something that isn't supposed to be here; inside all of this gaudy celebration, one solitary intake of breath.

She pushes through a screen of leaves and finds her. In a small clearing, a pregnant deer lies on the ground, gasping. Eyes deep brown, belly rolling with life, the animal's every impulse is to run, but what has been done to her prevents her from doing so.

Each of her four hooves has been cut from her, her legs only raw bloody stumps.

CHAPTER 68

E mely stands shocked, staring down at the hurt animal. "The Wrong One's back," she instantly thinks. "He's the only one who would do this to an animal." She hears Chipkorie's sharp intake of breath as she comes up behind her.

"Stand back granddaughter," Ogotu orders, stepping into the small clearing. "Don't let any of this wrong blood touch you. What we have to do is send this animal to her final sleep." The old woman moves to the head of the deer, sits down, and, so tenderly she could be holding her first child, pulls the animal's head to her lap. The deer's eyes are wide open but are dimming quickly.

Ogotu lowers her face, gazing into the deer's eyes. "I'm sorry," she says. "You should have had the chance to deliver the new life growing in you. Much, much later we would have continued your spirit by eating your flesh and giving thanks to the Mother for your life. This is how it should have been. But now this has happened to you. Even in death your bones won't be right."

The animal is losing the rhythm of in-and-out breath, but still, glimmering in its eyes is the why, why, why; it asks that question with each blink of its eyelids.

As Emely watches death move inside the animal, occupying more and more space, each of its ragged breaths cracks against her and pulls her into a vast fear. She doesn't know how she knew to come here to this small clearing finger-painted with blood.

Death is quickly becoming the dominant presence inside the animal. Ogotu is now only inches from the deer's eyes, ushering the animal toward her final breath. Something that can't be said with words finally passes between them.

"Go," the old woman whispers. "Go and become the great beyond."

The passing of life is like watching a day end: you're never really quite sure the exact moment day has turned to evening. Death is soft. This animal who once moved mild and free through these trees, flicking her delicate ears, growing fat on green grass, this animal who slept in secret, shadowed nooks, takes her last breath and moves into the final forever.

More potent even than when the deer was alive, a charged vacuum fills the clearing. Without the deer's breath to belong to, fragmented, broken, and alone, the people who stand in the clearing can't quite look at each other.

Ogotu leans over and closes each of the deer's eyes. "No more innocence," she finally says with heavy sadness. "Just one death, but nothing will ever be the same."

Lifting the deer's head from her lap, she stands and walks over to the trees, breaks off four leaves. "When you kill even one animal this way, you kill something inside yourself," she says, almost to herself.

Returning to the deer, she places a leaf against each stump where its hooves should have been.

Emely turns to her. "Did the Wrong One do this?" she asks.

The old woman raises her head and looks at her with the same focus with which a few minutes ago she looked at the deer. "Yes," she says. "What I've been worried about for some time has come true. The Wrong One is back in the forest."

Emely has no chance to think about what the old woman has just said, for at that moment her brother Kareem bursts into the clearing.

CHAPTER 69

Panting, covered with bruises, one eye black and swollen—someone has hurt Kareem badly.

"Kareem," Emely gasps. "What are you doing here?"

Hands on his knees, trying to catch his breath, he doesn't answer.

Ogotu swings her eyes to Emely. "You know who this is?"

Barely able to believe what she sees before her, Emely blinks. "He's my little brother," she says, "but I have no idea how he got here."

"He's hurt," the old woman says, approaching him. Very gently she runs her fingers up and down his body. "I don't think anything is broken, but somebody has beaten him badly." She turns to her granddaughter. "Get this boy some water."

A short time later, Kareem is greedily drinking from a long tube of bamboo, water splashing down his chin.

His eyes hunt for Emely over his clasped hands on the tube. "You're in big trouble, Sis," he rasps. "I had to find you and tell you. There's a police chief here in the forest with a lot of soldiers. They want to kill you."

"Me?" Emely is stunned. "What are you talking about?"

Though one of his eyes is swollen shut, she can tell he is avoiding looking into her eyes. He takes another drink from the tube of bamboo.

"I was arrested," he finally confides in a low voice. "The soldiers brought me into this forest. Police Chief Kenti wants to kill you and everyone else who lives here. He even mentioned your name. I thought they were going to kill me, too, but then his men got really drunk, and when they weren't watching I was able to slip away. I know the ways of animals, know how to stay silent, follow signs. That's how I found you."

"Police Chief Kenti?" she exclaims. "Are you sure of that name?"

He nods. "Yes. I certainly heard it spoken enough. Why? Have you heard of him?"

Now it is her turn to not quite return his gaze. She tries to make a joke out of it. "Guess we're just a family of jailbaits. I was arrested too!"

"You?" he says. "What for?"

"It was no big deal," she says, shrugging. "I was a few minutes late getting to the youth hostel after my flight landed, and I was arrested for breaking curfew. That's when I met Chief Kenti. I talked myself out of jail though. When I told him I was part of the Land Reform Movement, he released me." She spreads her hands. "It was nothing. Really." She narrows her eyes. "Why were *you* arrested?"

Shame, guilt, pride, secrecy—an entire genealogy of feelings chase themselves one right after the other across Kareem's face, and when he finally replies, some of the secretive, angry brother Emely encountered on the bus ride home returns.

"Fat cats," he spits. "Friends of the president are taking our land, you know. They're in cahoots with big corporations. They could even take father's land. All kinds of backroom deals are going on."

"What are you talking about, Kareem?" she asks impatiently. "What does any of this have to do with you being arrested?"

"I fell in with some people at school," he says in a low voice. "We wanted to make a statement. We were planning five simultaneous explosions at five different government-owned businesses around the country. A Five Point Star, we called our action. I was going to blow up the quarry near our home. It's government-owned, you know." He raises his head, meets her eyes. "I wasn't going to hurt anybody."

She's astonished, asks the first thing she thinks of. "But how do you know how to make a bomb, Kareem?"

"I looked it up on the Internet," he says, almost proudly. "I got a piece of PVC pipe and loaded it with dynamite from the shack in the quarry." Even swollen with bruises, his face grows soft and dreamy.

"There's a girl," he says. "Her name is Eshe. . . She's so beautiful. I just wanted to show her how brave I was."

Emely doesn't know whether she wants to slap him or put her arms around him. "Oh, Kareem," she says, "how could you be so stupid? You could have gotten yourself killed!"

She remembers how, when Kareem was little and one of his animals died, he would crawl into bed beside her, the blanket he always slept with clutched in his hands. "Why does everyone always leave me?" he would cry, and she would comfort him as only a big sister can. "It will be alright," she would croon, until finally he was able to sleep. But then one day she was no longer there to crawl into bed with. When she left for boarding school, Kareem must have taken all that tenderness—the way he hurt when that fish died, or when a kitten stopped breathing—and turned it into raw anger. He dropped his blanket and took on the world.

But buried beneath all those purple bruises is the achingly sweet brother she has missed so much. She hears it in the way he says the name Eshe, pledging his heart to a love so beyond reach it was bound to eventually hurt him.

Ogotu's shrewd, traveling mind puts it together first. Both the place that begins the question and the answer arrived, she speaks quietly. "The one you call Police Chief Kenti is my nephew, the Wrong One. He is the one who did this to the deer. It's a message for me, announcing his arrival back in the forest."

She moves her eyes from Emely to the dead deer, then to her granddaughter's face, and then back to Emely. "Your brother is right. The one you call the police chief is going to find us, and when he does he'll kill us all." She squints her eyes, raises her head. "There is only one thing to do," she says grimly. "Though the moon is not quite full, tomorrow, at the first blush of the sun, we will cut Chipkorie. It is the only way to shove back this wrong."

Suddenly somber, older, Chipkorie immediately moves to her side. "I'm ready, Grandma," she says. "Don't worry. I will dance all night long, make myself clean inside."

"I know you will," Ogotu says, and she puts her arms around her. She gazes at Emely across her granddaughter's head. "And you, Amely, must spend the night praying to the Mother so that you will be clean enough to cut."

"I've told you a million times, I'm not going to have anything to do with the cutting," Emely says, almost spitting out the words. "That's not the answer anyway. This is an out-of-control police officer who's abusing his power. I have to get on the radio, contact the professor. He'll put a stop to this immediately."

When Ogotu raises her arm and points a finger at her, the skin under her arms quivers indignantly. "You must spend the night praying to the Mother, so that when I hand you the cutting glass in the morning, you will be able to slice quickly."

Ogotu and Emely are so entangled with the battle they are waging, they forget about Kareem for a moment; both are startled when he speaks.

"Does this have anything to do with female genital mutilation?" he asks tentatively.

The old woman looks as though she wants to give him another black eye. "Do not speak of women's things!" she snaps.

But he persists. "I think I might know something about this," he says. He turns to Emely. "Right before I was arrested I found a cave. I had never seen it before. It was really deep, and I climbed down inside of it because I heard a lot of voices way down below. Mama was down there, and she was sobbing. Everyone was there—Auntie Bulu, Afrua, all the women in the village—and they were talking about you!"

"Me!" she exclaims. "Why were they talking about me?"

"It was right after you had just come home. They were going to find you and keep you in the cave and perform what they called the biggest cutting of them all. That's why Mama was crying. I think it has something to do with . . ." His voice trails away.

"Female genital mutilation?" Emely nudges.

He nods. "Mama kept offering her own blood, but they said it wasn't the right kind. She said you would die, and she was crying really hard, but they said you couldn't go into the forest unclean. It sounded as though they wanted to cut you a long time ago, but Mama outsmarted them by sending you away to the boarding school."

Dead deer buzzing with flies, brother blooming black roses planted by soldiers' fists, Ogotu in a frenzy to cut, and a crazy man with a shiny, vindictive mind coming forward to slaughter them all . . . but what does Emely do? She falls to her knees, shot straight through the heart with love, everything she thought a moment ago has just been proven untrue. Mama does love her—loves her so well, in fact, that she sent her away to save her. A deadly secret beats away beneath the benign surface of her village: the women who raised her still practice the ancient cuttings. That is the reason Mama sent her away to boarding school; that is the reason she sent her away that last morning. Not once, but twice, Mama has saved her from being cut. She has placed her face in the black wind of village criticism to protect her.

Mama, Mama love, comes on the light. For the first time in what seems like years, Emely becomes calm inside, the motherless vacuum inside her, so long empty, now filled. It's as if she can see her mother from inside of herself; she now understands the secret that made her so frightened.

Mama, Mama, Mama. Pushed into the safe harbor of her life by big-time, sturdy Mama love, Emely Matei, oldest daughter of Ebele Matei, is finally home.

Until Old Tempi's face breaks into her mind, that is. *Amely*, he calls in spirit voice. *You have to come get me.* Face a full moon, eyes wild and frightened over lips so still. *I've never been so scared. Many soldiers. They came and dragged me here.*

Two realities at once, a duet of inside and out; at that moment Mentegai bursts into the clearing as well. "Soldiers," he yells. "They have the old man!"

CHAPTER 70

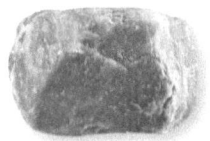

*I*n all this smeared night our new Stone Woman thinks she is only one *leaf falling,* the dead say, *but she is not alone. Lantern songs, that bright. Cradle songs that will rock her to sleep. Hearth songs to curl around and feel their warmth. Our songs run through her blood.*

It is time, time for her to know us. If she listens, we can help her.

Back in the cave, Ogotu is in a frenzy. "It is time," she says. A frantic, embittered energy burns in her eyes. "When the sun rises tomorrow, we will cut." She locks eyes with Emely, and everything that has been lurking beneath the surface of all those long, flat days begins to spin, moving closer to this, her demand. "Tomorrow I will hand you the piece of holy glass, and you will bend between Chipkorie's legs."

Emely doesn't even bother to reply, just goes to the back of the cave and turns on her radio. "CD1245, come in, sir. Base camp here. Come in." The glittering coinage of all those important-sounding words.

The old woman places her hand against Chipkorie's head. Against its clean perfection the old woman's arthritic fingers look even more crooked, as though each finger is attempting to escape.

"We know time from the very beginning," she says, caressing her granddaughter's head. "When our bones were shaped differently, our fingernails were scales, and we could breathe underwater." Though she speaks to no one in particular, the words move into well-worn ruts; somehow Emely knows they are the ancient words used before cuttings.

She will use her important-sounding words in response. Once again she picks up the radio's microphone. "CD1245, come in please. We have a critical situation here."

"Our green is only as small as the pupil of an eye," Ogotu says.

It is a war between words and gadgets. Hands on the radio's dials, turning, hands on the young girl's head, turning.

The old woman raises her head, imperious, streaks her eyes across the paintings of the cave. "What happens when the world doesn't re-member how it began?" she asks rhetorically. "What happens when the old stories are no longer told?" Though she seems to be trying to reach for some kind of regal authority, fear burns deep in her eyes.

She's scared, Emely suddenly realizes. *She's as scared as I am.*

No answer from the paintings, of course. Chipkorie is vacant and gone, her body already commercialized for the old woman's needs; and now this microphone, too, is dead in her hands.

And then one more time the old man breaks into her head. His skin also blooms Kareem's garden of black roses. *I'm dissolving*, he says, his voice weak. *I'm only rain on water. Please come, Amely. You're the only one who can save me. I'm sorry I didn't believe you were the Stone Woman.*

The old woman comes close, squinting hard, twin fires of hysteria in her eyes. "You're hearing from my husband, aren't you?"

The old man floats for a moment in Emely's mind, his face a full moon against the empty sky. She nods her head.

"You must cut this girl," the old woman snarls. "It is the only way to get my husband back."

"You know it's the last thing in the world I would do," Emely says, speaking hard. She now knows what she has to do. Didn't Mama stand up against her husband, Father Joseph, and all the women in the vil-lage? The place that has been hollow inside her for so long is now filled with the essence of her mother. She will use all of that courage for what she knows she has to do next. "I'm going to go out and talk to the police chief," she announces. "I'm going to convince him to give me back the old man."

"No, Emely," Kareem immediately cries. "He'll kill you."

And then the heat of Ogotu's scorn. "You think that you can just look into that man's dead eyes and put the sound of an upright walking stick into your voice, and he's going to listen to you? He's the Wrong One. Your brother's right. He's just going to kill you, and then he's going to turn around and kill my husband. The only thing that is going to stop this is Chipkorie's blood."

"Maybe this is all just some kind of mistake," Emely says. "I've managed to talk sense into him once before. If I did it once, maybe I can do it again."

"He wants to kill you, Emely," Kareem says. "Be careful."

Avoiding her brother's pleading eyes, Emely turns and grabs Mentegai's hand. "Will you walk me as far as the clearing where the soldiers are?" she asks. "I need to talk to the chief alone, but I would love some company along the way."

By way of saying yes, he squeezes her hand.

Before she leaves, Emely puts her arms around Chipkorie. "I'll try to get your grandpa back," she whispers. "You don't have to cut yourself." But the girl isn't listening. She's already gone deep inside, moving toward a faraway place Emely can't reach.

CHAPTER 71

As though reluctant to generate light for this night, the moon's thin light falls broken to the ground. The land is tired, like overchewed meat. Smoke fills one part of the sky; chainsaws growl on the horizon.

Old man, she asks in spirit voice, *are you there?*

Nothing. Nothing except her hand in Mentegai's.

Mentegai leads her deep into the forest, pausing once to help her climb over a tree that has fallen across the trail, stopping another time just to stroke his hand across her head. They reach the edge of the clearing where the soldiers are, peer out from behind a tree.

A massive tent has been erected in the middle. Men are everywhere, a surf of incessant movement spiked with diverse acts of violence. Each soldier seems to be engaged in some kind of demolition against a tree. Some light fires against the massive trunks, others use chainsaws, some swing axes—the only difference between each man is the method of destruction he holds in his hands. A cluster of yellow flowers spangle the gloom at their feet, their blooms more eloquent and forgiving than any face she sees before her.

Emely feels the police chief's deadly mind out there, waiting for her in the tent. Despite her confident promise to everyone, she's more frightened than she has ever been in her life.

Light suddenly hoses the tree they stand by.

"Get down!" Mentegai hisses in her ear and pulls her to the ground. She presses her head against his chest, hears the measured beat of his heart. Curtained by dreads, it's the safest place she knows, more sheltering even than the cave. The light passes on.

"I'm so scared," she whispers.

Mentegai leans back and inspects her face. "You can do this," he says. "Think of what you did yesterday with only your breath."

The world out there is like a giant x-ray divested of any kind of color, only desolate, skeletal information revealed. Each soldier a cardboard cutout hinged to his shadow.

"Sometimes in my dreams my body becomes part stone, but in the daytime all I want is you," she murmurs.

"I know," he says, and when she lifts her face to his they kiss with the intensity of all the times they have wanted to but haven't. She feels how muscular his body is, how warm his skin, and the feeling that rises from their joined bodies is the only true thing in all the world. As they kiss her body fills with an ecstasy very different from the one she feels when she is tall and running, and she surrenders completely to the feeling, falling into this new and persistent physical hunger.

In the clearing before them a giant tree falls, taking with it all the younger trees below it. Birds flutter and fill the air with sound, alerting the sky and each other that one more home is gone. Emely and Mentegai break away from each other, panting slightly.

"I love you," he says, gazing into her eyes. He sends the words into the brutality and chaos of the falling trees and smoke. "I'll be waiting for you right here."

Paired with the in-and-out gallows of his breath, she wants to stay here forever, but he won't let her. He pulls her to her feet. "Hurry back to me," he says, kissing her on the forehead. "The faster you do this, the faster you'll be back in my arms."

Fortified with new love, fledgling Stone Woman, the future Dr. Emely Matei, steps into the clearing.

CHAPTER 72

The first thing she sees is a truck tearing up the red wound of the road, bristling with half a dozen soldiers. As though attached to a string, at the same time all of the soldiers turn their heads to look at her.

"Look," says one of them, standing unsteadily. "It's an animan!" He takes a swig from the bottle he holds in his hand. The alcohol shines with the color of young wood. "Ugly little jungle creature, isn't it?" he says with rubbery lips. He wipes the back of his mouth with his hand. "Guess we're smoking them out!"

She reminds herself that the night behind her is still kind, tries holding Mentegai's "I love you" close.

"Animan," says another soldier.

"Monkey eyes," says another.

The other soldiers take up the chant. "Monkey eyes, monkey eyes," and the venom in their words moves into the space left behind by chainsaws.

Why didn't she remember to clean herself up for this encounter? As if she's holding up a mirror, for the first time in weeks she sees herself through exterior sight. A colobus monkey skin drapes her shoulders;

she wears a necklace Chipkorie made for her, fashioned from seedpods; Ogotu has stained her cheeks with blue; and her hair is beginning to spike like tiny exclamation points all over her head.

And she will be the one to remind the police chief of their country's constitutional law? Moving toward the tent, she unwraps the monkey skin from her shoulders and drops it to the ground for its final sleep.

No warm animal to snuggle her shoulders, the moon too far away to be good company, what she sees when she enters the tent knocks the breath out of her. A cluster of candles burns at the base of a giant cross, and a heavy fragrance fills the air—an opiate replete with forgetfulness. Though the light is soiled with smoke, there is no question that a man stands a few feet away from her, and she doesn't need to see his face to know who he is.

"Amely Emely," he says. Gleam runs along the bottom of his voice. "I knew you would come. I have the old man and now I have you." His voice licks her skin. Just its sound and her body temperature lowers.

More skull than face, so many medals shine on the police chief's chest it looks like a computer keyboard.

A feeling of incredible malevolence steals over Emely, and she can't find one single word of the argument she practiced. "Are you the Wrong One?" she whispers.

His eyes light up. "Yes!" he responds. "I am Police Chief Kenti and I am also the Wrong One." He speaks in a strangely intimate way, as though he knows something about her she hasn't yet discovered.

"Did you cut the hooves from that deer?"

"Yes," he responds. "It was a message for my aunt to tell her I'm back."

A new kind of silence fills the tent, different than the one that fills the night outside; no laughter, no songs, no questions, it's a silence laced only with malice. When the chief speaks again his voice moves dirty through the thick air. "My aunt kicked me out long ago," he says. "But I always swore I was going to come back and show her that my power is so much greater than anything that moves on wind chimes and breath. I even let your brother escape; I knew he would try to find you. And then I told my soldiers to take the old man because I knew you would rise to the bait and try to get him back."

As if trying to find its own individual vigor, the smoke from the candles curls for a moment, but then the thick, prevailing absence in the tent sponges up even that small piece of life.

"Amely Emely," the police chief says. "You stand where I should be. You live in my family's heart—but not for very much longer." His voice festers with old resentments, deep wounds. "In a matter of hours I will burn these trees. And when I find my family I will kill them." He reaches up and theatrically slashes one finger across his neck. "I will watch them die, and then, finally, no more family, no more trees, no more Mother."

He begins to pace back and forth.

"Twenty years ago my aunt pushed me out of the forest. I lost my home, my family, my life." Hate burns deep in his eyes. "For twenty years I have lived the lie that is Police Chief Kenti, plotting, strategizing, assimilating the power I needed to implement my plan. But now it's my turn! I'm going to destroy her world. My aunt will suffer as I have suffered. I am going to watch her face as she dies." He punches the air with his fist. "The Wrong One is back!"

Is it a trick of the smoke? Right before her eyes, the chief's shadow seems to expand, completely swamps one side of the tent.

"I will slash light into the heart of this dreary forest," he continues. "I will cut all the trees, and when all is flat, everything I see before me will belong to me."

She remembers how her grandmother warned her about this man the first night she encountered him in the police station. *He plays with bones not breath*, Grandmama said. *He crawls into the darkest places, loves the midnight things. But most of all what he loves is to kill.*

"You can't just come in and take someone from their tribal home," Emely says. Though they are the words she practiced, her voice sounds thin even to her ears. "It's against international law. There are laws to protect the rights of indigenous people. The professor will put a stop to this."

She remembers what Ogotu said: "You think that you can just look into that man's dead eyes and put the sound of an upright walking stick into your voice, and he's going to listen to you?" The old woman was right. All the arguments Emely practiced seem to have melted away under the power of the chief's malicious gaze, all of her words reduced by his cruel, corrupt mind.

He barks the sound that is his particular laugh. "The professor?" he scoffs. "Haven't you figured it out yet, Emely Amely? No one cares about the rights of indigenous people, especially not your precious professor. The only thing he cares about is finding the tablet. Hasn't he

300 o JEANiE KORTUM

been hounding you about finding it in every single radio transmission? 'Find the tablet, find the tablet!' That's the reason he had me slip that GPS unit into your backpack when you were sleeping at the police station. The moment you found the tablet we were going to come in with my soldiers and confiscate it. It's all he's ever wanted. The gathering of scholarly information was only a ruse to get you into this forest. The only reason you were hired is that your grandmother has ties to the forest and he thought maybe that might bring him a little closer to finding the tablet. He was trying to manipulate your guide Mentegai, too because his mother and father came from this forest, but he slipped out of his grasp."

He crosses his arms. "I pretended to make an alliance with him," he says. "It's so easy to manipulate greed, you know. He was so predictable. The professor thinks that finding the tablet will make him rich. I've used that greed, even sent him a statue made from the clay from this forest just to underscore the fact that I had ties to this place. I fed him just enough information to inflame his ambitions, and in return he pulled the political strings necessary to install me in a position of power. I needed men, you see, many men, to implement my plan. But here I am," he says, thumping his chest emphatically. "Police Chief Kenti. Full authority to send in my soldiers, burn all the trees, and slaughter my ex-family."

"No," Emely says weakly. It is as though he is some powerful force of nature only temporarily wearing flesh. Staring into his dark heart, she can't think of one thing to say. Slowly, purposefully, he is divesting her of any outside reinforcement. She closes her eyes against the sucking hole of him.

Because she heard the truth in what he had just told her about the professor. All their recent radio transmissions: "Never mind the fate of that young girl," the professor said. "Pretend to be the Stone Woman. Use their beliefs to find the tablet."

The sour taste of betrayal fills her throat. She now fully understands that Police Chief Kenti is right: the professor has just been using her.

"Finally my aunt will know my power," the chief says. "I alone control shadow and sun, not the precious Mother I heard so much about when I was growing up. There will be no one left when I finish. Violation, death, punishment, and hate. These are my children. This is what I love above all else."

Emely tries to swallow but can't. This man, so broken, he needs the world to be broken as well, what power does she have to fight him?

Trying to find some embryonic part of the man that is still good, she stares at him. Suddenly she remembers the statue in the sculpture cave of the little boy with the dimpled bottom. Is that little boy still inside of him? Can she find him?

It is as though he knows what she is searching for; his eyes light up, and he rubs his hands together delightedly. "You won't find it," he says, answering the question she hasn't even spoken aloud. "I have spent my entire life divesting myself of anything that is good." He takes a step closer. "You know, Emely Amely," he says, "you are as much a part of this plan as I am. You need me just as much as I need you. We hold each other in balance. I am dark to your light, shadow to your sun, sickness to your health, wrong to your pretty kind of right. We are more alike than you know." His brutal mind seems to light up the insides of the tent. He takes a second step toward her. "Have you ever considered that you fostered some of this chaos yourself?"

Is it some kind of inflamed telepathic force? Now he isn't just moving into her mind with thoughts; somehow, he is filling her head with pictures. A forlorn landscape—no trees, just red dust swirling in the wind. Ogotu, Old Tempi, and Chipkorie pushed by soldiers with rifles; Mentegai, his hands shackled behind him, pulled along by a rope. Right before her eyes he falls, is dragged a few feet before scrambling up again. Behind them the forest crackles with flames.

"Join me," the chief croons. "Think of it! You and me, Emely Amely. Together we could own all of sun and shadow."

She reaches for the stone in her pocket, runs her fingers across its smooth surface. *Ogotu*, she prays, *Grandmama, Mama, can you come? I'm so scared*. She tries turning her prayers into sharp arrowheads, tries this way to penetrate the thick, brackish gloom that fills the tent, but everything she speaks is quickly extinguished.

Eyes riveted on hers, the police chief is taking away everything that is good, pursuing her down into herself until her very bones vibrate with his evil.

It is only when she is so small she is just a cast-off splinter of herself that she remembers her grandmother's necklace. "Hold it in your hand," her mother said as she slipped it over her head the last morning they were together, "and when it is warm with you, you can send us your thoughts. We will hear them, and then all who are alive and all who are dead will come to you."

She reaches for the necklace and grips it tight; her mother was right. Suddenly she knows what to say. "The only opposites we need are our songs against the outside thoughts, feelings against the ax, the intake of breath against its release," she tells the chief. "These are the twins that compose our world."

She remembers something Ogotu told her the other day. "When you admit what you don't know, that is where the Great Mother will begin." *The old woman was right*, Emely thinks. As she holds her grandmother's necklace, the words flowing through her are of her and not of her all at the same time, so powerful they billow out the sheath of the tent.

"The Great Mother," she says, "She is the sound of her name and yet she is all names. The still air that follows her fury says more than she ever can with just one bolt of thunder."

The police chief knows what is happening before Emely does. His eyes light up. "The Great Mother!" he says. "She's here."

The words so brilliant they throw off their own light, she lives them as they cross her throat. She now even knows the bargain to make. "How about instead of killing the forest people, you give me two weeks to convince them to leave the forest?" she asks. "Won't that be more satisfying than a quick massacre that could ultimately get you in trouble?"

Eyes ice cold, the chief is watching her.

"The forest people will be moved onto a reservation. They'll suffer for the rest of their lives, remember you every day. Then you can come in and bulldoze all these trees, burn it all down."

When he smiles, he releases a cold current of energy. "That sounds like a good idea," he says. "And can we agree to one other component of this agreement? Can we both give Chipkorie what she and Ogotu so desperately want?"

Emely hesitates. "You mean the cutting?" she finally whispers.

"Yes," he says, crossing his arms triumphantly. He smiles down at her from what seems to be a great height. "As the reigning Stone Woman, it will seal our little bargain. I will save their lives only if you cut her."

She slowly releases her grip on her grandmother's necklace, balls her hands into tight fists at her side. "You know that's the last thing in the world I would ever do," she says.

He shrugs. "I'm through playing games then"—and, turning, he begins to walk toward the door of the tent. Light from all the candles flickers against his skin.

Emely realizes she is trapped. Chipkorie's beautiful face floats before her. Refuse and the soldiers will come in and slaughter everyone; agree and even if Chipkorie survives, she will be forever altered.

"If it means keeping everyone alive, I'll do it," she calls after him. "But only if you give me back the old man."

He turns, blazes a smile as bright as the candles. "It's a deal!" he says. He slips outside, and a moment later Old Tempi is dragged into the tent.

CHAPTER 73

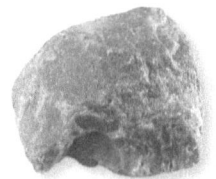

Barely conscious, the old man keeps falling as Mentegai and Emely drag him back to the cave. But it's not so much his wounds that concern her; it's the new absence spinning deep inside. The old man is gone. She can't even reach him with spirit voice.

As they near the cave, Ogotu appears out of the dark. Just as she had with Kareem, she passes her seeing hands across every part of her husband's body. "He's inside," she says, more to herself than anyone else, "but he's fiercely disappointed in the world." She looks up at them. "I can get his body to heal with my herbs and rest, but I don't know about his mind."

No questions about how Emely got him back, no thank-you, either; her entire focus is her husband. Ogotu helps Mentegai bring Old Tempi to the fire, lowers him carefully to the ground, then begins to gently sponge the blood from his body. The bowl of water she uses quickly turns a deep opaque rust color. When she once again lifts her head, however, it's to issue her familiar refrain, the relentless drive toward cutting.

"Amely," she says, "you must begin to make yourself a piece of the moon, clean and bright. We have my husband back but the Mother still needs blood."

"Ogotu," Emely says, exasperated. "I don't want to talk about this."

Shame punches her hard. She thinks of the agreement she just made. In a matter of weeks everyone will be led out of the forest, forced to live on a reservation. Would they even agree to it? Even the fact that she has agreed to cut Chipkorie won't soften the cruel bargain she has just made. And she didn't know if she could bend between her friend's legs and cut her with a piece of glass.

And the professor! How could she ever have been so naive as to trust him? He doesn't care about her. He has just been using her to get to the tablet.

She tears herself away from the old woman's gaze, moves to the mouth of the cave. Betrayed by the professor, pushed into the small confines of the terrible bargain she has just made with the police chief, she catches a glimpse of the world tipping on its axis, cut away forever from the web of the past. All of those trees out there will be burned down, rows of chemically engineered crops will strip the land, no more songs and stories of remembering will rise into the sky. The umbilical cord that connects the world to its beginnings will forever be severed.

What has she done?

She jumps at the sound of Kareem's voice in her ear. "I really thought I would never see you again," he said. "How did you get the old man back?"

She answers more sharply than she means to. "I don't want to talk about it," she snaps, and turns back to the fire.

Chipkorie sways back and forth before the flames, her body already ready to be used. As though to narrate what is to come, the old woman extracts a knife from her furs, glides it quickly across her arm. A bunched red rose immediately blooms on her skin. She transfers that rose to her mouth when she brings her head down to drink from the severed artery—then, approaching Chipkorie, she dips her finger in the blood, draws a line across the girl's forehead. More slashes—one on the left cheek, one on the right. The crazy old lady is finger-painting her granddaughter with blood.

And then Mentegai's voice in her ear. "You have to find the tablet. It's the only thing that will save us."

She doesn't want to turn and see the faith shining in his beautiful eyes. She hasn't told him about the bargain she had made with the police chief, or the professor's betrayal.

"Why is it all resting on me?" she says—again, more harshly than she means to. "I have no idea where it is. It's not like there's any kind of treasure map or something like that."

"You can find it," he insists. "You're the Stone Woman."

"I don't know if I even believe that." Something hard has arrived in her voice. "It could be just one of your father's drunken stories."

His face seems to move in on itself; hurt swallows the edges of his open, loving expression. One last time the burn of his beautiful green eyes, then he turns and goes back to the fire.

Now she is truly alone, so lost she has become brutal herself—irrefutable proof that she is a low-down, mean person, capable of doing low-down, mean things.

And just when she thinks it can't get any worse, the police chief's voice fills her head. *You will die tonight,* he says.

You said we had two weeks! she exclaims back in spirit voice.

His voice hums in her head. *Did you forget who I am?* he cackles. *I'm the Wrong One! I break everything, especially my word. Of course I would have loved to have seen you cut the girl, but what I love most is watching people die. Tonight I will watch light slip from my aunt's eyes, hear my family's last cries. My soldiers and I are close now. Do you see me?*

Sure enough, she sees fire curling against the sky a few miles away.

She turns to look at the people in the cave. Ogotu raises the knife, cuts herself once again. Chipkorie sways before the fire, eyes closed, Kareem watching her. The old man sleeps. Mentegai stares glumly into the flames. In a matter of hours they will all be killed, and she has no idea what to do.

And then, just as it happened in the dream her first night in the forest, a hand reaches toward her through the veils of life and death, grabs her wrist. *It is time to dream again,* says a voice as soft as flower petals.

She knows who it is immediately. Grandmama's back. But this time Emely doesn't have time for ephemeral ghosts. Tonight people are going to be killed.

She tries to pull away, but it's just like the first night when her grandmother taught her how to fly: her grip is strong. Emely is pulled out of the cave and into the clearing.

CHAPTER 74

The moon lacquers the clearing's miniature beauty; the sky is so bright it is as if it alone carries hope for the night. Emely blinks in the sudden light.

Listen to me, granddaughter, her grandmother says. *You must do exactly as I say.* Like words floating across water, her voice floats back to her slightly dislocated.

"Please, Grandmama," Emely pleads, "let me go. I don't have time for a dream. Police Chief Kenti is back in the forest, and he's going to murder us all!"

Grandmama wasn't large in life; in death, however, she is powerful. Emely can't break free of her grip. *I am your best chance for staying alive,* she says. *I've come back from the other side to paint you for the ones who are lost.*

One more time Emely tries to pull away. "I don't know what that means, Grandmama," she whines. "Please, let me go."

No answer. Her grandmother just begins to pull her into the trees. The air thick with the nocturnal campaigns that usually knock against her sleep, gripped by a powerful, gauzy hand, Emely stumbles forward. It's a neighborhood she is not part of; the forest is so dark she thinks at first they are moving through long silver ribbons hanging from the sky. *No*, she realizes a moment later, *they aren't silver ribbons; it's moonlight pouring down the sides of the enormous, dark trees.*

"Where are you taking me, Grandmama?" she asks. Her grandmother doesn't answer but the world does. Wet stones, a poured, determined sound, the silver tassels of river plants—she realizes they are close to the river.

Ogotu has brought you this far, her grandmother says, *but she is still made of flesh. The dead on the other hand have the wider, more complicated thoughts that will protect and guide you.*

One more time Emely tries to pull away. "I don't have time for this, Grandmama. Soldiers are coming! Don't you see that fire over there?"

Stop thinking so much, Amely, her grandmother snaps. *That's always been your problem. You think you can control the world with your frightened thoughts, but it's only in the silent places in between what you know that you'll find the answers.*

They stop at the edge of the river, and her grandmother turns to her. *Take off your clothes and that necklace I gave you*, she orders, and it doesn't matter that Emely can see right through her, that she is made only of moonlight and gauze—just as it did when she was alive, her grandmother's voice holds the expectation of obedience.

Do it! she says again when Emely hesitates.

"But why, Grandmama?" she asks. "I don't understand."

Don't argue with me, Amely! The Stone Woman wears no clothes or jewelry.

More to get it over with than anything else Emely pulls her T-shirt over her shoulders and head, takes off the necklace, her pants and underwear. Her grandmother, in the meantime, is busy prodding the clay on the riverbank. Finding a consistency that seems to please her, she scoops some of it up in the palm of her hand.

Lift your arm, she instructs, and when Emely complies, the old woman rubs the white clay of the river into the hollow of Emely's armpit. She shivers. "Grandmama," she exclaims. "It's cold!"

Her grandmother doesn't answer, just begins to smooth the pale clay across her body—up to cover her face, down across her breast and pelvic region, down over one arm, webbing it between her fingers, and then all over one leg and between her toes. But all only on one side.

On one hand it feels good to be loved and stroked by her grandmother; on the other hand, she doesn't understand any of this. "What are you doing, Grandmama?" she asks once again. She needs to raise her voice to be heard over the sound of the rushing river. "How is this going to help?"

I am painting you for the ones who have strayed so far away they don't believe in magic anymore, her grandmother replies. *It is easy for them to take an ax and chop down a tree that is older than their great-grandmother. But something new will begin when you stand in front of them and dance. There will be more room inside to find out what it is they have forgotten.* She reaches up and pushes white clay into the roots of Emely's hair.

"But how is a little bit of mud slapped on me going to stop them from killing us all?" Emely asks. She knows her voice is shrill but can't help it. "Mud can't stop bullets, you know."

I'm painting you with the Stone Woman's palette, her grandmother responds. *Do you remember your dreams when you run tall through the forest at night, part flesh, part stone?*

"Yes, but they're only dreams, Grandmama, kind of like this." The clay dries quickly in the night air, begins to crack.

Hold still, is all her grandmother says. Moonlight shines through her, her eyelashes spike shadows. She layers more clay into the web of skin between her granddaughter's fingers.

Emely hears a small metallic click on the wind, knows instantly what it is—the release of the safety on the trigger of a gun. A tremor runs through her body. "Do you hear that, Grandmama?" she asks. "They're close."

But her grandmother just continues calmly, spreading the clay across her body. *What begins bad often brightens into something good,* she says, rubbing the clay into the troughs between Emely's ribs. *Tonight you will raise your knees high into the sky and touch your other family, the stars. If you turn your questions into prayers, they will rise and meet the warm, receiving heart of the Mother.*

"The soldiers are going to see right through this little charade," Emely says, her voice rising into a shriek. "I'm just a naked person wearing some clay. They'll know I'm not the Stone Woman." Her mouth is so dry with fear she can barely swallow. "They probably don't even believe in the Stone Woman anyway." Behind her she hears a tree falling.

One more time her grandmother wraps her bony fingers around her wrist and begins to pull her up the path. Emely tries to reach down for her jeans, but her grandmother is too strong. *No,* she says, shaking her head. *In order to do what you have to do tonight, you must be naked. It is only by swinging your hips and dancing with everything you are that you will stop those men.*

Moonlight slants against the long pole of Emely's thighs; her hipbones jut new shadows. A branch scrapes against her skin and a patch of clay falls to the path behind. She's lost a lot of weight these last weeks in the forest, and her skinniness makes her feel even more naked.

She is being led to certain death. Even if the soldiers did believe in the Stone Woman, in her "tall one" dreams she is made of stone and flesh, her parts sinewy and paired. This is only dried, flaking mud—a caricature of her dueling parts.

She tries one more time. "Grandmama," she says, "a few wispy stories from the past is not going to save the Okino. In a matter of hours, everyone's going to be slaughtered." She stumbles on the path. A patch of clay breaks away, the brown continent of North America is born on her belly. Another patch of clay breaks away, this one Africa. She is starting to come apart.

You have a great light, Amely, her grandmother says from somewhere in front of her. *I saw it first when I scraped the juice of birth from you.*

A piece of moss drags a lascivious tongue across her naked skin. More continents born.

We who are the dead watched you blow on stones the other day. I was so proud of you. You took what you didn't understand and combined it with what you do know, and looked what happened! The same thing will occur tonight. You must trust in the goodness of the world.

"I'm not going to become the Stone Woman just because you've slapped a little clay on me," Emely protests, but she's discovering by the moment that the dream life of the ghost doesn't offer much opportunity for argument. She doesn't appear to have a choice in what is happening to her.

Her grandmother leads her up the path toward an opening between the trees, and when she finally stops Emely sees she has brought her to the edge of the wind clearing.

She turns to her one more time. Light shines through her desiccated face. *I want you to dance tonight as your great-grandmother danced,* she instructs. *Dance with everything you are, all of your opposites—old and young, modern and ancient, what you know with your mind, what you feel with your heart.*

Emely feels like she's going to faint. Her grandmother is trying to reach for transcendence, but they are only facing tragedy. One more time, very faint. "Grandmama, this isn't going to work."

Her grandmother smiles. *I have one last gift for you*, she says, and points a bony finger. *Look over there.*

A constellation of stars? Flying blossoms? What is it? The thing coming seems to carry its own light.

It comes closer, and she sees it's a cloud composed of hundreds and hundreds of white butterflies. Fairylike, carrying starlight on their wings, they come close, and then, as soft as a whisper, they land on her, blanketing the top of her head, her stomach, her thighs, filling in all those new and vulnerable continents with their pale, warm wings.

But all only on one side.

You are a bride tonight, her grandmother says. *Rise and dance with the source.*

"But Grandmama, butterflies and mud aren't going to stop bullets. You're sending me to a certain death."

They will if you believe enough.

"Grandmama . . ." she says, once more beginning to protest.

But when she turns, her grandmother is no longer there.

CHAPTER 75

The first thing Emely sees when she steps into the clearing is a soldier crouched behind a large rock, the long lean of his gun pointed straight at her. Another soldier appears, then another; in contrast to the wild, tumbled forest, their moves are sharp and calculated. Eventually each boulder holds the lean of a gun, each of those dark barrels directed at her.

And now, almost worse, comes the bright beam of their flashlights. "Looks like one of those animans," one of the soldiers says. "And she's naked except for some insects."

One soldier steps out from behind the rock, his silhouette a dark cutout against the stars. "No one shoots," he directs, "until we get instructions from the chief."

The flashlight he holds in his hand disturbs the butterflies; they move restlessly against Emely's left side. The soldier holds a walkie-talkie, pushes a button. "I have something strange to report, sir," he says. "I don't see the rest of the tribe, but one of these monkey animals is standing right in front of us." His voice holds derision but also the snapped efficiency of a salute. "It appears to be a female," he continues. "She's naked and one half of her is covered in insects."

As he waits for an answer he idly reaches up and tears the sail woven of leaves and thorns.

Emely tries to look beyond the flashlight's trespassing light, tries in this way to touch the stars. "What happens tonight rests with you," her grandmother had said, "and just how wide and free you make yourself." In a preliminary way, feeling ridiculous, she moves her hips to the left, to the right. The torn sail slaps desolately in the night breeze.

"What are your orders, sir?" the soldier asks. "Should I shoot?"

Emely hears the cackle of the Wrong One's voice. "Wait for me," he says. "Don't do anything, but keep your guns trained on her." Even through the walkie-talkie she hears his glee.

Above her, the stars swirl in circles like someone is stirring the sky with a spoon. Below are the soldiers, their anger unyielding, pitiless, and cruel. She's so frightened she can barely breathe.

It has come down to this moment. How is she supposed to get big enough, brave enough to fill the breath of the sky with a dozen guns pointed at her? One more time a swing to her right, once more a swing to her left. Trying to find a place to land, the butterflies flutter up and down on her body.

It is a soldier's hard laugh that halts her swinging, an ugly, falling-down sound that holds both phlegm and derision.

"Not much meat on those bones," he jeers. "Looks like she should have eaten a few more monkeys or whatever those animans eat!"

She swallows, tries to speak. "I'm representing the Land Reform Commission," she says, her voice reedy even to her own ears. "We're documenting our country's history. It is illegal to come in and violate the lives of indigenous people."

A butterfly rises from her cheek and flutters for a moment before her eyes. She raises her hand to flick it away. "I have an assignment from the government. It's the same government that employs you."

"Is that the required dress?" one of the soldiers jeers. "Moths?"

Laughter then, and behind the laughter, the broken gasp of the wind sail.

"Grandmama?" Emely asks under her breath. "Are you there?" She explores the place where she should be. Nothing. The sky is unoccupied.

The guitar tree is the next to be destroyed. A soldier reaches up with a knife, cuts the strings. They snap in the wind. Next the windmill tree, its blades cracked one right after the other.

No grandmother, Mama too far way, Mentegai turned away from her, no solidarity in this night . . . nothing. Even the sky doesn't want her. She doesn't belong to anything greater than herself, and now, in a matter of minutes, she will be shot.

She's not really surprised when a soldier steps forward—not really surprised when his remarks gradually swell from idle derision about insects into the sharper menace of lust, either.

"She still got some curves under those moths," he says. He takes another step forward.

Her throat tightens with fear. Behind her the broken breath of all those many inventions snipped, stopped. She turns her head, tries to sip a little moonlight. It doesn't work.

Another step. Laughter as concentrated and dark as the pupils of all those watching guns.

"I've never had an animan before." Inflamed, what he says flows into the gasps of all those broken inventions, and she knows without a doubt that the man standing before her is going to step forward and use her, give himself the precious inside place of her to wear, and none of the other soldiers will do a single thing to stop it.

"No," she moans. "Please." No magic here; not even the restless spell of the butterfly wings can keep her beautiful. The irises of all those guns watching.

The soldier's close now—hooded eyes, sour breath, a rubbery smile on his face like a cast-off rubber band. "I love women," he says. "See?" The sound of his zipper, cold and metallic against the murmured prayer of leaves, and now his erection, another horizontal line leaning into this night. As he touches his erection, she hears the intimate sound of his heavy breathing, breath very different from all the formerly buoyant gadgets and musical instruments in this place.

One more time she tries to use her voice. "Please," she says, faint. "Please don't"—and that's when he leans forward and runs one finger down the cheek without butterflies. Emely experiences a shocked intake of breath. Just the slide of a finger but it holds all the violation of what is to come. *Grandmama?* she silently pleads. *Can you help me? Please come.*

Despite everything that is happening in front of her, she still wants to believe what her grandmother foretold, that tonight she will dance for the soldiers and somehow, magically, she will become the Stone Woman and rise into the celestial sky.

But that hasn't happened, has it? No prayers answered, nothing out there to make her larger, all potential for sky's cleansing union diminished . . . she is only one more small and broken thing in this place of broken things. Her grandmother used her energy to come back from the other side just to tell her to dance naked in front of these men like some kind of vulgar lap dancer.

But then the soldier with the empty eyes leans forward, tries to kiss her, and something sparks inside. She rears back, slaps him so hard the butterflies rise from her skin for second.

Stunned, the soldier puts a hand on his cheek. His expression slowly changes from lust to anger. "Fuck you, bitch," he snarls. Hate bubbles in his voice.

"Spider walks, spider walks, spider walks all day long." From a time almost before memory, a slip of a song comes to her, one she used to sing in childhood. "Spider spins her silver web all day long."

With the small part of her brain still working Emely asks herself why, in the middle of this danger—guns pointed at her, a man about to rape her—she is singing a song from childhood, but even that part of her chooses to hum along.

"Spider spinning. Spider spinning its web all day long."

The soldier is reaching for her again when she first sees the silver line. It's hanging from the sky and slowly moving toward her, dangling its silver thread, something of rescue in this lawless night. She stretches out her throat a little bit more to welcome the song, inviting it toward her, this little piece of innocence that is hers from childhood. She even manages to move her hips a little. "Spider web, spider web, all day long." The line dangles a little to the left of the soldier as he brings his erection closer, pumping it with his hand.

She knows she is turning when she begins to have a deep affinity for light—where it is in the clearing, where it isn't, where it sprinkles the ground before her. Light fills the crevices of that rock, bunches against trees, shines on grass blades, sparks against an actual spider web, making it jewelry for one night.

Emely feels a rush of excitement. Never mind that pumping penis, the barrels of all those watching guns, and the Wrong One coming close—light, this light, she can dance with it, wear it, sing it, this knowledge so slight but so huge all at the same time.

It hasn't yet reached the soldiers, this light that is almost emotion, but she knows it soon will.

And now here it comes, the sweet rush of things formally separate now joined. Like the wax walls of a honeycomb, those walls of carefully kept-apart information, all the separate compartments of scholarly fact and grandmother knowledge, tall one running and master's degrees, the separate geography of Africa and America, even the horror of what the man was doing in front of her, taking something private and tender and turning it into a weapon, those walls melt, and all of Emely's different experiences rush together, flooding her with a sense of wholeness and hope.

Sometimes it's the only thing to do: rock your hips, receive, and rejoice. Sometimes that's the only way to keep the feeling going, and this is what she does. Of course she is still perfectly aware of the soldiers, that one in front of her thumping himself toward orgasm, but something else is beginning to happen.

She's beginning to rise into the sky, so tall now that that pumping penis, all those guns, are now only little-boy slight.

Though she is fractured with doubt, as cracked and broken as everything else in the wind clearing, somehow, illuminated with the deep, animating principle of light, she is becoming whole.

The moon shines on the reflection of its wrinkled grandmother floating on the surface of the river. She raises one arm, gathers them both. "More," she says. More acreage for light to lean against. And now she's grown so high what those men are doing down there is merely foolish. Some of the soldiers below her are staring up at her, beginning to rub their eyes. Even the soldier who has been pumping his organ stares up at her, mouth agape.

Yes, oh yes, she is rising. There's a tickle in her throat that will eventually erupt into a full-blown, deeply felt laugh. Grandmama had been right after all.

She sees suddenly that beneath their machismo the soldiers are still boys, still frightened of their mothers, their grandmothers: "Yes, ma'am, no ma'am." She sees how that soldier hiding behind a big pile of stones over there stood in front of his mirror this morning adjusting his beret so it would be just right. That one over there is worried about his oldest son; he's hurt when the boy tells him he just wants to be alone. She even sees how the one who has been pumping his organ is utterly alone, how he has turned his penis into a weapon because nobody wants it for love.

All of her is being used, and the light begins to thicken. She makes beauty where her body is, and sometimes in the places where it isn't. She raises her knees to touch the moon. She touches gradual things, shy things, leaves just unfurling, new seasons just beginning. She dances with love for the forest people, for Mentegai, for her mother and father, even these men standing before her, fast sliding back into the boys they used to be.

Cave, city, night, day, Africa, America, Amely, Emely—she dances with all of her parts, loving the soldiers' ugly green uniforms, the starched ironed creases of their pants, their self-prescribed importance. She loves their hands, not long ago used against the taxi driver, Old Tempi, and Kareem. It is just as her grandmother told her. She can use this light to love the soldiers back into the boys they were when they climbed mountains just to feel the wind, back into the feeling they've had when they've taken their young children into their laps or nonchalantly wrapped their arms around their best friends as they walk down the road together.

She loves the soldiers back to the times when they were still kind, hadn't yet fallen in love, fallen out of love, been hurt, turned hard—in short, she loves them back to who they used to be before they met the Wrong One.

And it works. Awestruck, one by one, the soldiers lay down their guns. "The Stone Woman," they say, and then, one after the other, the boys they once were and now are again turn and disappear into the night.

CHAPTER 76

T his dark, breathing night. The leaves on the trees shiver like whispered prayers. Every now and then, Emely sees the frisky jazz scat of a shooting star.

Why was she ever afraid?

There is something solid beneath her feet. Emely leans over and pokes her fingers into the dirt. Even before picking it up, she knows what it is. The tablet, the sacred tablet! It has been under her feet the whole time.

She can't say she's really all that surprised. Wearing only the trembling vestment of butterflies, wasn't she the one to grab that line of silver from the sky, reach for the moon, and turn all those life-hardened soldiers back into who they really were inside, little boys needing both a miracle and their mothers? And she had done it *her* way, with beauty and magic.

Now, she knows what to do next. Two handprints, made thousands of years ago, are imprinted onto the surface of the tablet. Just as promised by all those old stories, she places her hands into the ancient troughs and finds it's a perfect fit.

Then, she begins to rise again.

High, then higher. Moonlight fills the chamber of the world, rain talks against her skin. She can see all the way to her family's village; she imagines her family sleeping curled against each other, and smiles. A butterfly lands on the dome of her shoulders, its wings a delicate tent, its underside washed with the color of stars.

"Beautiful," she says. Everything fits, even her, moving up into the sky, rising into light before it was used by human beings, rising, bringing with her all those facts and corners of academic equations, the so-called "noise" that Ogotu tried to banish.

A disdain-flecked laugh stops her. "You turned out to be a more formidable foe than I expected," the police chief says. He rubs his hands together gleefully. "I'm actually having a bit of fun with you." He doesn't seem to be upset in the least that his soldiers have run away.

Emely speaks to him from her great height. "You broke your word to me," she scolds him. "You said I had two weeks to convince the forest people to leave their homes peacefully."

Light gleams across his shiny medals. He shrugs, then offers her a cocky grin. "I must be living up to my aunt's name for me. Of course it would have been fun to watch you bend between the girl's legs and cut, but look, it's happening anyway!"

She looks down to see the old woman pulling Chipkorie across the clearing. "Blood will run into the grass," Ogotu says. "We are bringing our initiate forward." She can no longer speak her granddaughter's name; in order to do what she must this night, she has already traveled the distance from loving family member into the impersonal.

The chief crosses his arms triumphantly. "Now you understand," he purrs. "Disorder and chaos are my kind of power, so much stronger than yours. And you don't matter. Even now you're shrinking and there's nothing you can do about it."

It's true. There is no more light to wear, and nothing will stop her fall. She's the height of the top of the tree now, sliding down toward its middle branches. As is her habit when she is upset, she reaches for her stone, then realizes once again that she is naked. No stone, no pocket, no necklace—only vulnerable flesh, covered with a tenuous veil of butterflies.

Remembering the statue in the professor's back bedroom, she reaches up and tries to fill her curved hand with the moon, but can't. Her fingers are empty; the moon is too far away.

From somewhere down below, a drum begins to beat, the drummer's live fingers against long-dead skin. "It will be a good cut," Ogotu announces proudly. "Our Great Mother will finally drink what has been denied her for so long."

No stone, no moon, no necklace, but Emely still has her voice. "No, Ogotu," she calls. "Don't do this!"

The old woman still possesses some of her formidable power; the look she sends Emely abruptly brings her crashing to the ground. She is once more her normal size.

"When our initiate's lips are placed on the holy leaf, our Mother will become strong enough to push back the wrong," Ogotu says. The piece of glass she holds in her hands glints in the moonlight. "Here is our initiate, the moon in the sky, and all is as it should be."

Driving hard, moments away from the only solution she knows, the old woman is trying desperately to assume a kind of historic grandeur, but her voice quivers with age and fatigue.

The police chief chuckles. "I presume the wrong you're talking about is me, Aunt."

The old woman ignores him and cuts a banana leaf, then places it on the ground.

The chief turns back to Emely. "Where is your precious Mother now?" he jeers. As though sponsoring the cruelty before him, he stretches out his arms triumphantly. "Yes my soldiers have run away but the wind clearing is chopped down, in a matter of seconds that young girl is going to be cut, and there's nothing in the world you can do about it. Look around, your world stands in ruin."

The old woman reaches down and places a stick in Chipkorie's mouth. "When I was cut, no one had eaten any part of an animal for forty moons," she says. "Our Mother received my blood, and on the fourth moon Tempi brought to our fire two antelopes. This is what all of our songs sing; this is what all those brushstrokes on the paintings say. If we believe in the Mother and honor what she needs, she will take care of us."

Ogotu wedges herself between Chipkorie's legs.

The night darkens. Bereft of mercy, the moon hides behind the clouds.

A flick of the old woman's wrist and Chipkorie's clitoris is cut. The girl's anguished eyes rain tears. Blood, so much blood, the most intimate of all.

The old woman turns, drops the clitoris on the leaf, and goes back between the girl's legs. One half of Chipkorie's labia minora is cut. Her legs shaking violently, the girl arches her back in agony.

No temple of kindness to live under; now, all is sad. Even the butterflies are still. As though it can't be witnessed in its entirety, everything is illuminated only in brief flashes of light, but Emely knows, watching, that she will always be branded by the night's horrific images.

She has lost. True, she made the soldiers run away, but Chipkorie's womanhood has been cut off, the girl mutilated for life.

It is only a thin-winged sound, but it alters everything that is to come. Startled, Ogotu freezes, hand raised, holding the glass.

Emely doesn't know what it is at first, but here it comes again, a slight, slender sound gradually sharpening into a word.

"Nooooo . . ."

It takes a moment to link up Chipkorie's anguished eyes with that small, traveling sound, but when she does, Emely understands. Just like her mother before her, the girl has done the one thing guaranteed to stop the cutting. She has said the word "no."

"No," the girl says again. Just one thin sound, but the same way a crescent moon cups the full round of the moon, that one, tiny word encompasses the girl's full resistance. "No," Chipkorie demands again, her voice now stronger. And again. "No, no, no."

The police chief is thoroughly enjoying this new development. "All that spying on women's ceremonies when I was a little boy has paid off! They said a girl must never cry out or the ceremony would be cursed. Now my aunt can't go in for the last cut!" he snickers, rubbing his hands in delight. "And what we both know is that her sacrifice means nothing. Everyone will still die tonight!"

Her head in her hands, Chipkorie now rocks on the ground, the world glimpsed only as bars through her fingers. "No, no, no," she cries, putting more body into that one word than anything she has left.

But now Emely knows what she must do: she will match Chipkorie's act of courage with her own. Pushing past the police chief and the old woman, she runs toward the girl, and when she's at her side, bends over and folds her in her arms. She rocks her back and forth, singing the melody of her name over and over again—"Chipkorie, Chipkorie, Chipkorie," she chants, voicing the only whole thing that still belongs to the hurt child. *Don't die*, is what she's thinking.

She doesn't realize at first that she is rising. All she knows is that she wants to put more distance between the girl in her arms and those mutilated parts of hers left on that leaf.

Rising, rising now into an immense and intricate blackness; she still holds the tablet, heavy with time, and Chipkorie seems to grow lighter and lighter.

They are rising into a world without regrets. Wings creak, fish rise to nuzzle the sky, she sees small bonfires of the moon's light burning inside the many watching eyes. From her great height, she can see new gaps in the forest where the soldiers have burned down the trees, but each space is still replete with self; what is not there is just as palpable as a tree.

Like Chipkorie. Cut. Hurt. This girl in my arms just wants to be a girl, intact, not someone missing half her vagina.

Rising.

Rising into a world before her, into time that has not yet been used.

And now, finally, comes the voice. *You, the tall one, are you listening?* Part music, part spoken word, the voice stops her in her tracks.

"What?" she asks and turns. "Who's there?" Just the act of turning causes spores of herself to travel on the wind. "Are you . . . the Mother?"

Yes, replies the voice. *But because I am all things—that tree, wind, dirt, each and every raindrop, even that damaged child you hold in your arms—it is hard to respond as merely one. I have been waiting for your questions to grow large enough to let me in, but now, finally, I think you are ready to fill your empty spaces with me.*

The voice is so calm it immediately lowers Emely into her own quiet inside.

All these centuries of silence, and now at last I have a Stone Woman who brings me a cut girl, not her cut parts. Now, finally, I have a Stone Woman who can hear what I have to say. It is your very opposites, the way linear facts rest against your intuition, prose brushes up against poetry, ancient wisdom intersects with modern thought . . . the fluid line between exposition and pure, pure listening . . . these are the opposites that have made you who you are. You even have two names!

Emely can hardly breathe, so attentive is she to this presence.

There is a time coming when anyone who believes in my magic will be called "misled," "paganistic," a "devil worshipper," the voice continues, *and, as in years before, they will be named witches and sent to fire. What happens* under my great trees will happen no more. *You must take back this warning to the flesh ones.*

Mutely, Emely can only nod her head.

I have never been this warm, the Great Mother continues. *Industry and smoke, you are cooking me alive. Dirty air, I cannot breathe. Even my love for you will not be able to keep you alive much longer. Birds enter my sky trying to find a place to know flight, but they can't fly; in some places, the air is too dirty. There are dead places in my seas where no fish can swim.*

A new night is coming soon. No more Grandfather Rain, Mother Thunder, no more twin sisters of the Moon and Sun. If you do not listen, terror will clot your ears and you will no longer be able to hear. Terror will fill the caverns of your eyes, and you will not be able to see. This is what will happen if you do not heed my warnings.

Emely whispers her next question. "The old woman down there, the one who cut this girl, says you need blood to keep you strong. Is that true?"

Stars hiss and the wind whips a little harder. The Great Mother is angry. The voice changes, becomes fierce.

The cuttings of women's parts will never be sanctioned by any force that honors life, she replies. *How could this be? What I require is clean air, the repeated blush of my sweet dawns, the honoring of the flesh of my sweet girls, not its destruction. I speak my dreams for this planet through my women, who bring new life.*

"Have you ever needed blood?" Emely asks.

No, the Great Mother replies. *And now, finally, I have a Stone Woman who understands. When one defiles my girls, they defile me. Nothing beautiful or strong comes from bodies that have been cut. When a women's sexuality is sliced from her body, it creates anger, pain, resentment. This is not what I wish for my women. I want them to live full, lusty lives, speaking with all their parts, singing the music of their sighs. I want them ardent, moaning, praying, crying, kissing, and coupling.*

The voice seems to come from all directions at the same time. *The defiling of my children's bodies must stop, now and forever.* The voice swells. *All those centuries with Stone Woman rising into my sky, offering me the parts of cut girls. Even your great-grandmother came to me holding cut parts in her hands. Why would I want the only organ grown by my women for her pleasure to be cut away? Have all these women never seen that when they cut away part of their daughters and granddaughters, they are cutting away a part of themselves?*

Could it be that I finally have a Stone Woman who understands? This is a crime so sinister, so well designed, it is perpetrated not by the oppressors but by the oppressed themselves! The world must know that this terrible practice must stop . . . now!

Emely doesn't know if it has arrived with the voice or rests in the spaces between, but suddenly something new is in the air: the lament of things left behind. Snakeskins, feathers, shells, birds' nests, the sound of yesterday's rain . . . some of it is beautiful and part of life, but some is ugly—all the cuttings from women left to sing their laments beneath the dirt.

Can all of this actually end? The world, this planet, her breath?

Everything Emely has considered entrenched and permanent buckles beneath her, and she begins to weep as never before, her heaving sobs matching those of Chipkorie a few minutes ago.

"How can I be your next Stone Woman?" she asks, so sodden with tears her bones feel soft, so bereft her skin is now only a rind. "I couldn't even protect Chipkorie."

But the Great Mother has an answer for her.

Place both of your hands on the tablet. Bunch time between your fingers. Reach across every single evolutionary step, each year of war, advancement, discovery, and error. Then, stretch your hands through all of that longing toward your own beginning. Have you done it, placed your fingers into those troughs made by the first human being? This is the only way to give back to Chipkorie what she has lost. This is where magic happens.

Emely looks down at her hands, resting on the tablet. Her left hand is made of stone. Her right hand, too, is stone. Still, not a word from Chipkorie.

But something is happening. A new, soft light permeates the girl's face; in Emely's arms she turns and sighs softly.

And that's when Emely understands. She is not just reaching backward into time, she is reaching forward toward wholeness, the magical property inherent in the wheel of time activated by her fingers on the tablet. Chipkorie has grown quiet because the Great Mother has returned her to her birth anatomy. Initiated by the Great Mother through Emely's hands on the tablet, in a night replete with restoration, this is the most telling renewal of all. Together, they have unleashed new petals of flesh—Chipkorie is healed, the beautiful, cursive folds of a full-petaled orchid bloom once more.

The Great Mother hums her gladness. *Let this girl, now whole, be a message to all women, dead and alive. There will be no more cuttings. It is not the way to keep life in balance. If you continue this practice I will send no more game, only storms, destruction, and chaos.*

You are my new Stone Woman, the great voice continues. *It is your mission now to tell the world to stop cutting my girls and my trees. Will you do this?*

Clutching Chipkorie in her arms, Emely nods. "I will. It will be how I spend my life."

She will do it for this girl sleeping in her arms. She will do it for all the mothers trying to push babies through the scar tissue sealing their cut vaginas. And she will do it with Mentegai.

"Mentegai." Just his name spoken aloud fills the creases of her body with lust.

Touch your face on both sides, the Great Mother says gently.

Tentatively, Emely raises her hand. Rain runs water down one cheek, mixing with dirt and tears. Her cheek is stone.

Ancient light from the stars runs down the other. She touches it as well. That cheek, too, is stone.

And that's when she understands. She is stone, both sides, and what she previously thought was cold and solid and gray is not; stone, all stone, her body is now filled with the flickering colors and movement of a deeply committed life.

The bullet that emerges from the Wrong One's gun travels quickly, but she does not remove herself from its path, simply clutches Chipkorie a little tighter in her arms. It doesn't hurt when it hits her belly, but she is surprised when it ricochets off her stone form and speeds back to the police chief, where it hits him square in the chest. With a cry, he staggers back a few feet and then falls to the ground.

"Nephew!" Ogotu calls, and springs across the clearing. When she reaches him, just as she did with the dying deer, she leans over and pulls his head into her lap. "Nephew!" she cries out again, curling over him. Cradled in the lap of the woman who banished him from this forest years ago, the chief stares up into his aunt's eyes, and the hard thing that has lacquered his face begins to melt away. Like those sculptures in the cave, he falls back in time, for a moment twenty years old, then sixteen, now ten—he's tumbling back through the seasons of his life into a final, beautiful softness.

"I'm sorry, Auntie," he murmurs. His voice rises an octave. He is now the little boy he was when he lived in these trees. "I just wanted you to know I was strong."

Ogotu runs one finger down the edge of his face. "I know," she murmurs. "You're home now."

All stone now, staring down at the scene below her, by this time Emely should know about miracles, but she is still surprised by what the old woman says next. "I'm sorry, too, Nephew," she confesses. Her voice is heavy with sadness. "Maybe the old ways aren't just for women. I should have tried harder to teach you."

She is leaning over him, her hands cupping both his cheeks, when all goes quiet behind his eyes. "Auntie," he says softly, then takes one last breath, turns his head, and slips away.

And Emely, still wearing the sheen of stars, lands on the ground, once more her own size.

CHAPTER 77

Eyes huge with fear, Kareem runs toward Emely. "Will Chipkorie be alright?" he asks, lifting the girl from her arms.

"Yes," Emely says. "She just needs to rest."

Her brother takes Chipkorie to the fire and lays her down gently on some furs.

And now, covered in the chief's blood, here comes Ogotu; shells clinking, tassels from her colobus monkey skins flying in all directions, hair a swirl of weather, she is a dangerous confetti of glitter and light.

Emely remembers what the Great Mother has just proclaimed and braces herself. Is the old woman going to insist that Chipkorie be cut again?

Maybe it is some special "Stone Woman sight," but suddenly, deep inside the circus tent of her furs and shells and feathers, Emely sees a frightened old woman. She begins gently. "Ogotu," she says, "I'm really sorry about your nephew."

"I'm sorry, too, Amely," the old woman responds. "Maybe I was wrong to keep the Stone Woman ways from him. Bitterness corrupted my nephew's heart. Magic can turn to hate, you know. It mutates and fills hearts with rust. Maybe more men should know the secret ways of the Great Mother worship."

She shakes her head, looks at Chipkorie sleeping by the fire, and somehow she knows. "My granddaughter . . . is she truly whole again?" she asks. "You and the Mother have made her as she was?"

"Yes," Emely says. "I know that this is going to be hard for you to accept, but the Great Mother says no more cuttings. She doesn't want blood, has never wanted blood. She says that all these years, she has never wanted the offerings from young girls."

She doesn't know how the old woman will respond. Will she fight her, try to go back in and cut Chipkorie once again?

But Ogotu reaches into her furs for her cutting glass and, to Emely's surprise, draws back her arm and with a mighty heave throws it as hard as she can into the trees. Then she turns to her, a beautiful smile on her face. "You were right all along, Emely Amely! And my daughter-in-law and your mother were right. Chipkorie's womanhood returned is final proof. All those cut lips, all those sacrifices, all those Stone Women rising, holding in their hands the parts of cut girls . . . How could we have been wrong for so long?"

Once again she shakes her head, then answers her own question. "Up to now all we've been able to do is rise with our offerings. But when you rose you were stone, all stone, and you were able to speak with the Great Mother! I've never seen anything like it!" She stares deeply into Emely's eyes. "None of the songs we have ever sung, none of the paintings we have ever painted, have spoken it. Your outside noise, all the things I tried to push away, have made you exactly who you are: the most powerful Stone Woman of all time!"

The tassel of her monkey skin is the first to move. "No more blood," she says. Another tassel catches the conversation. "No more blood," she repeats. Her cheeks fill with color, her finger snaps, and she smiles the radiant smile of someone set free. "No more cuttings." She moves to the fire and sits down by Chipkorie. Still smiling she sighs deeply and, staring into the flames, lovingly strokes her granddaughter's head.

CHAPTER 78

Mentegai is the next to appear out of the night, his beautiful green eyes filled with tenderness. Emely immediately runs into his arms.

"I'm sorry," she says. "I didn't mean that about your father. It wasn't just a drunken story; it's true."

"I know," he says softly. "I watched as you climbed into the sky."

"Will you help me with the tablet?" she asks. "I need to bury it for the next Stone Woman."

"Of course," he says.

They dig a hole, and she lays the tablet carefully in the dirt, wondering whose hands will touch it next. If she has a daughter, will she inherit the gift?

And then more hands touching: Mentegai reaches for her, pulls her to her feet, and, their bodies pressed tight, they kiss. Two conversations inside her one body; two different kinds of belonging. *Can I do it?* she wonders. *Drop from the Great Mother, the top of my head brushing the cosmos, into this conversation of bodies? Will I one day make children with this man?*

She kisses with new skill, already an expert, her desire exhaled in one long rush of air. *How do I know these things?* she marvels. *How do I know how to make a man hunger for a mate?*

She draws back, breathless. "The Great Mother says I must go out into the world to share what I have learned, and try to stop the cuttings."

"I know," Mentegai says softly, smiling. "I know you are the Stone Woman and that you belong to the world—but do you think you can save a little of yourself for me?"

She looks into his eyes, sees for the first time an entwined life where things that are unknown can reside next to the known, and stone can live side by side with flesh. *Can I do it?* she wonders one more time. *Pledge my life to this man?*

Then she reminds herself that in all the world she is only truly home in Mentegai's arms. *I can.* Reaching up, she kisses him again, tasting possibilities. *And I will use all my body to speak this promise.* She remembers the Great Mother's words about her wishes for women: *I want them to live full, lusty lives, speaking with all their parts, singing the music of their sighs. I want them ardent, moaning, praying, crying, kissing, and coupling.*

She lays her head against Mentegai's chest. *No problem*, she thinks to herself and smiles. She will seize it all, speak it all, use it all. There will be no more parceling it out. No longer will she allow fear to fracture her into dislocated parts. From still, motionless time she has arrived, happened, become; she has met the Great Mother, and met herself as well. She is both her doctoral thesis and her great-grandmother's name carved on the walls of the cave. She is what is at the bottom of oceans jostled by tides, what holds up mountains.

Stone, all stone.

CHAPTER 79

Emely speaks through the stones:

Sister Women, you who are the dead and you who are alive, can you hear me? I send you my song of prayer. The secrets are exposed now, no longer sheltered by superstition. I will match Chipkorie's brave "no" with one of my own. All those pieces of glass scabbed with a young girl's blood, all those girls delivered trussed, stitched, and paired for a man, the entombed light of sexuality stitched forever inside of tattered vaginas . . . no more! Girl, woman, future mother, and grandmother, the more I deepen into the assignment of womanhood, seasons notched with my own story, the more I understand the seriousness of what has been cut away. I will speak to every woman inhabiting the blank world. I will speak through these stones to the women who are both dead and alive, and use words of fire. No more cuttings, I say. I am the new Stone Woman. Do you hear me?

The women respond:

We hear you, Amely Emely. We will do as you say. Dark are the cuttings, dark are the women who cut. We will move into the ears of mothers and granddaughters and daughters, telling all who are alive, all who are dead, that the Great Mother ordains that the cuttings must stop. We will no longer be silent, as our silence serves only those who cut. They are we and we are they. When it is done to one, it is done to all.

Dreaming our dream of wholeness, our women finally set free—this is our incandescent song for our sisters, our daughters, ourselves. This is our prayer of stone.

ACKNOWLEDGMENTS

This book is dedicated to my husband Michael. Deep gratitude for my Fairfax, San Francisco, Petaluma and Irish families, both inherited, married into, and adopted, with special mention to my beloved children, Crystal Stermer and Lenny Kortum O'Mahony. Special gratitude as well to Tommy, Margaret and Danny, Dugald Stermer, Chums, James O'Mahony, Max, Si and Maxine Durney, Lucy Kortum, Florence and Libby Durney, Helen and Sara O'Mahony, Helen Schneider, and my parents.

It has taken me a long time to write this book. Here are some who have helped me on the way.

Maureen Healy, Anne and Mark Dowey, Anne Lamott and Pam Nyham, Blake Hallinan, Alex and Mars Rivera, Julie Catton, Kate Misskelly, Isabel Allende, Lori Allende, Janice Schopfer, Mark and Elena Boylan, Margaret Brodkin, Hilary Burrage, Lorraine Koonce, Dave Nelson, Deirdre English, Shelly Erceg, Claire Gerus, Suzanne Girauldo, Virginia Hubbell, Joan Semling Bostian, Gabrielle Rileau, Bev Gherman, Sharon Johnson, She Writes Press, Eve Pell, Leo Litwak, Leah Garchik, Dr. C.K, Eve Zimmerman, Neshama Franklin, Tobe Levin von Gleichen, Brian O'Neill, Bob Matthews, Rose Messina,

Laurinda Ross, Pat Coyle, Doris Ober, Penny Wright, Beth and Annie Perry, Luther, Rhoda and Kathy Nichols, Steve Proctor, Jan Sarvis, Sean and Kate Murray, Bosque hill citizens, Shao J Thorpe, Sheila O'Sullivan, Steve Westfall, T.Sunish, Terry Strauss, Therese Kristenson, Donna Vozar, Gerrie and Joe Walsh, Suzanne Warner, Deborah Benson, Kim Rosen, Ellin Kavanagh and Barbara Meyers.

ABOUT THE AUTHOR

Jeanie Kortum is an award-winning author, journalist, and humanitarian. She founded A Home Away from Homelessness for homeless children in partnership with the National Park Service and ran it for almost twenty years. Her philanthropic work has been widely recognized by a long list of awards, including the Jefferson Award, the San Francisco Foundation's Community Award, the Commission on Women Making History Award, the Espiritu Award from the Isabel Allende Foundation, and the 2006 Lifetime Achievement Award from the San Francisco Urban Research Association. She has been the subject of two CBS national news profiles and rights to her life story have been sold to Warner Brothers. Kortum's award-winning first novel, Ghost Vision, is loosely based on her experiences living at the top of the world in a Greenland village. She researched Stones by living with a hunter/gatherer tribe in Africa, during which time she witnessed a clitoridectomy. This experience compelled her to bring awareness to Female Genital Mutilation (FGM) and assistance to young women forced to undergo the procedures. Kortum lives with her husband and adopted son in Northern California and Ireland.

Author photo © Anne Dowie

SELECTED TITLES FROM
SHE WRITES PRESS

She Writes Press is an independent publishing company founded to serve women writers everywhere. Visit us at www.shewritespress.com.

Light Radiance Splendor by Leah Chyten. $16.95, 978-1-63152-178-2. Set in Eastern Europe in the first half of the twentieth century and culminating in contemporary Israel and Palestine, Light Radiance Splendor shows how three generations of the Hebrew Goddess Shekinah's devoted mission keepers grapple with betrayal, forgiveness, and redemption.

Faint Promise of Rain by Anjali Mitter Duva. $16.95, 978-1-938314-97-1. Adhira, a young girl born to a family of Hindu temple dancers, is raised to be dutiful—but ultimately, as the world around her changes, it is her own bold choice that will determine the fate of her family and of their tradition.

A Cup of Redemption by Carole Bumpus. $16.95, 978-1-938314-90-2. Three women, each with their own secrets and shames, seek to make peace with their pasts and carve out new identities for themselves.

Elmina's Fire by Linda Carleton. $16.95, 978-1-63152-190-4. A story of conflict over such issues as reincarnation and the nature of good and evil that are as relevant today as they were eight centuries ago, *Elmina's Fire* offers a riveting window into a soul struggling for survival amid the conflict between the Cathars and the Catholic Church.

Pieces by Maria Kostaki. $16.95, 978-1-63152-966-5. After five years of living with her grandparents in Cold War-era Moscow, Sasha finds herself suddenly living in Athens, Greece—caught between her psychologically abusive mother and violent stepfather.

Singing with the Sirens: Overcoming the Long-Term Effects of Childhood Sexual Exploitation by Ellyn Bell and Stacey Bell. $16.95, 978-1-63152-936-8. With metaphors of sea creatures and the force of the ocean as a backdrop, this work addresses the problems of sexual abuse and exploitation of young girls, taking the reader on a poetic journey toward finding healing from within.

www.ingramcontent.com/pod-product-compliance
Lightning Source LLC
Chambersburg PA
CBHW020932260626
47169CB00006B/1690